Dying to Read

Dying to Read

by
Mark R. Sneller

Published by Fresh Air Press

This is a work of fiction. Names, characters and incidents either are the product of the author's imagination or are used fictitiously. Any resemblance to actual events or persons, living or dead, is entirely coincidental.

Copyright © 2020 by Mark R. Sneller

All rights reserved. No part of this book may be reproduced or transmitted in any form or by any means, electronic or mechanical, including photocopying, recording, or by any information storage and retrieval system, without permission in writing from the author.

Visit Mark's website at
marksneller.com

This edition was prepared for publication by
Ghost River Images
5350 East Fourth Street
Tucson, Arizona 85711
www.ghostriverimages.com

ISBN 978-1-7330238-5-6

Library of Congress Control Number: 2020919832

Printed in the United States of America
November, 2020

Other books Mark R. Sneller:

A Breath of Fresh Air

Greener Cleaner Indoor Air–a Guide
to Healthier Living

Toxic Exposure

The Mars Virus

City Beneath the Earth

In Progress books:

The Fight at the Poker Game and Other
Stories

The Magical Powers of Lazlo Pearce

Dedication

To my grandparents who raised me from the age of three.

To my grandmother from Odessa, Russia, who permitted me to allocate my growing collection of paperbacks to a little cupboard in a little hallway in our small home, and who fed and cared for me. She endured me well, especially while I wrote and read to her my first one-page stories.

To my grandfather who grew up on a farm in Lithuania and who worked his small dime store in a poor section of Los Angeles. He overcame holdups and worked six days a week and ordered me to stop playing baseball in the streets and help him in the store.

My greatest regret? I never asked them about their own stories.

Author's note

This novel is a work of fiction and any resemblance to persons living or dead is purely coincidental. The idea for this book was based on a dare for me write a story that was *different*. The idea was expressed within a few seconds, although the story continued to grow over a period of years.

The science upon which this story is based is real and this has permitted my imagination to create the various scenarios, which may stretch the truth, but not to any extent that I would consider to be significant. The truth be told.

Acknowledgments

The author would like to gratefully thank the staff of Tucson Newspapers Incorporated for their guided tour of internal plant operations and their patient explanations to his questions. Thanks are given to Lorrie Cohen, then editor of the city desk of the *Tucson Citizen* for arranging the tour.

A grateful acknowledgment is also given to Robin Tanamachi, Department of Meteorology at the University of Oklahoma, for explanations regarding thunderstorm and tornadic activities in the central Oklahoma area.

The author expresses his encouragement to the staff, legislators, and developers of the Oklahoma City National Memorial & Museum, on the site where the Murrah Building once stood. These dedicated persons have contributed to that profoundly touching memorial. His feelings of bereavement go out to the families and friends of all those who perished in that tragedy.

The author would also like to gratefully and publicly thank the National Institutes of Health for awarding him training grants for his doctoral and post-doctoral research. This was in pursuit of his dreams of helping others in any small way he could.

Perhaps writing about it a little for entertainment value fits in there somewhere.

The author would be remiss if he did not thank his daughter, Jessica Dufour, who assisted him in the research and writing of *Greener Cleaner Indoor Air, Toxic Exposure*, and her critiques of his other writings.

PART ONE

1

Stanley Albert moved from California to Saudi Arabia to crystallize pounds of aflatoxin, a task no one had ever accomplished. He didn't need to know the intended purpose of the poison. Only one reason existed to make that much fungal toxin: to cause a great deal of suffering and death.

He checked in to one of the five-star penthouse suites in the Riyadh Royal Hotel, albeit for a short couple of hours. Fifteen hundred square feet of the world's finest carpeting from Persia, an indoor sauna and Jacuzzi, and picture windows overlooking downtown Riyadh and its airport were all his for viewing pleasure, until somebody came to pick him up.

The hardest thing Albert would have to tolerate would be the absolute nothingness of his new life. No real pleasure, no real release. Even if one were only an occasional drinker, a person would have no way to hide it.

Albert had already received a million tax-free off-shore dollars and would receive another million a year. This money served as adequate incentive to sign on the dotted line. An airtight contract stipulated that he would lose all monies if he reneged on any aspect of his work, or, if anyone were ever to discover his activities. The latter portion of the agreement concerned Albert. By definition, the future held no promises, yet, he signed because it beat anything else he had to look forward to.

A principal player in this particular effort was Vladimir Mikhailovich Ochenko, presently on-site, another foreigner, a former chief scientist for the largest pharmaceutical firm in the old Soviet Union. Ostensibly, Ochenko awaited him with all the necessary equipment required to complete their mission.

Albert showered leisurely and then changed into cooler attire. Hopefully he would not have to spend too much time outdoors in the blistering heat.

A knock at the door pulled him away from the window and the view of half-completed hotels and idle building cranes. The years of collecting billions of petro-dollars were over—most of it wasted on the rich. Saudi Arabia remained another second, if not third world country.

Albert opened the door to a handsome, dark-haired middle-aged man who seemed totally at ease with himself.

The man appeared to have great physical strength. He wore a lightweight tan suit and a thin, light-blue cotton shirt, open at the collar.

"You may call me Rashid, sir." The man spoke with a British accent.

Albert merely nodded, not knowing what to say. He followed Rashid down the hall to the elevator, then out into the blast furnace of the Saudi summer. A porter followed behind, bringing Albert's single suitcase and small carry-on.

A black Rolls-Royce Silver Shadow stood before them at the entrance to the hotel beneath the portico.

Rashid entered the passenger side and said, "You can drive. I presume it will be a new experience."

Albert gave a slight nod as he circled the vehicle to the driver's side. His sensory circuitry warned of overload. The element of surprise had been used up—or so he believed, until Vladimir Ochenko would enter his life a short while later.

Albert attempted to negotiate the Rolls through the wide tree-lined streets in the modern metropolis, while Rashid laughed uproariously. Back home, Albert drove Hondas and Toyota pickup trucks. To drive the behemoth Silver Shadow became a challenge.

"Oh, don't speed here," Rashid cautioned, "especially not on the open highway. They have unmarked patrol cars, and in addition to paying a fine, you'll spend a day or two in jail. No civil rights allowed. No such thing as a phone call. In time, you'll find things are pretty absolute here."

Albert hoped Rashid wasn't speaking from personal experience. From all appearances. Hopefully, the man carried enough weight to rescue him from an emergency, if it became necessary.

At Rashid's direction Albert drove east about ten miles. Occasional industrial buildings appeared on the right and left, interspersed with sand dunes. It reminded him of pictures of Las Vegas in its early years, when casinos along the Strip were separated by long stretches of desert.

At last Rashid told him to pull into the asphalt parking lot of a facility. It looked like many of the other structures they'd passed. An inconspicuous sign on the front of the building read, S.A. PHAR-MACEUTICALS in English with scrolling underneath. Albert took the letters to mean the same words in Arabic.

Albert glimpsed perhaps three large buildings and a smaller domed structure. The entire complex might contain perhaps twenty thousand square feet of interior space alone.

Rashid unlocked the front door of the building and led Albert to a device similar in appearance to an advanced airport-type metal detector. As he did so, Albert deposited the car keys and his belt in a basket, mentally searched himself, and cleared through first.

Rashid reached behind him, pulled a semiauto-matic handgun from a holster in his waistband, and placed it in another basket. He also removed a dia-mond-encrusted Rolex and money clip.

After scanning, a male receptionist thoroughly searched both men while an armed guard stood by watching closely, carrying a machine pistol. Albert surmised the pat-down was necessary, as plastic guns and plastic bullets were coming to the fore in the new technological world.

These guys play for real. On the other hand, so do I, he considered. His sense of pride grew. He felt honored to be treated thusly.

The guard also wore a semi-automatic on his hip with spare magazines, nightstick, handcuffs, walkie-talkie, and Taser. He approached the visitors and gave a slight nod of acknowledgment to Rashid, who pulled out a laminated identification card with his picture on it.

"I'll help you with the paperwork to get you checked in," said Rashid with a smile.

Albert completed mandatory fingerprinting, being photographed from four sides, and filling out a detailed information sheet, which was compared with what they retained on file. Once Rashid received a final nod, he collected his possessions including the car keys, and departed, taking the Rolls with him. Rashid left Albert with a future only to be guessed at. The penthouse suite would soon be a distant memory.

The guard silently led Albert down a long corridor and through a set of double doors. He spoke a few unintelligible words into the walkie-talkie and departed.

Albert found himself in his place of employment. Large windows set at the higher portion of the east and west walls of a warehouse permitted entry of the almost perpetual daytime sunlight. Most importantly, five large industrial fermenters dominated the scenery.

Each of these machines measured six to eight feet on a side and stood eight feet in height, with a catwalk about one foot up in the front portion. This design let the operator pull the various levers, flip switches, and read dials covering virtually the entire front side.

At the heart of each fermenter was a twenty-gallon bell housing. A small hand-operated forklift raised the bell housing into place to be bolted on. With water, proper nutrients, and mold spores added, the machine would warm and mix the stew, thus encouraging the spores to sprout and grow. A port at the bottom allowed a person to drain off a small portion for analysis.

The smell of growth media felt refreshing as if he were back in California at his old workplace or back in graduate school. Numerous workers in beige jumpsuits tended to the machines under direction of a single man wearing a blue jumpsuit, with his back turned to him.

Albert also noticed a separate large room with windows facing him. He walked up to the room and examined it through the windows. Inside he saw advanced scientific equipment alongside a large freezer and two refrigerators. Two desks were present, and a filled bookcase stood against one wall. Papers and notes were neatly piled atop one of the desks.

Curiosity pulled him through a door into a pleasantly air conditioned room where he was destined to spend the bulk of his working hours. He found one of the refrigerators contained agar slants labeled with the names of the *Aspergillus* strains he had ordered to be sent over. He did not recognize many of the others.

In the book collection, Albert found texts related to antibiotic and fungal toxin production and advanced biochemistry, some of which contained several of his own publications.

A computer stood on each of the desks. Albert played with one of them and soon found it linked to the world's scientific literature base, and multilingual translation capabilities were at his fingertips. He would need this literature.

Although Albert felt important, this feeling of identification with his hosts was supplanted by the force of a realization—emotions such as self-importance or pride could cause him to lose focus and get him into trouble. Mistakes could be made.

After several minutes, the man in the blue jumpsuit checked his watch, looked around, and saw Albert inside the room.

Ochenko smiled as he walked through the door of the lab. He stuck out his hand. "Vladimir Ochenko," he said. His voice inflection and the cant of his head presented curiosity at what he saw.

Each man might have been looking into a mirror. The only real difference between them was that Albert wore a rough-hewn beard and the Russian was clean shaven and perhaps fifteen to twenty years older. Each stood with a medium build at five feet nine inches in height. Each possessed an unruly mop of dark hair, similar eyes, nose, and mouth along with a slight paunch.

The men were to discover common ground. They shared the same attitude toward life in general and lacked the normal internal regulatory mechanism of conscience which served to separate civilized humans from barbarians.

After the fall of the Berlin Wall, East German scientists went to the highest bidder. The Chinese and Russians hired many of them to develop undetectable performance-enhancing drugs for competitive sports participants. After the fall of the Soviet Union, various countries hired a number of Russian scientists to create weapons of terror. Weapons of mass destruction had been present since World War I and before. That niche was occupied, although new ideas were always entertained.

One primary architect of the new terror weapons was microbiologist Vladimir Ochenko, who signed on with a backer from the highest-bidding country, Saudi Arabia. In the old Soviet Union, Ochenko had earned the highest honors in microbiology and biochemistry and who believed business transcended all.

Ochenko pioneered the production of mycotoxins for contact dispersal. His theory held that to injure a target population, three strategies should be employed. The first called for a relatively small number of people to be affected. Unless there was a specific target, this method served primarily for its entertainment value. Not causing any great harm, it allowed the population to wonder if a big event would be forthcoming.

The second strategy involved targeting a large number of persons to cause great injury over a relatively short period of time. Fear would self-reproduce exponentially. Neither method could guarantee success in disabling and destabilizing the population, so both were employed. This approach required a very large amount of fungal toxin.

The third strategy would require a massive exposure to a large contained population over a short period of time.

Those decisions were not his to make. He was hired as a project chemist to decide which mold would produce the highest yield and to produce the yield requested.

Ochenko chose aflatoxin as the agent of destruction because of its incredibly high degree of potency. It would also be hard to detect because the symptoms would disguise its presence. Also, it would be an unlikely possibility that anyone would look for it. A major problem remained: How to grow enough mold to produce the quantity of mycotoxin Ochenko was hired to manufacture? This task was akin to single-handedly finding the right strain of *Penicillium* that would produce the most antibiotic and then multiplying the production by ten-thousand-fold.

His investigation led him to Stanley Albert through Albert's publications on purification techniques for fungal toxins. After background checks on the man, it became only a matter of negotiating a price for his services.

Albert took Ochenko's hand in a strong grip. "Stanley Albert," he said.

The two men looked out over the facility as workers added water and growth media to one of the fermenters, cleaned another, and performed modest servicing to a third.

"How long have you been here?" asked Albert, totally engrossed in his new surrounds.

"Little over a year," answered the Russian. "Got a nice high-yield strain of *Aspergillus flavus* I'm testing and playing around with the equipment. So far, got over one hundred grams, a tenth kilo—call it a quarter-pounder." Ochenko laughed at his joke.

Albert considered what his new associate said, turning down both sides of his mouth as a show of respect for the unbelievably high yield. The man definitely knew his business. In the old days, several grams of pure mycotoxin could have been worth its weight in gold. Now the man was producing an unheard of amount of the poison.

As if reading his thoughts, Ochenko said, "They want lots of hundred-gram amounts of crystal packed into tenth-kilo packages, say around twenty-five packages altogether. Got a big project coming up in Africa—something they've been planning for a long time—and we have to do the math, personally. Then they want several times that amount for another project."

Albert quickly ran the numbers through his head.

The task would be daunting. At last he said, "Fine with me, but doesn't anybody here know how to use a computer besides us?"

"Plain old math works fine with me. I don't need to lose all my data because some machine malfunctioned and besides, computers don't have any common sense," the Russian replied with a combination of British and Russian accents in his speech.

"Saw you sent a few of the beasties yourself," Ochenko added. Albert smiled, showing teeth.

"Yes, I shipped over a couple of killer strains of *A. flavus*. One I found growing on a rotten log. It is truly magnificent. I maintain it on wet wood chips to keep it viable. And surprise, surprise, I can't find any other life forms on those chips. You get enough of this crystal, and it'll kill almost anything living. The other one is a strain the WHO isolated from Uganda growing on a large amount of USDA rice. You may have heard a while back about numerous government officials catching cholera in over there."

"No. Some people have to work for a living," the Russian said, too flatly to be taken seriously.

Albert laughed. "In one region, the natives were so happy to get so much rice they cooked up a huge batch and left it out for people to eat it at will. They invited the same government sent officials, who were the ones who horded the original rice shipment, to join them in a party. By then, *A. flavus* and other aflatoxin-producing species also took their share and joined the party. According to estimates, more than two hundred people either died or got so sick they wished they could have died. So the United States got blamed. In the U.S. it hit the news as a cholera epidemic."

Ochenko said, "Breaks my heart. Thanks for nothing foreign aid. It is so much bullshit from the start, whoever gets involved: the Russians, the Arabs, the Americans, the English. I don't care. The people never get anything. Don't get me started."

"I suspect our average citizens are going to get something special this time," said Albert facetiously.

Ochenko shook his head vigorously, as if to dispel evil spirits. "Look, stay out of it. We're here to get rich and do a job. We can't dick around. How you say...'This ain't no party'. These guys are big players. So let's play. It's their game.

"Word is, you're the king of crystallization," continued Ochenko, a hint of tease in his voice.

"That's me," responded Albert, without a trace of humility. "The king of purity. It's as clean as my mind."

Ochenko laughed. "If you're like me, that's a scary thought." Now Albert laughed in turn.

Ochenko became serious. "I'll need you to clean up my batch, and then we'll give it to Rashid. We need to keep everybody happy."

Through experience, the men understood that if oxygen could be pumped into the bell housing, the gas would support fungal growth throughout the entire twenty-gallon tank. This permitted the production of a massive quantity of toxin because the mold grew three-dimensionally, not only on a surface, such as when it was grown in a typical laboratory on agar, or on stationary liquid, or on cooked rice.

Ochenko needed Albert's expertise to help separate the toxins from look-alikes also excreted by the mold, to purify the poison, and to turn it into crystals.

"What do we do with all the left-over pounds of mycelium?" asked Albert.

"I asked the same question of Rashid, and he said to put it into the big freezer. Don't ask me why," answered Ochenko.

Albert nodded knowingly. "I'm guessing they have plans for it. Anyway, are these guys treating you all right?" Albert waved an arm to indicate the entire country.

"No worries, mate," said Ochenko in a poor imitation of an Australian accent. The Russian appeared congenial, good-natured.

"They leave me alone as long as I give them monthly progress reports. They pay on time. One year to the day past my hiring they put some good money in my Bahrain bank account, as promised. Hell, man, to these guys a million dollars is like a hundred dollars to us. No reason to stiff us with play money. Their motto is: Do what we hired you to do and everybody will walk away happy. Nothing complicated."

"What do you know about this Rashid guy who brought me out here?" Albert asked. "He seems to be an interesting character. I get the feeling I wouldn't want to mess with him."

"Rashid, the Brit?" said Ochenko. "A watch-dog—a go-between us and the multibillionaire at the top of this job; a guy named MaHoud. Right now he's here to ensure this particular project goes smoothly and you and I work together well. He's lived in Saudi for years, is fluent in Arabic, and is wired into the top level of government. He's also a friend, someone who can get you things, although I wouldn't trust him with personal secrets. Who knows when he might use them against you? That's a good rule of thumb no matter who you work for. As for the rest of it, good old Rashid knows the circuit. My guess is he's got a lot of garbage floating around in his head I certainly don't want to know about."

Which makes two of us, thought Albert, beginning to wonder, not for the first time, what new hand fate had dealt him.

Ochenko motioned upward with his head toward the south and put his hand on Albert's shoulder. "Come on, Stanley. This is a small portion of our setup. I'll show you the rest that will be our playground for the next three or four years. We've got our own cafeteria, a small mosque, of course, and our own home. If you're like me, you got some spending cash for vacations. Forget it. You'll never get a chance to use it."

"Stan's fine," said Albert, feeling the strength of the man's hand. His new life felt overwhelming. "What do I call you?"

"You may call me Ochenko. Oh, it's okay if you

lose the beard. It won't get you anywhere around here. You're an outsider no matter what you look like."

Albert liked this Russian. Maybe his fears were for nothing. Living in abstinence and maintaining one's sanity at the same time might be possible.

Ochenko smiled broadly. "Come on, my friend. I'll show you around to our quarters. Oh, one more thing." He stopped walking and touched Albert's arm. "A note of caution. Don't get overenthusiastic about anything here, unless it's pro-Islamic, anti-American, or anti-Jewish. The pendulum always swings two ways."

Albert produced a quizzical look.

Ochenko almost whispered in his ear, "It means, my friend, it can come back to bite you. Word has it that Rashid's boss funded the 9/11 attack on America and made a little profit on it too, so let's do our job and get the hell out of here."

2

With Albert closely on his heels, Ochenko walked to the rear of the warehouse and unlocked a steel door set beside a set of double sliding doors, both of which had escaped Albert's notice.

Albert opened his mouth to say something about the need for keys, when he realized the answer. Somebody had invested heavily in this project, both in terms of dollars and probable political gain.

They exited and crossed a fifteen-foot span of concrete. To the left lay the open desert with the nearest building a quarter mile away. To the right lay a smaller building with a cupola, which Albert took to be a mosque.

Ochenko consulted the key ring affixed to his belt and unlocked the door to another smaller building, a miniature of the one they had just left, but without the lab. This facility also included attendants who were operating various pieces of equipment, doing their best to maintain a dust-free environment.

"It's all backup," said Ochenko. "Once in a while, a piece of equipment needs serious repair. Instead of facing downtime, we move in a fully operational piece that we know is working."

They continued walking south and exited another metal door set aside yet another set of large sliding doors, to confront a third warehouse. Albert saw within it a complete newspaper printing operation suitable for turning out thousands of copies a day. Workmen were printing a small four-page newspaper with black and colored ink in some of the inserts.

"What is this about?" asked Albert. He'd never seen such an operation before.

Ochenko laughed. "This, my friend, is what we are all about." He explained their mission statement in some detail.

"These guys are not stupid," concluded Ochenko. "The people who hired us took my idea about ways to use our product and are running with it. We are scientists, are we not? These newspapers have the formulation. Among our other duties, we need to test this ink to ensure it is up to standards. We also need to run tests on the ink after it is printed, compare the amount of aflatoxin we get back with what we put in, and, if it is less, find out why. Then we fix the problem."

"Oh, good, I'll do that in my spare time," snorted Albert.

The two men exited the rear of this final warehouse to face a low apartment building. "This is your new home," announced Ochenko.

Once inside, Albert stared at the expensive dé-cor. He saw two leather armchairs and a sofa, coffee table, wall TV, dining table, marble-top kitchen and bathroom counters, and satellite TVs in the two large bedrooms. Each bedroom had its own full bath along with spacious marble-enclosed showers. His luggage stood near the entrance.

The views from the living quarters were limited to the newspaper printing building to their north and desert to the east, west, and south, albeit through picture windows.

"I'm impressed. What do you do to blow off steam?" Albert asked.

Ochenko led him to a door at the south end of the main living room. A complete gym greeted the men, with stationary bikes, treadmills, universal weight machines, and free weights. Mirrors lined the walls. Yet another large wall-mounted TV faced the exercise machines.

"One question," said Albert. "If I'm staying here with you, why the grand show at the Riyadh Royal Hotel?"

"Oh, that. They're trying to impress you with their muscle. They did the same thing with me."

"I'm impressed, all right." Then Albert lowered his voice. "Aren't you worried about bugs here? I mean..."

"I know what you mean. And no, no listening devices. You don't live where I've lived and work where I've worked without knowing how to search for them. And believe me, we've been thoroughly vetted. There is no reason for them to spy on us. Besides, they don't need to get us pissed off if we found out. Men like us are hard to replace. No, they need the project to get finished and nobody needs trouble.

"One last thing. I really hate to say 'kill or be killed', but you might want to keep that in mind. It's their philosophy and mine too."

3

Before the Saudis hired him from his job in Los Angeles, Albert worked as a graduate student in the same laboratory as Jeffrey Shenero, another graduate. Some twenty years earlier, Albert's ego got him into trouble when a particular batch of purified toxin came out with less potency than he expected. Instead of chalking it up to a loss, Albert altered the data in his lab book to reflect the desired results.

At that time, Albert and Jeff worked on the same project. Jeff needed accurate data to design the next stage of the experiment, but found it would be impossible for Albert to have obtained the results he claimed. Jeff raised the question to his lab partner, while Albert argued and told Jeff he resented the accusation of him lying about the data. Albert's angry retort occurred the same moment their major professor walked in. Each man pleaded his case, and the professor took both students' lab books. Albert left for the day, incensed at Shenero.

The next day the professor called Albert into his office. He remained there for an hour and left the building.

The following day, the professor called for a meeting of the committee which oversaw the work of the two doctoral students. The committee called both men to attend in one of the vacant classrooms.

Albert claimed that the fault lay with Jeff's data which he was working off of which caused him to miscalculate.

Albert listened to Jeff explain his side and had no problem laying the blame on someone with whom he had partnered for two years. While they may not have considered themselves the best of friends, Albert couldn't admit to failure. If he had done so, the matter might have been resolved easily. Instead, he found his career at stake.

The committee requested both men to leave the room while they convened in private to discuss the issue. After a considerable length of time, thee professor called Stanley Albert back into the room where he was summarily expelled from graduate school. Jeff went on to finish the project and gain fame for the discoveries made by himself or under his direction. Albert never forgave him.

In the long run, Albert's creative talents paved the way for his present station in Saudi Arabia with money in the bank. Yet, a person doesn't lose out on a title of doctor without a certain amount of unexpressed anger.

At the time of the incident, Albert worked part

time at a pharmaceutical company in Oklahoma, which became full time after the rift. Within the year, the company transferred him to a branch in Los Angeles. Years later his published papers and expertise in the field of purification techniques kept his name at the forefront of scientists who appreciated solid original work. Ochenko was one of them.

A plane ticket and a promise of great wealth sent Albert overseas for an interview. Subsequently, he resigned from his job and readily accepted the money offered to work in a fully equipped laboratory with no income tax to worry about.

One day in the warehouse, Albert's ears burned when he overheard the name of Oklahoma City during a conversation between Ochenko and a visiting superior. He began to daydream of hurting Jeffrey Shenero in a very real way, not as an event reduced to a recurring fantasy.

Nearly eighteen months after joining Ochenko in Riyadh, Albert seeded two barrels of magenta ink with the toxin mixture dissolved in a special solvent. The on-site printing press aided greatly in their ability to refine their techniques.

Someone above the two men chose Tunisia to be the recipient of the ink. At the conclusion of the experiment, the hard work would begin in earnest in preparation for the attack on the United States.

Albert and Ochenko shut down the fermenters one by one and began the cleaning process necessary for the next round of activity.

The project required that extra colored ink be supplied to the Tunisia press run. Two workers used a forklift to lift the barrels of colored ink onto pallets, including two specially marked barrels of Magenta. The pallets were transferred onto waiting flatbeds while the two men walked back to their residence to take the evening off. Their schedule included eating steak and lobster at home, catching up on old John Wayne movies and whatever else they could find on satellite TV, and sleeping in.

Unfortunately, a late breaking story told of an imminent major sandstorm due to arrive in the early-morning hours. Not prone to watching local news in Arabic, the men were clueless as to the coming event.

The howling wind woke them at first light. The pair looked out the window to the east and saw the city cast in a yellow fog. A huge tidal wave of orange-brown sand roiled over the horizon obscuring the taller buildings. The men were not at all prepared for this particular storm, which appeared to be unusual in its severity.

No words need be exchanged. Time beckoned. Several things became evident. They would not be able to go through the two buildings separating their residence and the main warehouse because the southernmost doors were bolted from the inside. They would have to go down the north-south walkway fronting the mosque where they would have partial shelter at the west end of each building. Between the buildings they would be sand-blasted.

Also, no workers would be present because they would have been forewarned of the storm to remain home. Indeed, public transportation would have come to a standstill.

A third reality presented itself. If too much sand entered the warehouse doors and windows, ostensibly tightly sealed, the fermenters and the other equipment would be ruined along with the project, and themselves. Their bosses would want to know why they weren't prepared. What were they doing when sand got into millions of dollars of equipment? Their contracts stipulated they be prepared for all eventualities. The project must and would succeed.

Scoured and battered, the men now walked completely backwards in the face of the storm in order to reach the very front of the warehouse.

At last Ochenko unlocked the door and faced the receptionist and the armed guard, both men loyal to the core.

Once inside, with no time to relax, the men saw a fine layer of grit covering every horizontal surface in the warehouse. Countless microscopic and submicroscopic particles hung in the air as a fog, most as small as a virus, to make their eyes water and their vision blur.

Ochenko gave Albert a directive. While Albert covered all tabletop equipment with light plastic sheeting kept in rolls for such a purpose, Ochenko turned on a full dozen large air scrubbers, known in thee remediation business as hogs—high-volume HEPA air scrubbers used in the remediation business to remove a large percentage of particles from the air. This technique worked for most practical purposes. The highest percentage of particles were actually smaller than even the HEPA could remove and were a thousand to a million times more numerous than the filtration capability of the machine. These needed to be removed by moisture application.

Ochenko began hosing down the floor and hand-wiping the machines, doing his best to avoid splashing water into the motors that powered the precious fermenters.

Much later, their tasks completed, Albert began working on the second warehouse and the backup equipment while Ochenko moved to the newspaper printing area.

By early the next morning, it was a given they would have to oversee the staff when they returned to work. They would all spend the next several days detail-cleaning the three warehouses and the equipment they contained. Only then would they know if the storm had destroyed anything.

At least the Tunisia project got off the ground. However, if no more mycotoxin could be produced, their time and efforts would all have been for nothing. The Saudis would take back their money, whether it was their fault, or the doing of a greater power. The men could soon be homeless with no plane ticket home.

4

Situated in North Africa, the Republic of Tunisia is bordered by Algeria to the west and Libya to the southeast. The country enjoys nearly seven hundred miles of oceanfront property along the Mediterranean Sea on its northern and eastern borders. The country approximates the size of the U.S. State of Georgia, with a population of ten million. The country celebrates a modest tourist trade, substantially aided by their prideful wines.

Mohammad MaHoud had chosen Tunisia as the target for a number of reasons. After Habib Bourguiba's domination of the country for thirty-one years, his successor continued the government's relatively liberal policies and did not return to Islamic fundamentalism, a matter of concern for other fundamentalist nations, including its neighbor, Libya. However, business is business. When the offer of an extremely large sum of money donated to the president's personal account was privately offered, he could hardly say no to the deal. The almost certain downfall of the West got mentioned as the object of the so-called loan.

Most males over the age of fifteen could read and write in Tunisia. As such, the country enjoyed a relatively high literacy rate. Calculations for the experiment were made based upon this figure at a newspaper dispersal rate of approximately two readers per copy, similar to that found in the West. Thus, ten thousand readers meant some twenty thousand exposures.

Two cities were chosen for the experiment, both interior cities; thus, the foreign tourist trade of the coastal resorts would not be affected. Although a significant drop-off in tourism elsewhere could be expected during any time of crisis, financial compensation allowed for that factor.

The first city targeted was Tozeur, with a population approximating 100,000, slated to receive a high dosage of poison. The second city was Gafsa, located one hundred miles north of Tozeur, with a population of 325,000. Because of its location and with little else to offer, Gafsa lacked any significant amount of tourism. This city would receive a relatively low dosage of poison.

Small local papers were printed in both cities and were selected as the vector. These were chosen because Gafsa papers produced regular features prepared with soy-based colored ink and the city already possessed the infrastructure necessary for the experiment.

Mohammad spent a small fortune to modernize the presses to run color for the experiment. Between the two papers, theoretical high-and low-end exposures were now bracketed thanks to the different concentrations the men had prepared back in Riyadh.

Ochenko wanted more cities added to the test run. Rashid consulted with MaHoud and returned to say that if they included more cities, they might receive undue attention. And infecting the populace of too many cities created other problems, such as insurrection and unnecessary military activity. That aspect would be saved for the United States.

The populace in general and clinics in particular were closely monitored during the experiment. Within twelve to fourteen days after exposure, preliminary symptoms of rashes appeared in both cities. Those of Tozeur were much more profound and faster developing than those of Gafsa. In Tozeur these symptoms lasted for a month, and numerous deaths were recorded, ostensibly because of toxic poisoning. Yellowing of the skin mirrored the onset of jaundice as the liver began to shut down. At that point, the colored-ink supply was changed to fresh, uncontaminated ink. In the infected population, the symptoms spontaneously disappeared as the victims' bodies slowly rid themselves of the poison.

In Gafsa, initial symptoms were less intense, and after one month of exposure, symptoms included a wide range of complaints, less severe than those found to occur in Tozeur. At this point the World Health Organization attempted to make an entrance.

Another two years passed after the conclusion of the Tunisia project and a very large amount of crystal awaited shipment to America.

Mohammad MaHoud stood in the open doorway of the warehouse, the workplace of Vladimir Ochenko and Stanley Albert. Next to him stood Rashid.

Backlighted, the two figures cut entirely different silhouettes. Rashid stood a full six inches beneath the Saudi and weighed sixty pounds less. The dark-bearded MaHoud wore traditional Muslim clothing, giving him the presence of greater girth.

In front of them at several yards distance stood twenty-two drums of ink on pallets, each with the English word MAGENTA stenciled on the side. Twelve of them would go to twelve newspapers in ten cities, and ten would go to the ten publishers of *Your Good Dining* in the same cities. These inks would join their cyan and yellow brethren along their way to the States.

On this day numerous guards, wearing vests and carrying an assortment of weaponry, watched every aspect of their surroundings, both indoors and outside the building.

Rashid spoke in Arabic to the nearest worker who wrote destination tags for each of the ink containers. Then he returned to speak with his employer. The pair walked to the rear of the building to watch as forklifts began to carry pallets of ink containers and loading them onto a line of waiting trucks.

Soon Albert and Ochenko would begin working on another aspect of their job description. This phase would take them another month—decontamination—a lengthy and tedious process.

After the work it would be time to decontaminate; a lengthy and tedious process.

The past years proved to be more difficult for the two scientists than Albert could have imagined. First, they needed to take regular samples from the different vats to follow the amount of toxin produced by the mold as it grew.

The chemicals used to extract the toxin from the liquid were always a potential problem. Most of them were flammable and explosive. This necessitated keeping them indoors and out of the heat. The unpredictable added to their woes, threw off their timetable, and kept them working longer hours than they preferred.

Although Ochenko and Albert could trust the workers to draw off samples from each of the vats, common sense dictated they do the analyses themselves. In addition, sometimes an all-night vigil required one of them to be present when a peak yield was imminent in one of the fermenters.

Then came the laborious task of isolating and purifying the vast quantities of toxin requested without becoming exposed to the poison themselves

All of this left little time for leisure. The mold in the vats took two months to mature. The time period between the completion of one batch of samples and the startup of the next theoretically could be as little as two weeks. Reality dictated three to four weeks.

In addition to their other responsibilities, enough stock cultures had to be grown and maintained in order to seed the vats at the beginning of each run.

The men could not travel together during that time period. Necessity insisted one always remain at the job site.

Finally the years of their slave labor and drudgery ended. Now the time for them to enjoy life could begin.

Ochenko and Albert traveled to St. Petersburg, the city of the Russian's birth. Awash in money, the partners traveled for weeks until they finally purchased a grand home and settled in an upscale area of Puerto Vallarta, Mexico, with false documents and real money to burn. With a monetary exchange rate of twenty-to-one they began to live like kings.

5

While murdering pirates were commonplace on the nether world of the seas, on this particular voyage, the merchant ship *Silent Night* ran free and clear of trouble, an occurrence not unexpected, considering her owner.

The *Silent Night* was one of forty thousand similar merchant ships that plied the vast oceans of the Earth on any given day, in addition to perhaps a million pleasure craft. A single owner had purchased her in Hong Kong for fourteen million dollars. The country of Panama, looking for such a ship, leased her from the owner.

Her registry noted Liberia as her parent country—a country that actually lacked a seacoast, let alone a port. The ship was subleased at a substantial profit to the South Koreans, who then subleased her to the North Koreans. The ship flew the flag of India and shipped a crew consisting of bedraggled seamen of various nationalities, including Thai and

Vietnamese. All members of the crew spoke a form of broken English, the language of the oceans and minor seas.

She was a pretty vessel, with her sides, cranes, and derrick painted dark blue and the single funnel painted in light blue with a red stripe around its upper periphery.

The *Silent Night* had undergone four name changes in an equal number of years, not unusual for ships engaged in covert activities. Only her captain, Sergei Dufour, of Russian and French heritage, knew the owner of the vessel, and he wasn't talking.

On this journey the merchant ship took on several tons of electronics in Malaysia off the dangerous South China Sea. From there she journeyed to Sri Lanka for a load of tea; followed by a trip to Madagascar, where she deposited the electronics and picked up a load of coffee, vanilla, and sugarcane. From Madagascar she sailed to French Guiana to take on one last load.

This last load included forty-four colored-ink containers, each filled with more than three hundred gallons of yellow, cyan, and magenta ink in toxin-free soy oil. These would complement the twenty-two toxin-laden totes of magenta ink on- board. Now jammed to the gills, the 420-foot-long vessel sailed toward the port of New York.

Nearly one hundred thousand miles of coastline exists in the United States, and about one hundred ports of entry could handle the ship's size and her amount of goods. Captain Dufour's orders were to become lost amid the traffic entering the Port of New York daily. Once in the harbor, she waited for a vacant pier to off-load the cargo. Another week passed.

Eventually the colored-ink totes were off-loaded onto semitrailers and transported to an Oklahoma City warehouse, fifteen hundred miles to the west.

From New York the *Silent Night* departed port and headed to Curacao, where she changed names and colors once again.

Four days after the *Silent Night* had deposited her cargo, the MaHoud brothers, Alan and Harry, anxiously supervised the unloading of the ink supply from the line of 18-wheelers as they arrived over the next several hours at their general warehouse outside of Oklahoma City. With a truckers' strike set to begin only hours later, receiving the entire shipment was imperative.

The warehouse complex served as the central hub for all ink supplies used by twelve newspaper and ten *Your Good Dining* magazine printing plants located in ten cities throughout the Midwest.

This included the colored ink for the printing of the newspapers owned by the brothers, the *Oklahoma Storm*, the *Oklahoma City Mirror*, and the *Tucson Times*. Color features occurred on Sundays along with inserts and coupons.

Your Good Dining Weekly Magazine Corporation also received the brothers' ink for their publication because they specialized in high-resolution color pages.

The ink supplied by the brothers also supported occasional smaller press operations through special orders.

Alan felt a sense of pride, as though he were watching the birth of his first child. He knew Harry felt the same way. They had waited literally their entire lives for particular birth. Forklifts raised each pallet from the truck, slowly and carefully handling the goods, as if they were eggs.

While Alan directed the forklifts to a specific location in the building, he felt a sense of wrong, a perception of foreboding. He instantly shoved aside that sense the instant it began.

The brothers managed to find one driver who accepted a very large amount of money to take a chance he wouldn't be blackballed by the union with the strike due to begin momentarily. He volunteered to transfer six ink containers to Tucson, Arizona, three for the newspaper and three for *Your Good Dining*. They found another who would haul six more a few miles further into Oklahoma City to the newspaper plant the brothers owned.

Except for the poisonous contents of one-third of the ink containers, the delivery appeared to be similar to any other delivery day. On those days, rolls of blank paper were received, or necessary machine parts might arrive, or their shipment of ink for all their users would be delivered—basic materials and supplies necessary for the operation of a large newspaper complex.

The night's work completed, the brothers smoked

a last cigarette in a congratulatory toast to the near future and then drove back to their separate homes. Today was Friday. Sundays were always reserved for color features on the front page, occasional inserts, and in coupons. Now the color would be used on Thursdays, an additional day for them to show their stuff.

One week from this coming Sunday, the ink would be changed out for the new and improved variety. The Tunisia project had provided Ochenko and Albert the final pieces of information they needed.

Once a person began to handle the ink, the poison would be absorbed into the body. It would take a period of time to incubate before symptoms occurred, similar to any infection. In this case it would be about two weeks of handling the ink on a regular basis. Reactivity would depend on the person and their lifestyle.

Therefore, Day 1 would begin two weeks after the ink supply was changed out.

By Day 12, after only three or four exposures, including the two Thursdays, the reading public would begin to notice the effects of their work. Some people might die by then. After that, things should move along nicely.

Although Alan and Harry were of Saudi descent, only three persons knew of this lineage. One of them was their true father, along with their father's brother and his wife, their foster parents.

Their true father, Mohammad MaHoud, was

named after his own father. MaHoud the elder, was a wealthy anti-American who sponsored terrorist activities directed toward the United States government and its citizens. He raised his children to follow in his footsteps.

Mohammad the younger and his two young sons were in-route to a family meeting in Belgium to finalize the master plan when their vacation home in Brussels mysteriously exploded. Everyone inside was killed. Authorities claimed that a propane gas leak had leveled the home. Mohammad the younger knew differently.

The death of most of his family gave Mohammad vast power and wealth at an age considerably earlier than anyone could anticipate. The event did not affect the larger plan at all. In MaHood's eyes, the plan could move forward, this time with him at the helm.

With only a brother and sister-in-law remaining and now residing in London under the names of Abrim and Malia Hood, they arranged for his boys, then aged three and five, to live with them as surviving relatives. Using British passports, the family of four moved to Oklahoma City. The four obtained American citizenship, and the boys began their schooling.

Mohammad did have great misgivings about having his sons raised in America, but his long-term vision included this as part of the grand plan. So what if Alan and Harry were westernized and reared in the Midwest. Their guardians would also serve as the boys' trainers.

After moving in with their guardians, the boys went through formal education and eventually joined various writing groups in high school and college. They married American woman and became fathers.

The Hood family possessed money and lived well, not ostentatiously. The boys' male guardian was a jeweler with his own business. Many guessed he was a millionaire. The amount in his domain was actually many billions, money that could be traced back to the Saudi oil fields.

While in college, the sons developed skills in both journalism and business. They began serving as junior apprentices with the Oklahoma City newspapers, working part time.

Mohammad did not want undue attention drawn to the family; thus he stressed hard work and dedication, even while his sons' attitudes were adjusted to appreciate the ways of true Islam.

The sons worked their way through college as reporters. Over the next twenty years, they learned the various aspects of the newspaper trade in Oklahoma City. That particular enterprise held a particular attraction to the Mohammad. One reason was because of its great ink distribution network. Another was the potential availability of a company owned by Daniel Kirk and his wife Lorraine for over thirty years.

The boys occasionally saw their father at his getaway mansion in Malibu, California, when their guardians, and later the brothers themselves, made business trips to Southern California.

While Alan was logical and cool like his father,

Harry turned out to be impetuous from an early age. He became involved in numerous fights throughout his school years. As a result, after high school graduation, the foster parents and the two children took a two-month trip abroad. That was when Mohammad MaHoud had a lengthy and stern one-sided talk with Harry regarding his heritage, his allegiance, and his actions. When they returned from vacation, Harry was a different man outside, although Alan could see he was seething beneath the surface; Harry possessed a craving to destroy something large, something on a grand scale.

The Hood brothers made a solid offer to the Kirks and after negotiations, the purchase was completed. The Kirks were pleased two of their outstanding and dedicated employees wanted to buy from them.

Now that the future was here, the brothers had seen to the safety of their families by moving them far from coming events.

Time also dictated that the brothers take a moment for personal matters. One of these included a meeting with their father in Malibu, a meeting they dared to miss.

The father and his two sons lounged poolside and drank iced tea. Mohammad MaHoud wanted to raise his children in the strictest of Muslim traditions; reality led him in a different direction. The death of his family some forty years earlier had left him no choice but to have his sons raised in the West if his great plan was to succeed. They would have to be trained properly while living among the enemy—not an easy thing to do. He might have to pay the price later.

In Mohammad MaHoud's eyes, philandering was permissible. Women were meant to be used and abused; especially Western women. Unfortunately this planned victory over the Americans would not free him from the curse of many religious leaders within his own country and throughout the Muslim world because of his lack of total faith and the lack of total faith of his sons. While this bothered him somewhat, he was willing to let it slide a little longer until the project concluded. He was a practical man and would worry about atoning for it later.

He'd spent most of his adult life building on the fortune his father had left to him and his brother, and programming Alan and Harry for this moment. Soon the Americans would be just another page in the history book, and his people could take control of the land they already occupied, as countless of his faction came into the country among the millions of immigrants who had streamed inside, ironically with government protection. This country would belong to the Muslim people sooner or later. He preferred it to be sooner. His personal scheme for post-apocalyptic America definitely did not include Anglo rule.

Palm trees decorated the interior grounds of the home, and servants bustled about, cleaning the pool, trimming hedges, and planting flowers. An armed guard carrying a submachine gun patrolled the house grounds, moving randomly, unpredictably.

The trio discussed the ink project at some length, and Mohammad closed it out abruptly by saying, "I gave you an assignment, Hari. What did you find out?" Mohammad preferred to use his sons' given names when in private.

Harry set his drink of tea on the table, took a moment to pull out several papers. He said, "PolyWrap is the largest wrapping and bagging company in the country. Based in Los Angeles, the company manufactures and distributes countless millions of polypropylene and cellophane bags and a million yards of sheet films per year. They directly employ a thousand people with another five thousand in ancillary outlets.

"PolyWrap supplies bags for bread-making companies and supermarkets for the bagging of fruits and vegetables by customers. It provides sheet film for covering fruits and vegetables, packaged and frozen meats, coverings for record albums, CDs, DVDs, videotapes, cigarette packs, candy wrappers, toothbrushes, and literally a thousand other uses.

"A subdivision of PolyWrap furnishes the ink labels for their products, which include special orders for supermarket chains and any products requiring a special label. I also know that buying out a company such as this would be a good business investment, however it's much less expensive and more time-efficient to buy off key personnel instead.

"Good so far. Go on," said Mohammad, impressed by the depth of his son's research. He wanted his sons to become schooled in business, mathematics and the art of stealth. Loyalty was a given.

Harry admired his father and tried his best to emulate the man. This would include his lack of regard for anyone but himself. Life was a business and should be run as such, not run like a touchy-feely democratic society that functioned more on emotion than on practicality.

Harry continued, "I could give you the background check on their chief technician. I am certain he will take the money. However, the physical aspects of the project won't work. The way cellophane is made, cellulose fibers are treated in strong alkali. The mycotoxin can't be added at this point because the agent would be destroyed. The paste of cellulose is forced through a slit and comes out as a sheet. This is sprayed with sulfuric acid. A large amount of mycotoxin present would be destroyed during this process.

"In addition, in the preparation of the stretchable and regular plastic sheets used for holding and wrapping products, high heat is employed. While the toxin can withstand the heat of home cooking, it cannot survive this process. Therefore, although we have the weapon, it cannot be deployed here."

"And the talcum powder?" inquired the father.

"No-go there either," replied Harry. "While talc is used in chewing gum and aspirin, in addition to its use as a powder, there are some thirty brands out there and more than one source. I don't see it as a prospect worth pursuing."

"I'll accept that. Good job," said Mohammad.

Mohammad said, "Ali?"

Unlike his younger brother, the handsome Alan MaHoud already looked like his father's brother, the man who had raised him. At the same time, Harry couldn't avoid feeling the odd man out, though his father had treated both sons equally through the years.

Alan, too, reviewed a number of papers in front of him. "The toothpaste industry is two billion dollars a year strong. While there are many brands, one company is responsible for three-quarters of the toothpaste sales. That company is Marker General Foods. Toothpaste contains about fifteen different ingredients. Oh, Father, get this." Alan became enthusiastic. "Propylene glycol is added to help stop mold from growing."

Alan and Harry began laughing. Their father merely smiled.

Alan went on, "The beauty is the relative simplicity of adding our own special ingredient. This can be done at any one of a number of stations during the manufacture of the toothpaste. We can also coat the inside of the tube during its manufacture.

"Normally, some twenty percent of toothpaste users get canker sores from the sodium laurel sulfate that is typically added. I think we can help raise the level of canker sore formation to one hundred percent and greatly increase the size of the sores.

"Here's another good point. No acids, strong bases, or heat of significance are applied in the processing of toothpaste. And finally, the chief scientist at

Marker is a man named Benjamin Posner. Recently battered in a bad divorce settlement, Posner is completely tapped out. His marriage lasted nearly ten years, and his income for the next several years will go toward monthly payments to his wife and children. It will leave him enough to pay the rent and not much left for food.

"Marker reneged on their promise to give him a significant pay raise after the ten-year mark, so he's really strapped. Posner took the one hundred thousand dollars in cash our man offered him two weeks ago. He wants to leave the country for Argentina. As you requested, he was told that another hundred thousand will be banked in his name anywhere in the world he requests."

"No doubt it was impressed upon this Posner the need to complete the task," said the father as a statement rather than a question.

"Very much so," said Alan. "Posner knows the stakes, and it's too late for him to turn back. I asked Luis Alvarez, our Spanish friend from Madrid, to fly in, make the deal with Posner, and fly out again. None of us are involved anywhere."

Alan went on to describe another plan he was prepared to put into action: the poisoning of women's face cream. He concluded by pointing out other options, such as adding it to eye shadow, eye drops, shaving lotion or perfume.

His father took a strong drag of his opium-laced cigarette, tilted his head backward, blew out a cloud of smoke, and leaned forward to look the brothers in the eyes. "My sons, let us understand one thing. We are not on an exercise like a soccer team in practice. I want these Americans dead and their sons and daughters dead. Hari, help your brother with his project. I do not want either of you to fail." He did not have to elaborate.

After Alan's presentation, Mohammad raised his arm, and a moment later a servant came over. "Put these documents in the safe," he told the man in Arabic. The man bowed and did as directed.

DAY 1–Tucson, Arizona—twelve days after first exposure and end of incubation period

Percy Butler was one of the first cases of the epidemic. Affectionately known as the Old Wino, he checked himself into the clinic, conveniently located down the street from his place of business.

Little Darlin', a short-haired terrier, now approaching eight years of age, always accompanied her master. Her plastic milk crate home lay on its side covered with newspapers and padded inside with more newspapers to offer her a place of comfort and shade from the hot Arizona sun while she maintained vigil over her master. Percy had placed the milk crate in the center island of a thoroughfare where he was identified as a city fixture, replete with beard and good nature, for all to encounter as they crossed the street or drove past.

The city permitted him this and allowed him to

sell newspapers to motorists who stopped at the red light of his intersection situated at the cross streets of Tucson and Broadway Boulevards. In fact many of the motorists actually wished the light would turn red on them so they could buy a paper, say hello to Little Darlin', and hand Percy a water bottle on the fly with a quick and always cheerful wave of the hand. Occasional traffic jams occurred at "Percy's Station—A Public Landmark," as one Sunday edition of the paper proclaimed several months before.

Percy looked the part of the classic vagabond. To most, he appeared homeless. That was far from the truth. Only occasionally shaven, he tried his best to wear relatively clean clothing and maintain a modicum of personal hygiene. He never drank on the job. His plethora of legitimate ailments included the presence of shrapnel lodged next to his spine he obtained while serving as point man for his platoon in Vietnam. Once drafted into the war, he accepted his fate philosophically. Within only a few months of entering the Asian country he was wounded yet managed to carry another wounded man away from the field of battle into the arms of a medic who saved both of their lives. Percy was awarded the Purple Heart.

Percy was never a good student and even though the GI bill was available to him, he opted against going back into formal education. More than one teacher had told him he wasn't very bright and to seek a life outside of an educational setting.

After the war Percy was offered a job as a carpenter by an old friend, which he accepted. After only two months of carpentry work, Percy lost the index finger of this left hand in a freak accident with a circular saw. Insurance compensated him. On the advice of friends, Percy invested the bulk of the money into Texas Instruments, a small company his friends believed would grow substantially. This proved to be a good choice, and over time, Percy quintupled his money.

With his money well hidden, Percy worked a number of odd jobs, always living an austere life, preferring life on the lower end of society.

"Try as they damn well might, the two things the government can't take away from me are my freedom and my poverty," he was heard to say on occasion.

In those days, although Percy liked to foster the notion of his being a very poor man, he lived in a studio apartment for which he paid eight hundred dollars a month, including utilities, a short bus ride away from where he worked as a cleanup man for a landscaping company.

Then, while riding with a friend one day, their car was struck on Percy's side, and he was permanently disabled with a neck that wouldn't stop hurting. He turned to alcohol as a painkiller. It took the combination of years of alcohol abuse and bad luck for Percy to find five years of happiness at his present station in life working on the street corner.

In the grassy neighborhood of the clinic, the early spring air in Tucson smelled as fresh as newly mown lawns. Homeowners dotted the neighborhood, cutting, trimming, bagging, painting, and planting, all as a hormone-driven calling which caused them to flutter about their nests.

Percy tied his Jack Russell terrier to an African sumac tree in the shade in the front yard of the clinic only two hundred yards from his corner. Whispering a few words to her to behave, he entered the air-conditioned freshness of the reception area.

This Monday Dr. George Haskell would see his patient in Exam Room 3. Percy had begun to see him regularly for the past three and a half years, shortly after Haskell had joined the clinic.

"Hey, Percy, how's everything going today?" asked the bespectacled Dr. Haskell, only four years out of medical school.

Always genial, the doctor still found time for exercise. He had a full head of dark-brown hair parted down the side and a well-trimmed mustache. A slightly shorter height didn't seem to bother him. He always maintained good color to his skin, which spoke of outdoor activities in the desert community. Married with children, Haskell maintained the innocence of a man not too experienced in the ways of the medical world. As a new clinic doctor, he loved to play word games with his patients and became a popular doctor because of it.

"Not so good, I don't think," said Percy, this day sorely in need of a shave.

"Back acting up again?" asked the doctor.

"That's always there, Doc, but something funny

is going on." Percy displayed the fingertips of both hands and the angry redness on both forearms.

"Have you looked in a mirror lately, Percy?"

"Not if I can avoid it," said the Old Wino jokingly.

"You've got more redness around your lips, your nostrils, and the edges of your eyes."

"Let me see," requested Percy. Haskell handed his patient a mirror.

"I saw that yesterday," said the patient, examining his face from various angles. "The eyes are new, though. I thought there was something funny going on."

"You can say that again," said Haskell, comfortable enough around his patient to make the statement.

Percy laughed.

"How's your pup?" asked Haskell, as he examined the rashes carefully, noting that the skin in all the areas was beginning to slough off. The forearms were the worst.

"Little Darlin' has got something bothering her nose and her tongue. I need to take her to the vet," replied Percy.

Haskell didn't respond to this and called the nurse to collect blood and urine samples from the patient, and then he left to examine another patient.

The nurse entered the room and gave Percy a urine cup. He knew where the bathrooms were located.

A short while later, Percy exited the bathroom

and returned to Exam Room 3, where he gave the sample to the nurse, who labeled it and left.

Dr. Haskell returned to ask, "Do any of these areas itch, Percy?"

"No, they burn. It's worse on Sunday and Thursday. Trouble was you were closed yesterday being a Sunday and all.

"How long has this been going on, Percy?"

"Oh, seven or eight days," answered the patient.

"Most likely it's not an allergy," said Haskell. "I'm going to put anti-inflammatory cream on these rashes, except for the red areas around your eyes. I don't want you to rub the cream into them, so you'll have to suffer there. The redness should go down within an hour or so. Try icing an area and see if it helps. Check back with me next week, and we'll take another look. "First, though, I want pictures."

Haskell pushed a button on his desk phone and asked for a particular nurse to meet Percy in the photography room, where a large whiteboard hung on one of the walls for a backdrop.

When Percy returned from having his photographs taken, Haskell met him at the door to the exam room.

"I'm not going to lie to you, Percy. I think you have some real trouble. As you know, according to blood testing over the past year, your liver will stop working sometime in the near future. Add this rash business to that problem...suffice it to say, I'm concerned."

Percy shrugged carelessly. "I'll do better tomorrow."

Percy was satisfied with his station in life. With his local fame, a place of prominence, and enough money saved and invested to draw on for any of his daily needs, Percy felt very comfortable. He needed to show love and feel love, and Little Darlin' filled the void.

"Thanks, Doc," he responded, after Haskell presented his opinion regarding Percy's rashes. "After you fix me up, I'd better get back to work."

Percy left the clinic, untied his dog, and took another look at her red, irritated nose. She kept licking at it. He noticed her tongue appeared to be red and swollen.

Percy returned with her to their place of employment and finished out the workday. In the evening, Percy permitted his pet to lick his forearms. In the past he'd found that when she licked his paper cuts and other occasional wounds, they seemed to heal faster. In this case nothing seemed to help.

"Sorry about your nose and your mouth, sweetie," he said, lying on his bed with his pet next to him.

Percy finished his spaghetti and meatballs dinner, but his companion hadn't eaten for several days. Now she wagged her tail and cuddled up in her master's arms, running her tongue over her nose.

The following afternoon, Percy left his station early and took his partner to the veterinarian, who could not pinpoint the cause of her problem. He gave her an injection of nutrients and put her on a special diet, hoping to reduce the amount of swelling around her oral cavity. Percy paid cash for the visit and decided to place his pet in critical care at the vet hospital. After several days she improved and found herself back in her master's arms.

Percy didn't improve. Feeling too ill to care for his pet, he left her with a neighbor for the night and returned home. When he didn't return to pick her up the next day, the neighbor paid a visit and found that Percy had died in his bed.

Authorities discovered Percy's will in his apartment whic had been recently notarized. He'd left all his cash and investments and Little Darlin' to Dr. Haskell.

Day 1–Oklahoma City, Oklahoma—twelve days after first exposure and end of incubation period

At the same time Percy Butler was reporting his problems in Tucson, Margarete Hutchinson was incurring her own issues in Oklahoma City, while preparing for her seventy-fifth birthday.

Described by her children as intelligent and witty, Margarete had a fetish for much younger men. Living most of her life in Oklahoma City, she could dance and party with the best of the over-sixty-five crowd. A pack-a-day smoker, Margarete's life was filled with riches until the death of her husband fourteen years earlier. After coming to terms with that tragedy, she sold their spacious home and moved into an apartment building in the south portion of the city, which they also owned.

One of her new neighbors, another widow, asked Margarete how she had coped with the death of her husband. Margarete responded by saying that after his passing, she began dating a number of older men, but gave it up because they had nothing intelligent to say other than time-worn philosophies, always angling their conversation toward sex. So she shifted her attention to younger men who possessed no philosophy other than sex. She now enjoyed her privacy and, if necessary, could contact a number of friends, when the need arose.

After her primary physician diagnosed Margarete with lung cancer, she underwent a heavy bout of chemotherapy but continued to smoke, not unusual for those whose eyes saw the inevitable looming on the horizon.

Margarete's dearest possessions were her books. A farm woman from near Green Bay, Wisconsin, she was a diehard fan of the Green Bay Packers, and after the death of her parents, possessed three long-term season tickets to the games, worth a small fortune. She sold these to buy collector's editions of books.

Margarete went to the University of Wisconsin–Madison, majored in English Literatuer, and obtained a bachelor's degree.

In her senior year of college, Margarete met Benjamin Hutchinson, a self-described world traveler. They fell in love and were soon married. Benjamin was twenty-five years older than his bride and infinitely wiser and more experienced. He taught her the ways of the world as they traveled on his yacht from one port to another. The trade-off was that she would teach him classical literature. Her trim, dark-haired, and handsome husband eagerly accepted the offer. Two children resulted from the marriage.

Benjamin's home was based in Oklahoma City, where he gained his wealth from the developing oil fields.

After some forty years of marriage and Benjamin's death, Margarete vowed to remain a single woman, a vow she never regretted. She didn't want to go through the death of another husband and the freedom of doing what she alone wanted to do was refreshing.

Following the woeful diagnosis, her entire attention went toward learning as much as she could about the disease that spelled out her oncoming demise. Computer illiterate, she purchased newspapers and magazines and cut out any article she could find relating to the latest in treatments and possible cures. She possessed shoe boxes full of clippings, all organized in terms of subject matter. She reviewed the newest clippings regularly. As a wise shopper, she saved and catalogued countless coupons, relevant or not to her lifestyle. An aficionado of fine food, she regularly perused *Your Dining Pleasure* magazine to read the latest taste treats of nearby restaurants.

The irritating rash on her fingers and various areas of her face began almost simultaneously with the chemotherapy. Mystified, her physician, Dr. Jasper, took a blood sample and also requested a urine sample. He told his nurse to call him when the results were returned.

Three days later Dr. Jasper's nurse called Margarete and then transferred her to the doctor's line.

He explained, "Margarete, the results of your blood work came back yesterday, and frankly, I don't see anything here we can use to help you. "Do you have any idea what could cause this rash?" the patient asked curiously.

"I'm sorry, but not at this time," responded the doctor. "I don't think it's an allergy because there is no itching involved. Otherwise we could sleuth it down and I'd give you some cortisone cream. Unfortunately it's not that. I'm going to give you a referral to a dermatologist. For now, let me give you back to the nurse, and she can make the arrangements.

Margarete hung up the phone, picked up her latest newspaper, and lit a cigarette. Her fingertips on both hands were red with rash, as were the insides of her fingers. And they burned. Portions of the skin around the rashes were peeling. The outside of her fingers were unremarkable. There was also a rash on her right ear, including the lobe, areas she'd always rubbed out of nervous habit.

A mosquito or bug had attacked her inner thigh which was red with rash and it both burned and itched. The more she scratched it the more the rash developed. Then, like her fingers, the skin around it began to peel. Topical antibiotics were no help at all.

She checked her page-by-page calendar, which

she always used to keep track of events in her life, large or small. The redness started two Sundays ago.

She hadn't told the doctor because he would think she was losing her memory. In actuality she was. She couldn't work her crossword puzzles anymore and she had headaches. Her moods were sullen at times and exaggerated at others, and her eyes hurt. Strangely enough, her liver hurt when she pressed on it, as though it were inflamed. She knew a thing or two about chemo and this stuff didn't fit. She decided not to mention the symptoms to her doctor who might view her as a complainer.

Who could she tell about this who might understand? Her children were coming at the end of the week to join her in a birthday celebration. She could discuss it with them.

Two days later she died from a stroke.

Drs. Haskell and Jasper chanced to meet at a medical seminar in Denver. During the meeting the two doctors exchanged stories about strange cases they had encountered, a normal topic of conversation at medical meetings. The doctors shared verbal notes and could not find a common denominator between Butler and Hutchinson.

What they did not know at the time was that each of them had experienced one of the earliest recorded cases of the epidemic. Once the epidemic broke only days later, they reported their respective cases to the CDC.

PART TWO

Totally ignorant of Percy Butler and Margarete Huthinson's demise, Jeffrey Shenero was busy telling colorful stories about the various exotic fungal diseases known to the world of science. Many of the tales were borrowed from his own experiences and adventures.

His medical mycology lectures were scheduled for seven in the morning on Mondays, Wednesdays, and Fridays. All fifty-four of the students in class were present on this day when Jeff told his famous story. These students represented three laboratory sections of eighteen students each.

Jeff stood behind a long counter. A large whiteboard hung behind him on the wall. In the tray were a variety of water-based colored markers. He looked out over the tiered seating arrangement where most of these students awaited his every word. He paused to take measure of the class, looking many of them directly in the eyes. He saw perhaps one bright scholar, many aspiring microbiologists, and a score of students who would make a living for themselves in this field.

He needed to excite them, to pour fuel into their souls and turn them into the hotness of independent suns. His aura added to the romance and poignancy of the moment. Unfortunately, more often than not, despite his aura his regular lectures were usually dull.

Many of Jeff's peers saw him in the same vein. Despite his accomplishments, many classed him as "high risk, high gain."

They were correct in their perception. To others, he was a man who might apply for patents or a person who was on the verge of something wonderful, perhaps one who might make a great and wonderful discovery. They would also be correct.

"Permit me to take you right now to another universe not so far away where a certain exotic mold was discovered here in the States."

On the screen he presented a video.

The students sat transfixed. This was the famous lecture.

Jeff began. "Pratlong Gullulong first went to the University of Texas as a graduate student from Bangkok, Thailand. Quickly inaugurated into the university party scene, the electrical engineering major, affectionately known as Pratfall, might have downed a few too many drinks and took off his shirt during a weekend fraternity party.

"With black-light strobes flashing, Pratfall stood out among the numerous dancers because the scaly patches on his chest glowed in the dark whenever the strobe flashed."

The renowned professor paced back and forth at the bottom of the lecture room as the students watched the glowing dancer freeze-framed in the strobe. "In fact Prat's sheen was so magnificent that his partner and the other dancers and onlookers stopped whatever they were doing and stared."

Student's heads lowered in attempted sleep began to rise. "According to what Prat told me, he thought they loved his dancing. Referred from the University of Texas at Austin to the University of Oklahoma, Pratlong fell into my lap for a diagnosis. No medical doctor could find his problem. It's not their fault or the fault of their training," Jeff apologized for the medical community.

"If a man or woman from Botswana came to you, how would you diagnose their particular problem? Unless you were experienced in diseases from that area of the world, you wouldn't have a clue, so when when Mr. Gullulong came to my office, I did the same thing. After I turned out the lights and put a black light on him, he glowed in the dark.

"Then I took a skin scraping and examined it microscopically. I found what I was looking for." Here he flashed a microscopic picture of the mold growing in the skin.

"A daily application of sodium thiosulfate, otherwise known as 'hypo' to photographers, was suggested to cure the problem.

"Welcome to the world of the fungi and the molds," said the pacing scientist. "They can poison you to death or cure you. They can grow on you and in you. They can make you sneeze or bring down a building. They can cure whatever ails you or get you burned at the stake. They make bread and alcohol and at the same time destroy billions of dollars of crops each year. Do not underestimate them. And, by the way, welcome to *my* world.

"Now I would like to introduce you to two of my graduate students who have finished their own research and will be assisting you in bettering your laboratory skills. These would be Parker Johnson and Richard Smith."

Parker and Richard rose from their chairs in the front row as their names were called.

Although not particularly handsome, the unmarried, light-skinned African American was extremely smooth and dangerous around women.

The second graduate student to be introduced was thirty-two-year-old Richard Smith, a married man, thus far childless, who knew more about the inner workings of most advanced scientific equipment, including computers, than did the men who sold the equipment.

Richard's bio noted that constructed and repaired equipment and computers for a hobby. After reading the applicant's academic qualification and expertise with instruments, Jeff accepted Smith on a full scholarship.

Both Parker and Richard were finished with their coursework and research and were writing their dissertations prior to final oral exams.

Jeff's third graduate student, Marilyn Woods, was not yet ready for teaching. A master's candidate, she possessed a strong background in biochemistry and at the age of twenty, was the co-author of three papers in the fields of microbiology.

Raised in near poverty, Marilyn's father currently worked as the thankless manager of a fast-food restaurant while her mother babysat for extra money.

A straight-A student at her father firmly believed his beautiful brown-haired be-freckled daughter was meant for movie stardom instead of driving herself to become a hard research scientist. Yet regardless of her sex appeal, no current problem with Parker and Marilyn Woods existed; Marilyn was a simple woman of strict upbringing who wanted to save *it* for marriage.

Marilyn had the full package: high intelligence, wit, and delicate femininity. She was shy and reclusive by nature. Jeff clearly saw her potential as a graduate student and convinced her to sign on as a master's candidate.

With nothing but smooth sailing ahead, Jeff Shenero and his staff enjoyed the peace and tranquility that comes with being at the right place at the right time.

Day 10–Early morning—ten days after deaths of Butler and Hutchinson

The federal agents arrived earlier than expected while Jeffrey Shenero found himself behind schedule. He completely forgot about the appointment while writing a high-end grant proposal until Carmen, his office manager, called him at home about the presence of the two men. Fortunately he was dressed and the Rottweilers had been fed. Now it was only a matter of locking up the house and jumping into his Mustang.

Jeff had two offices, one at the university and the other, only blocks from the school, was his personal business office on Boyd Street off Campus Corner. It had once been an old small restaurant that Jeff had purchased and converted. In the front was a moderate-size meeting room, and through a door were two desks, a sofa, fridge, and other accoutrements necessary to operate a small business.

Frustrated because he prided himself on his punctuality, he dearly wished to get this business finished quickly. He had a class lecture to give at the medical school in Oklahoma City, not far up the interstate.

He pulled into the front lot. Alongside Carmen's Toyota Camry he noticed a black Lincoln Town Car.

Jeff took a calming breath as he stole one last look at himself in the rearview mirror. His vanity would not accept the process of going bald, so, years before, he began shaving his head on a regular basis.

His eyes were brown with a slight almond shape to them. He possessed high cheekbones, a trait not present in either of his parents. A strong, two-inch-long jagged scar ran from his left eyebrow into his forehead at a forty-five-degree angle, the result of a gouging from a stalactite while he was caving in Palau. To many, the facial package gave him a less than normal appearance.

Jeff flipped to a moment of self-denigration. He felt sullen and lonely and frequently thought about his ex-wife and the way she had left him. He could only blame himself for his anger, although he didn't know how to get over it.

His wife simply walked out one day citing irreconcilable differences, her term for her husband's marriage to his work. Jeff's outspoken nature led to her embarrassment at several luncheons and dinner parties. Professional scandals revolving around her husband continued unabated. She used to tell him that his *moral* compass needle pointed to true north, while his *oral* compass needle spun in circles.

Jammed with a heavy schedule, he also needed to plan for his upcoming lecture at the University of Arizona medical school in Tucson.

Pulling himself together, Jeff walked into his office. Two men stood there restlessly. Both wore conservative blue suits and standard Brooks

One of the men stood before a wall on which hung his various award plaques. The other man looked at an eight-by-ten color photomicrograph of *Penicillium notatum*, a picture the mycologist had taken years earlier through the lens of a microscope.

"Hello, gentlemen. I apologize for being a little late," he offered. He made a show of looking at his watch. He approached the man who was looking at the photograph. His hair was shaved into a buzz cut and his posture strongly suggested a military bearing. "It does look like a paintbrush, doesn't it? What you're looking at is the part of *Penicillium* that produces the spores.

He was about to explain how this same mold was harvested years later to produce the lifesaving antibiotic penicillin, but read the signs of distraction. The man only stared blankly at him.

These men are totally bored. This is not a good start to my day, Jeff thought.

The entire story about the discovery of the first antibiotic fascinated Jeff when he first heard it. It told of high adventure, intellectual challenges, heroes, and a chance to save lives. The bugle beckoned.

At the first opportunity, he began the pursuit of the study of antibiotics, the stuff of life, and mycotoxins, such as aflatoxin, the stuff of death—both the products of mold. His goal was to use them together as chemotherapeutic agents. His scientific papers describing the beneficial interaction between lifesaver and life-taker were legend.

The man to whom he was speaking turned and said, "Dr. Shenero, we appreciate your apologies for your tardiness, although late is late. My name is Robert Brewer. I'm with the Department of Homeland Security. My associate here is Dr. James Whitaker, who represents the United States Public Health Service."

"Please be seated, gentlemen," Jeff offered. "I'm afraid I'm on a limited schedule. I need to teach shortly."

This man Brewer radiated military. He was over six feet in height and broad shouldered. His eyes told of battle-hardened cunning and experience and a long career with the armed services. The man did not seem to have adjusted well to civilian life.

The other man, Whitaker, late fifties, was of medium height and sported a salt-and-pepper mustache matching his hair. Jeff had not heard his name. Doubtless, Whitaker had his connections to rise to his present level of authority.

In contrast to Brewer's hard eyes, Whitaker's, although severely bagged, glinted with geniality.

Whitaker said, "Sir, I, too, am a microbiologist. Actually, I recently retired as CEO of a major laboratory before being asked into administrative positions with the health services. Frankly I prefer the microscope rather than management. Now I've been called to duty in another regard to head this investigation." He chuckled, seemingly trying to bond with Jeff.

Jeff was on the verge of asking what investigation Whitaker was talking about when Carmen entered the room.

As was her custom, Carmen seated herself in a folding chair near the doorway to the inner office. Shenero introduced them to her turned his attention back to their guests.

The men stared overly long at this tall, leggy woman who might be Puerto Rican or Cuban with a trace of European in there somewhere. Her luxurious head of black hair hung in ringlets, her lips were full and moist, and her skin suggested an olive color absolutely blemish free. *Wrong woman for the wrong man,* each of them thought, replacing Shenero with themselves.

Brewer regained his focus. "Doctor, if you don't mind—no offense, ma'am—we need this to be private."

Before Jeff could say a word, Carmen smiled and returned to her duties in the inner office. Out of sight from any visitors, she donned a headset, listening and recording the conversation being transmitted from a microphone she'd hidden prior to the men's arrival. She did this on occasion when her boss believed he might need to review an important private conversation. In this instance they opted to use a standard digital recorder to avoid recording a discussion via computer. This included a conversation involving government representatives. A computer recording could be hacked, copied, stolen, or used against them in some indefinable way.

Jeff ambled over to a desk chair at a computer, Brewer took the armchair, and Whitaker the sofa. Each visitor set his briefcase on the floor next to him.

Brewer spoke first. "Dr. Shenero, we're here to talk about the epidemic that has hit a few of our cities that started about ten or fifteen days ago. I'm sure you're aware of it," he stated.

"Not the details," replied the mycologist. "I don't have a lot of free time get involved with current events."

Jeff saw Brewer react to his strong retort when the man instantly pursed his lips and narrowed his eyes. Jeff was accustomed to that reaction.

"Doctor, the press is reporting that numerous people are affected," Brewer said. "In fact, nobody really knows the truth."

"That's hardly what I would call a sweeping epidemic," replied the scientist. "How much of that is hype, and how much is real? Sounds like another flap that the media cooks up to generate news on a slow day. Not to be rude, gentlemen, but I feel confident you have a point to make, and I do need to get to the medical school."

Jeff's emotional pendulum began to swing back and forth in broad sweeps; not a good sign—an indication that life was becoming too complicated in a way not to his choosing.

Jeff disliked disingenuous people and purposely confronted them. He knew the difference between right and wrong, and on this occasion he deliberately chose to be rude. At the moment he didn't care. He was becoming frustrated. Social graces did prevail, however, and he backed off a notch, relaxing his tense shoulders.

Jeff's couldn't resist a perverse sense of enjoyment as he tweaked Brewer's sensibilities. He knew his type. Brewer was nearing the boiling point with red face and a trace of actual spittle at one corner of his mouth.

Whitaker entered the conversation not yet a minute old. To Jeff his body language was all wrong. He appeared tenser than he should be, and his heat signature was elevated when it shouldn't be.

Whitaker continued. "Right now it looks like the

count is approximately fifty in Oklahoma City and half that number in Tucson, Arizona. We believe there are many more cases in each city. We know of one death in each of them. Several cases are in Tulsa, and two or three are right here in Norman. There are a few in various areas extending beyond the hot spots, such as one as far south as Nogales, Mexico. I believe that's across the line from Nogales, Arizona."

"And?" queried Shenero, whose mind wandered to his upcoming lecture, until he processed Whitaker's words. If Whitaker were in the hierarchy of the United States Public Health Service, he would have beneath him the NIH, which, in turn, oversaw the CDC, or Centers for Disease Control and Prevention. This would mean he oversaw virtually every aspect of health, including chemical and radiation emergencies, natural disasters, mass trauma, bioterrorism, epidemics of AIDS, influenza, COVID-19, and the common cold. Tens of billions of dollars could under his control. In short, the man held a very important position, yet Jeff believed he wasn't being told everything about this purported epidemic.

Jeff's attacks on these men could cost him dearly in grant monies since many of his training grants came from the CDC. Wasn't writing a grant proposal to the agency only this morning the reason for his rush to the office for this meeting?

Jeff's head throbbed. "Help me here, gentlemen. What do I have to do with this?" He needed to publish to be considered for them.

Jeff didn't like Brewer. The man's statement about late being late was uncalled for in a professional setting of this informal nature. After all, they were the guests who had entered his domain.

Whitaker chanced a smile. "Your publications and the students you turn out have provided you with quite a reputation. You are the reason why we're here. The press you've obtained during the toxic mold trial and the Dunham Elementary School fiasco kept you in the national, if not international, limelight for quite a while."

Whitaker added, "Doctor, if may interest you to kinow that own Senator Evans strongly recommended you for the job."

They had talked to Senator Evans? Jeff and Evans had known each other since the time the senator hired Jeff. Apparently, Evans' wife discovered mold growing on the wall behind the bathroom vanity and Jeff fixed the problem, getting the senator's wife off his back. Now he could do no wrong in the man's eyes.

Whitaker had picked at a scab. The trial Whitaker referred to had concluded two years before and it scarred Jeff. This occurred shortly after his wife's departure. A greedy family, their lawyer, a self-proclaimed remediation expert, and a medical doctor with questionable motives all combined forces to sue him for seven million dollars. Their claim: he *didn't* find mold in the family's home. Although he won, that is, didn't lose, he rankled at almost every memory related to the case. He received a double hit with another job at the same time, which turned out to be tied to Dunham Elementary School, which legally got described as domestic terrorism.

Jeff composed himself and decided to hear more. After all, the men did travel a long way to visit him. Could Carmen feel the vibes while listening in on the conversation from the next room? He arose from his chair, walked to the door to the inner office, and opened it. He spoke briefly to Carmen. "Call Phillips over at OU Medical. Tell him I may be running a little late."

Jeff always tried to allow for a half-hour cushion between the end of his prep time and teaching a class. In this case, he could forgo the cushion, although calling Phillips would be the courteous thing to do.

Brewer wagged the foot on his crossed leg ever so slightly, and Whitaker shifted uncomfortably.

Seated again, Jeff pushed both palms outward, as if to establish a barrier, and said compliantly, "Okay. So far you're telling me we have two states involved, Oklahoma and Arizona. That makes the matter a federal concern, and the state health departments are now under your umbrella. Gentlemen, no offense intended, but localized outbreaks don't make it a national epidemic.

"I haven't really paid a lot of attention to it but, apparently, rashes are one of the disease symptoms. Not to deflate your balloon but we go through one or two adventures of this type each year. Fear is a great motivator for sales, the modus operandi of the media in general."

Brewer half opened his mouth when Whitaker responded. Evidently Whitaker owned Brewer, although Jeff could not fathom the hierarchy.

Shifting himself closer to the edge of the sofa, Whitaker told Jeff what he knew. "The primary symptoms are burning of the fingertips, mouth, nose, and lips. A burning sensation may also appear elsewhere on the body, but not always."

Either Jeff would assist these men or dismiss them. For the life of him, he couldn't make up his mind which it would be.

"You see," said Whitaker patiently, "we've analyzed the urine samples taken from as many subjects as possible. That's what red-flagged this epidemic. We found nearly every urine sample contains the breakdown products of aflatoxin. We wouldn't have found out if one of our researchers hadn't been a mycologist experienced in mycotoxin research and followed up on a hunch."

Jeff became deep in thought. *Burning rashes on fingertips? Around the mouth? Those were definitely not symptoms of mycotoxicosis. They should be looking for hepatitis and jaundice, along with immune suppression for starters. These symptoms would be accompanied by diarrhea, fatigue, dizziness, drowsiness, and a host of others. Liver cancer would come later.*

Now that he knew aflatoxin was involved in the issue, Jeff resolved to hear the men out. He dropped his defensive posture and relaxed.

Whitaker continued, "In fact, doctor, we have enough cases to report that 87% of those affected are women over in their mid-twenties and above."

Jeff countered, "That doesn't compute unless they're the only ones who are eating the bad food."

Jeff leaned slightly forward, facing Whitaker, eyes glued to the man, totally ignoring Brewer, fascinated, trying to learn more. "I mean, it is possible there's a restaurant chain that specializes in products or services catering to women."

Whitaker and Brewer shook their heads in unison.

"Okay, no is no," said Jeff. "Have you screened commonly used products made from soy, wheat, barley, corn, and nuts? How about figs and tobacco?"

"That was the first thing we did," interjected Brewer, as though he were speaking to a child. "You might recall a recent similar situation in a couple of cities in Tunisia."

Suddenly Brewer stopped his presentation as Whitaker gave him a sharp glance, which Jeff caught.

In his medical mycology class, Jeff taught that mycotoxins could be listed as either poisons or antibiotics, depending on the point of view. The same could be said about antibiotics. Couldn't a person go into anaphylactic shock or extreme itching over their entire body once they had been injected with penicillin? Like penicillin, arsenic, or spider bites, mycotoxins were not gender specific. Yet these government agents were telling him that more women got this disease than did men.

Jeff rubbed the back of his head. "In your opinion, Mr. Brewer, how does a smattering of people in only two disparate and unrelated cities in this country, no less, get mycotoxicosis?"

"We're hoping you could tell us," responded Brewer.

Jeff said, "I can think of several examples where ingestion of foodstuffs can cause toxic poisoning, going all the way back thousands of years up to the recent past, which would include the Salem witch hunts in the late seventeenth century. Many years later we discovered that the bread had been prepared with moldy rye grain which led to ergot poisoning—never mind the Catholic versus Protestant or rich versus poor issues.

"Therefore, poisoning in the outbreak you are describing is most commonly due to toxic people.. These would include contaminated meat and fish, peanut butter made from moldy peanuts, people working in silos who inhale dust from moldy grains, laboratory accidents, and some miscellaneous causes. That about covers it."

"Those were the first things we researched," said Whitaker. "Except for an infrequent bad episode of neglect in product selection and processing on the part of the manufacturer or purchaser."

"Have you checked personal care products?" Jeff asked.

"Yes," responded Whitaker. "We tested every item in the refrigerators and pantries, as well as products found in under-sink areas. Of course we paid them for what we took. No mycotoxins were present in any of them."

"Interesting. I'll have to think about this," said Jeff. He wanted to be flippant, but reason prevailed. Something might actually be going on here. On the other hand, why get sucked out of his comfortable routine? When he made a motion to stand, Brewer uncrossed his legs and placed both feet firmly on the floor. "I'm afraid we don't have time for thinking," he said, suddenly changing the tone of his voice from conversational to a timbre of a hard man used to action and respect.

"Let's get down to business. First, Doctor, I take it you know Paul Anderson in your mathematics department."

"The epidemiologist? I've known Paul for years, although he's a little too smart to suit me," Jeff replied.

"Good, then you'll be working with him," said Brewer. "And with us."

Brewer then looked over at Whitaker and gave the slightest of nods, as though handing over a phone to another person and saying, "It's for you."

Whitaker took the handoff. "A few outliers in Washington believe we have some people playing jokes on us. We have another dozen theories to check on. As you can imagine, we try to keep a close eye on things."

Brewer snapped open his briefcase and took out three items, holding them up one at a time. "This CD, prepared from data gathered so far, has all the information you should need to get you started." He set it down on the small table in front of him.

"To preempt your next question," Brewer said, "we spoke with your department chairmen, both here at the university and at the medical school, and cleared your paid absence from teaching duties for an indeterminate period of time, starting as of this moment.

"We gave Dr. Anderson the same CD I am giving you. It contains almost every data set we have, although, as you can understand, things change from moment to moment. It contains all the social aspects on the disease we have so far, starting with its discovery about a couple of weeks ago. You'll get an updated version every two or three days, including Sundays. Please make yourself available."

"Who's going to write my papers for me while I'm working on this pet project of yours? I've got deadlines," Jeff protested.

"Find somebody," said Brewer curtly. He held up a second item. "This is a laminated card with a laser-imprinted three-dimensional picture of you on it. Don't lose this.

"Also on this card are two call numbers. The first will connect you with our offices for any reason twenty-four-seven. The second number will get you on any domestic airline or any rental car anytime. When you show up at the airport, ask the shift supervisor to call the number to verify your status, and you will be admitted onto your flight. Don't worry, they're used to it." He set the card on the table next to the CD.

Brewer held up the third item. "This is a check for five thousand dollars to cover any out-of-pocket expenses you might need for the next month. You will continue receiving your regular teaching salary. We all hope this epidemic will not last another month. If it does, you will receive another check in the same amount one month from today. If it doesn't, please return what you don't use along with receipts of your expenses." He set down the check with the other items.

Jeff grimaced. "Look, there are a hundred medical mycologists out there. Have you contacted any of them?"

Whitaker appeared to choose his words carefully. "The reasons for our selecting you and Dr. Anderson are both simple and complicated. This entire investigation is under government control at the level of top-secret security clearance. You both have previously acquired that clearance through the World Health Organization and with the Department of Defense.

"The fewer people who know what we know, the better. So far, the press can only guess about what is happening, no different than us. That's their prerogative. We won't tell them how many people are involved because we don't know, and if we did know, we wouldn't tell them."

In truth, Jeff's interest was piqued, now that he had been relieved of his teaching duties and no longer felt an urgency to conclude the meeting. He said, "You mentioned the CD and the listing of demographics it contains. What can you tell me now?"

Whitaker said, "As I mentioned, the highest incidence of infection is among those over the age of twenty-three. Most of them are women, and the fewest patients are among the lowest wage earners, although there are exceptions to this. Part of the reason we don't believe the disease is communicable is because we don't have enough data points. And we don't have a clue as to how the disease appeared in two cities a thousand miles apart at almost the same time."

Jeff argued, "Sex distinction is no big deal. The flu pandemic early in the twentieth century selected teenage girls above all other groups." The morsels in front of him were tempting, and he wanted to view the data.

"We've considered that too," said Whitaker, without elaboration.

Jeff assimilated Whitaker's words. On the minus side, he didn't need to take on another project. Grant proposals needed to be finished and indoor air quality projects always needed his attention. Cash he had. The hardest part involved a restructuring of his time schedule. He needed to ensure his obligations to the university and his overall business would not suffer from a new commitment. The money and privileges didn't interest him right now as much as did his mental stability.

The more he thought about it, what first sounded like his time might be tied up for a lengthy period now sounded like a project he should be able to complete in a week or two, especially once Anderson joined him.

That said, if the entire government got involved in the investigation, the job might never get done. After all, didn't the uniquely designed Susan B. Anthony dollar coin go through seventeen congressional committees before it came out looking like a quarter?

Jeff wavered between curiosity and the desire to escort the men to the door. Neither man could claim to be his drill sergeant or his mother, nor could they force him to do anything. He made a decision.

"All right. I'll consider taking on the project once I look at the data on the CD. As of right now, I'm not totally convinced. Since you've looked at topics I've mentioned and don't have an answer, what can I do that you haven't done?"

Brewer leaned forward, with eyes that speared Jeff's. "Fix the problem."

Jeff accompanied the two men out of the building and watched his visitors walk stiffly down the path toward the building's parking lot. He followed them with his eyes until they got into their dark rental sedan and drove away.

Jeff lingered a moment outdoors, smelling the clear crisp air of the morning, longing for a jog, then returned to his office where he locked the outer door. He retrieved the wireless microphone from the underside of one of the coffee tables and brought it into the inner office where Carmen waited for him.

Carmen had her own demons. After completing medical school in Guadalajara, Mexico, she came to the States to serve her internship at the University of Oklahoma Medical School. Soon thereafter, she succumbed to mononucleosis, the curse of the overworked, and had to take a break. She met Jeff at a conference held at the medical school before she had taken her break and later when he lectured at a class she forced herself to attend. After he expressed concern as to her status, she explained her situation truthfully. He thought for a moment and asked her if she would accept a position with him until she could get on her feet.

Down to a few meager dollars and having an interest in his business and knowing his reputation, she accepted the job. Once her strength returned, she found herself torn between completing her medical training and her new life working for Jeff, which she thoroughly enjoyed.

Carmen worked the job hard, trying to ignore Jeff's pending divorce, learning the lingo of the indoor air quality trade and the scams perpetrated by fear-mongers. According to her mentor, there was no lack of medical science sharks who freely cruised the varied waters of the Internet. They sniffed out prey in order to contaminate whatever they touched with their false claims.

Initially, Carmen considered Jeff to be stalwart, athletic, macho, off-center, and erratic at times. She never changed her mind and learned to accept him for what he is, indeed, respect him for what he is.

Carmen placed the microphone in her desk drawer and sat at her desk only a few steps from his. The headsets were already stowed.

Jeff asked her to call Phillips at the medical school and confirm the fact that Jeff would not be present until further notice, as per government declaration that he work on the "epidemic" issue. He also instructed Carmen to place his personal projects on hold. Then he said, "Okay, let's hear it again."

Carmen turned on the recorder, and the two of them listened to the conversation in its entirety. After several minutes, Jeff commented, "I didn't like their interplay. They were correcting each other."

When the recording ended, Carmen said, "It's not logical. I've seen a lot of food poisoning, probably more than you have. I've seen people mix bad flour and handle wet and contaminated grains out in the villages. There will be some irritation and maybe a lot of people with stomach problems. This is different. So you're right, ingestion will cause distress and that's not what they're talking about.

"And it's not Hantavirus or anthrax or Zika or the other diseases in the news. Those are insect or virus related."

Jeff pondered, "Something bothers me about the dynamics of our situation here."

"TV news has something about this every day now," Carmen told him.

"I have to go to Tucson anyway for the lecture

at the medical school. I might as well take Paul with me. We can do some investigating at the same time. I'd invite you along, but people might talk," he quipped, with a ring of truth to the words.

Carmen understood. Her tagging along would be a problem from a number of standpoints. A professor who went on tour with his secretary for business-related reasons smacked of enough unprofessionalism to cause predictable problems.

After she had finished her tasks, he asked her to come over to view the CD with him. He loaded it into the computer and they spent the hour becoming familiar with the contents of the disk and reviewing the list of symptoms reported.

In addition to the onset of rashes, a number of patients reported headaches, malaise, inability to concentrate, sleeplessness, poor taste, and dimming eyesight. Blood tests, when available, found a low white cell count. Carmen confirmed that these symptoms are recognized as signatures of mycotoxicosis at one time or another.

Diarrhea had not entered the picture as it would in the case of typical food poisoning. Poisoning by moldy food could do the same thing, yet it had not occurred. Jeff's head spun.

The office landline rang. Carmen walked over to her desk and picked up. "It's Dr. Anderson, boss." From her desk she could turn her head to the right and see the doorway to the outer office, to the left and see Jeff's desk, and on the far wall behind her, the sofa and fridge.

Jeff pushed the button on the extension. "Shene-ro," he said unnecessarily.

"Jeff, it's Paul. I tried you at the U. When nobody picked up, I figured you were at your private office. Are you free?"

"Yes. We're headed back to the school. See you in twenty. Our friends have left," replied Jeff.

"Oh, it that what you call them. You could have fooled me," answered the mathematician.

Whitaker slid behind the wheel and waited for Brewer to climb into the passenger side. A few weeks before, his personal bills were in the seven-figure range for his six-year-old daughter's heart transplant. His wife was near a nervous breakdown and was giving him grief until one day when Senator Rossman called. Rossman headed the subcommittee on Crime and Terrorism and asked him to head an executive committee for some health issue that might be coming down the pipeline. Money problem solved. There would have to be a trade-off, of course. Whitaker then appointed Brewer.

Brewer learned of his own appointment while on the golf course as he was approached by a donor who made him an offer in Whitaker's name.

For his part Brewer had been seriously stressing. After twenty some years in the military he lived little better than a pauper. The administrative position he held with Homeland for the past several years didn't go far enough to help pay for a daughter in her first year at Columbia and a son on his way to Harvard.

As quickly as it is to say yes, the tuition problem went away, plus his acceptance of other incentives.

The directive was clear. Stall for a few weeks and to look the other way whenever a problem might arise during his watch, as a member of the committee that oversaw the investigation into the epidemic. He was familiar with the procedure of looking the other way.

Traffic moved rapidly with the absence of the heavy haulers since the strike began. Foods and medicines were no longer reaching their destinations, and those available were marked up in price. A black market in sales of these necessities began to flourish.

Whitaker casually drove toward Interstate 35 in no particular hurry to reach Oklahoma City and Will Rogers World Airport, a forty minute drive from Jeff's office. From there they would catch a flight back to Washington, DC, where they were both stationed. They found no joy in having to fly to Norman and return the same day without a couple of days of R&R between arrival and departure.

"I can confirm the fact that after you meet him in person, Jeff Shenero has lived up to his reputation," said Whitaker after several minutes of driving. He tried not to think about the next several hours of airport time and travel boredom.

Brewer responded, staring straight ahead at the light traffic, trying to take a few deep breaths and unwind after their meeting with the two men. "That's being diplomatic, Jim. I can't stand the prick. I don't like his smart mouth or his cavalier attitude. Too bad the bastard wasn't in my platoon ten years ago. I don't like his disrespect, to put it mildly. May the gods grant me a chance to cause him great harm."

"Come on, Bob. We don't have to enjoy him, only employ him," said Whitaker, not pleased that neither of the men had declined to work for them. Couldn't they have said no and be done with it? They had everything was under control until Senator Evans stuck his nose into it. After the appointment of Whitaker, Evans suggested they try to recruit Jeff, a mycologist, and a second man, an epidemiologist, from the school the senator graduated from way back when. Hey, if the new recruits didn't get exactly all the facts, or perhaps received a little misinformation and misdirection, who would know? And if they found out the truth in a few weeks, it would all be over anyway.

Brewer said, "I spoke to the provost of the university a couple of days ago to get more background on this guy. You can be sure his reputation has reached to the top and beyond, and I'm not talking about academic accomplishments; we're talking rough edges here.

"Which gives me an idea. A buddy of mine was in covert ops. Maybe he'd like to have a little fun keeping an eye on these two—you know, see what they're up to."

Whitaker laughed. "It's a little early to get paranoid, isn't it? Anyway, we've got the committee in tow. What with Reynolds handling the press, and

Schmidt and Simon handling the statistics, we've got this thing solid."

Whitaker suddenly got serious. "Changing the subject, why did you bring up Tunisia?" He turned his head slightly to face his passenger.

"You got a point there," Whitaker agreed.

"Well, you're right, Jim, I wasn't thinking. Don't worry. He'll never pick up on it. Anyway, it's Anderson who scares the hell out of me, not Shenero."

Whitaker snorted. "Paul Anderson? A tall skinny math major with a bow tie?" He laughed heartily. "You must be getting soft, Bob. How can that man be a problem?"

Brewer ignored his friend's rebuke. "Let's put it this way. When most single men throw a party, they invite their girlfriend and a number of other friends over for a barbecue and beer and to watch a game on the tube—or a variation thereof. Am I right?"

"Right," said Whitaker.

"Not Anderson. He has puzzle parties."

Whitaker shook his head quickly, not comprehending.

Brewer said, "The dean told me the man has boxes full of them, mostly the one-person types, like the Rubik's Cube, huge search-and-find erasable posters on a wall, jigsaw and crossword puzzles. Doubtless, he probably has every Chinese puzzle ring ever created and, from what I'm told, knows how to take them apart and put them back together blindfolded or behind his back. So people who come over to his house to party actually come over to play with his puzzles, and they love it."

"What's scary about that? Sounds like wholesome innocent fun to me," said Whitaker, checking his rearview mirror as he punched the gas and merged onto the interstate. "Might try it myself," he mused.

"What's wrong? Puzzles, Jim. He lives for puzzles, whether they're toy, word, or mathematical types. An hour or so before we met Jeffrey Shenero, we served up a silver platter and handed our mathematical genius friend a real-life puzzle in his personal area of expertise to dissect and to solve. Do you think he's going to treat that any differently from any of the others? I don't think so."

"Shit," responded Whitaker in the serious tone of a man who might have just stepped in it.

"My sentiments exactly," said Brewer, concerned about his own plight.

Day 10–Late morning

Paul could have arrived in five to seven minutes, which left plenty of time to stop at the student union for a coffee and jelly roll.

Paul Anderson emigrated from England as a teenager. His relaxed demeanor, baby face, tousled brown hair, and trustworthy personality were attractive to women wherever he traveled. He took full advantage of these attributes. In addition, the tall man lacked obvious character flaws, a disturbing fact to his colleagues. According to those who knew him, what you saw was what you got. Paul believed that if a man's hormones drove him to run or go to the gym, he wasn't getting enough exercise in bed.

A scar ran across his left forearm, the reminder of a confrontation with a broken bottle as a youth; however, when responding to an occasional question about the scar, he failed to mention the rival gang member had wielded the bottle.

Paul wasn't shy about admitting his ignorance of areas he knew little or nothing about. He possessed a vast knowledge about his areas of accomplishment and treasured the times he and Jeff would go out on jobs together so he could learn about the life of fungi and especially the common molds. His bachelor's degree in molecular biology gave him a strong base of support before he turned his real talents to mathematics and epidemiology.

Once he finished his snack, Paul sauntered over to Jeff's office to find the couple hard at work.

Jeff recently moved into a newer office at the university. The room was large enough for two desks with computers, several bookcases, and a table that held a printer and a fax. Jeff added a small refrigerator he kept stocked with a variety of sodas and juices.

Today the mathematician wore a tan jacket, navy-blue slacks, white shirt, and blue bow tie. He always looked fresh and preferred to dress cleanly and neatly, including shoes that required laces, in contrast with Jeff, who preferred a polo shirt, khaki slacks, and loafers.

"Just a second, Paul. I want Carmen in on this."

Paul smiled, knowing they were both instructed to keep this information to themselves, but Jeff trusted Carmen as much as he could trust any person.

Carmen rolled her desk chair over to where the men were talking.

Paul pulled a soda from the refrigerator and took a comfortable seat in the only armchair in the room.

Jeff inserted the CD into the computer. "Okay, let's see what we've got."

The label on the CD read Middle Eastern Flu Epidemic with a time stamp from the day before/ It contained an expanded database with close to one hundred persons officially affected, along with the two deaths.

"Frankly I don't see any connection in terms of disease transmission. Not in Oklahoma City or in Tucson," said the epidemiologist.

"Not communicable," stated Carmen.

"Correct," answered Paul.

"It almost seems random," opined Jeff.

Paul said, "Except that we've got a lot more women than men with the disease. Before we go any further, I do need you to educate me about mycotoxins so I have more than a general idea of what to look for," said Paul.

Jeff leaned back in his chair. "If there is a batch of moldy peanuts that gets processed into peanut butter, there's a chance you're going to get aflatoxin in the peanut butter, depending on what the mold is, of course."

"Aflatoxin?"

"It's named after *Aspergillus flavus*, hence, A-fla-toxin. It's possibly the most potent naturally occurring poisons known to man—cancer causing, liver destroying—nasty stuff. The chemical was discovered back in 1960 when one hundred thousand young turkeys died within months in the south and east of England, your own country. On one farm alone fourteen thousand ducklings died because they ate moldy grain.

"In California the same year, an outbreak of trout liver cancer occurred. The fish were inspected and the disease was traced to a commercial hatchery where their food source consisted of moldy grains. Today's extensive use of farmed fish worldwide, with similar feeding practices raises the same issue, especially in fish farmed overseas.

"Many different fungi, including several species of *Aspergillus* and other mold genera, produce similar toxins. Many animal types succumb to these poisons, with the liver as the primary target organ. Breakdown products can appear in the milk and urine of cattle and humans. Dozens of other fungal toxins exist."

"Spare me," said Paul. "I'd rather remember somebody's vehicle identification number than have to try to pronounce a bunch of your Latin names."

Jeff laughed. He'd heard that by the age of six, Paul could play with numbers like Mozart could play the piano. After Paul's bachelor's degree in molecular biology, he went straight into a PhD program at MIT.

Jeff continued his explanation. "Most of what we know about fungal poisons, and antibiotics is learned through experiments with animals. We also learn a lot by dissecting animals that eat the bad food, such as horses, cattle and bad hay; chickens and moldy grain; farmed fish and moldy soy. With humans we see a lot more of it in less developed countries.

"Our problem is this: The database on the CD doesn't support what they're telling us. Brewer and Whitaker told me they were in the process of tracking various foods, but so far there was nothing to go on. If mycotoxin poisoning in food is the problem, the food should show up like a red light. Not only that, but there would be a lot of people reporting stomach problems.

"I'm willing to bet more people go to the doctor for bowling injuries in these two cities than are affected by this epidemic."

Paul smiled. He knew his friend. When Jeff went into sarcastic mode, the man was completely thinking through a problem with whatever information he had at hand. He could almost predict what Jeff would do next.

Jeff suddenly changed demeanor and became instantly serious, like a batter who got hit by a pitched ball. He went through the list of reported symptoms. "You know how these things work. The most sensitive persons will react first. Typically, a lot more people are exposed and are affected than report to their doctor."

Paul said, "What I don't understand is why we have randomness where we should have patterns. This doesn't follow any disease course I know of. There is no epicenter, no spread from an original case outward. If it's bad city water, everybody would get sick. Although Oklahoma City and Tucson do seem to be focal points, the increase doesn't follow a pattern of poisoning either by food or drink."

Carmen said, "Let's say there is a food problem. Then why is somebody saying this might have to do with terrorists? You can't control the amount of bad corn or peanuts eaten by certain groups in a population. Or can you?"

Jeff began to to slowly nod his head. He froze an instant, then suddenly spun his chair from the computer and stood. "Let me get something."

He went to one of his file cabinets and recovered a document.

"This paper is from the CDC titled 'Biological and Chemical Terrorism: Strategic Plan for Preparedness and Response'. It discusses the uses of toxins, gases, and chemicals that can be used as weapons by terrorists, so they've been thinking about this for some time. It discusses various methods the bad guys might want to use. It's quite fascinating."

"How did you come up that thought?" asked Carmen.

"Because they didn't mentioned it at all," Jeff replied. He handed the paper to Paul, who skimmed through it as Jeff took his seat again. Jeff once asked

Paul how many words a minute he could read, and Paul answered, "About four thousand." When Jeff asked if Paul could show him some speed-reading tricks, Paul told him he didn't feel he was qualified to teach because he had never finished the course.

"If you breathe some kind of poison, your trachea, lungs, sinuses and entire respiratory tract will react. So we can rule out an airborne attack. And most fungal toxins have a much higher molecular weight than, say, formaldehyde. Therefore, mycotoxins are not going to evaporate much, if at all, compared with acetone in nail polish remover or gasoline vapors or fragrances or any other of the hundreds of products we inhale daily."

Jeff scrolled through the CD to the section labeled "Foodstuffs."

Jeff said, "They've looked at natural and processed foods containing corn, all grains, tomatoes, sugar, and all manner of nuts, and so forth. There are literally a hundred products that have been discovered to have mycotoxin in them at one time or another. None have come up positive for fungal toxins except for a bad lot or two which is what we expect. As an educated guess, I'd say that many of these foods are more closely inspected now than ever before."

Paul said, "I didn't see anything in the heavy metals category. Did you?"

Jeff pulled up the category and scrolled through arsenic, cadmium, gold, lead, mercury, nickel, selenium, and zinc. "So far, they've found no correlations with metal in the water or in the food. The symptoms don't match, anyway."

"I want to see the demographics again," said Carmen. "Go back to the beginning of the epidemic. Take a closer look at the first cases."

They scanned the Butler and Hutchinson files.

Jeff stood and paced the room. While he did so, Paul pulled up a map of Oklahoma City and another of Tucson. Green dots marked the regions of disease outbreaks, and two red dots marked the areas where a single death occurred in each of the cities. No obvious pattern of infection or death appear.

"Do you think there might be a contaminated product that is shipped to these two cities?" Carmen asked.

"It could be, but again, the symptoms don't match," responded Jeff. "We know it's real because they continually find breakdown products of aflatoxin in the patients' urine. That's the convincer for me."

"Which eliminates mass hysteria," Paul contributed, a veiled allusion to Jeff's involvement in the Dunham Elementary School case.

"Look at this. What do you see here?" Paul declared a moment later, after pulling up the statistics of the cities most affected, including Norman.

Jeff leaned closer to the screen and said, "It looks like both Oklahoma City and Tucson have close to half-million population. I'd say we can double that number, if we include their outlying unincorporated areas. They're split down the middle with almost exactly 50% of each sex. Norman has about 120,000 population when OU is in session. So how do you get a two-to-one ratio?"

"We're not seeing the forest for the trees," Paul responded.

The puzzle master had hit on one of the universal truths of investigation, indeed, of all research. They weren't seeing the obvious glaring them in the face. Paul continued, "Let's see, what else. Hispanics, Blacks, and American Indians are among the poorer minority groups in the country. In Oklahoma City we have thirty percent minorities, and in Tucson it is forty-two percent, predominantly Hispanic. But few people in these groups in the two major cities have the disease."

Paul sat back in the chair. "It's almost as if there is half the exposure in Tucson," he said softly.

An instant later Paul asked, "I know you've visited Tucson. What do you know about the city?"

"Actually quite a bit. I've been there several times. Most recently a couple of years ago when I taught a summer course at the University of Arizona medical school. I'm going to lecture there in a couple of days. So we might as well leave today. We'll check on the epidemic situation at the same time."

"Okay, mind if Carmen comes along?" said Paul teasingly, testing the waters.

"Not a chance," growled Jeff, somewhat more intensely than he'd intended.

"Anyway, about Tucson...," Jeff rubbed the back of his neck as a nervous gesture in response to his sharp answer. "It's a quiet town south of Phoenix by about a hundred miles. The University of Arizona is known for cancer research as well as having some of the world's greatest astronomers and telescope mirror production facilities. It has excellent sports programs.

"The city has little in the way of industry per se, unless you want to call retirement an industry. It does have an important air force base, and one of the nation's largest defense contractors is planted there. It has a single newspaper, the *Tucson Times*."

"Just one paper?" asked Paul.

"A lot of cities have only one major newspaper. Anyway, I don't see any point in spending too much time interviewing people. We have their medical summaries on the CD, and we have plenty of sick folks right up the interstate in Oklahoma City."

Jeff wanted to move fast and wrap up the investigation in record time so he could get his life back. "In Tucson, though, I really want to interview the doctor who treated Percy Butler. He was the first case and an alcoholic. Apparently, he was also the first person to die from the mycotoxin and had rashes."

"To complicate matters, the second death was Margarete Hutchinson and her drinking habits were not unusual," added Paul.

Paul closed his eyes and placed the fingertips of both hands against them. "We're missing something. If alcohol doesn't fit, let's leave that one alone for now. Food and heavy metals don't fit in either."

Jeff said, "Now that we've been essentially drafted, I don't mind telling you both I have a bad feeling about this. Usually an inner voice speaks to me and provides a little direction. Not here. I can't help thinking there are going to be a lot of very sick, if not dead, people before we're done unless we can, as Brewer said, 'fix the problem'.

"So far, the difference in the number of newspapers between the cities is the only two-to-one ratio. How that ties in with anything we're doing is anybody's guess. And it's probably a stupid idea."

Jeff scratched his head. "Something's bothering me." He picked up the office phone and punched in a number.

"Who are you calling?" asked Carmen.

"Parker Johnson," Jeff said.

Jeff spoke into the phone. "Parker, I need you to find out what happened in Tunisia a couple of years ago." He paused. "Yeah, I know, I lot of things happened. What I'm talking about is some kind of epidemic. I'll be out of town for a couple of days. Call Carmen if you need to get in touch with me."

"Guess I'd better go get packed," said Paul.

Jeff said, "Definitely. And don't forget to bring your passport."

"My passport? For Tucson?" Paul's eyes widened in surprise.

"No, for Mexico," Jeff stated flatly. "We'll fly out later, check into a hotel, eat lunch, and drive down to Mexico. I want to talk with an outlier, Maria Carrasco in Nogales and be there when she's back from school in the afternoon. The day after that, I have the lecture to give at the medical school. When I'm free, we can try to find out about Percy."

Day 11–Afternoon

The men had picked up a couple of hours during the flight west. Jeff parked the rental car in a public lot and the men began walking the quarter mile to the turnstiles that led to Mexico. On the way Paul made a quick stop at a Wells Fargo bank.

"Be right out," he said. "In case I need some money for the unexpected."

Once across the border, they noted a line of cabs. "One's as good as another," said Jeff as they got into the back seat of the first cab they came to.

Jeff bargained with the cab driver in both English and Spanish and gave him an address. The cabbie drove them only a mile or so to a quiet residential area. The homes looked middle class, most of which were built of adobe or wood frame, many dating back to the 1930s or earlier. The houses were decorated with flowers in their front and side yards and green laws were common.

The two men climbed out of the cab, and Jeff told the cabbie to wait for them.

The outer door to the home stood open. Jeff knocked gently on a screen door. A moment later a middle-age woman appeared.

Jeff spoke to her in Spanish. "Excuse me, ma'am, we're from the health department of the United

States, and we are hoping to speak with your daughter, Maria Carrasco, about her medical problems. We're trying to help. Does she live here?"

The men displayed their new credentials.

"Yes, this is the Carrasco home," returned the woman in Spanish. She turned in response to a man's voice that questioned who was at the door. The woman turned her head slightly and repeated what Jeff had said. The voice told her to let the visitors in.

The interior of the home felt warm and comfortable. The powerful smell of freshly made tamales was heavy in the air. Both men took a deep breath of the delicious aroma. Paul looked at Jeff and gave his friend a smile with a quick eyebrow raise as if to say, "Man, I would give my left nut to get into that kitchen."

An old nineteen-inch TV was set on a small table against one wall. A sofa, a rocking chair, and several smaller chairs occupied the brown-carpeted family room. This adjoined a simple dining room consisting of a wooden table surrounded by seven chairs. The sofa was entirely covered with a crocheted spread of brightly colored six-inch squares that took every bit of half a million stitches, Jeff surmised. To this day his mother made shawls using the same pattern.

One wall of the family room and the fireplace mantle was covered with both black-and-white and color photographs of family members. Some photographs appeared to be ancient, based on their yellowing and the clothing worn by the subjects along with their statuesque appearance as they posed in a stony posture befitting the times. The voice of an older woman could be heard in the kitchen, upbraiding the children who were begging her for treats.

"We are surprised by your visit," said Mr. Carrasco. He was a smaller, gray-mustached, and dark-skinned man with a full head of graying hair. He smiled warmly and spoke in Spanish. "You are fortunate to catch me at home. I finished my afternoon meal a little while ago and was leaving for my store."

Jeff exchanged cordialities with them both, displaying their credentials once more along with their passports and driver's licenses in order to gain the family's trust. Jeff repeated to Mr. Carrasco in Spanish what he had told his wife a moment before at the door.

Mrs. Carrasco asked their guests to sit on the sofa while she stood next to her husband, who remained seated and inspected the credentials.

Mr. Carrasco called for Maria and a young girl dressed in a blue school uniform skirt with white blouse entered the room. Her clothing was neat and spotless. She held a schoolbook. The girl appeared to be the reported thirteen years old.

"Come here, please," said Mr. Carrasco. "These men would like to talk to you."

The girl came forward and said in Spanish, "About what, Father?"

Mr. Carrasco looked at his houseguests and said in halting English, "She speaks English good."

Jeff leaned forward in his seat. "Maria, we are

American professors and heard about your medical problem. Could you please tell us what happened?"

Maria looked at her father, who nodded for her to explain.

The girl began her story and spoke in excellent English. "I was always a good student and got a scholarship to go to a top charter school across the line. I got a permit and went to school in the mornings. In the afternoon I worked. Two or three weeks ago I got this problem on my arms." She displayed her forearms, which were red and irritated. Some of the rashes appeared to be fading.

Maria continued, "And also on my fingertips and a little on my face. We went to our doctor, my uncle. He was trained in America, and he has a very modern office, but he didn't know what it was. He said that polish on the desks at the school might be making my arms get red. But it was only me who had it. So the doctor told me to stop going there and to stay on this side of the line and go to school here and see what happened. That's what I did, and now it's going away." Maria had paused occasionally in her narrative to translate her words to her parents.

"So your doctor took tests. Is that right?" asked Paul.

"Yes. He took a blood test and sent it off to a laboratory along with a report. He was out of the country when we tried to reach him."

"That's too bad," said Paul. "It would have been nice to see the report."

"Oh, my uncle gave us a copy," she replied. "He

told me he was a little worried about my symptoms because they were not normal, and to be safe, he was going to send one sample to an American lab and one to the disease center."

"Centers for Disease Control?" asked Jeff.

"Yes, that's it. After a few days a man came from your country to talk to me."

"What did he look like?" Jeff and Paul glanced at each other.

Maria described Brewer. Then she explained to her father what she had said, and he motioned for her to get the report.

Jeff couldn't believe his ears. The family actually had the doctor's report. He thought, *Serendipity happens when you follow up on a lead. This is candy from left field.*

The girl returned with papers in hand.

"Do you mind if we photograph this report, Maria?" asked Jeff.

Maria asked for her father's permission for them to do so, and he consented.

Using their cell phone cameras, the men photographed the papers, thanked Maria, and returned them to her.

"Maria, do you mind if we take a few pictures of your arms and fingers?" Jeff asked.

She shrugged and her father nodded yes. He said nothing, but watched carefully.

Jeff asked the girl to hold up her forearms, and took several pictures of them at different angles.

Nodding and smiling Jeff announced, "As thanks,

we would like to take a picture of your family for you, if that's all right."

The father became animated and enthusiastic. He gathered the four children and the grandmother. The seven family members, at Mr. Carrasco's direction, left the house and went to the grassy backyard. Here they lined up against a bougainvillea trellis as a backdrop, while Jeff shot photos of each person, the four children, the parents, the grandmother, and the group as a whole. Then he promised to send them copies of the pictures.

The men were about to return to the cab when Paul said softly, "We really got nothing."

"I know," replied Jeff.

Suddenly Jeff turned to the girl. "Maria, I almost forgot to ask you. Where did you work after school?"

"I sold newspapers," she said.

"What newspapers?"

"From the city."

"From Tucson?" he asked.

"Yes, the *Tucson Times*."

Serendipity. "Where did you sell them?"

"I talked to the owner of the big drugstore, who is my father's friend, and he let me take an armful of papers and walk the streets and sell them to anybody. I did that after school and also on Sundays after church. But business was slow so I didn't sell many."

"Well, thank you. You are all very gracious," said Jeff.

Paul walked over to Mr. Carrasco and made as

if to shake his hand. The father reached out. While shaking his hand, Paul slipped five folded fifty-dollar bills into it, a small tip for the courtesy they'd received and the information they'd gained. Then he quickly turned away before the father could reply. The two men left the premises and climbed into their waiting taxi.

"Why wasn't any of that in our database?" asked Paul the instant they seated themselves in the rear of the cab.

Jeff gave the driver the name of the restaurant he wanted to go to and the man pulled away, heading back toward the border. "It might have gotten overlooked," he said, a supercilious answer he fabricated to get Paul excited. It worked.

Paus responded. "Right. You mean accidentally on purpose it got overlooked. You don't overlook this case. Let's see. An obscure case down in Mexico got lost in the shuffle. And tomorrow we're going to see a doctor in Tucson about another initial case for which we have no data."

The driver drove up to Pepe's Diner, where they served "The best food and drinks in all of Mexico" and "Tequila specials every night."

Shenero bargained with the cab driver, paid him, and walked indoors with Paul at his side.

They took a seat by the window and looked out as few Americans, indeed few Mexicans, were present on the sidewalks. Many stores were closed. The economy was depressed on both sides of the border. At the popular restaurant, both men ate heavily and drank lightly.

Jeff let Paul drive onto I-19 North back to Tucson.

Paul looked over at his passenger, now staring out the side window at the cactus with the low purple mountains in the background. He'd seen his friend come and go out of his mood swings over the years, none as severe as his present funk. It really hurt Jeff when his wife walked out. He appeared to be a man scrabbling up the side of a gravelly hill, only to backslide to the bottom and scrabble upward again.

Despite his bravado, Jeff must have felt like the poster boy for America's least wanted. He could see John Walsh appealing to America, pointing his finger at the audience through the TV screen. "Folks, here is a picture of Jeffrey Shenero, a loser, a man with a big mouth whose wife left him. A drunkard in the making. For a few nanoseconds he can be brilliant, remember anything, and accomplish anything. After that, forget it. Don't bother looking for this guy."

But Jeff would never stay down; the man's pilot light burned too strongly. From appearances, it wasn't quite time for him to climb up again.

The only time they stopped on the way back to their hotel in Tucson was when the traffic cones and speed-reducing signs forced northbound traffic to stop at a Border Patrol checkpoint.

Back at their hotel room, Jeff connected the camera to his laptop and rubbed the top of his head. "What I want to know is this: Why is she in this database?"

Paul nodded absentmindedly. "Spot on. The report said nothing at all about taking a urine sample from her and sending it in for analysis. Didn't Brewer tell us that all cases in the database were positive for mycotoxin?"

"All they *thought* were positive, I think he said," Jeff replied. "They included Hutchinson only because she had the same rashes, but nobody tested her. Tomorrow's another day. We'll sleep on it and see what happens when we visit this Dr. Haskell."

Day 12–Morning

The two men went down to the open-air breakfast bar of the hotel that overlooked the pool. Several children were diving from the springboard as each tried to outdo the other in a splashing contest.

The men breathed in the cool morning air. The sounds of ditch digging, the pounding of jackhammers, and the beeping of trucks in backup mode served as a poor replacement for background music.

Jeff ordered scrambled egg whites with a fruit salad and stared at the mountain of food in front of Paul.

"In case you're interested, I like my sausage and bacon pure and uncontaminated with extraneous flavors. I try to ignore the growth hormones and pesticides as long as the food tastes good," said the mathematician.

Paul went on. "I've got about 30% of our national population most susceptible to this disease, if we count those over sixty, those two years old and younger, pregnant mothers, and the immuno-compromised, that's more than a hundred million potential primary victims."

Jeff contemplated. *Why am I a sudden believer, a new convert into the religion of possible terrorism in the smaller community? Why am I getting pissed off at something I didn't believe in a couple of days ago?*

Jeff took a strong pull of his black coffee and offered, "According to Carmen, once symptoms develop, the young and the old and those who have the most exposure will react the most quickly and the most severely. The entire body will develop a variety of symptoms, and eventually the patient will die from the disease. The latest CD tells us of more deaths. That's why the most severe symptoms are showing up first in patients with weakened immune systems, like Hutchinson because of the chemo, or the disease is enhanced in the case of Butler because of the alcohol.

"In my view, Maria is a typical patient. She healed after her exposure stopped. I expect her to recover completely. For the rest of the population, once the mycotoxin level builds up beyond what the liver can detoxify, the entire body will become poisoned, including and especially the liver. Liver cancer will occur. The aflatoxin is poisonous to the liver itself.

"To me it's dermal, plain and simple, and my first suspicion is newspapers. I don't know anything beyond that. But it does explain the two-to-one ratio, the rashes on the hands and the other parts of the body, such as the face. The toxin can be spread through contact transference, sort of like ringworm."

"I'm with you on the newspaper part, but not the ringworm part," Paul confessed.

Jeff explained. "Look, ringworm is caused by common molds that have adapted to grow on skin, hair, and nails. If you get it in one place on your body and scratch that place and then scratch another part of your body, the spores and mycelium beneath your fingernails will transfer to the new area. Poison ivy works the same way. Simple contact transfer would explain rashes on the faces of the subjects and in infants."

The men finished their breakfast in silence, left money on the table, and drove to the University of Arizona for Jeff's lecture.

Every seat in the small lecture room was taken. Doctors and students of various disciplines were present, along with a few members of the public and several reporters. A video feed sent the proceedings outside the room.

Dr. William Cartwright, from the allergic diseases division at the medical school, stood at the rostrum to introduce Jeff, a professional colleague whom he respected.

Dr. Cartwright began: "Thank you all for attending. I'll get to the point. We are honored today to have with us the famous and outspoken Dr. Jeffrey Shenero from the University of Oklahoma."

Jeff stood and walked to the podium. "Thank you, Dr. Cartwright," he began, smiling genially. He faced the audience without notecards, "Today I'm going to discuss the views I presented in my latest book, *Toxic Exposure*, as some of you may have seen on national TV.

"From what I hear, the academic world and the public have a morbid fascination with my views. These views go against the mainstream of current thinking. In fact, one commentator recently stated that 'Dr. Shenero is so far outside the bubble, he doesn't know where the edge is located'."

Here the audience chuckled.

Jeff stood at the rostrum at the bottom of an inclined room that had seen the scientist present other topics on mycotoxins, antibiotics, and terminal illnesses. Now he railed against the charlatans, the uneducated, the self-serving, and the ignorant. He ranted against the pretenders, including the doctors and the lawyers and those who preyed upon the public after manipulating the press, the wannabees, and the insurance companies that served as prey to the predators. He gave examples. He told stories and gave his audience something to take home with them.

Jeff paused to take a sip of water, scanning the audience as a matter of habit. He enjoyed a connection with those who wanted to connect with him. On the top row Jeff saw Stanley Albert, his old lab partner some two decades before.

Albert possessed a baby face. It never changed. He might have a few lines beneath the eyes and around the nose-to-mouth connection, but basically he appeared to be the same person of old. His weight was the same and he still combed his hair the same way. In the briefest flittering of moments, their eyes met. Jeff stored the vision for later review.

What he really ached to do was to talk about the epidemic and why it wasn't an epidemic but a systematic poisoning of the people, and how he believed the government was misleading them, about how he was being lied to and being misled, and no, he didn't really have any good evidence but he strongly believed it. He was on the verge of discovering the truth.

That type of presentation would be more in keeping with his style, what his audience came to expect from him. But he didn't trust himself. Once he started, he wouldn't be able to let it go. And if he was wrong, he could kiss his job at the university goodbye and life as he knew it would come to a very embarrassing end.

From his vantage point in Mexico, Albert watched with fascination as the news of the epidemic filled the Internet. Jeffrey Shenero's name was rarely mentioned except in the context of a lecture he was to present in Tucson. Albert felt like the positive pole of a strong magnet being attracted to the negative pole of another. He felt a palpable hatred for Shenero. Albert wanted to see Jeff again, to see what had become of the man with whom he'd spent his lab years. Albert's pulse raced with the excitement of impending danger. *Yes, sir, I know you very well, and you owe me.*

Day 12–Afternoon

The two scientists parked at the clinic lot on Tucson Boulevard, what used to be a main thoroughfare of the city. At one time the roadway served as the eastern limit for the city. Now, the boulevard actually resembled an average street with tree-shaded homes and some businesses lining both sides of the street.

Under a clear sky in the heat of the desert sun, the men walked to the clinic entrance.

After receiving their names, the receptionist made a single phone call, then requested the men to wait for a few minutes.

The men took their seats on folding chairs in the overcrowded reception area. With the exception of a man and a women seated next to each other, a dozen adults were seated, many of whom seemed to be locked into some kind of stasis, almost as though they were regular travelers on New York subways with their inscrutable facial expressions. Others played with apps on their cell phones.

Jeff mentioned in passing, "Funny thing. During the lecture I saw an old graduate school partner of mine in the back row."

"What's funny about that?" inquired Paul.

"Well, we parted on unfriendly terms. I haven't heard a word from him since, and here he is sitting at one of my lectures. The main thing I remember about him is the toothpick he always had in his mouth. I don't mean sometimes, I mean always. Stuck right there between his gums and cheek. Either side. He switched when you least expected it. You could always see it poking out. I asked him about it once. He told me he preferred the round toothpicks to the flat ones because the flat toothpicks were too easy to break, especially when they got wet."

"Maybe he takes it out on special occasions."

"Sure, like eating, sleeping, and kissing," responded Jeff, stoically.

"Now you're getting intellectual on me. Does that mean you're thinking about getting a toothpick?"

Jeff laughed. "That kind of logic is similar to the smoker who read so much about the detrimental effects of smoking he finally gave it up."

"He quit smoking?" asked Paul.

"No, he quit reading," replied Jeff.

Now Paul laughed.

Soon, an enthusiastic Dr. Haskell arrived to greet them in the waiting room. "I'm sorry I couldn't make the lecture, gentlemen, as per your invite, but patients come first." Haskell gestured to display the filled waiting of men, women, and children.

Haskell led the men to his office where he motioned for them to take a seat in the small armchairs across from his desk. "I blocked out a few minutes for this meeting," he said smiling. "I know both of you by reputation, I must confess.

"Dr. Anderson, during my undergraduate years, I majored in mathematics before switching to biology, and your name came up repeatedly, even in the biological sciences when we studied the tracking of epidemics. This is an honor for me.

"And Dr. Shenero, I've seen videos of your lectures before. As for the epidemic, you're not the first to visit me about it. I'll help any way I can."

Jeff pulled out a business card and handed it to Haskell. On cue Paul and Haskell did the same.

"Now, as to Percy Butler." Haskell opened a manila folder on his desk and began thumbing through the pages. "I can give you a few generalities, but, unfortunately, confidentiality prevents me from giving you this file to peruse. And, yes, gentlemen, confidentiality also applies after the demise of the patient. I'm not trying to be difficult, you understand, but it's the law.

"Percy Butler was a Vietnam veteran who sold newspapers on the street corner and came to me with various ailments. We accepted Percy as a regular patient, and we all liked him. He was going downhill fast in terms of general health. Shortly before he died, he presented with rashes, and I have photographs of them. I am not revealing any secrets here. I understand you gentlemen are aware of all this information anyway, and the rashes are typical of the ones reported every day in the press and occasional ones I see here in my office."

Haskell looked at his watch. "Please excuse me, gentlemen, while I tend to my patients. Give me, shall we say, ten minutes?"

Haskell left the room. The closed file remained on the desk opposite his guests. Paul reached across the desk and slid the file between them. Without saying a word, Jeff pulled out his phone and photographed each page, as Paul turned pages from one to the next. Within three minutes, they completely recorded the twenty-two-page folder, including photographs, and had returned the folder to its original position in front of Haskell's chair. They refrained from commenting on what they saw in the interest of time during the work-in-progress and now were free to speak about it.

"Those forearm rashes are not the fingertip rashes shown in the newspapers. Nor are they consistent with the reported symptoms of the disease," whispered Jeff.

"Or as presented on the CD," Paul replied. "Not only that, but on our CD, Butler is listed as an unemployed vagabond."

Jeff said, "They gave us less on Maria Carrasco than they did on Butler. Yet, these are the only two cases with forearm rashes I've seen. There may be others, but no mention is made of them in the database. Why not?"

Dr. Haskell returned. He quickly glanced at the

Butler file folder before regaining his seat. "My apologies again. Now where were we?" Haskell held up a finger. "Oh, wait. I forgot to tell you about Percy's dog." The doctor took a moment to relate that portion of Percy's tale.

"Obviously it's not here in the patient's record," the doctor said, pointing at the file folder, "but I thought I'd throw it out there for what it's worth."

Paul said, "Thanks, we'll make a note of it. Now, Dr. Haskell, you said we were not the first to ask you about the Butler case. Can I ask who else came in before us? I mean, if everybody is doing the same thing, we are not very efficient, are we?"

"A Mr. Brewer was here about ten days ago with a subpoena with him for the file, so I made a copy of it in his presence and he signed off on it. Do you know him?"

"Robert? Of course," replied Jeff. He took a quick glance at Paul. "Glad to see he's on the job."

"Between you and me, I didn't like the man," said Haskell, grimacing. "Gave off the wrong vibes, bad heat signature—call it what you want."

"That's Robert, all right," said Paul. "You have to get to know him. He means well, despite his character flaws." Jeff nodded in agreement.

Both men were eager to dissect the wealth of information they'd received in their short visit to Tucson and Nogales, but more work awaited before they could enjoy any meaningful relaxation.

Sensing an end to the interview, Jeff asked, "Doctor, if you could spare the time, could you show us where Percy sold his newspapers? You know, the place you mentioned to me on the phone when we were setting up this appointment."

"Of course, come with me," replied the doctor.

The doctor stood and the two others followed. The three men walked out the front of the clinic. Haskell stopped and pointed to an intersection a couple of hundred yards to the south. Percy's old intersection was barely visible between a stand of paloverde trees with their green trunks and branches.

They shook hands in departure and the men got into their car. Paul drove to the intersection and found a place to park at a restaurant. He maneuvered the car so that it faced the intersection. Jeff pulled out his phone and spent several minutes videotaping the vendor. Then he got out of the car, waited for the signal to change and walked across to speak with the man. He bought and paper and returned to the car. "Rashes on his forearms, mostly on the left with more on his fingertips," he reported.

"I figured as much," Paul said. "While you were gone, I Googled the location of the newspaper plant and punched it into the car's GPS."

"Let's go," Jeff directed.

Twenty minutes later, Paul turned into the parking lot of the plant. The men exited and walked into the front office. Ten minutes later, they were carrying two Sunday editions and several daily editions.

Paul said, "I'm trying to figure out how the dog fits into this."

"It's looking more and more like it has something

to do with the newspapers," Jeff commented. Truth presented itself in its naked glory, but the detective in him told him to be careful and not to get sucked into a bad hand.

Jeff felt like a ball in a pinball machine, racking up points as it got bounced around the table. What did all their important information amount to exactly? The Carrasco and Butler cases were crucial to the investigation and definitely were poorly recorded and poorly reported. But beyond that, he was at a loss. One step at a time.

"Let's get back to our room and look at what we've got," he said.

A short while later Jeff connected his phone to his laptop and the men reviewed the Butler file.

Jeff said, "Note there are no sharp lines of demarcation in any of the rashes as there might be, say, with hives." He scrolled through Haskell's findings. Paul hooked the phone to his laptop.

The men read Percy's medical history and reviewed his charts along with Dr. Haskell's conclusions, which changed over time. *At first I thought it might be a food allergy, but as the disease progressed, I settled on a contact allergy and finally ruled out an allergic reaction altogether.*

"I'm going to send some of the pictures to Carmen." He did so and minutes later received the text that read, "No sharp edges so no hives."

He showed the text to Paul, who said, "Looks like Carmen and Haskell are in agreement."

"It's a type of contact dermatitis, all right. I've

seen plenty of those," said Jeff. "See, the facial irritation tends to strongly support Haskell's conclusions. The mucous membrane and the tissue around the mouth, nose, and eyes appear to be very sensitive. And look at the upper eyelids where people tend to rub when their eyes are sore. There's a little reddening at the right temple where he might have scratched. They're all touch-related locations."

The mathematician nodded. "True. I'll bet if we'd seen the corpse, we would have found other signs of transference."

After several moments of quiet, Jeff said, "Effing Brewer hid information from us. Didn't want anybody to see Percy's photos or to know details about Maria. What a butthead."

Paul said, "Here's a puzzle. How can people become world champions in something when only a couple of people play the sport? I mean, how many people in Ethiopia play beach volleyball or use skateboards? And how many people in Nigeria play baseball and make it to the World Series?"

Paul continued playing mind games with his friend. "Here's another one. How many people understand this disease when only a few people are making the rules? Our two government friends are covering up something they doesn't want anybody to know about. I think we know the what. The questions then become: Why and for whom?"

"We need to find out," said Jeff.

"I agree," responded Paul. "Let's go home."

Day 13–Morning

Paul knocked on Jeff's door and walked in to find his friend busy at work on the computer. "Where's Carmen?" he asked.

"She left early for a doctor's appointment," Jeff responded.

Both men knew a long shot when they saw one, but Jeff directed his graduate students to work on the Tucson newspapers to find out if they contained fungal toxin anywhere, whether it be in the ink or the paper itself. The next step would be to figure out how it got there.

Three days after their receipt of the last CD both investigators soon received a new database dubbed "Middle Eastern Flu Epidemic." Once again the time stamp was from the day before.

The death toll mounted. Experts were checking on the possibility that their government had dropped a mysterious substance from the skies over the two cities. The men weren't surprised to see these same experts chasing their tails, possibly under a directive to look everywhere except for where the problem actually lay.

Throughout the lower forty-eight, food, medical supplies, and all manner of trucks were scarce. The harbors backed up ships with no way to off-load their cargoes. The funnel had been closed at the othe end. Dockside bars, however, were filled to capacity with the owners having to drive their own vehicles to pick up supplies.

Many governments had conducted experiments on their citizens. Events of this nature were amply recorded, both in the United States and abroad. Jeff considered himself a conspiracy theorist, and to his way of thinking, these experiments were continually ongoing. Was the ongoing epidemic one of those? Yes, he told himself. Worse, might it be one of those gone wrong? Perhaps even Brewer and Whitaker did not have all the information they needed to solve the problem and could only pass along what they knew.

U.S. Air Force denials of disease agents dropping from the sky made their proclamations appear similar to those of Area 51 regarding flying saucers. "There ain't no such animal" only reinforced the suspicions that nefarious government activities were in operation.

"Look at what they're telling us, Paul. We are within the central circle of it all, and they are feeding us BS. The skyfall theory won't work, if all we're looking at is skin rashes. I mean, everybody gets rained on, not only women or readers. Don't the people who belong to the lower level of society walk under the same sky as everyone else?"

"And why doesn't the top of the head or neck get affected if it's dropped from the skies?" added Paul.

"Precisely," Jeff said emphatically. He leaned back in his office chair. "Let's go over it again. First, Maria and Percy are and were part of the economic lower class, the class that doesn't read the papers as much as those in the middle and upper classes. In their cases, although they didn't read newspapers, they carried them. Forearm rashes were present on both.

"But how would the toxin get into the ink? You can't add it because the chemical structure of aflatoxin won't allow it to dissolve in the ink to the extent we're seeing here. The two don't mix. I mean, whoever did it could hire attorneys who might argue that it is impossible to make so much aflatoxin and we'd say, yeah, but we found it. Then what?"

"Jeff, forget that for a minute. Newspapers are just an option when we consider the two-to-one ratio and the way it spreads out among the various people who might handle them," contributed Paul.

Paul turned to the computer. "Here, look at this interesting correlation. Do you know that twice as many people with college degrees have the disease, male or female, compared with those who have less education? I read somewhere that the ratio is the same when you look at people who read newspapers. The more educated you are, the more time you spend reading, Internet aside. There's your class distinction."

Jeff shook his head. "Trouble is, our situation is different. Here we have a lot more women who are sick compared with men."

"Spot on," replied Paul.

The office phone rang. Jeff picked up and spoke with Richard a few seconds and hung up.

"They found aflatoxin B1 in the ink," said Jeff. "They found it in the colored ink of the two Sunday papers and in the one Thursday paper we brought. It wasn't in the black ink or in the paper itself."

"Well, I'll be dipped and lit. Bingo," responded Paul. He lapsed into silence for a moment and suggested, "You don't mix aflatoxin and newspapers together by accident."

Jeff stared at his friend. "No, sir. There's only one way that can happen."

"Are they still in the lab?" asked Paul.

"No, it didn't take them long. Richard had to run home and Parker is prepping for one of my classes. I'm thinking that if the ink contains mycotoxin, contact dermatitis would certainly be expected along with the transfer factor to another person, especially infants and possibly to pets. It would explain a lower incidence of the disease among the poor. They don't buy the paper on a regular basis. It would also explain the presence of the excretion of mycotoxin in the urine."

Jeff's mind whirled with deductions. "It would also explain our original two cases. Old Percy handled newspapers on the street corner every day. So did Maria Carrasco. And let's not forget Margarete Hutchinson, a third case, who underwent cancer chemotherapy. She centered her life around cutting out and reading every newspaper and magazine clipping she could find about her disease."

Paul said, "Yes, it would also explain the problems with Percy's dog, who licked her master's rashes, according to what Dr. Haskell told us. If nothing else, the doctor is thorough. It's a good starting place."

Paul had discarded the bow tie since the visit to Arizona after Jeff told him he wouldn't protect him if he insisted on wearing it if they should go into a cowboy bar. Jeff hoped his friend would become a convert to standards of dress that fell within acceptable bounds, as he viewed them.

"Since no one is using the lab at the moment, we're going to do a little extraction. I'm going to get set up. Can you pick up three copies each of the *Norman Gazette* and the two Oklahoma City newspapers? Make sure you get copies with color. Let's get more evidence. Oh, and bring copies of the school paper too. I want to have comparison controls. If my hunch is right, the smaller papers won't have the mycotoxin."

"I'll help for a while," said Paul. "But I have to make some calls to make reservations for a date I have tonight."

"A date as with-a-woman-type date? I'm jealous, admitted Jeff," whose emotions were torn between undergoing a bad divorce and the need for female companionship.

"Yes. I have a life, you know."

"Who is she?" Jeff asked.

"She likes to ride bikes."

"A biker? I didn't know you rode a bicycle," stated Jeff.

"A biker, as in Harley-Davidson."

"Oh. Where are you going?"

"You're not old enough to understand," answered

his friend. "But if you must know, we're going to dinner and then dancing."

Jeff couldn't picture Paul dancing, but the vision conjured up memories of Pratlong Gullulong dancing in the video he always presented each semester—Pratlong dancing to the strobes, the fluorescence of the mold in his skin glowing under black light.

That was when the inspiration hit Jeff. Unable to hold back his excitement, he took the stairs to the third floor where most of the laboratories were situated. Jeff inserted the card key, heard the click, pushed open the door, and turned on the lights.

To any serious researchers, a laboratory is its own reality, a world separate from all others, another dimension where careful use of instruments and hard evaluation of the data could lead to new discoveries. It meant isolation, organization, and tedium intermixed with insight.

This particular laboratory held a special place in Jeff's heart. In this room he had spent a thousand hours and shed a million tears. Any time he wanted, he could use it at will. Two marble-top counters topped with equipment ran the length of the lab with storage above and below the counters. Desks sat at each end at the far wall with a long worktable in the center of the aisle. He had long ago bonded with each of the pieces of equipment.

Filled with charged emotion, Jeff waited for Paul to return. For now they wouldn't need the big stuff.

Paul appeared several minutes later with gloved

hands and carrying a load of newspapers.

"Paul, let's go across the hall to the conference room. I'm going to get something first," said Jeff excitedly.

A moment later Jeff appeared with a handheld black light and said, "Let's lay down what we have, face up."

Jeff turned on the black light and then turned off the room lights. He held the ultraviolet light over the newspapers. A slight glow appeared in the colored portions of the newspaper but not in the black ink.

Jeff said, excitedly, "Our first clue. Now, the only way to know for absolute certain is to do chemical extraction."

Essentially, the cutting involved cross-slicing the sample materials into small pieces until a total of ten grams of each were cut, the weight of ten pennies or ten packets of sugar found at a coffeehouse. These pieces would be placed in a small beaker and treated with solvents to remove the ink and any toxin.

They next coated glass plates six inches square and placed a drop of their test solutions onto it, then added a comparison control from Jeff's refrigertor.. The plate was placed into a solvent bath which migrated upward carrying the drops with it.

When the drops finished their migration upward, the men saw that the colored ink had separated into its red, blue, and yellow components. At the end of their climb, some of the drops were very circular, others not quite as perfect. At the top of the migration, a single spot matched the height of the aflatoxin control.

"It does appear we have some aflatoxin in the Oklahoma City papers in the color, which matches what your grads found in the Tucson newspapers," Paul said.

"Thus, we have the answer to the problem with the epidemic. And," Jeff continued, "not in the black ink of any paper. Looks like colored ink is the culprit, which confirms what Richard told me. So now both cities are implicated."

Jeff stared at the spots, trying to discern any messages they might be hiding.

"Good job," said Paul. "You start at the center of the maze and work yourself outward. A lot of times it's a lot easier to find your way out than to find your way in," responded his puzzle-loving companion.

"Aren't you supposed to start at the outside of the maze and find your way to the center?" asked Jeff, curiously.

"Most people would. Not me. Why limit yourself to finding a solution to a puzzle unless the game's directions are to do it a certain way. That's not our case here. You find the answer any way you can. Stretch the mind to find a solution."

Paul continued, "Now, the *Norman Gazette* and the school papers lack mycotoxin in the colored ink because the papers aren't using contaminated colored ink. They could be using an old batch of ink or they get their ink from someplace where there is no mycotoxin. And the disease is present in Norman because they do sell quite a number of copies of the

Oklahoma City papers here." "Damn, this stuff is *pure*," Jeff whispered, tota

"What do you mean?"

Jeff stared at the spots at the top. "Do you realize there are no tailings on the round aflatoxin spots we got from the color in the newspapers? Look at the circles. The aflatoxin from the newspapers is more pure than the control sample we got from our supplier and better than we can make. We've got perfectly round circles on the TLC plate with fluorescent glow from the black light."

From a drawer Jeff pulled out a magnifying glass, looked carefully at the spots and gave the glass to Paul.

"Nobody makes crystal that pure. Spots have tags and tails, even if they're tiny. Not here."

"Okay, we did a good job in our extraction process," said Paul, not feeling as confident as he tried to sound.

Jeff dropped his head forty-five degrees and looked at his friend with upturned eyes, as if to say, "Yeah, and I'm a monkey's uncle." Instead he offered, "Let's prepare a report and then call Whitaker and tell him what we found. It's better than not telling them what we found and then it turns out we should have said something."

The men decided to wait an additional day before they made the call to Whitaker in order to retest as much as they could to be sure of their results. The researchers were confident their efforts would change the path of the investigation. That would be the end of it, as far as they were concerned.

Day 13—Late Afternoon

Jeff and his team took their seats around the oval table in the third-floor conference room of the micro-biology building. The group included Paul, Carmen, and Jeff's three graduate students, Parker, Richard, and Marilyn.

After Jeff explained what he and Paul recently discovered in the newspaper ink, confirming his students' find, he said, "Parker, why don't you go ahead."

Parker pulled up his ever-present laptop and opened a file. "I am now going to give you the in-formation about the Tunisia epidemic, compliments of the World Health Organization. And Dr. Ryan sends her regards. Much of this she gave me over the phone. She emailed me a written report. I printed out a copy for you.

"To begin, according to her, the WHO didn't get involved for perhaps three weeks after the outbreak of the disease. Authorities in Tunisia didn't report the disease as quickly as they should have and then dragged their feet once the report was filed.

"Innocently, I asked Dr. Ryan if they'd checked for fungal toxins in the urine and she told me this is not usually done by anyone in their standard panel of testing procedures, unless symptoms relate to eat-ing toxic foods."

Jeff reflected, "In the case of Percy Butler, our first victim in Tucson, only blind luck on the part of the urine analysis team allowed for the discovery of mycotoxin in the sample because the technician was also a mycologist. He went for it on a flier and hit pay dirt."

"So Dr. Ryan doesn't know about our mycotoxin findings or our theory?" asked Marilyn.

"Correct. She did ask why we were curious. I told her you'd get back with her on that. She trusted you to inform her, if you found out any more about the issue," replied Parker.

"Anyway, in Tunisia," Parker continued, "two cities were involved, Gafsa and Tozeur, both located inland. Gafsa is the larger of the two with maybe a quarter million population while Tozeur was the first to report the strong outbreak of rashes on the fingers, hands, eyes, lips, and nose. The Gafsa symptoms were nearly all gone by the time Dr. Ryan and her group showed up.

"Tozeur got hit heavily and several thousand people became ill with nausea, headaches, loss of memory, and neurological problems. Liver disease became the common factor."

"Isn't liver disease a red flag suggesting aflatoxin poisoning?" asked Marilyn.

"Yes," answered Parker. "It's common in humans, poultry, fish, and other life forms. Supposedly, local officials reported that they traced the entire affair to a batch of moldy peanuts imported from Malaysia. Dr. Ryan also told me that the peanuts actually appeared after the onset of the epidemic, not before the epidemic, a claim denied by the Tunisians. Malaysian authorities vary in their response. Some say they shipped the peanuts; others deny it. She thinks the peanut scare was a diversion for something else, but they couldn't figure out what it might be.

"She also told me something else. A follow-up study found a number of stillbirths and deaths of babies younger than one month occurred during the same time period. This correlates with the effects of many fungal toxins on the prenatal processes.

"There's more," added Parker. "According to her, the WHO was beset by other problems. Aside from not being able to determine the source of the disease, they also couldn't determine when it started. All they knew was that women, the elderly, and the educated were the most severely affected, and their number increased over a few weeks. Then there occurred a mass effect among the population as a whole, with the first group beginning to die off.

"From start to finish, she'd never encountered a case as garbled as this one."

"It was a goddamn test run," Jeff stated emphatically, pounding his fist onto the table. "I knew it. One of the reasons why the infants died could be due to aflatoxin's presence in mothers' breast milk, a normal occurrence."

"Right you are," agreed Paul. "That's why we have two cities with two separate rates of disease and it's not spreading. If they had used smallpox, the disease couldn't be contained and it would become global, what with international travel as available as it is. With mycotoxins, it stays localized. It's rarely spread from person to person."

Jeff took over. "Aflatoxin and other fungal toxins are considered to be poisons like mercury, lead, strychnine, and mustard gas, unless they're used as very low-dose antibiotics, like we do in our research. In our problem nobody is eating the poison, and babies don't handle newspapers. They do suckle, though. They can also develop a rash after being touched by their mothers who do read the paper and touch the ink."

"You're saying we're paralleling the Gafsa disease trend with Oklahoma City and Tucson?" Marilyn queried.

"That's what I'm saying," said Jeff. "I'm thinking that in Tunisia somebody miscalculated the dosage, or they got the information they needed and stopped the disease themselves."

"Wow. Nobody knows what we know," said Marilyn.

Richard said, "Do they or don't they?" Here he glanced at Parker's computer.

Richard Smith was of appearance in terms of height and build, with black hair parted down the middle. His face was designed such that it always possessed a perpetual smirk. He frequently wore blue jeans, sneakers, and a Tee-shirt with a saying on it. His favorite shirt stated on the front "Gold's Gym, New York City." The back of the shirt read, "400-Pound Bench Press Club." When challenged about this claim of great strength, he confessed to lifting 20 pounds a day for 20 days. Thinking like the machine people accused him of being, Richard asked "Parker, what computer did you use to communicate with Dr. Ryan? One here at school or one at home?"

Parker pointed to the laptop in front of him. "It's one and the same. This one here. It's my best friend. Normally I write my dissertation in a certain carrel at the law school library where it's nice and isolated. Except for you people, nobody knows where I hole up.

"To answer your question, first I emailed her and set up a time to Skype from home, using this computer."

Richard scratched his forehead. "Chalk this up to my suspicious mind, but do you ever leave your computer unattended at the library?"

Parker shrugged, "I guess, Rich. I mean the place where I study is so isolated. Okay, once in a while I'll go down for a coffee or take a pee break."

"Parker, may I?" Richard requested, reaching out to pull the laptop to himself.

"Sure," Parker said, "but why?"

"I'm going to close this out and check some programs, all right?" Richard said.

Parker looked around and saw the others' eyes on Richard.

"Fine," agreed Parker.

"What's your password?" asked Richard. Parker told him, then cleared his throat.

"Yeah, Parker, like we need your stupid password," said Marilyn sarcastically. "It's not like we didn't already know it."

Everyone laughed, and Richard grinned, even more than his face normally allowed. He shook his head. "How many times have I told you to memorize a string of numbers intermixed with small and capital letters so you won't get hacked?" His fingers flew over the keys, and various screens appeared.

Moments passed in silence. Finally Richard said, "It wouldn't have mattered if you were the sole owner of the greatest password in the world, Parker. Looks like somebody stuck a thumb drive in here and inserted a worm. Maybe it happened when you took one of your breaks."

"Where did you learn all this, Rich?" asked Paul, definitely fascinated and amused.

"Oh, let's say the law taught me a lesson about staying clean," answered the graduate student.

"Obviously it didn't teach you enough," Paul retorted.

"Fortunately for us," Jeff quipped.

"What about our phones, Rich? Are they bugged too?" Jeff, asked, acutely concerned.

"I don't have the equipment to check. I can get it if necessary. In general, though, it's safe to say that university computers and phones are very secure, even with budget constraints."

"So what if somebody hacked him?" asked Marilyn amusedly. "What are they going to get, his Facebook likes?"

Richard replied, "They can get anything they want. No doubt somebody tracked Parker's the keystrokes. It's a program that can be inserted into the computer. It permits external access to your emails; actually, whatever is on your computer belongs to them. It can also cause emails to be routed to another address."

"Why me, Rich?" Parker asked.

"Because you're the go-to guy on this project, other than Dr. Shenero and Dr. Anderson," Richard responded. "And you're the one who walks around with a laptop all day."

"How would they know I do and why would they care?" Parker turned his hands to display the palms. "I mean, does that mean I'm being followed?"

"You were but not anymore," Richard responded. "They probably got what they wanted."

"It doesn't matter why," said Jeff. "Rich, can you debug Parker's computer?"

"It'll take me a little time."

"Go for it," commanded Parker.

Richard Smith, microbiologist turned instrumentation expert and computer hacker, began working the keyboard again. "Okay, will do. But first, let's see if we can find out who did it," he announced almost in a whisper, as if the invaders of Parker's computer could hear them now.

Day 13–Evening

Carmen had Stage 1 non-Hodgkin's follicular lymphoma. Her prognosis was good because an early lymph node biopsy identified the problem at its early stages. Over a month before, she began her chemotherapy treatments. The doctor confirmed the presence of the cancer, which was now in rapid remission.

Together with her primary care physician, they decided on chemotherapy without radiation. The doctor preferred the more aggressive approach, but Carmen made the final decision. Another treatment the day before left her nauseous, tired, and depressed.

As she sat in her Toyota Corolla in her driveway, Carmen realized she could go nowhere for solace. She did have a few friends, but she didn't need sympathetic pats on the back. She needed to get through this setback without self-pity.

Her luxurious hair had begun to fall out, almost increasingly each day, and worse the past two or three days. She knew it would happen. In the past she could hide it by wearing a scarf as a fashion statement. The days of hiding it were over. She began to cry. *Sometimes you have to toss a rock in the pond if you want to get ripples*, she could hear Jeff say.

But I don't have a rock to toss. Casting bread upon still waters still requires bread, she thought, feeling more alone than she'd felt in a long time.

How alone is floating outside of Earth in free space with a questionable life-support system?

Now what? Go back to the office and write reports? Sure. She decided to reorganize. Or get re-disorganized, as Jeff would call it.

Suddenly she felt wild and reckless, free. The feeling wouldn't last, and it didn't matter. Nothing did. *Live for the moment.* That's what Jeff always said.

Carmen went into her home and, despite recommendations, took a quick glass of wine and entered the shower. Hair began to clog the drain. When she saw the hair fall, she screamed, dropped down on all fours and let the hot water pummel her. She began to pull at the remaining hair. More loosened and fell to the floor of the shower.

Carmen sobbed for a few moments, and something grabbed at her. *Not like this; I won't go like this.* It can always be worse.

After the tears stopped, she felt a hot new resolve course through her as she stood and let the shower soothe her. She dried herself and took one of her razors and shaved her delicate scalp. She laughed at the sight. She chose a mauve-colored blouse that melded with a skirt decorated with Comanche Indian runes, and put on stylish flat sandals. She completed her outfit by loosely placing a red scarf over her head. She forced herself to smile. She would tell Jeff she cut her hair off so she could look like him.

With credit cards in tow, Carmen headed out to Juliette's, an upscale fashion store for women in the

Norman Mall, a quick fifteen-minute drive from her home. Two shopping hours remained before the store closed, and the first thing she planned to buy would be a turban. Although she tried on numerous wigs, her head didn't feel comfortable with any of them. Besides, she didn't like their look.

Carmen went on a fling. She purchased nearly two-thousand-dollars'-worth of dresses, blouses, slacks, shoes, and a new watch.

She likened the alien growth inside her to the growths inside people in Sigourney Weaver's *Aliens* movie. In her situation the real alien was called cancer.

She remembered what Jeff always said: *The aggressive will win over the weak, a positive attitude will win over complacency, and drive will win over placid acceptance.*

Recalling his words brought thoughts of her own. *Does scared out of their skin win over stupidity? Does "What the hell did I do to deserve this?" win over status quo?* No, dammit, she wasn't going to weaken. *Stick to your resolve. If a storm comes up, only then is it time to reorganize. So do it.*

Carmen left Juliette's, not having purchased all the items she'd wanted, but her emotional gas tank was nearing empty. Using her credit for such extravagances had been a new record for her.

She had nearly completed her list of things to do before she crashed on this Thursday night. She considered: *Only one more day at the office this week. Should I call in sick or should I show up looking like a hag?*

Her self-respect wouldn't let her do either of those. Instead, she made the decision to party and let tomorrow take care of itself.

She loaded her purchases into the trunk of her Corolla and walked over to the Complete Steakhouse, located in the same mall as Juliette's where she enjoyed a complete steak dinner, which began with an appetizer and a glass of white wine. Unaccustomed to drinking alcohol, she then made the unfortunate decision to drive home without calling a cab.

Three blocks from her house Carmen got pulled over for crossing over a white lane line several times. Her blood alcohol level measure .08, the borderline for a DUI vs. a DWI in Oklahoma. She spent a considerable amount of time being questioned and taking sobriety tests before being handcuffed and helped into the back of a squad car.

Now in jail in the company of two hookers and a junkie, Carmen tried to think about her present life. She knew men were attracted to her thin and well-proportioned body, at least by traditional American standards. She was affable and fluent in English with enough of a Spanish accent to add charm to her speech.

Although her parents had taught her not to question authority, Jeff taught her to question everything. Analyze what authorities say, they are often wrong, the press is wrong, and science is only right for a brief period. First salt and cholesterol are bad, then they're not, and then they're only bad for certain people. Newspapers are owned by a few people who follow a party line and specialize in propagating bad news to sell copy. How many politicians ever worked a nine-to-five job, but are authorities on telling us how to live? TV advertisers promote unsafe products, and for the consumer, it's a seller's market. If you don't ask for the truth, you have only yourself to blame.

Do I really have myself to blame? What happened to my internship and my license to practice medicine, something I'd wanted to do since childhood? Where's the tradeoff?

Is jail the big trade? Or is Jeff the big trade? None of it means a whole lot, except for one thing. What does Jeff like to say? "Sometimes you need to reshuffle the deck to get a new hand." If she were to quit Jeff, she'd better do it soon and get back to medicine before too much more time passes and it's too late.

If she does decide to stay with him, then maybe—no, definitely—Jeff is going to be the ace in that new hand.

Day 14–Morning

The truckers were hanging tough despite federal arbitration. A full dozen men occupied the arbitration table, most of them lawyers for each side. For the truckers' union and their attorneys, there would be no compromise.

The local newspapers reformatted to create larger editions. A few of them decided to increase their production runs with extra color thanks to the epidemic and the strike providing a boost to sales.

The evening of Carmen's arrest Jeff went to bed late. He received her call on his cell not an hour later. His secretary needed to get bailed out of jail.

Hurriedly, Jeff made a few phone calls and dressed. Then he went to his safe where he kept emergency cash. At least he wouldn't have to wait until the banks opened.

Carmen was released to Jeff at 8:00 a.m. of Day 14. No bail was required because of Carmen's first offense and no injuries or vehicular damage had occurred. She still wore her turban.

Once outside the police station, Carmen surprised Jeff by wrapping her arms around him. "I can never thank you enough for being there for me. I'm forever grateful to you for this," she said into his ear, then kissed his cheek.

Jeff paid the fee required to get Carmen's car released from impound, then drove her to the impound lot where they found her Toyota. A light rain had fallen the night before and served to raise the level of odors from automotive greases and oils in the lot. They talked.

He had never seen Carmen so determined, so absolutely certain about herself. Not a tear in her eyes, not a hint she had spent the night behind bars. On the way to her car in impound she told him about her companions for the night. She didn't get along with any of them, *which might explain two of her broken nails,* he conjectured, in awe of her strength.

"Are you okay to drive?" he asked, opening the car door.

"I'm fine, Jeff."

"Where are you going now?" he asked. He did not try to mask his concern.

Carmen gave a brief shrug. "I'm going home. Jail gives a person a lot of time to think. All I'm dealing with now is tendrils. You call them spin-off. Even the DUI is a tendril, although I don't think it will look too good on my resume."

"Don't worry. I think we can get that expunged," Jeff reassured her."

Carmen continued, "Aside from that, it's all part of my great escape. You taught me about looking my enemies in the eye and calling them out. I'm going back to the house to change. If you want to follow me, we can go to the office from there. No reason to go to bed now. I can use a good meal, though, if you care to take me out. Then it's business as usual."

Jeff followed her to a small brick home surrounded by dogwood trees in a shady and relaxed neighborhood. Carmen parked in the driveway, and Jeff parked in the street in front of the home, where a porch and a swing awaited the next visitor.

Carmen walked to the trunk of her vehicle and removed boxes and bags containing her purchases from the evening before. She handed Jeff several of the packages. The lawn sparkled from the light rain of the evening before.

Carmen went into the master bedroom to set her packages onto the bed. Jeff followed and did the same. She threw her turban onto the bed and began to undress, pulling her blouse out of her skirt and unbuttoning it while slipping out of her sandals. She walked to the bathroom in her bra, unhooking it as she walked. Jeff watched, fascinated with her resolve and her sexuality.

The shower ran for several minutes and then stopped.

Fifteen minutes later Carmen reappeared wrapped in a towel, with makeup newly applied. She dropped the towel on the floor of the bedroom and began to dress. She picked out a new pair of panties and khaki slacks. Then she pulled a new black-lace bra from another shopping bag, put it on, and retrieved a new blouse.

"You have the price tag on the blouse," Jeff told her as she began to button it, gently grabbing her arm from his seated position on the bed. He stood and leaned toward her neck, turning her around gently to gnaw off the plastic line that held the price tag onto the collar of her blouse, then pushed through the remaining line.

"There, that feels better," she said. She didn't specify whether the feel referred to the shower or to Jeff's gnawing more at her neck than at the tag.

"Shall we go?" Jeff asked.

"Oh, one more thing." Carmen turned completely toward her admirer, wrapped her arms around his neck, held him hard against her, and kissed him deeply and passionately on the mouth. Releasing the stunned man, she said, "Now, as soon as I fix my lipstick, we can go."

Jeff didn't speak as Carmen grabbed the turban from the bed, positioned it on her head, checked herself in the mirror, and took him by the hand to lead him out the front door. Her movements were unhurried.

Jeff had enough discipline to know that his professional half did not permit him to accept his true feelings for Carmen. Now he really wanted her in her entirety, and it was all he could do to keep himself contained. What added to the aching within him was the knowledge they would return to a solid working relationship once they reached the office and put this little affair behind them.

They climbed into Jeff's Mustang, and he drove toward a café on the way to the school office. During the ride he joked, "In my next life, I want to be a developer and make up my own names for streets."

"Really?" said Carmen. "Like what?"

"Penis Parkway?" Jeff chuckled.

"I get it," Carmen giggled. How about Via Voluptuous."

"Boobs Boulevard," offered Jeff.

Carmen laughed louder.

She said, "We could name the development Sensual City."

They continued to laugh and offer more suggestions for street and development names. Finally they became silent.

Then Carmen said, "Thanks, Jeff. I needed a laugh."

"We both did," he replied. *Actually, I need a lot more than that*, he wanted to say.

"Who would move into our neighborhood?" she asked.

Our neighborhood? "I suspect the names would attract a certain clientele who might not be to *our* liking. What was the old Groucho Marx statement? 'I refuse to belong to any organization that would have me as a member'."

"And I refuse to have sex with any man who would have me as a girlfriend," she quipped.

Jeff paused to think about her statement. He'd been so cold and objective toward her for so long he occasionally wondered if she could personally own up to any feelings she might have for him. *Does she realize what she just said? Of course she does. First she kisses you and then she slides in a little comment. Let it go.*

At the café they both ate a hearty breakfast of waffles, bacon, eggs, coffee, and juice, but Carmen's heart ached. She understood why Jeff felt betrayed. He believed in honesty and he completely trusted her. She had broken the bond of trust by not telling him of her cancer. She felt his hurt, his angst. Tears welled up in her eyes.

He moved around the booth to her side, slid next to her, and held her hand. "Carmen, you're on the way up. Those clothes are a great start, and I'm here for whatever support you need and for whatever I can give."

Pleased by his words, Carmen turned to him and gave him a light kiss on the cheek. "Jeff, it's all over. I had the final treatment yesterday."

"Look, right now you're confused, I mean with the cancer and the DUI and all, so now is not a good time..." Jeff began stumbling over his words, surprised at the kiss, but knowing all along it was what he wanted.

"I'm not confused," Carmen stated flatly as she pulled back. "I know exactly what I want, and who I am now. "You're the one who's confused, Jeff."

"I am?"

"Yes,you are. You're still wearing your divorce on your sleeve. It's not the great secret you think it is. Your anger became greater after the divorce. So did your confusion.

"For me, I thank God for what He has given me and for what He has taken away. It made me a stronger person and then you come into my life and you helped me to see so many more good things. I consider that to be a present."

Jeff sat dazed and confused.

Carmen softened her tone and put her hand on his arm. "Jeff, you're a full-contact fighter, right?"

Jeff nodded silently. The mood had turned serious.

"Well, the way I see it, another black belt looked you hard in the eye and called you out, but you decided to pick lesser opponents instead of facing your man."

Jeff's mind spun. "You're not a fight, Carmen."

"No, I'm not, but I am a distraction and you have to fix an epidemic. That's the fight you have to face now. So how about if we get back to work until this problem is fixed and you get down to business and kick some serious butt. Then we let the dust settle and talk about you and me afterward. Okay? And if you don't want to, well, I guess that's okay too."

Jeff slid out of the booth and helped Carmen out.

"Come on, woman, let's go to work," he said as objectively as he could, stung deeply by the truth of Carmen's words.

Five minutes later Jeff parked behind the microbiology building, and the pair walked to his office. He unlocked the door and went directly to the microscope.

Carmen walked directly toward her desk.

Typically, Jeff took in good money each month from his private consulting firm. In addition to Carmen, a single employee worked for him, a certified industrial hygienist, or CIH. The man worked out of his home and performed the bulk of the inspections and air monitoring. Many required Jeff's personal attention.

Jeff functioned best under pressure, yet he couldn't stay ramped up too long without a break. A good long run would definitely help.

After a long silence, Carmen said, "Along with my own savings I'm going to start living."

He wanted to hold her, but he accepted her wish to keep him at arm's length for the time being. He didn't want to admit his love for her, and he didn't need another rejection. He remained silent for several minutes and then said, "So start living."

Jeff had thought about giving her a substantial pay raise for some time, yet didn't think this moment would be a good time to announce it. She would think he was placating her or trying to buy her off and to keep her working for him. He knew otherwise. She filled gaps in his life he desperately needed. It behooved him to tell her before she decided to leave.

"I'm ready for a late lunch," she offered at last.

"Minimum daily requirement of cholesterol. New federal guidelines. It looks like it's the two of us. Paul's at meetings."

"In that case, if you want to have colorful dreams, I suggest we go to the Bigger Burger," she suggested. "I like their salad bar."

"It's a date," Jeff replied, with the guarantee his dreams would indeed be colorful tonight, burger or not.

The TVs were on at the restaurant and the face of Billy Kirk filled the screens. Billy and Jeff had become close friends when they lived together during their college years.

"This is Billy Kirk with GNN, your Global News Network," the popular TV anchorman began.

His penetrating blue eyes looked directly into the camera, thrilling his female audience as they had done for years. He stood in front of the state capitol in Oklahoma City, the city of his birth.

"Whether or not we might call it a time of tribulation, America's attention is focused on the epidemic threatening to sweep the nation. So far it is confined to two major cities, with several cases in outlying areas. Experts are predicting the disease will soon spread across the country. Foreign leaders have expressed concern and are threatening to block American air travel to their countries unless the epidemic is stopped. Experts involved in disease control describe the deaths caused by this one as mysterious.

"We are unable to confirm the exact number of persons infected or dead. The official government statement is that a new and unusual strain of flu has emerged, perhaps a variant of Covid-19, although no virus has yet been isolated. Some say the disease is coming from poultry or swine. Others say it is from God. Almost all experts are in agreement that we were forewarned, ever since the great flu pandemic of 1918, which killed twenty to thirty million around the world.

"Our contacts with the Centers for Disease Control in Atlanta tell us that serious government oppression of information is occurring. This is supported by the fact that a military alert has been ordered. Sergeant Robert Brewer, a military spokesman for Homeland Security, stated that this is a normal procedure whenever an epidemic occurs. Our sources are checking on the validity of this information.

"Unnamed sources suggest we are under terrorist attack. Government spokespersons scoff at the idea. We will present updates throughout the day. This is

Billy Kirk with GNN reporting."

After lunch, Jeff and Carmen returned to the office and met with Paul. They called Whitaker and faxed him their report. Whitaker said he'd call them back in a couple of hours. When he did he told the men to be prepared to take a conference call in the OU Media Center the next morning at seven thirty, Oklahoma time, to which Jeff consented.

Day 14–Afternoon

Jeff cut short his afternoon ten-kilometer jog, changed, showered, and drove to his university office, anxious to escape the feeling of loneliness that suddenly gripped him during his run.

The moment he walked in, Carmen hit the hold button on the phone and turned to him. "Boss, it's another complaint from Big Sky Apartments."

Jeff had personal obligations in order to make his mortgage and insurance payments on time. These required cash flow, and government grants weren't targeted toward the payment of one's personal needs.

Big Sky meant big trouble. Nearly half the units belonging to the complex were seriously water-damaged and contaminated with mold. Bad outdoor siding hit by sprinkler systems, along with roof and plumbing leaks resulted in a sizable number of smelly and moldy units. The occupants were frustrated, but they lacked the money to move elsewhere. Like a roach motel or a time-share, you might move in, but you wouldn't be leaving.

Under instructions given by the property owner, reputed slumlord Manny Bolton, the management ignored the tenants' complaints. Bolton's method of dealing with the complaints was to send out colorful fliers twice weekly to all the residents to update them on such matters as improvements in the laundry room, new parking regulations, and household cooking tips. Fliers were also distributed throughout the campus areas to recruit students.

Mold growth could be commonly found under sinks, on ceilings, behind baseboards, on bathroom walls, behind pictures and furnishings close to walls, and within wall cavities—areas where humidity was the highest. A few of the renters knew about Jeff and got a number of other occupants to hire him as a group, if he would accept their proposed group discounted rate. He accepted their offer to inspect and monitor their units and relegated the jobs to his on-board CIH assistant.

Jeff believed Manny Bolton possessed all the necessary qualities as an example of what not to be, akin to ambulance-chasing attorneys or the classic depiction of the used car salesman. The man possessed unbridled arrogance and did not care about the human beings who signed his leases. Bolton had moved to Norman from Boston years before and spoke his r's like a doctor using a tongue depressor who would ask a patient to say "aaah." When Bolton said "car," it came out as "caaah," and apartment came out as "apaaahtment."

At fifty years of age Bolton's millions came from apartments such as the Big Sky. He always employed a single attorney, newly graduated from law school, who quashed complaints as soon as they arose and who also pursued those who skipped out on their leases. No one escaped. When the attorney left for a better job (or possibly to find another career) Bolton hired another attorney, also recently out of law school, who had his own loans to repay.

Bolton always appeared to be a man without a care in the world, despite being mocked on social media. Somehow, his business seemed to grow, if only because he received free advertising from the mockery and by providing among the lowest rents in town.

Bolton was married and owned a huge home with indoor swimming pool and spa out near Lake Thunderbird, a few miles east of the university campus. He also owned a motorboat, a yacht, and a small Cessna.

In the apartment complex, a prematurely born infant died in a heavily contaminated unit. Cause unknown. In an adjoining unit, a second child died within a few months of the first. Autopsy found a high concentration of spores belonging to a species of *Aspergillus* in the infant's lungs, similar to the findings in the case of first child. The management blamed the parents of the children for maintaining an unclean and dust-laden home. No correlation could be made between the mold and the deaths. The management pointed to countless children who lived in moldy homes everywhere and weren't harmed. Big Sky residents became outraged at the statement.

Big Sky had another problem. A mini-version of the epidemic had broken out among the tenants, with numerous persons reporting rashes which they claimed were due to mold in their apartments. They were right, but not in the way they thought, Jeff later realized. The city health department had no available personnel to assist them, but at least they knew Jeff worked with the government on the problem. Importantly, the government paid him to be a consultant, not them.

Jeff caught Paul up to speed on the apartment issue and asked him to review epidemic-related data collected by the health department while he worked with the tenants on their mold complaint issues.

The disease occurrences at Big Sky were a break for both the scientists who could obtain a great deal of information on the rash issue from a concentrated cluster of people. Big Sky needed repairs, and more importantly, Bolton needed to be forced to pay a large sum of money to provide safe housing for his tenants as per city and state regulations. At the present time, Bolton didn't appear to care, because newspapers were not read by college students to any serious extent. The men were confounded, as was Jeff's on-board doctor, Carmen.

In his fantasies Jeff saw Bolton brought up on charges of child endangerment or possibly manslaughter. But those charges would never stick. Proving the cause of the infants' deaths would be impossible.

However, Bolton was not immune to lawsuits. A jury trial would be the best way to handle the situation. Jurors would be more emotional than a single judge during a bench trial, Jeff knew from personal experience.

Then a singularly unpleasant idea struck him. Could trusted national and international health organizations, bought and paid for by terrorists, decide who might be poisoned and who might not be?

Insidious poisoning by mycotoxins could do the same thing, realized a newly enlightened Jeffrey Shenero.

Day 15–Morning

The OU media center was familiar territory to both men, conveniently located adjacent to history across a grassy oval opposite the biological sciences buildings.

This day, the men sat in low-back armchairs in a room that could hold up to twenty folding chairs. The work crew consisted of two men and two woman who were sworn to secrecy when they were first hired to operate the center. Too many private conferences were held there to chance a leakage of secrets.

Precisely at 7:30 a.m. or 8:30 Washington, DC, time, the large-screen TV lit up to reveal a small group of four seated at a rectangular table. In front of each appeared to be a copy of the notes Jeff and

Paul prepared which Jeff had faxed over the day before.

Present were James Whitaker and three other persons. Jeff noted the same dark circles beneath Whitaker's eyes, circles he had observed during the man's recent visit to his office.

Whitaker made the introductions. Few smiles were exchanged. The camera at their end panned those seated.

Andrew Simon, a microbiologist experienced in epidemiology, held the bragging rights of being Paul's physical opposite. In another life, the two men had presented papers at the same conferences. Simon was a short, overweight man with stubby fingers. With worldwide experience, he also worked and lobbied for various drug companies. After he retired, the Food and Drug Administration hired him as a go-between.

Gustav Schmidt, an elderly man of German descent, held the reputation of being an investigator with the European Health Organization. He recently arrived in the States to study the present disease outbreak. Call it the German scientific lineage, call it training, or both—Jeff appreciated that Schmidt would be absolutely and painfully meticulous in his work.

Marjorie Reynolds, press correspondent, was a female version of Simon in appearance. Small, overweight, frizzy haired, and mean spirited, the thirty-year veteran reporter and four-time divorcee was excellent at her trade. She handled the release of news items from the USPHS and the CDC. Her current directive was damage control.

Accomplished in his own right, Whitaker was out of his league in the presence of Jeff and Paul, the same feeling he had tried to hide during their first visit.

The screen split vertically, while another link from the USPHS fed to the Department of Homeland Security, where Robert Brewer faced the two. No coughs or background sounds could be heard from anyone. The man from the Department of Defense appeared to sit alone.

Linkup confirmed, a stone-faced Brewer waited until Whitaker finished the introductions and then, with a quick half smile, thanked everyone for their attendance.

Simon, the rotund microbiologist, spoke first. To his credit the man had a solid reputation as a respected administrator of his division.

He tilted his head downward and looked at Jeff over thick steel-frame glasses. "Dr. Shenero, I would like to read you a quote from a document you sent yesterday afternoon to Mr. Whitaker with a copy to Mr. Brewer." He then glanced down through the glasses at a page in front of him.

Simon read: "'Evidence suggests that two major city newspapers have mycotoxin in the ink. This method of poison transfer should be investigated. In addition, case histories suggest that ink may be the target vehicle for the aflatoxin agent since numerous persons were infected who were handling commercial newspapers. Signed, Jeffrey Shenero, PhD, and Paul Anderson, PhD, Department of Homeland Security, contractor numbers 3-146-4827 and 3-146-4828, respectively.' I reading that correctly, am I not? Dr. Shenero? Dr. Anderson?"

"Yes, sir, that is the memo we sent," replied Jeff.

Jeff looked closely at the image of Brewer, a man he had learned to distrust. He didn't like what he saw. The man appeared to be surprisingly at ease. Perhaps he could help change that look. He wondered whether their proposal might be so off the wall as to be stunningly stupid. Or were they right on and had hit on the mother lode?

Brewer said, "Gentlemen, this is not the first idea we've heard on this subject. Many qualified researchers have theories and findings to support them. We've checked them all out, and they don't wash.

"I'm afraid your theory is not very novel. We've investigated yours, as well as other possibilities in our own laboratory, and we don't find anything there. As you may know, I personally have experience in the investigation of terrorist activities, so you can rule that out here."

Brewer tried to impose a military bearing while speaking, but a trained eye and ear might catch a response all too ready—all too prepared. "I also believe that your research is rather shallow and, pardon me for saying this, amateurish, especially for scholars who have such great reputations. Do you have any theory about how this toxin got into the ink?"

Jeff looked at Paul in surprise. "Well, sir, I admit our study isn't conclusive, but we believe it has merit."

"Can you please answer a direct question with a direct answer?" shot Brewer.

"No, we don't," responded Jeff, beginning to feel defensive and confused with the unforeseen direction of the interview.

Brewer grimaced with apparent sympathy and shook his head. "I spoke with an old friend of mine, Alan Hood, who is co-owner of the Oklahoma City newspapers in question and where both the morning and evening newspapers are printed in the same facility. So, your finding really relates to a single occurrence, undoubtedly a false positive. And I might add, Mr. Hood is a responsible citizen and a trustworthy professional."

Brewer, now in his element, continued, "Are you questioning the integrity of Mr. Hood, who, I understand, actually purchased the newspapers from the Kirk family, with whom you are acquainted, are you not?"

Brewer had gone too far, bringing in the Kirks. Jeff responded, at first defensively, then with a trace of impatience and anger. "Does it matter how many occurrences we find? If it's there, it's there."

Brewer looked sorrowful, as if trying to prepare the new recruit who didn't yet understand the rules of the game. "I must tell you that Mr. Hood laughed at your suggestions of any toxicity associated with either of the papers or his facility, which I assure you, has passed OSHA and NIOSH federal worker safety and cleanliness requirements. Alan Hood is an American of the first order, and to cast aspersions against his newspapers is to cast those aspersions against him and his loyal staff."

Marjorie Reynolds interrupted and glared at both of the guests, looking first at the screen to draw attention away from Brewer's lead. "Please realize something. This is the American press you are attacking. I hope you are not suggesting that because you purportedly found mycotoxin in a newspaper, it is rampant throughout the country, because your own evidence says otherwise. How do we know it hasn't been in the ink itself for weeks, months, or even years? How do you know this mysterious contaminant doesn't resemble mycotoxin in its chemical reactions in your laboratory?"

"Yes," said Simon, "there are plenty of false positives where mycotoxin analyses are concerned."

"We always duplicate and triplicate our results. There is no doubt in our minds what we found," stated Paul.

Reynolds gave a slight smile. "Ah, in your minds." She permitted her statement to linger for a moment, then continued. "You do know that printing ink is also used on packages and labels. Untold billions of dollars could be affected by these accusations. The ramifications are that millions of books, weekly newsmagazines, and tabloids may be implicated in this plot. This is neither amusing nor practical."

Brewer took control. "Please, folks. Being a man of open mind, I am willing to hear more of your innovative ideas regarding this epidemic affecting—I hesitate to use the phrase 'sweeping through'—two of our cities—excuse me, three, if we count Norman and one or two cases in Tulsa.

"Understand this. Just because we have a few cases with mycotoxin in the urine doesn't mean we have an epidemic of mycotoxicosis precipitated by terrorists. In fact some members of the NIH continue to believe we have an ongoing viral infection that mimics symptoms of poisoning by mold toxins. There are other very promising leads, as well.

"And believe me, every idea passes through us and is reviewed by us or by our larger investigative team. There are other promising leads—perfume is one."

Then Brewer piled more manure onto the dung heap. "Do either of you gentlemen bother to read the papers or watch the news?"

"Well..." began Jeff, about to say they were fairly busy as of late.

Whitaker took over. "Because if you had, you would have known what we first believed might be a viral infection appears to be a problem with a new line of perfume, as Mr. Brewer alluded to a moment ago."

Jeff and Paul looked at each other, clearly confused.

"I can see you do not keep up with current

events," added Whitaker. "A new perfume manufacturer based in Oklahoma City is testing its brand there, where it has become popular, and they are also test marketing it in Tucson to a lesser extent. The product is made for the general public, and not for the high-end public. Therein lies the culprit in our mystery."

Although Jeff and Paul were thoroughly chastised, Jeff became furious, his mercurial behavior legend. The man on the screen in front of him had crossed over the line of honor. For the moment Jeff held himself in check, looking, hearing, processing, and digesting. The men now had to run through the findings and methodologies they used to arrive at their conclusion.

Brewer appeared surprised, even stunned, at the information he and Paul were presenting. He was not a man of science, but the presentation he heard told him the two knew what they were doing.

When in doubt, bail out. "Gentlemen, thank you for providing us with your information. Be assured your report will be reconsidered by our top experts," Brewer said dismissively.

"That's it?" said Jeff. To him, this sounded like the weak bespectacled government hack telling Indiana Jones at the end of *Raiders of the Lost Ark*, "Don't worry. Top experts are examining the Ark," as it was stowed at the back of a massive warehouse.

"Can you at least tell us the name of the perfume maker?" asked Jeff.

"I'm afraid not, doctor. They're under investigation, and we can't reveal any more information until we have all our testing completed," Whitaker responded coldly.

Then Whitaker drove the nail in. "As scientists, you should appreciate that concept," he said somewhat facetiously.

"That wraps it up," concluded Brewer.

"Not quite, Bob," Jeff snapped before Brewer's image could fade out of the picture. Jeff bored into Brewer eyes. "Maybe what you said is true, but we know what we found. You hired us, and you can fire us. I also know a few things about you that might accidentally get leaked to the press. I can't speak for Dr. Anderson, but I'm in this for the long haul.

"Oh, we also know a lot about Maria Carrasco in Mexico and Percy Butler and a whole lot about Tunisia as they relate to this epidemic. Do you want us to tell you now? No, wait. Let's save it."

Even while he said the words, Jeff wondered about the origin of his vitriol. It definitely was not part of his upbringing. Might it be a chemical imbalance? He'd have to check into it when he got some free time because the damn thing wouldn't go away.

Paul rose to the occasion. "I agree with Dr. Shenero. We know what we found, and we know where the problem lies—if you get my drift, Bob. Your attitude tells us we hit pay dirt, the jackpot. Thank you, sir, for confirming our findings."

The red-faced, somewhat glowering image of Brewer disappeared.

"Well," sighed Whitaker, seemingly embarrassed. If vitriol could permeate a TV screen, this was a defining moment for it to happen. "You'll have to forgive Dr. Shenero. The stress of the responsibility appears to be getting to him."

Simon and Schmidt clearly looked flabbergasted beyond words at what they had heard, and could only stare at the screen. Jeff guessed that none of them had suspected the easy-going Anderson would jump into the fray and he could write Reynolds' script for her before it went to press.

Whitaker appeared distressed. "I want to thank you gentlemen for taking the time to join us and I hope to be hearing from you again."

"Don't be condescending, Jim," said Jeff abruptly. "You will be hearing from us again and you won't like what you hear or the way that you hear it."

The screen went blank. The media crew emerged, moving as robots, resetting controls, probably thinking that it might be worth getting fired, sued, ostracized, and going to jail for relating to their friends what had just transpired.

"Man, am I pissed," said Jeff through clenched teeth. "We were set up, waylaid, shanghaied, jobbed, robbed, beaten, raped, plundered, and lied to."

"All because we responded to their request for help?" said Paul.

"No, because we found something they didn't want us to find. If there were any doubts before, I don't have them anymore."

Jeff hadn't been so angry and insulted since Willy Johnson stole his stamp collection when they were both in the fourth grade. His anger at Willy remained. In fact he wouldn't mind running into him again. Now Brewer was in his line of sight.

Paul said, "You heard Brewer. You heard Reynolds. It's the press we're slandering. We have such flimsy evidence to present. And did you notice Schmidt said he thought we had a novel idea in contradiction to what Brewer and Whitaker told us. This is his area of expertise. I think the man agrees with us, but couldn't flat out say so. Either somebody paid him off, or they have some dirt on him."

Jeff was adamant. "Hey, they're the ones who came to us asking for help. They're the ones who gave us their database and wanted us to contact them with any and all ideas. If they don't like the information they get, they might be able to tailor their request next in time which would include the request not to call them regardless of what might be found. You know, just take your paycheck and go away."

Paul said, "Actually, we really don't know when the ink was prepared or how the toxin got added or how long it sat around before it was used."

"Who cares? It's there, and thousands are affected," Jeff retorted.

"What's this business with the perfume? I don't know what to make of it. Let's get the CD recording of the meeting from the media crew along with the data from our pen recorders and get them to Carmen for safekeeping in case anything happens to us," added Paul, a touch of concern in his voice.

"As soon as we check them, I'm going to send

mine over to Billy Kirk at GNN for safekeeping—just because," Jeff said curtly.

"Fine, but I never heard anything about Tunisia. Where did that come from?" asked Paul.

"Tell you later," replied Jeff.

Jeff fed off bad opinions of himself, but in this instance, he had undergone a humiliating experience in a professional domain. Paul was right and he was right. Brewer absolutely told them they had hit home without having to state the words.

"Speaking of the teleconference, where were you coming from when you told Brewer you knew a few things about him?" queried Paul.

Jeff smiled. "Nothing. I felt like putting pressure on the son of a bitch and give him something to think about. I also wanted to force one or more of them into making a mistake."

Paul began laughing. "Jeff, you're a man after my own heart."

"And where did that mouth of yours come from?" chided Jeff.

"From your aura," answered Paul.

Jeff deliberated on Paul's off-the-cuff remark and decided there might be an element of truth to it.

Paul and Jeff then headed over to the student union for coffee. It wasn't yet 8:30. They loaded up with croissants and drinks and took a seat in their usual corner table. Paul added three sugars and two small plastic containers of cream to his. Numerous students were either eating, studying, talking, texting, or doing a myriad of things students did at the start of the day.

"Unfortunately, we haven't solved anything. We merely spotlighted ourselves as persons to watch, which is a little worrisome," said Jeff, beginning to cool after his heated outburst.

"And what was all that nonsense from Brewer about backing this guy Hood, the owner of the paper?" queried Paul.

Jeff took a sip of coffee. "To me, that makes Hood a player, an outlier to the puzzle."

"Or Hood might be close to the centerpiece," added Paul. "I say Brewer leaked information he shouldn't have. I'm hoping the bastard is probably banging his head against the wall right now and may blow a gasket during the night."

"You're right. I'm thinking Brewer can't stop from stepping on his own tongue. Anyway, let's see what we can find out about this Hood character," Jeff said.

Paul sighed. "In all honesty, we're going to have to think out our moves more carefully if we're going to have a chance of fixing this situation. It doesn't take a brainiac to tell me these people may not play nice."

Out of his temporary funk, Jeff's mood lightened. "That's exactly what I'm counting on."

Back in the conference room, Whitaker turned to the others and said, almost apologetically, "Dr. Shenero's medical history is varied. Rumor has it he's near a nervous breakdown. Apparently his imagination takes control and he forces others to listen to one wild theory after another. A control freak. I fear that stress at work, possible alcohol dependency, and a recent divorce are causing instability in the man. We strongly suspect he may be on drugs. He will be off the case soon."

Marjorie Reynolds declared, "Can you imagine their nerve to implicate the press in all this? Believe me, I'll never write a good thing about either one of them."

Whitaker felt secure in the knowledge that Marjorie Reynolds would never write a good word about anybody. That she had advanced to her present position by threatening certain people with a press scandal was an open secret, not a rare event in the business.

Reynolds's fertile mind probably spun webs of insidious news releases revolving around the frying of Shenero and Anderson. The time had come to make some trades with the mainstream press. The scandal magazines would spin off those stories.

Schmidt, microbiologist and a practical man, gave his view. "If I may say, it is a novel approach. As a theory it does bear limited merit."

Whitaker gave Schmidt a withering look. "Gustav, I haven't got time to chase after ghosts, and you don't either. You're being well paid to work so let's all forget this nonsense and get back to it and keep your thoughts to yourself."

Whitaker was only slightly disturbed about the entire affair. His CEO experience had prepared him for dealing with the unexpected. They had time on their side, didn't they?

With a flick of an unseen switch, a fuming, incensed Robert Brewer had cut off the interview. His temples throbbed. A rush of adrenaline evoked primitive urges to club someone to death and beyond, if it were possible. He already know about the contact of Shenero and Anderson with the WHO requesting information about Tunisia, as well as their flight to Tucson for who knew what, thanks to his covert ops friend who electronically tracked the flight and car rental cards he'd given them. This ink thing was definitely a surprise. Why did both of them go to Tucson and not just Shenero if not to check up on Butler and Carrasco? Which means they must have gone into Mexico during the time they were in Tucson.

What the true answer might be escaped him up to a point until the men sent the memo about their suspicions and wanting to schedule a meeting. He forward the memo to Alan Hood. Alan suggested a counter-strategy based on denial coupled with insult, two of his areas of expertise.

What a mess. He didn't need this. He regretted having been lured into the plot. Okay, he'd received a boatload of fresh green tax-free U.S. dollars safely ensconced overseas and his children were taken care of. He didn't need Shenero's mouth, and he certainly didn't need the aggravation. It wasn't good for his blood pressure. Worse, he couldn't get out of it if he wanted to. He had no way to retreat. The only direction was to charge forward into the maws of the beast and exit the country for good when he got the chance, given he wasn't turned over to Interpol, hunted and extradited.

A few minutes later, Brewer called Whitaker on a closed line to rant. "Jim, why in the hell didn't you tell them no conference, or a reasonable facsimile of the words, or tell them you were too busy, or some crazy-ass story? I don't like them."

"In case you've forgotten, I invited them because I wanted to hear their story, how close they are. Well, now you know, and does it matter one whit?" he concluded, rhetorically.

Brewer had never in his life been so shabbily treated, insulted, intimidated, and verbally assaulted except when he was in boot camp many years before. That didn't count; this did. That contributed to his betterment; this humiliated him and begged for a counterattack.

Let's deal with first things first, Brewer reasoned. There are certain natural strategic methods of dealing with confrontational problems. One of them is to cut the problem out of the loop. Isn't that what smooth sailing in business is all about?

Jeff did not enjoy reading the local newspaper, but when Carmen served it up in their university office that same afternoon, doing so became a distraction from the morning's hostilities.

"Look at this, boss," she said. This day she wore her designer jeans and a sleeveless pink cashmere sweater to match a pale-pink turban.

To Jeff, she appeared more striking in her appearance than ever. Jeff maintained a profound regard for Carmen, even while his marriage was somewhat intact. At the moment, however, he needed for her to soothe him. It seemed he needed female companionship more often as time passed.

Jeff was a self-contained man. He could be sent to a colony on the moon or to the darkest corners of the planet and survive. He knew without the smallest scintilla of doubt he would be physically active, inventive, and creative and he would make a discovery or two. However, given all that, he preferred having Carmen's company.

Burning from the morning's video meeting, Jeff was rereading all the data they had accumulated on the project, trying to find something they might have missed. He could think of no alternative explanation. The scar on his forehead stood out sharply in contrast with his slightly flushed face.

Jeff took the newspaper from Carmen just as Paul walked in. His eyes bore into the paper, intently following an article. "We've got a new wrinkle, Paul. Salem is happening all over again."

"The Salem witch hunts? Wasn't that a long time ago when people thought that certain people were witches?" Carmen said.

Jeff nodded vigorously, "Remember that the poor, never the rich, were singled out as bewitched. Authorities would proclaim them to be a danger to themselves and to society as a whole. A lot of it was tied to religious persecution."

Then Jeff pointed to the paper. "It looks like we're vindicated. Victims are starting to exhibit signs of disordered speech and convulsive fits and other symptoms of alkaloid poisoning."

"But we didn't identify any alkaloids," said Paul.

"Yes, we did. Mycotoxins are alkaloids. Furthermore, the combination of aflatoxin with drugs or medications in the patient's body may mimic ergot poisoning. According to the paper, a rapidly growing national movement is focusing on Satan as the cause of the epidemic and demanding that somebody pay for bringing him up from the darkness."

"Do they say who is to blame?"

"The Jews and the Blacks, of course," answered Jeff.

"I thought the Jewish faith didn't encompass Satan," Paul stated.

"No, but a lot of other people do, and they are jumping on the bandwagon.

"From the perspective of epidemiology and bacteriology, did you know that as the Black Plague swept through Europe during the mid-Fourteenth Century killing on average 70-80% percent of the population, a wave of anti-Semitism always followed in its wake?"

"True," said Paul. "Finding scapegoats is part of the human condition." He walked over to see what Jeff was reading. "All right, I give up. Who's behind the movement?"

"It says here the movement is spearheaded by an American right-wing Christian evangelist based in

Atlanta. The guy's name is Branch Hoag. His daddy is Parsons Hoag, currently doing time for stealing a few million in church funds. Apparently the son has quite a gift of gab and a lot of money behind him. Black churches and synagogues are being burned around the country."

"Oh boy, here we go," said Paul. "Maybe society needs to start blaming the weather for their personal problems."

"Right now I feel like they chose us," Carmen said, philosophically.

Jeff was concerned about Carmen. He'd told Paul about her cancer and didn't elaborate. But Carmen Ramirez was a good problem to have. Her new turban made her look even more attractive. Jeff never said it, but he totally loved sci-fi women with shaved heads. Put a uniform on her and he could become irrational.

Paul took the newspaper, scanned the article quickly, and then went to the Sudoku page, where he began practicing his meditation by mentally filling in the blanks of the daily puzzle rated as "very challenging."

The two men played the video of the meeting for Carmen. They needed her as an objective observer, a nonparticipant. News of the rebirth of the international anti-Jewish movement stung Jeff. His parents were Protestants from Europe who immigrated to the United States for freedom from religious persecution, and they had instilled strong feelings about this persecution in their son.

One of the reasons Jeff loved athletics was his experiences with water polo and martial arts. It was the camaraderie between sportsmen that transcended ethnic bounds. In sports one could call a close teammate to his face virtually any ethnic slur, and it would mean no more than hello said in friendly terms. Under those circumstances, the disparaging names connoted the breakdown of barriers between competitors and teammates, not a strengthening of the barriers.

Other people, like Branch Hoag, were always willing to choose ethnicity as a cure for their personal problems, as if wiping out an entire population would make those problems disappear. Right now the reverend was a little fish in a little pond, but very shortly, the preacher would be a big fish in a big pond—an extremely wealthy fish, judging by the millions of dollars supporters were pouring into this hate campaign.

Paul said, "Throw Brewer into the mix. He passed his own hatred down to us. We don't deserve that."

"As Clint Eastwood said when he shot the evil sheriff who claimed the same thing, 'Deserve's got nothing to do with it'," quipped Jeff.

Jeff's mood darkened as he looked first at Paul and then to Carmen. "Right now I feel like the bear that got shot with a twenty-two. The bastard got me mad and made a bad strategic mistake."

"I agree," said Paul. "Now let's go eat."

"Coming, Carmen?" asked Jeff, definitely not hiding his need for her company.

"If you want me," she responded teasingly.

He wanted her and she wanted him. So why did she insist so strongly they wait for the dust to settle before they talked about where they wanted this relationship to go?

Jeff knew she was right in doing so. But did she have to be so cool and collected about it? Yes, Paul was here and professionalism must prevail, but he needed to get her alone in an intimate moment without freight trains running between them all the time.

The trio left the university campus, crossed Boyd, and went another block up Asp into the heart of Campus Corner. They sought a new restaurant that had good reviews, but none of them had yet visited. So far, their government meal tickets remained in their possession, so they could eat on taxpayers' money.

Carmen saw a newspaper stand located curbside outside the restaurant where Big Sky fliers were stacked. She grabbed one.

Jeff quickly found a linen-covered booth near a window where he and Carmen sat together.

The waiter handed each of them a drink menu and dinner menu. It was nearly noon, early enough to avoid the lunch crowd. Smells of cooked lobster wafted through the air, seducing those who couldn't get enough seafood.

"Well, folks, what now?" Paul threw out to begin the inevitable discussion.

Carmen spoke first. "I checked around about that perfume thing. Honestly, it seems like a real possibility. The trouble is, the industry is so jammed with competition it might be impossible to find out if there is a new stranger on the street."

"It does seem to fit the parameters," said Paul. "If they're based here, they're going to sell more here and women will use it more than men, which answers the question."

Jeff stroked his chin lightly and slowly shook his head. "Let's forget the perfume. Let's concentrate on a strategy."

Carmen touched Jeff's arm lightly. "I think you've got somebody worried. My question is, who's pulling their strings and how high up is the pyramid, as we used to say back home."

"We don't have enough test results to float a balsa-wood boat. We only suggested a possibility, something they should look into," Paul offered, frustrated.

Jeff had rarely seen Paul this worked up, save when he attempted to explain one his incomprehensible models about intergalactic gravitational something or others. Now it seemed as though the man was wrapped up in a bigger puzzle with generalities being pieced in, but the overall picture couldn't be discerned.

"What's that?" Jeff asked, pointing at the flier.

Carmen passed him the tricolor sheet of glossy paper. "In case you need a place to stay. You know, after the government takes your job, your money, and your home."

Jeff looked at the flier, front and back, and passed

it across the table to Paul.

Paul looked it over and held it up to the light.

Jeff suddenly exclaimed. "I'll bet you ten to one the mycotoxin is in the ink, guys. The fliers are multicolored." He would have kissed Carmen except for Paul's presence.

"That's a random thought, Jeff," said Paul. "And where are they going to get those printed? Could be done on-site."

"Not Bolton. It's cheaper for him to have someone do it for him," answered Jeff.

"Carmen, call one of our graduate students."

Carmen already held her phone in her hand and held the other palm outward, giving him a sign to wait because she was ahead of him. A moment later she was directing a student to search around Campus Corner and get the rest of them.. Then she went outside and grabbed the remaining stack of sheets in the stand.

"Tell them to wear gloves when they handle the fliers," he told her. Carmen made a second call and repeated Jeff's words.

"Also, we need to wash off now," Jeff directed.

The trio got up from the table in unison and headed for the restrooms for a soap-and-water scrub.

The waiter brought their lunch of Alaskan king crab, garlic butter sauce, rolls, and a small portion of salmon and vegetables. Jeff looked at it as though it was a last meal before the guillotine.

Carmen said, "FYI, while you were both going over the data again, I remembered Brewer's statement in your conference call about Hood owning the papers, so I checked on the Hood family. Brewer was right. Actually, two brothers own the two city papers. They bought out Kirk's family about ten years ago and then purchased the *Tucson Times*."

Jeff said, "That is interesting. I knew Billy's family sold the business. I didn't know to whom until Brewer mentioned it.

"Can we go to the press or to Kirk's father? No. We might think we have enough hard evidence, but we don't. I know Billy's father, Dan, and he would be the last person to look into this. He's been tied to the industry all his life, and the implications of what we are suggesting are enormous.

"Marjorie Reynolds was absolutely right about one thing. We would be fighting the press, and we wouldn't stand a chance. Hell, we'd be lucky to get mentioned in the papers at all, let alone get to suggest our theory.

"Dan's a wonderful person and very dedicated. He's also strong-willed. You have to be a tough businessperson to survive in the industry. He travels several times a year to speak at newspaper and media conventions.

"Look at the position we would put Billy in if we tried to pressure him to present our version of the story. He's bound by code and honor to report the truth, but it would be going contrary to generations of Kirk dedication to journalism, especially since Reynolds's accusations have some merit. Anyway, we flat out don't have enough proof."

Carmen said, "Maybe you could you talk to Billy in confidence." She stopped speaking abruptly, then asked, "What's Billy's mother's name?"

"Lorraine," said Jeff.

"Oh, boy." Carmen's hand flew up to her face. "I think I remember reading the name of Kirk this morning when I was looking up people I knew to see if they were infected with the disease."

"You're kidding," said Jeff.

I hope I'm wrong," she replied.

"And what about your parents, Jeff?" asked Paul.

"They're okay. Dad's losing his eyesight so he only reads large-print books and Mom reads it online or catches it on TV."

After returning from lunch, the first thing Jeff did was to pull up the database with the names and scrolled down. Dan and Lorraine Kirk were there and were listed as critical.

"Why them?" asked Paul.

Jeff said, "Because Dan will read both papers seven days a week, and Lorraine is an avid coupon collector. Just because you have money doesn't mean you can't try to save it. Besides, coupons are a passion with a lot of people. My mother was the same way."

"It's another newspaper link," stated Paul.

"Carmen, see if you can find out what hospital they're at, if any," Jeff requested.

She Googled for a minute or two and reported, "They're in ICU at General Public."

"Ten to one Billy's there," said Jeff. "I'm going

to the city and talk with him about some things. I'll need you both to stay here. Paul, run the analysis on the fliers."

"I have a better idea," said Paul. "We set up an assembly-line procedure in your lab and test representative samples of print from, say, two weeks from before the start of the epidemic to the present time."

Jeff said, "Good. Carmen, have one of my students make a run to the newspaper offices and pick up back issues of both papers, including Sundays. Personally we need to stay in the background."

"How about the Norman Mall?" suggested Carmen.

Jeff thought of her shopping at the mall, the subsequent DUI, her night in jail, and of course, the kiss that followed.

"I know they have a stand where they sell papers from around the country. We can buy them out if we want," she offered.

"Good," replied Paul, enthused. "I'm thinking it might be a good idea to have a lawyer on board. Know any you can trust?"

A slight smile crossed Jeff's lips. "As a matter of fact, I do. Remember my old friend and roommate, Frank Bennett? He and I and Billy Kirk were tight for years. He and his family are living in Anchorage. Last time I spoke with him, his calendar was a fairly open and he wanted to come back to Oklahoma for a vacation. I'll call him tonight."

Day 15–Evening

Jeff found Billy in the hospital waiting room. He sat alone on an end seat. Jeff sat next to him. The man had clearly been there for many hours, but despite his disheveled appearance and without TV makeup, he still looked good.

Without Jeff having said a word, Billy said, "They're bad, Jeff. Their livers are shot. Along with the rashes—well, I suppose you've heard about it."

Jeff glanced at another couple sitting in the waiting room. "Let's find a private place to talk."

Billy stopped at the desk and told the nurse to call him on his phone if they needed him.

Jeff led his friend outside the double doors. A broad green well-mown lawn fronted the building. It offered little solace to the beleaguered friends. They stood to the side of the entrance. An occasional person entered or exited.

"Billy, listen to me. It's not what you think it is. And now I'm going to tell you what *we* think it is."

Jeff told him about Brewer and Whitaker and Paul. He went over their interviews and discoveries and their insults by the committee. He explained what they believed and why they believed it. He told him about Big Sky Apartments.

Billy looked at Jeff as though he were daft. "I can't run a story like that. It wouldn't get to first base with my producers. They'd laugh me off."

Billy's eyes sparkled blue in the dimming sunlight, as Jeff talked straight into them. He could not hide his frustration. "Excuse me, Mr. Kirk. I am not asking you to run the story. I'm asking you to take this into consideration so you can try and understand what's happening to your parents."

"You are nuts, aren't you, Jeff?" Billy stated, factually. "You're talking about Alan and Harry. Hell, man, I've known them for years. We even took journalism classes together back in the old days, and I'd seen them numerous times at one of our two papers until I spun off into TV.

"They're straitlaced guys and hard workers. We were all happy to see them purchase the business and now you come along and try to convince me these guys are poisoning people. Where do you get off doing that, Jeff?"

Billy made a move as if to return to the hospital. Jeff's hand stopped him.

"Have their urine tested for aflatoxin, Billy."

"So what if I do, and so what if it's in their system? Find some bad guys, not the Hoods," Billy said.

"And if you're so smart, tell me if they're going to make it," he said, as though Jeff actually knew any answers.

"I don't know," Jeff lied.

The liver cancer could be in the early, if not intermediate stage. They could look for it and start chemo. But their immune systems were already shot, and chemo might put them over the edge. They were at that point. So the answer was yes, he did know, and he saw in Billy's eyes that he perceived the truth behind the lie.

Jeff moved on relentlessly. "You know I feel terrible about this, but unless you really have to go in, I've got a couple of questions for you about the newspaper business."

"You sure know how to heap it on," Billy said as he leaned against the brick of the building. "Yeah, man, hit me."

Billy's parents died the next day.

Day 16–Morning

When Jeff's team completed the work, they found the presence of aflatoxin in three more samples: the Big Sky fliers and the two most recent local publications of *Your Good Dining* magazine printed in Oklahoma City.

His three graduate students didn't have to be told of the overall project mission; it spoke for itself. Jeff did ask them not to discuss this work with anyone because he knew they were in dangerous territory and so did they. He decided against asking them to give a vow of secrecy; the request would be melodramatic. To some, business was not a relative of trust. To him, trust should be considered a member of the family.

Having been apprised about the findings, Jeff walked into his office.

Carmen's first words were, "Hey, boss, look at this."

"What, again? Another Branch Hoag story?"

Jeff took the newspaper from her as the phone rang. Jeff grabbed it out of reflex. Paul was on the other line.

"Hey, Jeff, have you seen the paper yet?"

"No, because people keep asking me to read it but won't let me read it," was Jeff's terse reply.

"Call me back," said Paul.

"Yeah, yeah," replied Jeff.

On the bottom of the fold in bold lettering was an article, PERFUME BELIEVED TO BE CAUSE OF EPIDEMIC – SCIENTISTS ACCUSE MEDIA OF COVER-UPS, Written by Marjorie Reynolds.

Two professors, Jeffrey Shenero and Paul Anderson, both from the University of Oklahoma, asserted that the American media is responsible for the ongoing epidemic. This is according to James Whitaker of the United States Public Health Service and head of the committee to investigate the outbreak.

The men were adamant in their accusations and breached professional protocol, according to Whitaker. Neither man has responded despite numerous attempts to reach them.

Whitaker has disclosed that a new brand of perfume popular in the Oklahoma City area and test marketed in the Tucson area is believed to be the cause of the disease. Attention is being focused on testing the perfumes in question, but other perfumes may be involved. This testing will be finished as soon as possible, he said.

The brand names suspected cannot be revealed at this time due to the ongoing investigation.

According to our sources, the professors may be under investigation for making false claims and using the news media to promote their own gains.

Jeff got Paul on the other line and put it on speaker.

"Any comments?" asked Jeff.

"If this is on the wire services, you can bet Billy has it," Carmen said.

"As in Billy Kirk, your old college friend, right? Along with Frank Bennett," responded Paul.

"The same attorney who was with you when you went to trial. The one where you got sued because you didn't find any mold?" asked Paul.

"One and the same," responded Jeff.

"Look at the positive. At least we got some free press," said Paul.

"Either that or a free hanging," Jeff replied, who looked at Carmen and winked. She gave him a silent kiss in reply.

The light-complected, black-haired Alan Hood, born Ali Mohammad MaHoud, stood in front of the west-facing tenth-floor office window of the building he and his brother owned. The office was large and windowed on three sides. The drapes were drawn on two of them.

Today he wore black herringbone slacks and Italian tassel loafers, a white silk shirt open at the front to expose the dark hair of his chest, and a heavy gold chain. No pendant adorned the chain.

The setting sun glowed bright red and twice normal size thanks to breezy conditions that had prevailed throughout central Oklahoma the evening before.

Alan placed his right forefinger to his lips. Things were not working quite right. The unexpected had to be prepared for, yes, but undercurrents were at play here.

He went over the calculations for the thousandth time. Combined, his two Oklahoma City newspapers served 140,000 daily customers, not counting Sunday. Add an equal number in Tucson to total more than a quarter million. With a readership nationally accepted as 2.2 persons per paper published, this totaled more than a half million exposures per day. *Your Good Dining* was read and handled by tens of thousands more each week.

This was not a huge number of papers and magazines as these things went, but the money deposited in the names of himself and his brother in various out-of-country banks certainly could be classed as a very large amount. This amount actually exceeded the gross national income of more than half the nations on Earth. Huge deposits came from investor nations who would make their money back several-fold with the demise of America and the subsequent rise of Islam in the soon-to-be-dead nation. In the strictest sense, it was a simple business investment.

With stakes such as these, it behooved him to spend as much time and money as necessary to prevent discovery of the overall mission.

Unfortunately the bald mycologist, Shenero, and his friend, Anderson, breached the system. The senator wanted their hiring. Alan couldn't help that. But how the hell did they stumble onto the truth in such a short time?

He knew their reputation, and he'd heard that the damnable Shenero was like one of those large Gila monster lizards of the Desert Southwest that carried venom in its lower fangs. The lizard would turn upside down while clamped onto its victim to assist in draining the poison. One could cut off the lizard's head and it would continue to remain clamped on.

Another disconcerting thought entered Alan's mind. If loose lips sank ships, then so could loose cannons, especially in stormy seas. Once a cannon broke loose from its mooring, it could take apart both men and their ship with equal ferocity. A frightening thought struck him. Shenero is the classic definition of a loose cannon.

And the backstreet Brit with a criminal background, Paul Anderson—that was a blindside hit from out of nowhere.

On the upside, the article by Reynolds should neutralize the pair. Alan ran more numbers through his thoughts. Sixty million newspapers were printed each day, and a larger number on Sunday. Because of the multiplier effect, each issue reached 132 million people a day. Too bad they couldn't have the whole thing, but they didn't need to be greedy.

Initially Alan's father speculated that newly printed books, weekly newsmagazines, packaging and labeling markets, leaflets, and fliers, could serve as a nice adjunct to the overall plan. His sources couldn't get enough mycotoxin crystallized for the huge effort they'd wanted from the start, and they'd gone to great lengths to hire the best men for the job. Unfortunately, both the petro based black and color ink bound up the toxin to lessen its effect. Soy was the answer and he bought into it.

He would have to be satisfied with what he had. Like the 9/11 attack funded by his father, not every plane could be expected to hit its target, and public paranoia from the epidemic itself was working nicely. Once the Americans found out the cause of the disease, the country would fall. The entire printed word would become obsolete in the United States as a nice wrap-up to the deaths or sickness of a million or more. Then would be the time to kick them hard—when they were down and the second part of the plan could be employed. The third and fourth parts would follow.

He couldn't forget about the scarcity of food and medicine, the ports were backed up, food was rotting, and the truckers were both hurting and helping the plan's cause at the same time.

Forget that nobody was getting anything that trucks deliver. For his sake, the damnable strike needed to end soon.

The potential to serve God and history always

presented itself to the enterprising businessman. As the Americans said, "There is always room for a man who can make a better hamburger."

A soft knock on the door pulled Alan from his reverie. "Come," he said.

Harry Hood, born Mohammad Hari MaHoud and Alan's younger brother, entered the room. He held a single sheet of paper in his hand. Where Alan was tall, light, fit, and trim with a full head of black hair, Harry was shorter by two inches, a shade darker, and balding rapidly.

"I was hoping you weren't busy," said Harry.

"I am too distracted today to get anything done."

Harry held up a sheet of paper he carried. "Here's the copy of my conversation with Whitaker. He said you are the one who is responsible."

"I am?" asked Alan incredulously.

"Whitaker said they already formed the committee when you called the senator and asked him to find experts to help with the epidemic," answered Harry.

"Okay, okay, that's what I said. I was trying to stay on the senator's good side. What's wrong with a little kissing up? Besides, it doesn't matter. By the time they get hard evidence, it'll be too late anyway. So they got lucky."

"It's not a matter of luck," replied Harry. "Give Anderson his nightly sex toy and Shenero his stupid laboratory and they will be relentless. Take something meaningful away, and they will likely reconnoiter and attack all the harder. We need to figure out how to control these morons.

"Incidentally, I left the profiles for Anderson, Shenero, and his group on your desk. Did you read them?"

"I did. This Carmen seems interesting. She might get involved in a serious crime, or have an accident where a death is involved, something that will land her in jail for something more serious than a DUI this time," Alan replied with a lascivious grin bordering on a sneer. "Then our good doctor can make a choice, pay attention to her, or chase ghosts hidden in newspaper ink. I was ready to discuss my ideas with you, until I read the profile of one of Shenero's students. This new idea fits right up my alley and gives me a chance to have some great fun in a way that will accomplish several of our goals at the same time."

Harry smiled broadly, in the mood for merry-making. Relaxing in a desk chair, he leaned back. "I'm intrigued. Go ahead."

Both men laughed as Alan told of his plan, embellishing on it to their great delight down to the minutae. The best part? Mere hours remained until it could be implemented.

Day 16–Afternoon

Marilyn Woods, one of Jeff's prize graduate students, spent much of her study time in the Big Coffee Bar, a single block north of the campus. Marilyn rarely drank alcohol, but considered herself to be an expert in the tasting of fine coffees. She liked the ambiance of the bar, sipping mocha and studying, until fatigue overtook her. She could study with the jukebox playing bluegrass as she could alone in an isolated carrel at the back of the library. Where she could not study well was in the four-story student housing complex where she lived. Too many distractions: cute guys, chatty girls, continuous parties.

Alan Hood found Marilyn sitting alone in the rear of the bar. He put on a polite smile and summoned his best masculine charm. It was time to make her acquaintance.

"Excuse me, is anyone sitting here?"

Marilyn, intent on copying her class notes into a more legible format, looked up to see a handsome man standing in front of her, white silk shirt open at the collar, dark chest hair showing through. A chain of gold hung about the man's neck. His slacks matched the color of his razor-cut hair. A thin leather belt encircled a waist with not an extra ounce of fat. He wore no wedding ring, although a pale circle appeared around his ring finger. Newly divorced, she decided. He wore a gold, paper-thin Movado watch and manicured nails.

She looked around her at the other tables, many of which were empty, and finally said, "No, have a seat."

For some unexplained reason, she felt curious if not reckless. This was definitely against her nature to accept the invitation of a stranger to sit with her. It was as if an aura surrounded him and she needed to find out more about it. It was his dark eyes, she told herself, as she permitted herself a moment of what-the-heck attitude. What's the worst could happen?

The TV sets surrounding the interior of the bar were playing Oklahoma football and basketball re-runs on mute as the latest prerecorded pop music played in the background. On the wall was a sign that read, BUD WILKINSON CREATED THE MONSTER, I JUST FEED IT. Former OU football coach Barry Switzer's name was attached to the sign.

"I wonder if you could help me," said Alan.

"If I can," replied the young woman, her pale, freckled skin in stark contrast to the lightly tanned skin of the man seated across from her. The slightest scent of a musky cologne wafted across the table. "I'm lost, and I need some directions. I'm looking for the School of Business."

"Oh, are you a student or teacher?" Marilyn asked.

"Actually, I'm interviewing for a job, more of a hobby or pastime, I suppose. I mean, I don't really need the money, my import-export business is doing so well."

Woods took in this man, who appeared too real to be true with money, looks, and enough nerve to ex-press himself with honesty. Obviously conversation-al, her tablemate strongly suggested elegance along with a dash of foreign intrigue.

Marilyn found her voice. "The School of Busi-ness is right across the oval from my building. I'm in microbiology in the Biological Sciences Building."

"Really? You are in microbiology? How fascinating. I have always admired those wonderful men, Pasteur, Ehrlich, even the Dutchman Leeuwenhoek—didn't he invent the microscope?"

Marilyn stared at the man's penetrating black eyes. He knew of the great men who served as inspiration for her. What could be better than that? What wonderful talks they could have.

"What do you do?" she asked, somewhat breathless.

"I've got a fleet of ships. I deal with commodities on the world market."

Marilyn shook her head. "How does that work? I mean, commodities."

"Well, say Guatemala has a thousand tons of broccoli they need to sell or Chile has a couple thousand tons of tomatoes. I find out who needs what around the world and hook them up. It's quite lucrative. And, of course, it's a chance to help people. Sorry, I didn't mean to brag, but I like what I do," Alan told her innocently. "And business is growing so fast I have to keep hiring new staff all the time. Anyway, if you'll point me in the right direction, I'll go find my building," said Alan, baiting the hook.

"Actually," blurted Marilyn, surprising herself, "I'm going that way. I'll show you where it is."

"Don't bother yourself, I'll find it," said Alan, standing.

"No problem." She collected her books and papers, stuffed them into a flat briefcase, and stood.

They left the bar and walked south in the fading sunlight across Boyd to the university campus and the School of Business.

After a few minutes of walking, Marilyn pointed off toward the right and in front of them. "There's your building right across the oval. Mine's right here. It was very nice meeting you."

"Likewise. If you'll be around later, maybe I'll see you again," he replied.

Marilyn impulsively informed him, "I'll be there later this evening around nine. That's where I study a lot. I have a lot of important research to work on today."

"Well, I'll look for you later. If we meet again you can tell me about your research. If we don't meet again, thank you for your time." Alan Hood smiled charmingly, turned, and walked across the lawn without looking back.

Marilyn felt dizzy. This nameless man suddenly entered into her life and flitted out again. *Good luck doing any work today*, she thought. And tonight, would she see him again? Yes, she decided. She needed a little fun in her life. She also decided she was ready for a little romance.

That night, Marilyn chose to sit away from the migration of waitresses serving chicken wings, fried onion rings, and pizza. The jukebox played "Coat of Many Colors" by Dolly Parton.

She pulled a sheaf of notes from her briefcase, along with a calculator, and began to work on one of her courses.

An hour later Marilyn checked her watch for the fifth time and decided to stop fooling herself. She began to gather her papers when she heard a voice,

"Oh, there you are. Sorry, I got stuck on an international call."

And there he stood, as attractive as when she first saw him.

"May I sit down?" he asked.

"Uh, oh, no, please, I was putting my notes together," Marilyn stammered.

She felt very self-conscious and hoped it wasn't too obvious she had changed into a sweater slightly tighter than the one she wore earlier. "Let's see," she said, "where did we leave off? Ah, I never told you my name. It's Marilyn."

"And I'm Alan."

They both stuck out their hands and shook. To her, his grip felt both strong and gentle at the same time. His fingers were smooth, uncalloused. *He must be a man of intellect. He's compassionate, humble, confident, yet self-effacing. His eyes are like black fathomless pools*, Marilyn thought as she sought to define some unusual rising emotion within her.

Marilyn's pulse raced as the ebony eyes bore into her.

"You were going to tell me all about your research," said Alan, his eyes aglow with true interest.

Marilyn lost herself. "It's all so exciting. Where do I start?"

Day 17–Morning

"Did you get a CD today? Because I didn't," said Paul.

"Nope. It appears we've been abandoned, my friend."

"Well, as a backup, I requested the various health departments to email me their latest data, so I really don't think it matters whether we get their version of the information or not. In fact, I suspect we may have more accurate data this way."

Jeff and Paul had no doubt they had discovered a cause and effect. Without better information, they figured Big Sky was a regular customer of the Hoods for printing of their fliers. But where did *Your Good Dining* come into the picture? The feds weren't going to contact the two investigators, who in turn, were certainly not going to initiate another contact. They found that route to be a dead end. It was as if they had stepped on a land mine and couldn't step off.

At the same time, the national health watchdogs reported a connection between the perfume and the disease. Although symptoms might increase for some time—which could be expected due to the nature of the disease—it should soon go away.

Jeff had a sudden compulsive urge to contact Branch Hoag and side with the preacher. Witches weren't at fault here. Demons and spirits had been summoned from their dark dimension to run amok, to cause people to get the twitches and shakes and do irrational things. Who said mushroom-based poisons were present in the Salem bread? Nobody really believed that theory, did they?

When Marilyn entered the office to discuss her classes for the following semester, Jeff told her about the Big Sky fliers and the latest on their discoveries relating to the ink.

Wait until I tell Alan what we're finding out about the terrorists, she thought excitedly.

Day 17
Evening

After Jeff's wife left him, he suffered through the initial stages of a spouse's departure and then decided to be good to himself. He purchased a three-bedroom, two-bath brick home seven miles from campus.

Situated on two acres of forested land, a six-foot-high chain-link fence surrounded the home to give it a good half acre of usable space. He'd requested workers to remove the common wall between two bedrooms. The large room held a complete office, including a binocular microscope with a turret that held five different objective lenses.

Then Jeff contacted one of his clients who trained dogs, and told him about his needs and concerns. The trainer said to let him take care of it, which he did. He obtained two female Rottweilers from two different breeders. He explained they would bond with him more than they would with each other and would be more protective than pups from the same litter.

Each Sunday the trainer and he spent time with Suzi and Lila, as Jeff named them. Jeff ensured they knew Carmen as a friend who would feed them during his out-of-town business trips.

The wire fence didn't hinder his view of the birch and alder forest, and the yard was perfect for his pets to roam the grounds.

Jeff activated the automatic garage door opener, pulled his Volvo wagon next to his Mustang in the double garage, and hit the switch to close the outer gates, which he chain-locked each evening. That was the only drawback to this home. In inclement weather, the gates didn't open if blocked by snowdrifts. *Stupid, the things we worry about*, he thought.

Before closing the garage doors, he fed the two dogs with a large scoopful of high-nutrition crunchies and filled their large water bowl. Jeff entered the kitchen through the garage door, threw down a single notebook onto the kitchen table, and walked over to the wet bar located in the living room. Because he loved open spaces, he'd ordered double-pane picture windows installed on two sides of the room and another large window in the office/lab room.

He would not permit his mind to relax until he'd poured a single shot of vodka on ice and opened a cold bottle of beer. Then he walked out onto the large deck and sat in his favorite chair. When he whistled for Suzi and Lila, the pair came through their large doggie door and bounded forth to be patted and scratched.

Jeff scratched their ears and took a long pull of
beer. Then he took a sip of vodka and another pull
of beer. He set the containers into cup holders in the
chair's arms and scratched the dog's necks, one dog
on each side of the armchair. The early evening sun
felt soothingly warm.

Now he closed his eyes and tried not to think for
a moment. It didn't work.

Carmen. She wanted him, and he wanted her.
He'd told her all about his divorce. In many ways,
she went through it with him. Understanding as she
was, she never judged him and accepted him for
what he was. He tried to ignore the old caution about
mixing business and pleasure, allowing his feelings
and daydreams to sweep him away.

After several minutes, Jeff's mind switched
gears. He and Paul had been wined and dined, hired
and fired. Their discovery of the truth proved their
own worth to themselves. But there were missing
links. What were they?

They couldn't trust the Department of Defense;
certainly not with Brewer tapped into it, or the CDC,
à la James Whitaker. They could only trust each other and Jeff's students to confront an epidemic presently threatening the security of the nation.

Jeff nuked some left-over chicken, rice and veggie dish and sat down to eat and think. Should he
call Carmen to tell her that he loved her and ask if
she could come over tonight? Jeff decided that the

little alcohol he consumed a little earlier did not influence his wish and made the call.

"Carmen, it's Jeff."

"Yes, Jeff," she responded.

She sounded so good. He could almost smell the baby powder fragrance of the soap she used through the phone line. "I wonder if you could come over for a while, if it's all right...I mean to go over some billings." Jeff was starting to feel foolish at his own words.

He was about to correct himself when she said huskily, "Be there in an hour."

Jeff went out and opened the gate, and then he set a timer and dozed for a half hour. Feeling better, he took a long, hot, steamy shower while jazz played on the stereo. The music fed some undefined emotion. Could it be the jumble of events, the confusion of it all or might it be categorized as sexual expectation? Hey, all he wanted was company. Nothing more.

Jeff lazily opened the shower door, and Carmen stood in front of him dressed in a low-cut blouse and slacks. She was barefoot, braless, and carrying a drink in one hand and a white bath towel in another. Her turban was gone, and her hair was starting to come back.

"Service with a smile," she whispered seductively.

She set the drink down on the vanity and wiped his body, front, back, and front again. She began to detail her efforts, slowly and deliberately.

Jeff pulled her to him. They held each other and

kissed hungrily. Carmen led him to the bed where she took control of the evening's lovemaking. They both needed care and affection, but Carmen insisted on taking charge. Jeff offered no resistance.

Finally, thoroughly exhausted, they talked and shared the same emotions: love and guilt. Each admitted to loving the other and each confessed to a feeling of guilt about dissolving the bond that separated work from personal life. In the end they decided, not for the first time, to concentrate on resolving the epidemic problem first and worry about their personal lives after that.

Frank Bennett, hunting and fishing enthusiast, attorney at law, and former star catcher for the University of Oklahoma baseball team, had never served jail time, an oversight on the part of the law. As an undergraduate and former roommate of Jeff Shenero and Billy Kirk, he had shared with them a variety of adventures, most of which revolved around drinking and women.

Having passed his bar exams on the first attempt, at six-foot-two and two hundred–plus stout pounds, Frank Bennett got a job as an environmental attorney doctoring the books for a small airline company based in Tulsa. They gave him the ambiguous title of "legal accountant." There he spent the next several years skirting the edges of federal investigations for illegal dumping of toxic chemicals.

The airline had supported a subsidiary business of degreasing engine and wheel parts from airplanes with the use of trichloroethylene, otherwise known as TCE. This was a common and accepted practice, as long as one didn't dump the poison into porous soil to percolate into the groundwater aquifer. As the man responsible for making records of the dumping disappear, the new lawyer made very good money.

Frank had an ethical concern with this entire job. However, long ago he'd decided that money trumped poverty, having experienced both. Middle ground was to be avoided. Frank had put money in the bank and had married the daughter of the company vice president, a man who would soon become president.

Feeling increasingly guilty about his work, Frank was preparing to resign when a drunken evening resulted in his bedding a childhood friend from Seward, Mary Sue Megan Moore Tamsen. To her he trustingly confessed his earlier crimes and expressed his paranoia about being arrested. Mary Sue forced him to provide monthly blackmail payments to her unless he wanted his wife and the law to know about his illegal activities and their sexual encounter.

Frank paid her for years until her demands were ended and the matter settled. Then he quit his job.

After a few more years with his family living in Oklahoma, Frank took a job as an environmental attorney in Anchorage, where he and his family made a new home.

Day 18–Morning

Now Jeff, Paul, Frank and Billy sat in Jeff's private business office. Carmen, in her quiet elegance, attended the meeting. Smiling, she greeted the men and took a seat on a folding chair in her usual place by the door to the inner office. Jeff wrestled with the confusion that now underlay their working relationship. It added another layer of pressure and confusion onto his already overloaded mind.

Carmen, in her turn, felt more secure than she had felt in a long time.

When Jeff had called Frank in Alaska, he offered to put up the attorney at his house, shades of the old days. Frank said the call was good timing because his plans for the immediate future included a trip down to Norman. In fact, he had already made arrangements to house-sit for another attorney, Matt Collins. Matt and Frank had assisted and represented Jeff in the toxic mold trial, not long before the present state of affairs.

"From what I understand," said Frank, seated in the armchair, "you're originally from Great Britain."

"Indeed," said Paul. Although one inch taller than the attorney, Paul weighed thirty pounds less. "We came over right after my thirteenth birthday. Ever hear of the Teddy Boys? You know, your equivalent of a gangsta? You're looking at one."

"I didn't know that," said Jeff.

"Yep, I was one of those street boys who got into knife fights and committed crimes against the state."

Paul pointed to a scar running along his left forearm and then pulled up his right shirtsleeve to show an ugly scar across the deltoid. "I tell people I fell off my bicycle onto a broken bottle at an early age. The real truth is, as the saying goes, 'You ought to see the other guys'."

He continued, with a smile that presented a mixture of feelings. "My parents decided that my father's grocery store had seen enough robberies and no good would come of my life, what with me spending a lot of time in juvie and all. So my father made an arrangement for the three of us to emigrate. They saw I had a talent for numbers, and they didn't want the talent wasted. I can't blame them. They stuck me into school and sat on me hard until I came around."

Jeff smiled in understanding, then turned to the newscaster. "Billy, I really appreciate you joining us. I know you're hurting. You didn't have to come," said Jeff.

"I need to keep busy and let time pass," said the newscaster. "I'm on personal leave anyway.

"Everything you've told me about at the hospital smacked of enough truth for me to stick my nose into it. If it's true, I want these bastards. Now it's personal."

The men got down to business, with Carmen taking occasional notes. These could be shredded later. They opted against recording the meeting for the same reason they had destroyed the original tape taken during Jeff's first meeting with Brewer and

Whitaker not that many days before.

Like Jeff, Paul believed that a man's word was the bond to his honor, which was a bond to his soul. If a man couldn't keep his word of honor, he should be disgraced as a castoff. Neither of the two men they had met exhibited honor.

Jeff said, "Only the colored inks come up positive in Oklahoma and Tucson. This matches what Billy told me."

"Which was?" asked Frank.

Jeff nodded to Billy who said, "The newspapers served by them are supplied with soy ink for their color. Many papers use petroleum-based ink for black, but it's a pain to have to run two types of ink, so total conversion to soy is the wave of the future. Soy is more eco-friendly, more stable in price, has less bleed-through, and gives better color."

Jeff said, "Now we find out that tainted color fliers are present in at least one apartment complex along with a magazine. Carmen traced the ink supplies to Oklahoma City to a company called Mid-Western Soy.

"So why isn't it present in other apartment complexes?" asked Billy.

"Beats me," shrugged Jeff. "Could be a lot of reasons. They don't deal with these guys, they haven't ordered lately, or they do deal with them and we haven't identified it yet. But we know it's there.

"Anyway, after we found it in the latest edition of *Your Good Dining* published here, I asked Carmen to go to their office and pick up five back issues and to have the Tucson plant overnight us the same thing. "As far as the magazines and the newspapers from both cities, there is toxin in one or more of the ink colors going back four but not five weeks, right before the epidemic started."

"How many people have the disease?" asked Frank.

"Nobody knows," answered Jeff. "Clinics are turning people away. There is nothing they can do to alleviate the symptoms, which is a correct statement."

Billy said, "My producers will need more evidence than what you've given me by accusing two of the city's leading fundraisers for children's causes. Do you have any idea how much they've given out of their own pockets?

"Consider the stakes. America stops reading, stops buying books and magazines and newspapers? And stops buying any package with a label?"

Frank held up his hand. "Hey, look at the bright side. The public will watch more TV. We even get this guy's face up in Anchorage.

"Okay, bad joke. Right now, you have strong evidence, but not enough proof that to hold up in court.

"Enter Mid-Western Soy and their stash of ink," contributed Paul.

"Enter Billy Kirk, you mean," said the newscaster.

Jeff looked at Billy. "What I really need from you is to stand by and be up to date on this project if it breaks."

"If it breaks? From what you've told me, nobody's going to do anything," Billy said.

"Frank, we need you to defend us. Keep us out of jail, or if it happens, keep our time down to a minimum."

Frank raised his eyebrows. "Oh, is that all? I thought we were facing a real problem." He started to laugh, which triggered a round of laughter by the others.

"Billy, we need to know about commercial printing inks for newspapers and fliers too. Who the suppliers are and how often it is supplied," Jeff requested.

Billy explained, "The colored ink is supplied in what are called totes. By colored ink, I am referring to magenta, cyan, and yellow, a fact you already know. These totes come in steel drums that measure about three feet wide by six feet in height.

"The ink is supplied at various time intervals, depending upon the usage of each color. One delivery truck can carry as many as ten or more totes per truck if you wanted to stack them double. It's safer not to."

Billy went on. "The totes are supplied every four to eight weeks by contract. Black ink is a different story. It's supplied by tanker truck. Together, both of our papers here in the city use about seven hundred gallons each week, and they receive about an eight-week supply when the truck comes in.

"The tanker trucks pump the black ink into large holding tanks. Here in Oklahoma City, we have an east and a west tank. Unlike the colored ink, each tank holds about six thousand gallons of the ink."

Jeff dug deeper. "The paper. Where does it come from? In fact, where do any of these inks come from?"

"The paper itself is called newsprint. A single roll weighs one metric ton, and each roll measures nine miles in length. A city such as Oklahoma City will have a thirty-day supply on-site and a sixty-day supply that's warehoused as backup.

"You might be interested in knowing that all this paper must be at a minimum of ninety-five percent recycled. As far as paper suppliers, we buy from five different mills, for a variety of reasons which have to do with economics and availability."

Listening to Billy's recitation, Jeff mentally discounted the paper itself as a source of the problem because there were no lines of evidence pointing to it. *Follow your intuition. That's what it's there for.*

"As far as ink suppliers, we get our soy black from Mid-Western Soy. They manufacture it at their plant outside Oklahoma City. Our colored ink also comes from Mid-Western Soy."

A thought struck Jeff. Why soy and not petroleum? Does petro inactivate the toxin in some way or is because the Hoods own soy newspapers? He put the thought aside for the moment.

"What drives the need for colored ink?"

"Advertising sales and readership," replied Billy. "You get more ads on Thursday, when the fliers come out, and during various holiday seasons. It also depends on how much color you want to put on the front page."

"What an industry," commented Carmen.

Billy smiled, "Right now, the print industry is the second-largest industry in the world, behind medicine and ahead of automotive, though it's declining due to the electronic age Believe it or not, it's even ahead of weapons. Imagine your lives without being able to read anything non-electronic—no books, newspapers, tags on clothing, labels on packages, canned or bottled foods. No billboards, copying machines, printers, and medical information on prescription bottles...well, you can fill in the rest.

"Of course, then there are the magazines," said Billy absently, "and the distribution to the other papers."

"Which magazines? Which papers?" asked Jeff.

"I was about to tell you about magazines like *Your Good Dining*," stated Billy. "These are the slicks, the full-color weeklies or biweeklies that come out in most major cities in the country. Well, Mid-Western supplies the colored ink for them, as well as the color and black to another nine cities."

"Whoa," exclaimed Jeff. "They supply more cities?"

Billy scratched his neck. "Well, let me think. They may have added or deleted some since my day, but back then it was Wichita, Omaha, Salt Lake City, two in Dallas, Fort Worth, Albuquerque, Tucson, two in Denver, and two right here. Eight states in all and twelve newspapers."

"So the ink for all of those is supplied from Oklahoma City?" asked Paul.

"Yes, it's warehoused here and distributed outward," replied Billy.

"Then why don't we see the disease in those other cities?" said Jeff to no one.

"The strike?" contributed Carmen.

"Of course. Which strongly suggests the storage of a lot of ink totes in a warehouse waiting for movement," summarized Jeff.

"Come on, Jeff, that's a stretch," said Frank.

Paul ignored the exchange between Jeff and Frank. "Billy, you mentioned *Your Good Dining*. What can you tell us about it?"

Carmen stood up. "I've got one here," she said and went to her desk where she picked up the latest issue.

Billy shrugged. "We used to supply the ink to them. I don't know if they still do. Most people think all we did was to print papers. In fact, we did a lot more."

"How many did you print, or should I say are printed here in Oklahoma City?" Jeff asked.

The newscaster thought for a moment and replied, "About 20,000 a week. That's a fair number because they go to the middle class, not the upper class, like some of our competition. So figure three people per magazine as far as looking and handling—a lot better ratio than with newspapers. You can get them in doctor's offices, restaurants, and convenience stores. There's a bigger profit margin there compared with newspapers because the ads cost more and they're in full color. We didn't do the layout or sell the ads, we just sold the ink."

Jeff took the magazine and thumbed through it, careful not to touch the ink. The pages were filled with pictures of restaurants, their special dishes, contact information, and prices.

"Wait, hold on," Jeff announced. He went to the work bag he used for jobs and pulled out a small black light which he utilized on occasion to look for the presence of insects or laundry products that glowed under the light. He turned off the office lights and exposed the cover and the interior of the pages to the ultraviolet light. They all glowed blue-green.

"All right, Mr. Kirk, what now?" asked Jeff. Before Billy could reply, the phone rang.

"Boss, it's Jimmy Cantrell," Carmen said, holding the receiver out for Jeff, as if it were an agent of disease.

Jeff turned on the lights and quickly glanced back at Paul, who threw both palms into the air and canted his head as if to say, "I'm sorry it's you, but sure glad it's not me."

Jeff's rolling eyeballs communicated his feelings to Carmen. *Oh, jump for joy; that's all I need, the president of the university calling me. Let me guess what this might be about.*

Jeff and Cantrell had known each other on a personal basis for several years, and Jeff knew he wouldn't be fired. He brought serious high-end research money into the university and kept a lot of people employed. Despite this, it never feels good to get reamed out.

Reluctantly, Jeff took the phone from Carmen and said in the best suck-up voice he could muster, "Hello, Jimmy. How are you?"

"I've been better. I figured you might be over in your business office when Carmen didn't pick up on campus," said Cantrell. "Let's make this short, Jeff. I got a call from Senator Evans, who's being leaned on so he can lean on me and, by chain of command, I can lean on you. You know, big fish eats little fish. Here's the lean: What's going on with your end of the investigation, if I might be so humble as to inquire, never mind the smear against the university."

"Jimmy, all I can tell you is that all is not as it seems. On the bright side, Paul and I are making inroads," Jeff responded. Immediately and once again, he mentally slapped himself for stepping on his tongue.

"Making inroads? The bright side? That doesn't mean jack to me, Jeff. What are inroads—you're breaking ground, marking a trail, whacking the brush, pissing on a stump, paving a superhighway, staring into the sun?" Cantrell accused, dripping sarcasm. Jeff had sucked bad luck into Cantrell's territory as fast as a storm entered a calm.

Jeff thought about making a glib remark, but remained silent when he pictured Cantrell as an apocalyptic horse snorting fire. "We've got a handle on it and presented the facts, but we can't get the authorities to believe us. We need a little more time," he submitted weakly, glancing at the others in the room who watched and listened, trying to hear Cantrell's words through Jeff's landline.

"If the authorities won't believe you, whoever they might be, then you can try me," Cantrell stated bluntly. An instant later he added, "Dr. Shenero, is Marjorie Reynolds part of your conspiracy theory, too?"

Shit. Reynolds.

Jeff was about to reply when Cantrell said, "Is Dr. Anderson with you?"

"Actually, he is. We were discussing the project," Jeff offered, feebly.

"Good. You can both discuss it with me. See you in, say, ten minutes," concluded the university president, who then hung up the phone.

Day 19–Morning

Jeff awoke at three fifteen. He'd been mired in a recycling dream with the talking head of Brewer, eyes flashing and mouth spewing hateful and indecipherable words, now a fire-breathing dragon. He made every attempt to climb out of the dream. He tried deep breathing and wrenching free from the grasp of the man and yelling. Nothing worked. The mouth flapped, the eyes bore through him. Had someone been watching, they would have seen him twist the bed covers around himself into the wrappings of a mummy and heard him moan.

Finally, he forced himself to wake up. *What a monster to dream about*, he thought.

Not even Saturdays and Sundays were his own. When he wasn't writing grant proposals, he was beating his head against the wall about the epidemic or trying to run his private business. He found himself in exactly the situation he was trying to avoid at all costs.

How does he let himself get pulled into these things? Could it be that his inner drive and professionalism and an undefined part of his character dictated that he solve this problem.

He knew better than to believe the National Institutes of Health and the United States Department of Defense were against him. On the other hand, a number of their people were. In reality, and despite his confidence, he didn't have enough hard proof to try to blow this thing open.

To his credit Cantrell backed off when he and Paul explained about their discoveries and their dilemma. At the conclusion of the meeting, Cantrell agreed to ignore them as long as he could and as long as they came up with fast results.

The competition was unfair. They had the scum beat ten to one. This was Jeff's last thought before he fell asleep again. This time he dreamed the circus was in town—a three-ring circus without the animals or the rings—a random order of overlapping events otherwise known as a Chinese fire drill.

When he arose, he drank a bottle of water and ran an easy six miles to clean out the lingering trash.

Whatever poisons remaining within his being were only psychological.

Parker Johnson had the reputation of being a tireless worker, which was one of a number of reasons why Jeff selected him for his program. In addition to foisting his teaching duties onto Parker, Jeff asked him to get as much information as he could about the WHO in Tunisia, and more about soy ink.

Parker reached into his briefcase and extracted a number of computer printouts, file folders, and photocopies. His major professor sat relaxed awaiting the barrage of paperwork.

Jeff scanned the documents and called Paul, who came over to the OU office.

Parker began, "Today, about half of the dailies in this country's use soy to some extent and a large number use it exclusively."

"Now, there are hundreds of soy oil suppliers around the world. However, as we might expect, several large firms supply many of our local newspapers and newsmagazines. For the newspapers these firms are National Ink Suppliers, Mid-Western Soy, and Ink Industries, Incorporated, sometimes called Ink Inc. These companies will sell the complete ink or the ingredients so the companies can make their own."

Parker looked over at Jeff, whose eyes were looking off in space, a certain indication his wheels were turning.

"Soy makes good color, right?" asked Jeff, trying

to recall Billy's words.

"Sure, and coupons are handled more by women." Jeff looked at Carmen, who merely nodded in agreement.

Parker continued, "It turns out that all the inks we found with mycotoxin get their soy from one source, Mid-Western Soy. But there's a slight problem with the theory about tracing the mycotoxin back to this company. In the United States, federal and state regulations have controlled the technology of all inks since the 1980s. In reality, only a small percentage actually get checked for various reasons. These regulations include ink formulation, labeling, shipping, solvent type and content, emission of volatile organic compounds, heavy metal content, and so forth."

Jeff contemplated Parker's presentation and said, "Which doesn't affect the theory, Parker. Just because the EPA is supposed to inspect doesn't mean they do. Hell, they hire chemists who have close ties to the pesticide industry to conduct their pesticide approval testing, and the FDA hires people who have worked for the pharmaceutical industry to make decisions that will affect the firms they have invested in. These advisors help the agencies decide which company does or does not get to make a particular pesticide or drug.

"Because an industry is regulated doesn't mean it will always stick to those regulations. And name somebody who checks ink for mycotoxins. I'll bet anything it's like pesticide control—it may apply to products made in the United States; it does nothing to regulate imported fruits or vegetables or even ink. Was the ink imported?"

"I can partially answer that, sir," said Parker. "The complete ink, or the base to make the ink, is occasionally shipped in. Also, the Hood brothers own both Oklahoma City newspapers, the *Tucson Times*, and Mid-Western Soy."

Parker closed his briefcase and said, almost absentmindedly, "Rumor has it Marilyn's got herself a new boyfriend." He raised both eyebrows in a quick up-and-down motion suggestive of grapevine gossip.

"So that's why she hasn't attended our meetings and is so secretive about her activities lately," said Jeff, looking over at Carmen.

"Yes" said Carmen. "According to Marilyn, he's very rich."

Jeff added, "Well, her coursework has slipped and she may lose her scholarship if she doesn't get her head back in the game real soon."

Jeff considered those words might well be applied to himself.

Marilyn lost her virginity aboard a Lear Jet on a direct flight to the Florida Keys for a quick three-day jaunt. Full of wine, pleasure, and love, Jeff's young graduate student enthusiastically told her lover about the research she and others in her department were conducting on newspaper inks and the poison they contained, relating them to this incredibly wealthy, internationally renowned businessman who expressed his undying devotion and that he was falling in love with her.

For Alan Hood, it only took a few occasional tender moments to extract the latest information from Marilyn, who willingly gave her lover all he requested of her. Once he knew what she knew for the moment, he departed the bedroom and made his usual private call to his brother, then returned to his newfound toy.

Day 19–Afternoon

Jeff needed to think. He walked to his reserved space behind the microbiology building, lowered the top on his Mustang, and drove south down Classen Street, which bordered the east side of the campus. He drove slowly in first gear, then second gear, listening to and feeding off the music of the supercharger.

Soon he entered the beautiful south campus area with acres of cultivated lawns, the Lloyd Noble Arena, and various buildings related to earth sciences, not far from the National Weather Center. He drove into a strong cool breeze carrying a smell of moisture and fresh mown lawn. Occasionally, white puffball mushrooms the size of footballs would appear, ready for removal for slicing and eating.

He needed time for his brain to sort and merge the ingredients, as a stew simmered toward perfection. He needed a plan of action.

Jeff turned on the radio and punched the button programmed for soft rock. Instead of music he caught the disk jockey at the top of the hour.

"This is Johnny Helms, your king of soft rock, and as we announced earlier in the program, we are going to take calls from our listeners about the epidemic that has hit our city. Come on guys and gals, call in. The phone number is 1-800-SOFTROC.

"The boards are lit up, folks, so let's have a listen to what our native folk really have to say. Rick, you're on."

"Yo, dude. You there? Hey, I think it's the milk. I mean, I don't think we ain't got good milk here in Oklahoma. Anybody looking into it?"

"Rick, I hate to break it to you, but we already covered milk," replied Helms. "Read the papers and take a hike.

"Rita, you're on the Helms show. What say you?"

"The witches are brewing a big kettle of bones, and a bunch of us in Oklahoma City are in the kettle."

"If this is the best y'all have to offer," said the dynamic Helms, "take a hike. Any more intelligent calls?"

"Hey, Jimmy, I listen to you all the time," said a woman who identified herself as a housewife. "I depricate what you're doin'. My take is that the gov'ment's sperimentin' on us. I mean, like it wouldn't be the first time."

"Okay, that's better than the last two calls. We

need something to go on," said Helms softly. "I love you, sweetheart, do call back, won't you?

"One more call," offered the disk jockey, "then it's off to nine songs in a row of your soft rock favorites. J. S. from Norman, you're on."

"I believe the newspapers are behind this."

"You mean the American press is poisoning our attitudes?"

"In a manner of speaking, yes," answered the caller. "And how about them two professors?"

Helms said, "Heck, man, I'm a true American, and I refuse to accept that. I'd believe in the kettle of bones theory before I believed your newspaper theory. So take a hike." Helms ignored the comment about the professors.

Jeff hung up his cell phone and turned off the radio. Why did he bother? Why did he even try to communicate with the masses? Someday, he decided, he'd have to ask a psychiatrist why a person purposely went against he knew to be the right thing, because the call he made to the station was a bit of momentary silliness. Is it possible he wanted to play with fire, to tweak the nose of the devil?

For some reason Jeff felt a moment of actual relaxation. The public at large could always be counted on to maintain the good old American sense of humor.

He made a U-turn and drove back to the entrance of Campus Corner, then made a left to cruise the cool tree-lined streets. After several minutes of slow cruising, he headed east on Alameda in the direction of Lake Thunderbird.

As soon as he passed the last signal out of town, Jeff checked the roadway to ensure it was dry and clear of traffic, including the absence of police vehicles. Then, with a sudden fierce aggression borne of frustration mixed with a heavy dose of impatience, he downshifted and stomped the accelerator. The Mustang's Traction-LOC differential grabbed the rear axles that fed into the Yokohama CLAW-GRIP racing tires, and four hundred-fifty horses leaped forward simultaneously out of the starting gate.

He never did hit third gear when he backed down to fifty, the speed limit on east Alameda, and then down to forty-five, where he punched it again. With the need for speed temporarily satisfied, he cruised slowly the last few miles out to the lake.

Along the way he spotted an occasional fawn coming out of the woods to eat the grass growing by the roadside. Squirrels dashed down one tree and up another, most of them on the side away from him, sensing his presence.

Thoughts came to mind of Manny Bolton, owner of the Big Sky Apartments. He felt in his bones the man was evil, although he was a small evil as these things went. Right now, there were worse crimes being committed.

When the Mustang came to a stop at the lake, Jeff reclined the seat. He tried to relax and clear his mind of all extraneous thoughts. In the near total silence of a paved parking area, he watched the ducks fluff out as they nestled in the grasses by the lake. Birds and occasional motorboats in the distance were the only sounds.

Why don't they use aflatoxin in the black ink, whether soy or petroleum? Will aflatoxin become bound or inactivated in petroleum and not in soy? Was there a problem with concentration and a lot more aflatoxin was needed for any black ink because the vats were so much larger?

Jeff closed his eyes. Frustrations relating to the project were replaced by thoughts of Carmen, her creamy smooth complexion, her magical voice, with her trace of an Aztecan nose, her laughter like delicate wind chimes. He knew her medical career was on the line and it ate at him. Maybe he should let her go so she could find her life again. Carmen needed to know how he felt. Were his feelings actually true?

And why wasn't Brewer all over Cantrell to demand Jeff's and Paul's firing under one pretext or another? Perhaps he did call and Cantrell resisted. Cantrell knew Jeff could get anybody pissed off on any given day, but he also knew Jeff was loyal to the core. Could Cantrell see through the dark cloud that Brewer carried around himself? *I'm as good as dead if I lose my research,* he thought, and a great feeling of helplessness came over him. *Unless there was some way I could start my own lab.*

Eventually Jeff's mind gave up the electrical energy necessary to maintain consciousness.

An hour later rainfall signaled him to awaken in the descending darkness. He raised the top of the convertible and slowly headed back to town, suddenly remembering a dinner date he had scheduled with Paul.

A plan of action had begun to form while he slept, during which time the brain automatically created a solution to the problem. The possibility of death could not be ignored.

Jeff and Paul were placed in a rear booth of the steak house, a location both men preferred at the moment. Both men ate T-bones and baked potatoes.

This freaking mathematician is a contradiction, thought Shenero. *He eats an incredible volume of food, including junk food, yet eats it slowly and delicately. And when it's time to go he'll leave half the food on his plate. If you have the time to wait for him he'll eat it all.*

"I need to ask you something. Why do you leave so much food on your plate?"

Paul shrugged. "I don't mean to. The real problem is that the conversations are too short."

Paul looked at Jeff who was shaking his head slowly. "Okay, it's something I'm working on," he concluded, embarrassed at being confronted about a personal issue of his.

Jeff accepted the answer and contributed, "You know, somebody's got a very sick sense of humor."

"True. Like the guy who perpetrated the anthrax scare a few years ago," said Paul.

"Anthrax is a relatively innocuous disease and can be vaccinated against. We're dealing with a real disease that's killing people every day and making untold numbers of others sick. You can't vaccinate against mycotoxicosis."

"And there's no antidote?"

"Nope." Jeff swung his head in a no gesture. "I say it's time to take some action. I'm going to contact one of my press buddies at the *Oklahoma Storm*, arrange for a tour of their operations, and see if I can collect a few samples. It's time to go to work, go to the source of the problem. I'm getting real antsy."

"Okay, I'll stay here and find out all I can about the physical plant at Mid-Western Soy," Paul offered.

"Good. We need absolute proof before we make fools out of ourselves again," lamented Jeff. "There's something about public humiliation that rubs me the wrong way."

Paul cut off another small bite of steak. "We didn't make fools out of ourselves. They exposed themselves for what they are. The two dimensional puzzle just became three dimensional. That was the real beauty of what we did. And Hood won't be too pleased when he hears you're coming."

"Hopefully, I'll be long gone before he finds out. Thanks for the tip though, I'd better inform Frank first."

Day 20–Morning

Other than his single contact at the *Oklahoma Storm* city desk, only James Harper, head of production, knew Jeff would be paying him a visit.

Apparently the newspaper owners never considered Jeff bold enough to visit the site personally or to meet with the elderly and experienced Harper.

Jeff pondered whether, in actuality, the Hoods knew their papers carried the poison. He decided that, after his and Paul's video visit with the committee, they would certainly know. Was it possible the Hoods themselves were being framed? In the end he decided that stopping the flow of poison was more important than investigating the Hoods' involvement. Who did the actual investigation would be another issue.

Harper was reputed to have operated printing presses since he was fifteen, all of them in Oklahoma City. His employment record included many years working for Daniel Kirk, Billy's father, back when he owned the papers.

Wearing a New York Yankees baseball cap and overalls, rugged in his appearance, he was a man who took his profession very seriously.

Harper guided Jeff through printing, the area of the plant where the presses rolled, and led the fascinated scientist to the section where giant three-foot rolls of paper were fed into the huge machines and to another area where computers translated copy into print.

The workers all wore latex gloves—to keep the ink off their hands, Jeff surmised. But why, if there's less bleed-through with soy?

"What's in the big tank, Jim?" he shouted over the din of the presses. Harper led Jeff away to a quieter corner of the three-story room. "That holds our newsprint ink. It comes in by semitrailer and is transferred into this vat in the press room every two months. The tank feeds the presses for both newspapers, and we split the cost proportionately based on circulation. The morning paper has about 110,000 daily subscribers along with papers sold out of the boxes and convenience stores and hundreds of other outlets here and even in Tulsa and outlying cities. In addition we print 160,000 Sunday papers. The afternoon paper has about thirty thousand dailies. Most people prefer to get their news in the morning, hence better circulation then."

"How do you know how much ink you have left?" asked Jeff, looking at the huge holding tank.

"We know from experience. We almost always receive a new shipment of ink on the fifteenth of every other month. This is the sixth of the month, so this particular batch is about three weeks old. The exception is during the holiday season when we run more color specials and have more color ads sent to us by our advertisers."

"Which means you also have tanks for color, right?" Jeff took in the sights and sounds of this environment.

Harper pointed to his left and led Jeff to three large containers. "These are our color pigment totes. You can see the name and the symbol on each one: magenta, cyan, and yellow. The color totes hold more than three hundred gallons each and are brought in every other month—when the black doesn't come in. That avoids too many tankers in the yard at the same time and too much confusion." Harper tilted his head toward the double doors and said, "How about the lunch room? I'll buy you a drink."

They walked through a set of double doors down a corridor into a spacious lunchroom encompassing some 1600 square feet, including a full-size cafeteria with grill. At nine in the morning, the lunchroom was empty except for one person working on a laptop and another reading the paper.

"You're my guest. Can I get you a coffee?" asked Harper.

"Iced tea will be fine, Jim."

Harper went into the serving area and returned with two iced teas.

"Man, I mean, this is fascinating." Jeff had never given much thought about the magnitude of a newspaper printing operation. He was impressed, and so far what Harper told him correlated with what Billy told him earlier.

"That's why I stayed with it for nearly a half a century. But, hey, doctor, you're my hero. I not only print the papers, I also read them."

"Thank you. I appreciate that. So who's your ink supplier?" Jeff realized the question was abrupt and out of context. He struggled to rephrase it, but Harper answered the question.

"Only a limited number of ink suppliers dominate the printed media market. We get all ours from Mid-Western Soy right here in the city. This is perfect for us, and besides, the price is right compared with National out of Cleveland. Ink Inc. is in New Jersey, and they handle the big eastern papers, so I guess you could call them first in terms of population served. There are many others, of course, but these are the major ones."

"I take it soy's been around for a long time," said Jeff.

"A good half-century. Not everybody wants to make the conversion," Harper stated.

"So Mid-Western Soy provides for all your ink needs. Who supplies the ink for the Southwest, for example?"

"That would definitely be Mid-Western Soy, similar to Ink Inc., which almost exclusively serves the east. National has a number of branch outlets and supplies the tweeners. No question, it's a competitive business. We've used Mid-Western for our presses for years. They supply a lot of cities. Quite honestly I'm not sure what they all are."

"Let me get this straight, Jim. You use Mid-Western Soy for both color and black ink?"

"Yes. Since we switched to soy years ago with the Kirks and well before they sold the company, we haven't lost any customers other than normal turnover. That's what Mr. Hood wants—cleaner copy."

"Mr. Hood? He's the owner of both papers?" Jeff asked the question as innocently as possible. He knew the answer.

"Yes, he and his brother own Mid-Western Soy."

Jeff got the confirmation he needed.

"How is he to work for?" Jeff dropped his voice,

as though Harper might share an inside secret with a friend.

Harper laughed. "Hard as nails. Don't take nothin' from nobody. He doesn't give me any slack, and I'm okay with that. He has a business to protect."

Jeff needed to collect samples from the three vats of color. He knew only one way to do it. "Jim, I'd like to get a sample of each of the inks from these vats."

"A sample. For what?" Harper asked, as if Jeff were asking him for his first born.

"We're looking at landing a contract to develop a cleaner soy back in the lab so we need samples," Jeff said, nonchalantly and not far from the truth.

"I thought you did germs and molds and stuff," Harper queried, clearly stumped.

"Actually, we do all kinds of off-shoot things. We're like any business and follow any lead. A man has to earn a living. I'll be happy to give you a list of universities that have defense contracts to produce weapons." No lies there.

"Well, I guess you can take the color from the petcock attached to the Lincoln pump."

Harper saw the lost look in his visitor's eyes. "The Lincoln pump connects the ink line from the totes to the presses."

Harper went on, "Nobody's ever asked me that before, except for our quality control people. Need any containers?"

"No thanks, Jim. I've got my own," he said, tapping the briefcase on the floor next to him. They rose to go back into the print room.

When he returned to the lab, Jeff personally processed the samples. He soon obtained the information he needed and went back to his office to work the numbers.

Shortly after he finalized his notes, Richard and Parker entered to report their own findings. They had calculated the amount of toxin that was in the color they collected from the newspaper itself.

The three of them calculated backwards to determine how much mycotoxin an ink tote contained. Comparing it with his own findings, Jeff said, "With some variation between your figures and mine, I get about two hundred fifty grams in a tote of ink."

"Sir, that's a little more than half a pound!" exclaimed Parker. "Times how many totes?"

"A lot," said Jeff.

Richard stammered, "That's insane, I never thought...doctor, how can anyone produce so much crystalline mycotoxin? We have to go through how many cultures to extract milligrams of substance?"

Jeff stared into space and began nodding his head slowly in comprehension.

"Uh-oh," said Parker.

"I hate when he does that," muttered Richard.

Jeff said softly, as though he had entered another zone, "They grow the mold in large vats of oxygenated submerged culture; therefore, they have no space restrictions like we do."

He continued, "That's how they can produce so

much mycotoxin—the same way penicillin was produced in quantity. I think I know now why the disease is occurring, where it is, and why aflatoxin is being used as the weapon of choice."

Parker Johnson and Richard Smith stared at one another wondering what they had missed.

The phone rang. Carmen picked up. "Boss, it's the office of a Mr. Iverson. He's an attorney representing the Hoods and would like to speak with you."

Jeff grinned.

PART THREE

Day 21-—Morning

Jeff, Paul, and Frank sat in the office of Richard Iverson, attorney for Hood Enterprises. The dark mahogany wood, Berber carpeting, and imposing oak desk testified to the success of a man who commanded seven hundred fifty dollars an hour for his work. Two walls of the spacious room were covered with built-in shelves full of law books from several disciplines.

Iverson sat with his back to the picture window in the seventh-floor suite that looked out over Oklahoma City and the lakes and forests of the countryside beyond. The office held the faint aromas of furniture polish and cigar smoke.

Not overly surprised by the call, Jeff contacted Frank, whose law license in Oklahoma had not expired.

After introductions and greetings were exchanged, Iverson motioned for the three men to take seats in armchairs facing his desk. The brightness of the window behind Iverson served to blind the visitors and negate his facial features.

"Excuse me, Mr. Iverson," said Frank, "could

you please draw those curtains?"

"Yes, of course, Mr. Bennett." No apology.

Iverson stood reluctantly, walked to the corner of the window, and pulled the drapes closed, reseating himself. Standing perhaps five-foot- four including built-up heals, Iverson wasn't a bad-looking man, with an ample supply of dark-brown hair, razor cut and parted down one side. His eyes, nose, and mouth were somewhat small, which made his face slightly unbalanced with his head of hair.

"You gentlemen are here at the request of my client, Alan Hood, one of the owners of the *Oklahoma City Mirror* and the *Oklahoma Storm*. You are familiar with those newspapers, are you not?"

"Yes," responded Frank simply.

Iverson continued, "As my office explained to you on the phone yesterday, James Harper, our head of production, informed Alan Hood, that Dr. Shenero made a visit to the print room area of these newspapers where he took ink samples from the room.

"Doctor, can I ask you the purpose your visit, and why you took samples of ink from the vats or containers or whatever you call them?" He looked directly at Jeff with accusing eyes.

Frank had coached his friends prior to the meeting not to answer any question without his okay.

"Mr. Iverson, as an attorney representing these two gentlemen," said Frank, "Dr. Shenero's motives were expressed previously in a recent video conference call meeting at the request of authorities in Washington, not by him. He was at their behest.

That is why the samples of ink were taken. What he did with them is proprietary information."

Iverson looked at Jeff. "Doctor, I presume you know Robert Brewer?"

Frank interjected, "Excuse me, Mr. Iverson, this is not a formal deposition. Also, this is not a trial in a courtroom. Therefore, if you wish to avoid both of these, I suggest you feel free to discuss any issues you may have with my clients, rather than questioning them in such an offensive and accusatory manner."

Iverson grinned, somewhat sheepishly in a poorly disguised play act. "My apologies to all of you. Sometimes I get caught up in legal presentations. My wife accuses me of the same thing. She once told me, 'I'm your wife, dammit, not a hostile witness'."

They all laughed. No one was fooled.

"Anyway, Dr. Shenero, I asked if you knew Mr. Brewer."

Jeff glanced at Frank, who nodded.

"Acquainted, yes," said Jeff. "Do I know him? No."

"Do you know a Mr. Hood?"

"I don't know him, either. I've only heard he's the owner of our two largest newspapers," responded Jeff. He wanted to say that he'd never met Mr. Hood face to face, but they certainly seem to be bumping heads a lot lately. *I also know about the ownership of Mid-Western Soy by Alan and his brother, and a few other things you'll find out about in time*, thought

Jeff. *Hopefully, you'll go down with the ship.*

Iverson interrupted Jeff's reverie. "Doctor, it is my unfortunate position to inform you that Mr. Hood has communicated his concerns to Mr. Brewer, and as soon as Mr. Brewer recovers from a short illness, he will contact you.

"I am also acting as representative of Mr. Brewer, and, according to his instructions, you are both removed from the project as of this moment. Presumably you know what project he is referring to, because I don't."

Iverson's gaze caught Frank's as he raised his eyebrows and gave a small grimace, as if to say, "I don't know any other way to tell them."

Frank responded, "I will file an order to show cause with Homeland Security, as well as with yourself, Mr. Iverson."

Iverson looked like a man in the catbird seat. "Good luck with the Department of Homeless-land." He gave a slight chuckle at his trite joke. "It's quite a bureaucracy. Things are likely to get lost among the trees and the undergrowth. As for myself, I am only following instructions and don't have a clue as to what is going on as regards the project at issue here."

Paul suddenly interrupted Iverson, as he was about to continue. For his own entertainment, Paul spoke in as British an accent as he could call up. "I do say, suh, your comment smacks of a threat."

Iverson appeared to lose his stride for an instant and then he recovered. "Gentlemen, according to my sources, Mr. Brewer instructed you not to harass Mr. Hood. Pardon my direct approach, but that is how I speak. Can you please answer the question?"

"You asked no question," Frank told him.

"Quite true," replied Iverson, glancing at Paul for an instant before recovering. Did the man have a smile on his face? "Let's try again. Didn't Mr. Brewer ask you not to harass Mr. Hood?"

Frank placed a cautioning hand on Jeff's arm. "That is incorrect. Mr. Brewer supported Mr. Hood and spoke rudely to my clients. He gave no direction to Drs. Shenero and Anderson and did not tell them to stay away from the newspaper facilities."

"Given the truth to your statement, I will now give you that direction, doctors. I am handing each of you a restraining order. If you will check the letterhead, you will note that it really does come from DHS. We are all playing with fire here. A big fire. If we find either of you anywhere on the grounds of my client's newspapers, I will have you thrown in jail."

Surprised by the bold move, Frank and Paul did not try to hide the amusement on their faces. In his turn, Jeff grinned so hard it turned into a leer that yelled out at Iverson, "Catch me if you can."

Iverson took out a notebook, began to write, set down the pen, and leaned back in his chair. Jeff could tell he had stuck a nerve in the attorney.

Frank stood to indicate the meeting had ended at which point the other three men rose and wordlessly nodded their goodbyes.

Before leaving the room, Paul turned to Inverson and added, "Sir, I would expect a man of your caliber to smoke a better quality cigar than Swisher Sweets. My grandmother smokes those."

In silence the three visitors walked down the hall to the elevator and pushed the button. As the doors opened, Jeff started laughing.

"What was with the cigar crack?" Frank asked.

"I saw him grab the box off his desk and put them in a top drawer when we walked in," Paul answered.

"Well, what these bastards don't know may come back to hurt them," Jeff laughed. Inside, he did not feel so confident. What if Carmen were next on the hit parade?

Alan Hood could not hide his rage. Shenero had trodden on the sacred ground of his newspaper. He'd walked in and out, taking with him samples of his inks for laboratory tests.

To make matters worse, it turns out that the so-innocent-looking Anderson once had a juvenile career as street mugger from England. The archived police reports from London presented a psychological profile of the cool and smooth mathematician that made the hairs on his neck prickle. In another life and another scenario, he would be recruitable material for their own cause.

Jeff's graduate students were another problem he could not subtract from the equation. They'd do whatever their boss told them to do and do it efficiently. The entire pack knew too much.

The bunch of them needed distraction for a short

while longer. Glenn Lewis, General Manager at GNN, kept Kirk under wraps. Newspapers around the country focused on the epidemic along with the havoc wreaked by the strike. Sales were up thanks their expertise in keeping the nation scared.

A segment of Alan peaked out of the darkness and recognized Billy Kirk's loss as profound. He and Harry had known the Kirks for many years. They were decent and honest people whom they murdered in a gruesome manner—plain and simple.

Stop it.

Before the overriding voice of business-above-all could take command, Harry knocked and came in. He held a number of papers in his hand.

"I have some information and it may not be good news. Our tap on Parker's computer shows a copy of the documents the WHO emailed to him about the Tunisia project," Harry said.

According to Marilyn, Parker did Shenero's bidding. He knew from her and from Brewer that Parker had been in contact with the WHO and Harry had their documents to prove it. The mentioning of the Tunisia project was another one of big mouth Brewer's mistakes.

Alan took the papers and read the summary:

Initially, the disease begins with a skin rash on the fingertips and then spreads to the eyes, nose, and mouth. A burning sensation is reported, although little or no itching is involved.

In subsequent days, the redness ulcerates and is

followed by incrustation. These were the reported symptoms at Gafsa prior to the entry of WHO personnel. It is noted that spontaneous healing occurred in many instances.

In Tozeur, the situation became severe, and symptoms progressed beyond those in Gafsa. In both cities patients began to complain of insomnia, headaches, loss of memory, loss of small motor skills, occasional hallucinations, and general malaise. Nausea and blurred vision were reported. In more extreme cases, abdominal pain and tachycardia occurred, along with a steep rise in blood pressure. The disease is not contagious, and no causative environmental factors could be found leading to the symptoms, nor has a date for the first case been established in either city.

Disease symptoms persist and worsen over time. Especially noteworthy is the universal complaint of severe headaches, which suggest inflammation of the meninges surrounding the brain. Because we could isolate no microorganism from this tissue upon autopsy, it may be a nonbacterial and non-viral meningitis.

The disease begins spontaneous reversal after the patient has exhibited symptoms for approximately four weeks, although 447 deaths were reported most of which occurred in Tozeur. Those persons who were initially infected appear to have recovered completely, returning to normal health. However, without reversal of symptoms, the death toll had been projected to be exceptionally high.

The balance of the document dealt with demographics, medical descriptions and photographs, maps, and individual reports by the investigators.

"There's a lot more detail here than the national press received," said Alan.

"Good thing we stopped when we did. Another couple of weeks, and we'd have killed off a serious portion of the local population. Those are our own people, bro'," Alan said, using the vernacular of the day and not quite sure how he actually felt about any of it.

"It's on Father's head, not ours," rejoined Harry. He went on, "Look, we have enough ink for a six-week run—two weeks beyond the time we gave for Tunisia. By the time they figure it out, we'll not only own an island, we can return home and be welcomed as heroes."

"Don't be so glib," Alan chastised his impetuous brother. "We will be hunted down like dogs forever-more, and we sure as hell won't be going home. We will be two of the wealthiest and most wanted men on the planet. Sooner or later the Americans *will* find us. They always do. They'll either kill us or we'll be in solitary confinement forever. The same goes for Father. Our wives and children will have to change their names and go into hiding."

Alan's statement seemingly passed right over Harry, who merely shrugged. "And as far as our American troublemakers, I think you're much too soft. A natural calamity should befall one of them, preferably the bald one, or his secretary, to serve as a hint of things to come. It should convince him to back off. Let's see his file."

Alan pursed his lips whenever it became necessary to consider his brother's thick-headed attitude. He walked over to a file cabinet and retrieved the file labeled "Shenero, Jeff" and set it on the desk.

"Look Harry, don't do something stupid. A house fire is one thing; killing is another. That's a sure way for the pack of them to throw caution to the wind with us along with it. Then they'll scream fast and loud and attract undue attention to us.

"I know what you are thinking, little brother," Alan said, putting his arm around the shorter man's shoulder. "Trust Father. He's spent most of his life working on the master plan. Our friends in Riyadh are coming through nicely and the rest has yet to unfold. Are you ready for your California trip tomorrow?"

"More than ready," Harry said excitedly, glossing over his brother's concern. "Back to this Shenero character...I want to have a little fun; say, for the purpose of distraction. What do you think?"

"Go for it," replied Alan. "I've got the girl; you can have your own fun. Time is on our side. Honestly, Harry, Shenero is merely meddlesome, like a barking dog with no bite."

As he said this, Alan ardently wished he hadn't spoken so cheaply of the girl, and for an instant wished that he might have another life, one he might share with her.

He also fervently hoped the dog with no bite

would stay far away, just in case.

Day 21–Afternoon

"I think they've painted a bull's-eye on us," Jeff said in a genuine and cavalier attitude; his reputation when under extreme stress.

Jeff looked out the window of the student center to view a number of buildings across the grassy quad. A few early risers were strolling toward the building where he and Paul were seated.

To Jeff's consternation Paul ate a breakfast at dinner time as he poured maple syrup over his pancakes, cut them with a fork, then broke the yolks from two over-easies and randomized the mixture.

Jeff withheld comment on Paul's eating habits and said, "Billy told me he needs two things for him to break something new—solid proof from our end so he can stop parroting what every other news agency is saying, and he needs Lewis, his boss, to get off his back."

"You're thinking about making a visit to Mid-Western Soy, aren't you?"

"Yes, and I've begun to prepare for it. We'd better call Frank and tell him we'll be impersonating federal officials," Jeff added.

"I love it when you talk dirty to me," said Paul, dryly. He made a crack about his old criminal days of gang fights and home invasions. Then he excused himself to attend a departmental conference, leaving the remainder of his meal uneaten.

When Jeff returned to the office after breakfast, he found a box on his desk containing a number of small-to medium-size bottles of perfume, both square and round.

Jeff looked over at Carmen. "Is this yours?"

"They were when I bought them. Now they're yours," she stated, smiling cutely.

The scientist pulled out one bottle after another reading each label. "I don't get it."

"I went shopping last night," said Carmen, with a note of great delight.

"And?"

"Hon, they keep talking about the toxin being in the perfume, so I thought you might want some samples to test, especially those made locally. They're all middle priced, something the poorer folks wouldn't normally buy, so it fits into the trend. Who knows, one brand might be bad."

Jeff had an urge to tell her he didn't have time to waste on this perfume nonsense, but stoppered the bad nerve connecting his brain to his mouth. Instead, he sat down and thought it through.

If no perfume were involved, the issue could be a diversion from the ink poisoning. If poison were in the perfume, Whitaker and company were telling the truth. If so, why didn't they pull the bad stuff off the market? There are two reasons not to. They want it to remain in place to poison more people, and the perfume will serve as the perfect sacrificial lamb, if necessary.

And what's with that "honey" business on a workday?

He needed to get to the lab right now. "Where's Parker?" he asked.

"Teaching your class," she replied.

Jeff checked his watch. Another half hour.

"Where's Richard?"

"He and his wife flew back to Minnesota for a quick trip to visit a dying aunt in her family," Carmen said.

"Where's Marilyn?"

"Unknown."

"Call Paul."

"I can't. He's tied up in the department."

Jeff threw his hands in the air and looked around him, grimacing, as if to say to a viewing audience, "Damn, it's hard to get good help anymore."

"I'm going upstairs. Tell Parker to meet me there when he returns. Okay?"

"Got it, boss," said Carmen.

"So why are you smiling?"

Carmen gave the briefest of shrugs. "Oh, maybe because you might find toxin in one of the perfumes I brought, and that I feel good about being able to help you."

Jeff felt guilty. Why can't he be considerate of her feelings and why can't he be a man and thank her for her thoughtfulness? He could come to no good answer.

Day 21–Evening

Events did not go as well for the two investigators as they had anticipated.

While they made their final plans in their usual corner booth in the university commons, the late-afternoon sky darkened significantly. Jeff felt a great urgency to get back to the microbiology building to prepare for the upcoming evening.

Unfortunately, the weather service promised a severe thunderstorm to deliver a wall of water projected to occur sometime in the late-afternoon hours. His distractions had permitted Jeff to forget that the first part of May demarked the high point of the thunderstorm season, and the late-afternoon hours were the prime time of the day for the weather to turn.

The instability of the atmosphere, the presence of high wind shear, plenty of moisture sliding in from the Gulf of Mexico, and a source for uplift, necessary components of a severe thunderstorm—all were present in abundance.

Business will pick up as roofs leak and homes flood. Mold will be rampant. Actually, it already is, only not in the way anybody figured, Jeff contemplated.

As the rain fell, it evaporated and cooled the air significantly. As it did so, the rain also forced the air near ground level outward at a high rate of speed. Breezes lasted only moments and evolved into winds of up to sixty miles per hour surrounding the downdraft. Within minutes the temperature dropped twenty degrees. This storm did not occur in a desert and did not blow sand. Here it just rained and rained.

From his vantage point at the table, Jeff watched the rainfall follow the wind in ever-increasing amounts over the next hour. After this would fall hailstones large enough to terrorize dogs. With no place to hide, they might remain traumatized by every passing cloud for the rest of their lives.

The sky grew blacker and windier by the moment. A wicked witch in a cone hat riding a bicycle across the sky would not have surprised any of them.

Along with hail, the storm would down power poles and cause large-scale damage to mobile home parks. In this particular storm, a hook echo would be present, the comma-shaped portion of the severe storm found in the southeast area of the northeast flow, the part that gives rise to tornadoes.

Loose debris and broken tree limbs flew through the air, while students covered themselves in a vain attempt at protection. Lightning flashes scoured the sky. The day disappeared and another dimension appeared.

The wail of air-raid sirens began, warning residents that a funnel cloud had been reported. Although Norman had not seen a tornado touch down within the city limits for half a century, a few years earlier one almost completely devastated the nearby small community of Moore to make the national news.

At last the hail and heavy rain stopped. The peals

of thunder were fainter as the storm moved eastward toward Tulsa, leaving the sky to rain in a moderate and steady downpour.

Jeff and Paul left the student union to walk toward their respective buildings. Neither had a jacket, and they had to endure the cold breezes remaining in the storm's wake, as they gingerly stepped around obstacles that littered the campus.

Not normally given to superstition, both men considered the storm a bad omen. Jeff walked the hundred yards or so to his building, hunkering down to protect from the rain. He thought, *Brewer and Whitaker were absolutely right. I found mycotoxin in one of the perfumes Carmen had supplied.* This time he remembered to thank her for it. The label on the bottle held a brand name and beneath the name were the words TOUCH OF HEAVEN. Surprisingly, the product was not made locally.

TOUCH OF HEAVEN. *"I'll bet,"* Jeff said to himself, sourly.

In order to play the part, a coin toss won Paul the honors. He would drive. They took two cars to a rental car company in Norman, reasoning that once they returned, each could go his separate way.

Paul acquired a new black Chevy Monte Carlo and the pair headed out toward the fenced grounds of the twenty-acre site of Mid-Western Soy in the northern outskirts of Oklahoma City. Paul had completed his homework: he'd Googled and sky-watched the site.

However, their simple journey became complex. Downed trees and power poles, and the presence of emergency crews due to the storm, slowed them to the point that, more than once, they discussed the issue of returning home.

At last the presence of good pavement permitted easy travel as the men approached the site on pavement once well-traveled by heavy truck traffic.

Only a few lights were on in various warehouses of the facility during this post-midnight run.

Their car's headlights loudly announced their presence in the overcast night.

Paul slowly pulled the car to the side of a rear loading dock near a sign that read, ADMINISTRA-TION. They had decided to visit the facility during the graveyard shift because the shift supervisor would be there, not the head foreman. They thought a midnight visit might go more smoothly with less complications. This would prove to be a miscalculation.

Each man wore a suit and carried a briefcase and each man carried a pen camera in his lapel pocket.

Within seconds after they left the vehicle, a large, intensely bright light froze them in their tracks. A voice spoke: "Please identify yourselves."

This social visit is turning out to be too much fun, thought Jeff. *A forty-minute drive takes nearly three hours, and now I need eyeball transplants.*

"Patterson and Bentson from OSHA," Jeff said, trying to protect his eyes from the multimillion-candlepower handheld spotlight. He reached into his back pocket to retrieve his wallet and opened it to display an OSHA-authorized laminated card with his name displayed in bold letters accompanied by a photograph.

"Okay, Bernie, turn off the light."

"Got it, Wes." Bernie turned off the light.

Even as their eyes screamed bloody murder in the brightness of the light, the scientists saw that Bernie and Wes carried shotguns. One held a pump action and the other a side-by-side. Both guns were trained on them.

Wes, the man who had commanded Bernie, finally put his shotgun at rest. Bernie did the same.

"Sorry, guys, can't be too careful around here these days. Lots of bad guys running around anymore, know what I mean?" said Wes.

"No problem," said Jeff, unable to see anything. "In fact, we're glad you men are on the job. Can you point us in the direction of the shift supervisor?"

Wes gestured to a door a few yards away and told them they were looking for a man named Blackwood, The building could double as a warehouse. It occupied nearly a full half-acre of land. Occasional side doors and rollups garnished the exterior. Other warehouses and ink manufacturing facilities occupied the multi-acre site. Several flatbeds and 18-wheelers slumbered in a row nearby.

Upon entering the building, the men instantly sensed that the temperature might be twenty degrees higher than outdoors, as the building retained the heat of the day. The humidity now felt stifling, and perspiration began to bead on their foreheads.

A half dozen forklifts stood in a line parked along one wall, forks down, in perfect formation.

A large number of totes of colored ink, arranged neatly in three rows, stood toward the rear of the warehouse. Near them were a dozen or more large crates stacked against one wall.

A sign above all the totes and crates read, FOR SHIPMENT. Jeff disregarded the urge to check the ink supplies, as Paul pulled the mycologist along.

Three colored ink containers were located in front of the others in a section marked by a flag on the wall that read, EMPTY. Apparently the black-ink tanks were located in another warehouse where the contents could be pumped into tankers. These would haul the ink to their respective city and newspaper. A shudder ran through Jeff as he realized the potential for human destruction that lay before them, a silent death waiting to happen.

An odor of diesel exhaust and paint reagents permeated the air. A huge contingent of neon lights shone from the ceiling thirty feet above them. The lighting caused surreal shadows to emanate from the speckled steel grids of the railed five-foot-wide walkway wrapping around three sides of the building halfway up.

A galvanized steel stairway to their right led to a series of offices on the second floor of the building. Paul pointed toward the stairway and, as if they owned the building, slowly walked up the stairs. They did not speak and entered the office door marked WILL BLACKWOOD, SUPERVISOR.

The sparsely furnished office contained a large metal desk and worktable, a water cooler, and a few chairs. A heavy pall of cigarette smoke nearly obscured their vision. Windows opened onto the second-floor catwalk. An older man with a cigarette hanging from his mouth leaned over blueprints covering the table. He turned as they entered the door and looked at them curiously.

"Mr. Blackwood?" asked Jeff.

"Yeah," croaked the aged supervisor.

"Mr. Blackwood, I'm Bill Patterson, and this is Larry Bentson. We're with the Occupational Safety and Health Administration. I presume you've heard of OSHA?" Jeff pulled out his wallet and displayed a card stamped OSHA in bright red letters with his name, picture, and ID number.

He and Paul had picked up the cards from a local shop called Spies, Incorporated, in Oklahoma City. The store sold cards that read CIA and FBI, and it carried driver's licenses from every state and many foreign countries. It carried lock-pick sets, high-tech audio detection and recording equipment, hidden cameras, pen recorders, and other devices available to the up-and-coming spy. Stores like these were being shut down across the country because law enforcement saw how they served the criminals as much as they questionably served the public. A great deal of their business came from husbands and wives who wanted to know what their spouses might be doing at home during their absence or, in some instances, during their presence.

Blackwood gave Shenero a dirty look and glanced at his briefcase. He didn't give Paul more than a glance.

"What are you guys doing here anyway? I ain't been notified to expect you," rasped Blackwood suspiciously.

Paul took up the conversation. "That's the idea. We got a complaint lodged with our offices from this shift and are required to investigate."

"Who reported what from my shift?" inquired Blackwood with a mixture of hostility and doubt. "Ain't nobody ever complains 'bout nothin'. We take care of our own. 'Sides, ain't nobody here, or can't you see?"

Thinking quickly, Jeff interjected, "The complaint came in some time ago. It takes us a while to get the paperwork processed. I'm afraid we're not permitted to reveal the person's name. We'd like to take a look around and fill out our reports. To be perfectly honest, we don't like being here in the middle of the night, know what I mean?" he said, mimicking Wes's question outside.

Jeff thought his minor human confession would soften up Blackwood, whom he hoped would offer to take them through a tour of the grounds, but it only served to further irritate the supervisor. He stubbed out his cigarette in an overflowing glass ashtray.

"No, I don't know what you mean. Personally I like working nights. Doin' it all my life and wouldn't trade it for anything, if you know what *I* mean,"

Blackwood shot back sarcastically.

"Sir," said Paul, "we are authorized to look around on our own and ask questions of any workers we find, including Wes and Bernie, and do it with you or without you. Which would you prefer?"

"You guys are something else. Well grab those fucking hardhats from the wall there and let's get this bullshit over with," answered Blackwood gruffly. Clearly the man had his fill of government interference with his work and his life. "And if you want to throw me into jail for cussing in my own office, go for it. Make sure you add resisting arrest to the charges."

Works as well as if he were on the witness stand, thought Jeff. *Get the man angry, and he'll blab too much.*

The three men exited the office and walked down the stairs. "Where do you want to start?" asked Blackwood.

"We'll look around and ask questions. All you have to do is answer them," said Jeff authoritatively.

"Larry," Jeff said to Paul, "I'll start with the warehouse. Why don't you let Mr. Blackwood take you on a tour? I'll meet up with you later."

Once again, Carmen had it right. It would appear that the ongoing strike did prevent the shipment of inks to the other cities. Jeff stared at dozens of ink drums arranged in rows of three.

Now in the bowels of the huge warehouse and out of sight, Jeff opened his briefcase that held a number of small, wide-mouth Nalgene screw-cap bottles, each with a capacity of four ounces, and sheets of small, blank peel-off labels. There were two marker pens, a notepad, a hammer, a dishtowel, a score of heavy plastic spatulas resembling tongue depressors, along with the same number of self-sealing plastic bags.

The time available to him to collect samples would depend on how long Paul could keep Blackwood out of the warehouse. He faced a daunting task, since no dry runs could be made due to lack of time. At home and in the office, he could only practice by pulling the items from his bag one-by-one and go through the motions, clueless as to what variables lurked in the real facility.

Each of the remaining colored-ink totes contained a six-inch-diameter camlock at the bottom, which, when unscrewed, would reveal ink, that is, if it had leaked around a large ball bearing. This ball bearing sealed the hole to the ink supply. From this opening, the ink in the tote would be supplied to the main feed, which would lead to a separate petcock valve on the Lincoln pump system and from there to the presses.

According to Billy, a few of the camlocks would have sufficient ink on the inside to collect a sample; others would not. This would be his only method of collecting ink, unless he wanted to depress the ball and receive an unknown quantity of colored ink on his hands and clothing.

Jeff wrapped a cloth around the flange of the first

camlock and gently tapped it once with the hammer. It gave slightly, and he tapped it a second time. It gave more, and he tried twisting it with his hands. At last it spun freely. He removed a small plastic bottle and a clean spatula from the briefcase and unscrewed the entire mechanism. It slipped out of his sweaty fingers and fell several inches to the concrete floor of the warehouse with a small clang. Jeff's heart leaped. He froze, afraid to breathe, fearful others might have heard the sound. No one came into the warehouse.

He picked up the metal camlock and found no ink on the inside. No sample here and no time to lapse into anger or disappointment. He photographed the name of the ink color stenciled on the side of the container, made a note in his logbook, and moved on.

He quickly crouched from one tote to another, trying not to place his knees on the floor to make obvious dirt stains on his slacks. When he did find ink, he took a picture of it within the camlock and the ink color stenciled on the side of the container. He wrote the identification number of the tote on a label, peeled it off the sheet, and pasted it onto the bottle. Then he took a clean spatula, scraped the ink off the inside of the camlock, and transferred the ink into the inside of the respective Nalgene container. All the while the hardhat kept slipping down over his eyes or struck the edge of a container.

Each task took less than a minute. He placed the used spatulas into a common plastic bag for later disposal, screwed the camlock into place, tapped it down more tightly with the hammer, and moved on to another tote. Sweat dripped from his head onto the floor. His hands became slippery, and his shirt soaked through. More than once he paused to wipe himself with a tiny portion of the only rag he had brought along, trying desperately to keep ink off his face.

With knees aching, he kept a wary eye out for Blackwood and Paul, who could appear at any moment at the loading dock door.

He used the single rag to muffle the sound of the hammer. If discovered, he had not the slightest doubt that Blackwood and his men would turn violent in an attempt to protect their turf.

Heavily engrossed, Jeff heard men talking and instantly stopped working, concealing himself behind the ink totes several rows to the rear. He chanced a peek and saw two men he hadn't seen before enter the warehouse and walk toward the forklifts. They stopped to talk and laugh for several moments. Jeff found himself urging them forward, to stop wasting precious time. He tried to think of what he might say if he were discovered and couldn't think of anything plausible. He held the incriminating evidence in his hands.

At last each man climbed onto a forklift, started it, raised the forks, and drove out of the building.

Jeff went back to work, moving as quickly as he could, his heart pounding. His knees were in agony. He stood for a few seconds to stretch them out and went back to work.

He worried, not so much for himself and his friend, but for the project. If they were caught cold, they would surely lose the game and the Hoods would have it all. There would be no starting over. Instead of water and foam in the wake of their ship, there would be prison or death. He and Paul could easily be shot as intruders.

Paul had drawn Blackwood to the ink manufacturing plant and warehouse. "Mr. Blackwood, the complaint we received regarded the transferring of ink from one container to another; that, and the fork-lift operation of the colored-ink totes in your primary warehouse. Could you please show me how the black ink is transferred to the trucks?"

"Yeah, sure," said Blackwood with great rancor. He pointed to a vat labeled BLACK—10,000 GAL-LONS.

"We got lots of these," said Blackwood as he pointed to two rows of four vats each. Stenciled lettering on the vats read, SOY INK – BLACK. You wanna see our stockpile of soy oil and ink and where we mix them too?"

Blackwood continued speaking, with distain in his voice. "Hell, man, all we got to do is hook up a hose to the camlock. Gravity feeds it into a tanker truck waiting in the downstairs area. It's sort of like transferring gasoline into the underground storage tanks at stations where you buy gas. So there ain't nothin' to complain about, and ain't nobody gets hurt here. No emissions, no complaints." Blackwood turned around and began to walk back toward his office.

Paul needed to stall. "One more thing, sir." Blackwood stopped and glared at him.

"You do carry rolls of newsprint here, do you not?"

"So what? They're stored in another building," groused Blackwood, who was nearing the limit of his tolerance.

"Let's take a walk." Paul knew he was out of character when he found it necessary to order a person to do anything, and, as before, it took him back to his youth.

"Sure," Blackwood said sarcastically, "I got nothin' else to do."

"Your cooperation will be noted."

"Whoop-de-do," announced the shift supervisor, leading Paul out through the big doors to another warehouse.

The lights were off in the building, and Blackwood turned them on from a wall switch. Inside stood ordered rolls of newsprint, stacked according to their diameter, depending on the format of the press into which they would feed. "Happy now?"

"Quite," said Paul, who took more notes on his pad, stretching time. "So all those tanks of colored ink in the other warehouse are full? Or are they empty?" Paul asked.

"Both. And if you want to know, we're trying something new to see if it's more economical to buy from overseas—cost of labor being what it is. We fill them over there, so don't go looking at me about me about somebody fillin' 'em here."

"Where overseas?" asked the mathematician.

"Don't know, don't care."

Paul tried to become more conversational. "That's a lot of ink. I'm impressed. How many cities do you service?"

"Twelve, okay?" retorted Blackwood. "I got a feeling we'll be playing catch-up, as soon as we can get the trucks rolling. We're going to start loading them anyway in a day or so, soon as the ..."

Blackwood's mood suddenly became dark, as if he realized he'd said too much and saw the brightness of truth. He had reached his limit. "You know, I don't think this has nothing to do with worker safety. I seen lots of you guys before and they know all this before they come in. You're a piece of work, and I want to know what your buddy's up to. We gots us a problem."

Blackwood walked over to the huge loading dock doors and whistled loudly twice. Within moments, Bernie and Wes reappeared. "Wes, watch this guy. There's another one running around here somewhere in my building. Bring this one along. Shoot him if he runs."

Wes stayed several feet behind Paul with the shotgun pointed at his back. Paul fully believed these men would indeed shoot him without hesitation, if given the chance. His primary thought at the moment, however, was of Jeff. The success of the mission now lay entirely in Jeff's hands.

When the four men reached the main warehouse, Bernie began walking the rows of the totes, but he could not locate Jeff.

Finally Bernie opened one of the side doors and looked outside, where he saw Jeff casually leaning against the car, hardhat on the trunk.

Bernie pulled up his shotgun again. "Blackwood wants you," he ordered, waggling his gun.

Jeff walked toward the man. "For what?"

Blackwood appeared at his side with Anderson in tow.

"You could get in trouble for this," said Jeff in a cavalier manner.

"We'll see who's in trouble," replied the supervisor, grinning.

"Where'd you learn your manners?" Jeff asked.

"Shut up," said Blackwood. He looked at his men. "They say they're OSHA. They ain't no OSHA I ever seen. I don't care what their cards say. I'll run it by the boss."

Blackwood stepped over to the loading dock door where a phone hung from the wall. He punched in a several numbers, waited several moments, and then he spoke. Jeff and Paul couldn't hear the conversation, but from the cadence of his short, clipped words, they knew it couldn't be good for them. Blackwood looked at them and apparently gave their descriptions to the person on the other end of the line.

Blackwood returned to the group of four men.

"Relax, boys, the cops'll be along directly." Then he lit a cigarette, obviously gloating, and leaned against the wall next to the phone.

"Wes, see if they're packin'," Blackwood directed.

Wes leaned his shotgun against the wall for the pat-down while Bernie pointed his directly at the prisoners, back and forth, from one to the other.

Day 22–Very early morning

Jeff and Paul were processed into the Oklahoma City jail and their car towed to impound. They turned in the contents of their pockets and were photographed. Finally each man was permitted to make a phone call.

Paul reached a girlfriend and told her he got called out of town for a little while and would contact her when he got back.

Jeff desperately wanted to call Carmen and tell her he missed her and for her to call Frank. He resisted the temptation and made the direct call to their attorney, who expressed no surprise at their arrest and intimated that he was sorry he missed the excitement. He did promise to call Carmen first thing in the morning and let her know.

Jeff found floor space next to Paul in the overcrowded cell. Dressed in their business suits, the professors stood out from the other prisoners who wore jeans or ragtag clothing. Only Jeff's shaved head and scar on his forehead lent him an air of respectability in this environment, where tattoos were the rule, not the exception. Both men knew they were conspicuous targets. It was as if they wore Tee-shirts that read, "Support Your Local Police."

Metal bench seats along two walls were occupied by three prisoners each. A single harsh light caged in wire burned the darkness away. A semiprivate toilet was situated in the corner of the cell with a half wall in front of it.

In addition to Paul and Jeff and the six prisoners on the bench seats, five other men occupied the small space. Three were lying on the floor, trying to sleep, two were seated on the floor. To Jeff, they formed a class of persons he liked to call flagrant vagrants. He surmised that most of them had been captured in a single sweep.

Two prisoners seated on one of the benches had been whispering, and, within moments, one of them stood—a heavyset Hispanic male in a black AC/DC Tee-shirt with needle tracks down both arms. He approached Jeff and Paul.

"Hey, you got both my seats," he declared. "You look like lawyer types, and I got a thing about lawyers."

Jeff stood first. He faced the man of equal height who outweighed him by fifty pounds, including a beer-induced belly. Jeff's folded suit coat lay on the ground next to him on top of Paul's.

"Oh, I'm sorry, it's your mother's seat," answered Jeff ominously. He couldn't remember the last time he had been so hot and frustrated. His white shirt was sweat-stained and his tie and belt gone, compliments of the in-take procedure.

"Or is she in bed with your girlfriend, if you know what I mean?" Jeff silently thanked Wes for giving him his phrase of the day.

"You need to get your face fixed," said the assailant.

Paul rose and stood beside his friend as another of the men got up from the bench. He walked over to them, a man of medium height, slightly built, with bloodshot eyes. He looked to be the nastier of the two, with a face crisscrossed with scars, his neck and arms heavily tattooed with skulls and serpents.

"So what's your point?" asked Jeff, leaning into the man and whispering into his ear, "Word is your whore mother bangs lawyers for a living," Jeff backed off a full step.

The challenger's eyes widened. He gave a small cry and launched a punch at Jeff's face.

Jeff stood his ground, relaxed, awaiting the assailant's fist. Almost completely at ease, Jeff blocked the punch with his left arm and hooked and grabbed the arm, pulling the man into him while smashing a hard right fist straight into the addict's upper lip and nose.

The man fell. His nose released a geyser of blood as Jeff adeptly stepped aside to avoid the blood spatter. He flashed back decades to a similar encounter during his college years when a football player had invaded his space. The addict's partner charged forward, and Paul, standing to Jeff's left, shoved a hard right fist into the man's solar plexus. As the man fell, Paul stepped aside and instantly swung across with his left elbow and hit the man in the cheekbone. The bone cracked, and the man fell to his hands and knees, vomiting food and blood. The foul stench of alcohol filled the cell.

The defenders picked up their coats from the floor, dusted them off, and sat on the seats vacated by their assailants.

The incident lasted perhaps thirty seconds. Two guards arrived at the cell. "What's going on here?" demanded one who saw one inmate on his knees, retching. Another rolled around with a hand to his bloody mouth, chest heaving for air. Several bloody teeth lay on the floor.

Not a prisoner in the cell replied. The room remained stone quiet. The guards looked around, well-schooled in classroom misbehavior. One went into the cell. The second stood at the entrance while other guards hauled the hapless victims away for treatment.

The other prisoners either turned away or mumbled something about bad jail food.

Jeff and Paul hung their heads downward until the guards left. Jeff looked at the knuckles of his right fist. "Bastard cut my hand when I slammed him in the teeth. Now I'm really mad."

"Ah, Jeff, I'm really sorry. I'd file a complaint if I were you," said Paul sympathetically. "What's the world coming to? If I were to run a statistical analysis, I'd say my guy was out of shape. Sucker threw up when I buried my fist in his stomach. Indeed, he does need to work on strengthening his cheekbones more."

Paul rubbed his right pectoral muscle. "Think I'll start strengthening my upper body, especially if I have to get paired up with you on any more jobs."

Contemplating their present circumstance and wishing he were elsewhere, Jeff said softly, "Boy, did I need that."

Paul asked, "What did Frank say?"

"He said we'll be lucky to get out by this afternoon or evening." As they spoke, the pair acted like birds pecking for a morsel, looking around to ensure their safety, and then they ducked back down into conversation once again.

"So what'd you find out?" Jeff asked.

Paul snorted. "Plenty. They supply twelve newspapers, the same number Billy gave us. And, according to him, they were trying to be more economical by using foreign labor and they're importing the ink. The soundtrack on my recorder should have it all."

"Got it. Overseas shipment of ink," said Jeff, running the numbers through his head. Then he announced, quietly, "Paul, that accounts for all the containers of ink. Three go to each of twelve cities, and another three go to the presses at *Your Good Dining* in each city, which accounts for all it. One-third of the total is accounted for if only the magenta is tainted. And if they didn't get the ink yet and there is no news of the epidemic occurring in those other ten cities, we can assume it's all here in the warehouse."

"Given that it's tainted," added Paul.

"Yes, we need to find out," said Jeff.

"Which begs the question: Where are the samples you collected?"

"I threw the briefcase into the back seat of the rental. Good thing nobody noticed I didn't have it with me when they caught me," Jeff said quietly.

"Where's the cell phone with the picturs?" Paul asked, suddenly concerned, remembering Jeff's mission to collect evidence.

"It's in the briefcase. I'm glad you didn't lock the car. I put it there a couple of minutes before you guys joined me. Cops got my pen."

"No reason to lock the car in a good neighborhood." responded Paul, matter-of-factly.

Then Paul became serious. "How did you know we were coming back? Blackwood would have shot you if he'd seen you messing around with his ink."

"I didn't know," replied Jeff. "Luck of the draw, I guess. You'd stalled him long enough for me to finish as much as I could and I slipped out the side door. Besides, my internal alarm bells were ringing.

"This is serious, man," Jeff lamented, whispering and looking around. "We've got a terrorist attack going on, and nobody is doing anything about it. Not even us, not really. The time may come when we'll have to go public on our own. And I guess if we're wrong, we'll be in deep shit."

Paul guffawed. "Excuse me, honored guest of our most recent home. You might want to look around you and speak in the present tense."

The men were booked in at 3:14 a.m. After Jeff's phone call, it took Frank the better part of the day until he could post the necessary bond and file the papers required for their release.

Paul received his empty briefcase, and Jeff wondered about the security of his. After they claimed their personal possessions, Frank drove them to the police impound lot and got their car released. On the way the men quickly told their story to Frank what they learned during their visit.

"Did you call Carmen for me?" asked Jeff.

"Yep."

"What did she say?"

"She laughed."

"She actually laughed?"

"Yep. She said you have criminal record now, just like her."

Thankfully, Jeff found briefcase still on the back seat where he had tossed it. He placed it on the front seat and gingerly opened it, as if it were filled with explosives. Everything was there, including all the samples he'd painstakingly collected.

They returned the rental car, retrieved their own vehicles and each returned to their separate homes.

When Jeff did arrive at his house, he found the gate open with and Carmen's car parked inside the drive.

Jeff greeted Suzi and Lila, who bounded up to him. They waited to have their ears scratched, yet they seemed restless. He spent a few moments calming them, then entered the house.

Carmen waited for him. The table was set and the smell of a flank steak, eggs, and coffee permeated the room.

Carmen somberly greeted him. He was about to speak and hesitated. She didn't look too happy. "I know I look and stink like hell, but why so down? I thought you'd be happy to see me," he said as they hugged, briefly. She pulled away.

"Listen, Jeff. Something happened early this morning here."

"I'm listening."

"While you and Paul were in jail, a pair of intruders used bolt cutters to cut through the padlock on your entry gate. It looks like they pushed the gate open and entered the grounds."

Jeff cocked his head to the side in rapt attention. "Suzi, Lila..."

She placed her fingers softly over his lips and told him what happened.

In accordance with their training, Jeff's Rottweilers were silent as the intruders entered the grounds.

Once the men were inside the gate, the snarling dogs attacked. Human screams prompted calls to the police, who called Carmen when Jeff couldn't be reached. She met them at the house.

Carmen reassured the pets while the police investigated. They found a great deal of blood and two pieces of flesh. One appeared to be a large portion of calf muscle; the other might have been from the fleshy part of a hand between the thumb and index finger. A capped five-gallon can of gasoline lay on its side. Two trails of blood led from where the dogs had attacked the men, only feet within Jeff's fence, and led to the dirt road outside the fence. Tracks in the dirt suggested somebody had been crawling. Somehow they had managed to close the gate on the dogs, latch it, and drive away.

Hospitals in the area were alerted. Within minutes an emergency room responded and said one of the two men in question was scheduled for surgery to save a hand. The other man would lose a leg. Their IDs showed them to be from Oklahoma City. They admitted to their being hired to do the job and if they could ever find out who was behind their hiring they'd love to get even.

Now Carmen looked scared. "Honey, you kept the garage door closed when you left so they didn't know whether you were here or not."

"There are a lot of ways I can get out of my house, if I need to."

"That's not the point. They're after you."

Jeff noted the implication. They might be after her, too. After she related her tale, Carmen pointed at the food waiting for him and said her goodbyes. She wanted to leave him alone for his own sake to sort through events in his own way.

Jeff did not argue the matter.

Jeff had been trapped before in an underground cave off one of the islands of the Palau Archipelago.

Ocean water washed into the cave while he got stuck in a constriction while surrounded by psychedelic mushrooms. A gouge to his forehead by a stalactite during that misadventure gave him the scar he wore today.

On another occasion he got locked in a water-damaged bathroom with two others—a bathroom in which the entire floor was covered with black mold spores. And yet he found a way out of both dilemmas.

This was different. This was a corrupt portion of United States government putting the nation at risk and working hand in hand with mass killers and a jumbled series of events leading to death, sickness, and lies.

They had gotten into Parker's computer and no doubt had tracked them to Nogales. The teleconference debacle was followed by Reynolds' article along with all the misleading information they had been provided. Add to the stew a little dash of attempted house burning to raise the stakes. Their attacks had become physical and personal.

Jeff nodded slowly to himself. That can go two ways.

Day 23–Morning

When Frank and Paul arrived, Jeff relayed the story about the intruders at his home. They discussed the implications of the act until Jeff called an end to the speculation.

Jeff opined, "Along with the pictures and the evidence from the ink samples, we'll have enough when the time comes to put up or shut up."

"Jeff? Hello." Frank made a gesture of knocking on a door. "Forget the pictures for a minute. You're the one who needs to put up or shut. You're engaged in wishful thinking. Forget the fantasy. Honestly, as smart and industrious as you are, your naïveté surprises me at times. Didn't you ever hear the story about the wife who catches her husband in bed with another woman, and he absolutely denies having done anything wrong? His statement to her is, 'Sweetheart, who are you going to believe, me or your lying eyes'?"

Jeff and Paul looked at each other, not comprehending.

Frank continued, "My sources tell me the Hood family is reputable. They've given a great deal to their community over the years. That's why Dan Kirk sold out to them. All they have to do is lie with a straight face and say somebody jinxed the ink at Mid-Western Soy, which is a fair statement. You yourself told me that Billy said the print industry is one of the major money players in the industrial world. Look at the dollars in the medical and the automotive industries and all their spin-off products and services. So, do you think a competitor might have jinxed their ink?"

"They don't have any competitors," answered Paul. "And where would anybody get the mycotoxin?"

"That's beside the point, Paul. The real point is, how can you nail the Hoods with anything?"

Frank wasn't through. "And here's some topping for your ice cream sundae. The Hoods' lawyers are funded with unlimited dollars. They would take every cent you have and then some. My problem is, I don't know where to go from here.

"So, all your photographs and pictures and statements will only support the lie the brothers will tell if they are accused. I'm afraid rock-solid proof may not be enough to bring them down and stop the inevitable. And to tell you the truth, I'm starting to have my own suspicions about whether the Hoods are guilty of anything."

Jeff felt thoroughly chagrined and castigated. From one perspective, his friend's words had an element of truth. But true or not, Jeff knew that once the ink found its way to its target cities and got distributed, stopping the epidemic would be impossible. The infrastructure of the country would be in shambles, in financial ruin. Widespread panic would finish the job. Fortunately, for the moment, the ink was stored under a single roof, a possible advantage for them.

"Jeff, what's this business with perfumes they're talking about," inquired Paul.

"Perfumes and fragrances are made with so many ingredients It is possible. Maybe *Aspergillus* can grow on Orris root used in perfumes or on its iris leaves to produce aflatoxin when it grows. Bacteria and other fungi do.

"I mean, pot smokers will sometimes bury their baggies under the ground and retrieve them a couple of weeks later when they get good and moldy. They say it gives them a better high. Never mind the freaking *Aspergillus* growing on it. I suppose, hypothetically, the new company found some grain extract they're trying, and it happened to be contaminated, although I never heard of it."

Jeff changed horses in mid-stream and added, "I have heard of a smoke screen though, and I think we're looking at one. Otherwise why wouldn't they follow our lead? I know what they say they found and know what we found. Before I came here, Parker informed me that he and Richard were positive the mycotoxin is in the magenta ink. So am I. And let's not forget this fact: As of this date, nobody has pulled the bad perfume from the shelves."

Seemingly none of this mattered in the long run. The epidemic had spread to such an extent that authorities found it nearly impossible for authorities to determine which symptoms were real, psychogenic, or self-inflicted. Indeed, outbreaks cropped up in other portions of the country, so much so that even the Hood brothers began to wonder whether others might be introducing their own version of poison into the population.

Unable to separate spurious complaints from the real symptoms, the CDC changed direction toward damage control, being forced to spend a large percentage of their resources on the issue of mass hysteria, at the advice of Marjorie Reynolds.

Experts on TV and social media reviewed this topic of mass hysteria and its ample documentation throughout the civilized world in centuries past. The perfume and fragrance industry took a billion-dollar hit almost overnight. While expert talking heads on TV espoused their theories, the problem remained unresolved.

Richard's Tee-shirt read, "Best home Security: ISIS flag = Choppers + Feds."

As the group hovered around, Richard connected Jeff's cell phone to his professor's computer and downloaded the photos from the warehouse. One by one they examined the images of the rows of ink containers and pictures of their labels. Richard zoomed in and out and made the computer seemingly do the impossible.

"The resolution of this device is incredible," Jeff commented. "You can almost see the grain of the wood on the pallets."

Then he suddenly exclaimed, "Whoa, Rich, back up. There. Stop. What's on the very bottom of the picture in the corner?"

Everyone leaned forward for a closer look.

"Let's enhance it." Richard zoomed in on a yellow item stuck to one side of a magenta-ink tote. He centered the item and magnified it. "Looks like a white shipping tag. I'd say about four by six inches. Somebody left it on." He enlarged and printed the picture.

Everyone stared at the picture of the shipping tag and the writing on it.

"Looks like unintelligible squiggles and lines," said Richard.

"Looks like your handwriting," Jeff offered.

"No, it's too good to be mine," answered Richard.

"I say it's Arabic," said Paul.

"I concur," added Jeff. "Notice the height and sizes of the various letters."

"You know anybody who reads Arabic?" asked Richard.

"Hmmm, I might," volunteered Paul. "For a while I was dating a woman in linguistics..."

"And in physics and in sociology and in..." threw in Jeff.

Paul ignored his friend's intrusion. "Her name is Jeannette. She works in linguistics and we're on good terms. I'll bet if I call her and ask nicely, she can hook us up with someone in the department, especially if I tell her it's a national emergency related to the epidemic."

"Call her now, if you don't mind," suggested Jeff, with a note of arm twisting in his words.

Paul pulled out his phone. He walked out the door into the hallway and made his call. A long two minutes later, he re-entered the room. "We're set. How does today at three o'clock sound? The man's name is Matthew Edgemont. According to Jeannette, the man's been around the block several times, so we're going to need to be on our best behavior."

Jeff handed Richard a thumb drive and Rich transferred the pictures to it. No words were spoken as Jeff placed the drive in his pocket.

Day 23–Afternoon

Matthew Edgemont headed the Department of Linguistics at the University of Oklahoma. A distinguished scholar, Edgemont spoke a number of Western, Middle-Eastern, and Far-Eastern languages. Locked into his special microcosm of knowledge, he'd never heard of Jeffrey Shenero or Paul Anderson. Always willing to entertain visitors, he welcomed them.

Edgemont's desk was piled high with grant applications and administrative paperwork. Built-in shelves were packed with books written in a score of languages on a wide range of subjects. These included Solzhenitsyn's *The Gulag Archipelago* in Russian and Victor Hugo's *Les Misérables* in French.

A great black mustache adorned the face of the linguist which contrasted with a head of curly blond hair. Somewhat overweight, he did not fool his guests who recognized brilliance. Jeff and Paul had researched the man and found that he once served as a United Nations translator for three years in two dialects of Arabic to English, served as assistant ambassador to Morocco, and had written a dictionary of a little-known dialect only spoken in eastern Iran.

Jeff suppressed his amusement in the linguist's

office when he saw a book on one of the shelves with a red spine: *Teach Yourself Swahili*.

Jeff and Paul pulled up a chair at the desk opposite the professor. Edgemont looked over the eight-by-ten photographs of the shipping tag and the rows of totes. He twirled his mustache in contemplation, first on one side and then on the other. "These marks on the top line are the date written in traditional and not American style, that is, day, month, and year. So you've got the fourteenth of April, about six weeks ago. The writing is the reverse of ours and reads right to left, except for the date, which is left to right.

"The line below that says, 'From: Riyadh, S.A.,' followed by 'To: Cayenne, F.G.' Riyadh is the capital of Saudi Arabia, and F.G. probably stands for French Guiana, because Cayenne is its capital. French Guiana is a country of about 200,000 in the northern portion of South America.

"Finally," he concluded, "on the bottom of the tag is a stamp that reads 'MaHoud Enterprises'." The way Edgemont pronounced it, MaHoud came out as Maud.

"Maud?" asked Jeff. "What's a Maud?"

"In English it would be more like Ma Hood," responded Edgemont.

"Hood?" asked Jeff, like a parrot that could only repeat single words. He looked at Paul.

"Maybe their name really is MaHoud or some such," said Paul.

"Who's name?" asked Edgemont, confused.

"We'll tell you later," said Jeff.

"Mind if I copy these files?" Edgemont asked.

Jeff waved a hand in approval.

Something rankled at Jeff. Changing the subject, he asked, "Doctor, do you know anything about Tunisia?"

"Oh, a little. Passed through there once."

"How does a westerner simply pass through a country like Tunisia?" Paul queried, perplexed.

"I served with the U.S. State Department once upon a time in French Morocco because I speak both French and Arabic. They sent me all around trying to be the good American."

"That makes sense," said Jeff.

"Not really. A buddy of mine was fluent in Mandarin Chinese and the government sent him to Peru. Go figure. Anyway, in that part of the world, I'm not at all certain there is such a thing as a good American."

"How long were you in Tunisia?" Paul asked.

"Only a few days," replied Edgemont, reminiscing. "Stayed in a city called Tozeur, quaint place where tourists hang out and drink homegrown wine."

"Tozeur. Really. Did you happen to read the local newspaper while you were visiting?" Jeff asked.

Edgemont looked puzzled at the question, a definite non sequitur, and replied, "Of course. One way to know another culture is to go to their movies and read the funny papers in their language. You get to understand their image of themselves, which includes their sense of humor."

"I'll try to remember that next time I drive down

to Texas," inserted Paul.

Edgemont laughed out loud. "I'll have to remember that one."

Paul said, "What Jeff is trying to ask is this: Do you recall if their newspapers ran colored ink?"

"Why?" asked the linguist. "That's kind of a funny question."

Time to spill the beans. Jeff leaned forward and said, "Because we believe a recent epidemic that occurred in Tozeur is the same one we are having right here in our own city and in Tucson."

"Hot damn," exclaimed Edgemont. "And you think the ink has something to do with it?"

"We know it does," Jeff fairly bellowed in turn. "The question is, did they use colored or black ink in Tunisia? It doesn't change things here, but it does help us understand a little history of our current problem."

"Let me think," said Edgemont. A moment later he said, "I don't really remember. You got any dates?"

Jeff gave him the dates of the epidemic and explained that the ink may have appeared before the first cases were reported.

Edgemont wrote down the dates. "Tell you what. I'm going to have to shake a few trees to get this information. Why don't you meet me back here in, say," he looked at his watch, "two hours."

Jeff and Paul made the date and left for Jeff's office. They returned to Edgemont at the appointed time.

Tight-faced and deadly serious, Edgemont leaned back in his desk chair. "Well, my friends, from what I hear, you two are legitimate employees of this establishment and I also find that we appear to have a situation. It turns out that a couple of weeks before the epidemic began, the newspaper in Tozeur converted to full-color front pages and inserts, ran that format for several weeks, and then stopped the color before the WHO got involved."

Neither Jeff nor Paul mentioned anything about Gafsa. "Trial run is what we're thinking," said Jeff.

"A definite possibility," agreed Edgemont thoughtfully, "although I hear the culprit is perfume."

"Yes, that's what they're *saying*," Paul threw in.

Earlier on the way over the two men had decided to provide Edgemont with only the essentials. He didn't need to know all they knew.

"There's another problem, and it's a legal one," said Jeff. He explained to Edgemont that no matter what they found, it could be circumstantial as far as who they accused of adding the poison to the ink.

Edgemont listened carefully without comment and remained silent for the better part of a minute. Then he said, "Okay, you've got my attention. Let's not leave out the rest of it."

The men had nothing to lose at this point; their necks and those others close to them were out there flapping in the breeze, waiting for the next gust to blow them far away never to be heard from again.

Jeff said, "All right, sir, based on the timing of

events we've been able to put together, here's the time frame."

After several minutes of explanation, Jeff said, "Perfume is now involved. As far as the newspapers, it takes about two weeks for exposure to the ink for the most sensitive people to begin to react. Perfume is faster acting. When we got our first CD, it was labeled at the ten-day mark, which meant a total of twenty-four days of exposure."

Paul finished the explanation. "By my calculations, within a few more days death will begin on a grand scale. This is not counting the other cities where the epidemic will begin some two weeks later."

"What other cities?" Edgemont asked. ""What are you talking about?"

Jeff concluded as though it were a minor footnote, "Oh, almost forgot, you can add eight more cities to the list of where this contaminated ink is about to be shipped."

Jeff and Paul sat on a bench on the grassy oval in front of the microbiology building after their meeting with Edgemont in the later afternoon. For most people the day was winding down.

Jeff began to feel good physically once more. So good he'd thought about celebrating, but he knew that single act would open the floodgates. What did he preach during college? *You can't study and party both. It's called burning the candle at both ends. Therefore: burn the candle at only one end and party all the time.*

Not anymore. This project would be his new affliction. Frank was right about the evidence and the law. Jeff didn't care. The time had come for him to take chances and fight criminals with criminal acts, not with the law.

Totally resolute and focused, Jeff's pulled out his cell phone and stabbed a button on the speed dial. "Rich, are you busy? Can you meet me and Dr. Anderson here in the quad in a few minutes?"

How could the world be so screwed up and so normal at the same time? Today seemed like a Ray Bradbury story in which are children playing on a swing as a nuclear bomb explodes.

They were fighting an unconventional war now in which one side did all the hitting and the other side did all the receiving. Did that mean it is better to give than to receive?

"God, I want to hurt them, Paul," Jeff declared. The words came out softly and as one, almost as a sigh.

"Not to worry, we will. We have almost reached the solution," said Paul.

Richard sat down between them. Today his Tee-shirt read, "Help Stamp Out Stupid Tee-Shirts."

"I can't decide whether to love you or leave you," stated the graduate student, after examining the expressions on the faces of the two professors. Both men's faces were inscrutable.

"Rich, thanks for getting here so quickly, and thanks for helping us with this project." Jeff didn't try to hide his angst.

"It's not like I have a choice in the matter," responded Richard, now looking a little askance at his major professor.

"Here's what Paul and I have worked up," said Jeff. He presented an outline of a master plan. If it worked, it might win the war.

Richard said, "I could get into a lot of trouble for that."

Paul came to life, dropped his left arm from the back of the bench, and leaned toward Richard. "I know, Rich, and we won't force you to do something illegal," he said, in a manner of a magician forcing a subject to take a certain card. "Try to think of yourself as the only possible one who can save countless adults and children from dying a horrible death."

"Are these the same people who tried to burn down your home, doctor?" Richard inquired.

"We think so," said Paul.

"Yes is the correct answer," responded Jeff sharply.

Richard looked both bemused and mischievous, and his eyes narrowed and twinkled. His face held a "Game on" look. "I'll have to do it from home because my computer has a few features these university computers lack. Uh, and this is an independent project, separate from my degree, right? I mean, no graduate credit?"

"Unfortunately, not on the record," Jeff replied. "Although your doctoral oral exam might not be too rigorous."

"What do you think, Paul?" Jeff asked, leaning forward to speak across Richard's body.

The mathematician stroked his chin in an exaggerated motion. "Let me think about it... yeah, I guess we can keep it between ourselves."

"Okay," said Jeff. "Approved for the project."

Jeff felt no qualms about moving forward at full speed.

What the MaHouds were conducting and perpetrating was unholy and disgusting. These men were spreading evil with the same instrument Americans used for good—their own press. And who knew how many other products they'd poisoned besides the perfume. Doubtless the MaHouds had bought off key personnel in various agencies in charge of monitoring the well-being of the nation. He believed the Saudis were shareholders in one or more important news outlets in the nation and, as much as his good friend Billy Kirk wanted to help, the reporter was hamstrung.

Jeff noticed Richard looking inquiringly at his right hand, the first two knuckles of which were bloodied and beginning to scab over from the fight at the jail. Jeff said, simply, "House cleaning."

Day 24–5:00 a.m.

Paul slid out of bed. Alone tonight, he couldn't sleep. Thoughts of the worsening epidemic filled his mind with frightening images.

He put on a robe over his pajamas, stepped into a pair of slippers, and padded out to the dining room.

He ignored the paper-strewn table and sat at the paper-strewn kitchen counter where he did most of his best work—randomized calculations and doodlings, indistinguishable from one another to a layperson.

He pulled a clean piece of paper from the drawer, along with a sharp pencil, scratched his left armpit, and began to write.

At the top center of the page he wrote, "Riyadh, S.A., MaHoud." He circled the words and drew a vertical line downward a couple of inches where he wrote, "Cayenne, F.G., MaHoud." He circled the words and dropped down three inches below and drew another line to the words "Oklahoma City, Hood." From the latter he drew a final vertical line to the words "Tucson, Hood."

Paul thought for a moment and constructed a starburst of lines around the "Oklahoma City, Hood" designation. At the end of each line he wrote in the name of each city to which the remaining ink totes were soon to be sent.

Paul pulled out a fresh piece of paper and a ruler. Like a draftsman, he drew a three-dimensional picture of a puzzle block of wood that stood in front of him with holes of different sizes drilled through the sides and ends to interconnect inside the block where a single ball bearing was present. All of the holes were plugged save a single exit hole.

He tipped and turned the block. The ball clattered

as the gamer guided it through the passageways and into his hand, but not before he had hit a number of dead ends.

Then Paul referred to the first drawing he'd made of the movement of ink supplies throughout the network of cities. He looked at the drawing of the block of wood. He created a three dimensional picture of his own drawing and rotated it around. What the hell did the ball bearing represent? Product flow? Straight-line movement only. Hard corners. Take out the obvious.

In a few moments, Paul discerned the true center to the puzzle. It wasn't the Hoods and their network, the ink, or the perfume. It was the element of time. Time for distribution of poison to kill. Time for the ball bearing to roll from Riyadh to Cayenne and from Oklahoma City to the other cities, to go through its channels.

By his assessment, there were only days to go, and then the country would be out of time and the ball would come out of the hole. If a single aspect, a single wrong turn of their plan failed, it would all be over. The papers would shift to the new ink almost immediately, or soon after its arrival, and the poisoning would begin. Even if they were shut down within days after receiving the ink, tens of thousands of people could still be affected.

Paul returned to bed and lay awake. Eventually he fell asleep minutes before the alarm clock rudely woke him. Time was still in charge.

Day 24-6:00 a.m.

A multimillionaire with a purpose, one borne of hatred and vengeance, and with latex gloves protecting his fingerprints, Stanley Albert inserted the key card into the outer door's lock. He climbed the stairs to the third floor. Once at his old lab, he put his ear to the door and heard no sounds whatsoever.

Thoughts of Jeff began to take shark-size bites out of him, thoughts of the time they spend together in the lab, Jeff's exactitude in his research, his own personal excellence and concerted efforts in purification, surpassing even those of Shenero.

Albert inserted the card into the lab door's smart-key slot, gently turned the handle, slowly and warily opened the door, and entered. He then closed the door gently and turned on the lights. He took a moment to orient himself and went to work.

Deftly, he opened the incubator, pulled the cotton plugs from the Roux bottles and inverted them. The short, squat bottles were flared at the bottom to create a large surface area for mold to grow in the form of flat matt. The liquid was slated to be extracted for antibiotics or mycotoxins. Today the liquid poured outward into the incubator itself. Albert carried a small pouch containing a stout screwdriver, channel locks, and serrated shears. Silently, he went around to each piece of equipment, jamming, slicing, bending, twisting, and pouring acid. Eight minutes after he had entered the room, Albert walked out.

He casually descended the stairs and left the

building, pocketing the gloves until he found a dumpster behind the building next to his car and threw the gloves and tools into it.

There was nothing like a background check of campus security personnel to find out who might be in financial trouble and who would likely take cash money to get out of it. Two key cards, please, one for the building and one for the lab.

An hour later, Albert read a *People* magazine at Will Rogers World Airport in Oklahoma City and awaited the flight that would return him to Mexico, as he traveled under an assumed name with false identity papers.

Day 24–7:00 a.m.

Parker wanted nothing further to do with the law library for a while and decided to change his study location. His own desk at the lab was the safest place for him to go. Research was not ongoing at the moment so it should serve to be a good place for him to work.

The instant after he opened the door and turned on the lights, he called campus security and then called Jeff.

Security got there first and waited for Jeff to arrive.

The men stood in the doorway to the lab, staring inside. "I see no glass is broken," remarked Parker.

"The guy must not be too bright. If it was me, I

would have poured sulfuric acid, toluene, and acetone onto the floor to foul the air of the entire building. Then hazmat would become involved," said Jeff.

"It looks personal," the security man said.

"Yes, somebody knew what they were doing," Jeff agreed.

At first glance, Jeff calculated the damage to exceed eighty thousand dollars. Months of work could be lost unless he came up with the money to replace the equipment and do so quickly, in part because the best and brightest students of his years of recruiting were soon coming to join him.

Jeff shook his head. *Not satisfied with their first failure, now they destroyed my second home.*

"They would need a card to get in," the security man said. "I'll check and pull the data from outside and inside doors and find out what time they were activated."

Jeff looked at Parker. "How did they know the lab was unoccupied? How did they know how to jack the equipment in the way they did? They had to get into the building first. How did they get the two cards for the building and the lab?"

Day 24–10:00 a.m.

Present in Jeff's off-campus office were himself, Paul, Frank, Richard and Carmen. Parker was teaching one of Jeff's classes until Jeff went back on duty the next day.

Bleary-eyed from lack of sleep, Carmen accepted the invitation. Prior to the meeting she informed them what Jeff already knew—that her car had been stolen earlier in the night and had been found on fire in a vacant field half-way to Wichita, Kansas.

Now in possession of a rental car, she also informed Jeff that Marilyn had called her and wanted to go shopping in the afternoon. She hoped to get Marilyn back on track.

Evidently finished with them, Brewer, it seemed, no longer considered the pair to be a threat. They were also ordered via email to return their travel-free identifications and remaining monies shortly after their return back home from jail, with all receipts pertaining thereto. They decided to hold off on that bit of nonsense. It required to much time-consuming busywork. Hopefully Brewer would have other concerns to distract him from them.

Aside from Parker and Smith, who were not told, the others were cognizant of the fact that Jeff and Paul would soon need to appear before a magistrate. At that time, they would be arraigned on charges ranging from violation of a restraining order, criminal trespass, impersonating federal officials, and conspiracy to commit mayhem. The latter would be a hard sell, according what Frank had told them, because Paul was merely asking questions and the only time anyone had seen Jeff was when they had left him at the warehouse, or later at his car. Still, the pair faced years in prison. It didn't help that Marjorie Reynolds and the DHS had already marked them.

Richard related the story about the Hoods' foster parents' birthplace in Saudi Arabia and the American schooling of Alan and Harry.

"It's not like I stole this information. It's unsecured—unclassified. Second, the Freedom of Information Act permits the public at large to access the information, but you have to know where to look. Therein lies the trick."

Jeff didn't inquire as to where one would have to look or what the trick might be. He trusted Richard's judgment, and trust was a critical component of his persona. He passionately hated disloyalty, sedition, and traitorous acts, and he would never give a second chance to a person who deliberately wronged him, although he would allow for an honest mistake.

"Here's a more interesting part," Richard continued. He tried to be enthusiastic, but his eyes revealed he had spent a sleepless night, as had many there. "The World Health Organization requests all nations to provide a listing of any new antibiotics it produces directed toward antibiotic resistant bacteria, one of the great scourges of mankind. Saudi Arabia complies with the request.

"WHO wants the information because it's been over thirty years since anybody has come up with any new class of antibiotic.A new class is what every needs.

"Apparently, the foster parents have some investments in a pharmaceutical company in Saudi Arabia. When I tracked down the company, it turns out its primary owner is a man by the name of Mohammad MaHoud. He could be the father. When I looked further, it looks like this MaHoud got into pharmaceuticals about four years ago by purchasing a preexisting and completely operational facility.

"This is in Riyadh. He probably paid millions for the complex, which has a number of buildings, according to what I could find on Google and other sources. The problem is, neither he nor any of his enterprises list with WHO any antibiotics he manufacturers. Other companies in Riyadh list theirs, but not his. The firm did list before he bought it. Now his doesn't.

"Why not?" asked Richard, answering his own statement. "Because as far as I can tell, MaHoud's company doesn't produce anything at all, or doesn't report something they do produce."

Richard paged through his notes. "Now, has anyone here heard of Marker General Foods?"

Carmen said, "Aren't they a mega manufacturer and distributor? They own things we wouldn't normally connect them with. I mean, they're huge in Mexico."

"Correct," Richard responded. He reached into his backpack and pulled out a thick folder containing packets of a dozen pages each. He handed them out, keeping one packet for himself. Numerous notes in each of the packets were highlighted in yellow.

Richard explained, "They're into a lot of different products, from dog food to cosmetics to breakfast cereals. They serve every state and numerous countries. Their central warehouse is in Omaha. From there products are sent to regional distribution centers and then to individual states and so on. They have two distribution centers for overseas shipments, one on each coast."

The team thumbed through the pages and noted the list of products made and countries served by Marker General Foods.

Richard was now in his element. "Next question. Anybody heard of MyLady face cream or Brighter-Day toothpaste? They're the leading brands on the market. Both are manufactured and distributed by Marker."

"Sure, I use the toothpaste," said Frank.

"I do, too," said Jeff.

"And I use the face cream," contributed Carmen.

Richard leaned forward and dropped his voice as if, even in a private office, somebody might be listening. "Dr. Shenero, after I went to the newspaper offices, as you suggested, I got some information from Alan Hood's personal computer. I found a lot of email traffic between the Hood computers in Oklahoma City and Malibu, also some emails to and from Riyadh.

"It's all in English. They talk in vague generalities. Unless you know what to look for, which I did, you'd never spot the buzzwords they use. Marker is mentioned, and these two leading brands are specifically mentioned. From what I can gather, somebody added aflatoxin to each of the products, and a quarter million units of each are going to be shipped to

Omaha as soon as the strike is over. But they don't mention the word 'toxin' at any point."

Frank's mind twisted around legalities of every ilk and spoke his legal mind. "Richard, it's circumstantial at best, and it'll get thrown out before it gets to first base. Give me a single example of one email you're talking about."

"Okay," said the computer tech, who found himself in a place he enjoyed, totally fatigued, zoned, and operating at default setting. He leafed through some papers. "This one's from Riyadh. 'We are pleased you have found the ingredients of the cosmetics to be exceptional and authorize their purchase for our people. I am certain they will meet our needs and have every confidence you will succeed in delivering the products safely'."

Frank laughed. "That's it?"

"No, sir, it's not. It sets the stage," said Richard. "If you look at Marker's most recent monthly sales report, you will find their sales reached a half-million units of these items to the Saudi government through a buyer authorized by the Saudis to make the purchase. This is fine unto itself. It happens every day. Basic stuff in business. The problem is they were purchased near the beginning of the epidemic."

"So what?" asked Frank. "You just made my case for me. You've got nothing."

Richard fished out another document, building his case against the lawyer, "This one's from Marker General Foods to Riyadh. 'Dear Sirs: This is to acknowledge your purchase of 250,000 units each of MyLady face cream and Brighter-Day toothpaste. They are designated as batches 071205-85720 and 072831-92361. We look forward to a long and prosperous relationship with your country'.

"So I matched up the batch numbers, and they do correspond with those two products. The return from Riyadh reads like this: 'We are pleased to conclude the sale and know our people will enjoy your products. I am certain they will fulfill our needs and even exceed our expectations. We have every confidence they will all be delivered safely'."

Frank laughed. "What else? So the old man is trying to open up his country to new products?"

Richard said, "Well, sir, to my mind, it merely sets the stage. First of all, Marker has never sold to the Middle East. All their countries of usage are in North America, Europe, some in South America, along with Japan and China and some miscellaneous countries. For whatever reason, they don't sell to the Middle East, all except for Israel, where they buy breakfast cereals from Marker, not face cream or toothpaste."

"You said they sold to the Saudi government," said Frank.

Richard argued, "No, I said they sold to a buyer who *said* he *was* from the government," The record notes the buyer, not the country.

"The third thing is this. Those batch numbers coincide with a delivery scheduled to go to a number of Midwestern cities, including Oklahoma City and Tucson. They also include Denver, Dallas, and a few others where ink is delivered from Mid-Western Soy to the newspapers.

"The fourth thing is this: Alan Hood received a copy of the letter sent to Saudi Arabia."

"The guy left it on his computer?" asked Paul.

"Yes and no. I got it from his deleted file," Richard replied.

"What else did you find in his deleted file?" asked Paul.

"Don't know. That was the last thing I checked. I ran out of time. Since it matched with what else I'd found, I decided to put this package together for this meeting. My guess is there's a lot more there I didn't get to."

Frank inquired, "How did you find out where the batches are scheduled to go to?"

"Public records. It's simple. I can tell you what to look for and go to their web site. Dig a little, all legit, of course, and it'll tell you. To the uninitiated, it looks totally clean.

"Anyway, if you go to the Marker accounting department, there are no clear sales to any country other than to their usual list. Definitely none to Saudi Arabia. So why is Saudi Arabia acknowledging the purchase?"

"You're saying nobody bought the products?" asked Jeff.

"No, I'm saying there is no record of a direct sale I can find," responded Richard.

"Which suggests they were paid for in another way," entered Paul.

Richard continued, "One thing they could do is to sell in bulk to another company at a discounted price, a normal business procedure. The other player puts his off-brand name on it and sells it for less: same product, lower price. If the Hoods wanted to poison the stuff in bulk they would have purchased it in bulk. But they didn't. Instead, they bought actual individual units, a half million of them."

"Which tells us the products were poisoned before they were packaged or bottled," Jeff concluded.

"Exactly," said Richard.

"Or they're not poisoned at all," added Frank.

Paul looked at Frank. "Stop being the devil's advocate. You're suggesting the least likely probability based on the broad picture. There are several positive factors, each contributing to a solution, yet you want to negate one of them on wishful thinking. Play the percentages."

Sufficiently humbled, Frank became silent.

Jeff's head moved slowly in an up-and-down motion for several seconds as his eyes lost focus. Finally he said, "Rich, how does Marker keep track of their inventory?"

"It's all electronic, doctor. Each city has a code number, and so do each of the products. The number of units the city is slated to receive is included in the city code for that particular shipment.

"Clever." Paul offered, "If Rich can get into Marker's system, we might be able to do this thing with little further harm to the public, although we would be guilty of a little electronic fraud and violation of a dozen state and federal laws."

Jeff chuckled, "We think alike. Purportedly, the Food and Drug Administration regulates these products. Suppose we create sufficient reason for them to recall this latest batch of toothpaste and face cream. Hopefully, we can point the FDA in the right direction. We need to know under what conditions products like these would be recalled. Paul, I'd like you to help Rich find out."

Frank said, "Not to throw cold water on the happy party, but let's don't forget in less than thirty days, Jeff, you, and Paul must appear in front of the magistrate for local and federal crimes."

"Hey," said Richard, suddenly concerned, "I never heard about any of this."

"Better you don't, Rich," answered Jeff. *Now it's our time to return some favors,* he thought.

DAY 24–1:00 p.m. Oklahoma City

Alan and Harry looked out the window of Alan's office, over eight hundred square feet of luxurious sofas and foot rests, plush carpeting, and redwood paneling. Pictures of merchant ships hung on the walls along with photographs of oil rigs in faraway lands.

Harry's office, down the hall, stood in stark contrast. As impetuous as its master, its walls held expensive cubist art and one massive photograph of the Challenger space shuttle exploding in midair.

The brothers looked out on the remains of the Murrah Building—the building destroyed after the Timothy McVeigh's attack with a truckload of explosives in 1995, killing 168 people, including nineteen children, and injuring another six hundred. The blast was close enough to crack windows of the Hood newspaper headquarters.

Alan once visited the Oklahoma City National Memorial and Museum, situated where the Murrah Building once stood. Entranced, he'd spent over three hours lingering at the hundreds of displays in the self-guided tour. He examined the individually enclosed displays of each of the displays. Each held but a single small item defining the person: a baseball, a car model, a war medal, or a college diploma.

When he left the building, Alan Hood felt uncomfortable. He did not feel the same bravado he felt upon entering the memorial, a bravado tying him to McVeigh like an umbilical cord. Certainly McVeigh had been a man cut from similar cloth, although lacking Alan's class and ingenuity. Instead, Alan felt anger and hurt, knowing the memory of himself would far outlast the memory of McVeigh; that his name would be spoken in disgust forevermore, whether he lived or died. The thought did not give him pride. Instead, he recognized the emotion of shame.

In an instant, he realized the truth about himself. In the absence of his father from the equation, he would never have initiated this plot or any plot. He only wanted to live a normal life, however one defined it. He and his brother might be loved by their father, but they were also his play toys, a distinctly disturbing thought. They were his chattel, his owned property. Neither of them were ever their own men under the man, which caused him to wonder whether Marilyn was her own woman under him?

In addition, he wondered if the pressure had affected his brother's common sense. The man thought big and acted small. The two men he paid to burn down Sherero's house were nearly eaten alive by his dogs and made the local news. If it ever got back to them, they were finished. At the outset, when Alan asked Brewer if he had arranged the debacle, Brewer adamantly denied it. That left Harry as the last remaining suspect.

Alan was about to bring up the subject when Harry said, "We could be home and treated like royalty by now. All we have for our hard work are only two cities affected, and we can't move even a single container of ink."

"Harry, we were lucky to get the ink here in the first place and get it out to our own newspapers. All we were doing is what we always do, nothing different. That's the whole idea. But Father is tired of waiting for the strike to end and wants us to get a lot of large U-Haul-type trucks to carry the ink. He said we don't need flatbeds for this."

"What did you tell him?" inquired Harry.

"The truth. He should have told us to get the trucks right away and it would all be over. He said everybody kept telling him the strike would be over in a week, and then another week dragged by, and here we are nearly a month later and the papers are getting low on ink.

"Then I told him there isn't a U-Haul or any truck like that in the country available right now, because everything in the country has to be transported and ink is not a priority. Then he told me to use pickup trucks.

"I gave him the same answer and told him an ink tote and pallet won't fit into the bed of a pickup because it's too large, plus they weigh too much."

Harry responded, "Sounds like it's on him, not on us. Here's an issue I have with Father. He was wrong by insisting we use only the concentration recommended after Tunisia. He should have used a lot more, not the mid-range stuff that were used between the two cities."

Alan asked, "Did you ever talk to Ochenko or to Albert?"

"No."

"Well, I did," Alan stated flatly. "They told me the highest concentration used was as high as they could go without the toxin coming out of solution. That's why they bracketed the cities—to find a mid-point, based on Father's desires. If they went beyond the highest point, the concentration would be very low, exactly the opposite of what we want, and it could also foul the presses.

"Although things may look a little slow right now, Father believes the mycotoxin will take hold in the general population of our cities very soon, and you will get exactly what you want, little brother.

"Oh, and furthermore, it would take a hell of a lot more mycotoxin to put it into the black ink ...an impossible task, even for our experts."

Harry could not argue with his brother's words.

Alan put his arm around Harry's shoulder. "Look at the good side. Few groceries and pharmacies are receiving food or medications. They're chasing our tainted perfumes, not us. Stores are closing, and break-ins are at a record level. Come on, where else can you get entertainment like this?"

Alan did not feel as sincere as he tried to sound. In fact, his words sounded hollow to him and disconnected from his feelings.

Feeling like dirt, he took the plunge deeper into the dark, consuming waters. "And the secondary effects are a large bonus, Harry. Millions of Americans are complaining of real or imagined illnesses. No big deal. We have it covered. Does it matter? Endless streams of theories are being proposed. We are victorious any way you look at it."

Harry agreed. "True. And we've lost none of our staff, but a number of their family members are ill. I hope the staff doesn't decide to take sick leave or vacation all at once." One of Harry's duties was to supervise the hiring and day-to-day operations of the newspapers.

"How did you deal with it?" asked Alan. "I mean, how did you keep our own workers from getting sick?"

Harry seemed pleased at his own ingenuity. "At

the start of our operation, I informed them that three or four workers were complaining about ink bleeding through onto their hands even though we were using soy and it wasn't supposed to happen—could be a bad batch of ingredients. Therefore, we would supply latex gloves for continual use by every hands-on person in five departments. We're on their side. They're calling us heroes for taking care of them," Harry laughed.

Deep in thought, Alan now ignored his brother as he watched the Oklahoma evening sunlight turn the sky into a flag of ochre and blue stripes.

Harry asked, "Say, Alan, who was that guy going into your office wearing the baseball cap and coveralls carrying a briefcase?"

"Some geek," replied Alan. "He told me they got a call from our Internet server. He said some of the server's big accounts are complaining about their lines being tapped and hacked and whatever, and they wanted to make sure it didn't happen to us, so they sent over a technician to install new software. Before he left, I asked him if our lines were as secure as we ordered, and he said, 'Absolutely, even more so than ever'."

Harry looked at his brother questioningly. "Are you sure he was legitimate?"

"As legitimate as they come, with credentials to prove it—licensed, bonded, indemnified, registered, picture ID, whatever you asked for, the guy showed it. I even called the number on his card and they verified him. Knew his stuff too. Funny thing though.

The guy had this smirk on his face the whole time he was here."

Day 24–2:00 p.m.

Carmen and Marilyn sauntered into Annie's Boutique in downtown Norman. They made a contrast in appearances; the slightly taller and darker Carmen had a complexion of light chocolate without a blemish. She wore a turban, blue in color, with her usual designer jeans and sneakers and short-sleeve turquoise sweater.

In comparison, Marilyn's richly styled light brown shoulder-length hair framed her pale freckled face. She wore an expensive, heart-shaped sapphire pendant on a gold chain and a white pullover silk blouse tucked into cream-colored linen trousers.

Marilyn had called Carmen when she returned from a weekend in Scottsdale with money in her pocket and wanted the two of them to go shopping.

The women wandered around the boutique, talking and laughing together, each holding up items of clothing for the other's approval or disapproval.

"Alan's so secretive, Carmen," Marilyn whispered, "and romantic and incredibly sexy." She gave Carmen a little shove with her elbow.

"I take it he has money?" Carmen's eyes gleamed at the romantic tale. She wanted to hear every detail. She thought of her own relationship with Jeff. He so desperately needed love. She did too.

"He owns a place in Scottsdale, Arizona. He has some business there. We arrived on Thursday and made love half the night. We hadn't seen each other for three whole days. Then on Sunday evening we returned home. I'm so *sore*.

"And you know the beautiful part, Carmen? I feel in my heart he has honestly fallen in love with me, and I'm not being a total romantic."

Carmen's breath caught. Her mind flew off for an instant as she recalled the incredible night when she and Jeff slept at his house and what they did and said. She was definitely uplifted after Jeff examined her breasts and inner thighs for signs of rashes she may have overlooked. Marilyn's voice pulled her out of her lurid memories and fantasies back to the present reality "I can't wait to see him again."

"So that's where you've been disappearing to and weren't here all of yesterday. I told you Dr. Shenero is talking about you losing your scholarship."

"I know. I'll get back to it," Marilyn said lightly.

"When?" Carmen asked. "And if you're trying to get kicked out of the program keep doing what you're doing, girl." Carmen hammered the student, knowing all about losing out on a career. Marilyn appeared to show a momentary concern, but her eyes sparked as she described her first meeting with Alan at The Coffee Bar where she studied.

"He wanted to know all about me. After I told him what there was to tell, he held me in his arms and told me we would make love on his airplane, if I wanted to.

"The wonderful part is that when I told Alan it was time for me to get back to the lab, he completely understood. Actually, as soon as we're finished here, I do have a bunch of stuff to do for Dr. Anderson on the project. I do take a little work with me when we go out, and Alan doesn't mind. He even encourages me to do it. He's so interested in what I do, I tell him everything."

Carmen stared hard at her. "Marilyn, you're not supposed to tell people anything about what we're doing on this project," Carmen admonished.

"I know, but Alan is so different, always courteous, always interested in me as a person and the people I work with." Marilyn held a blouse across her chest and checked herself in the mirror.

"Where does he work?"

"Oh, all over. I think he owns a business in Oklahoma City."

"What kind of business? He's never taken you there?" To Carmen, something didn't ring right.

"World trading in produce and other goods. He promised to show me the business someday. I will admit, though, we did get into a little fight yesterday."

"What about?"

"He told me he couldn't introduce me to his family because they wouldn't understand," Marilyn answered.

"Understand what?"

"I don't know. He didn't say. We'll work it out. No worries."

"What do you actually know about him, his family; his background? Do you even know his last name?" Carmen asked mostly out of genuine interest and partly because Marilyn's story was beginning to unravel quickly.

"Alan Hood, but don't tell anybody I told you," she giggled.

Carmen froze.

"How do you know that's his real name? I mean, you can't be too careful nowadays," Carmen admonished. If fear had a scent, Carmen could smell her own. A cold chill raced through her vitals and her face flushed at the same time.

"Alan believes that honesty is the best policy. If he used a phony name and I found out, it would be like lying to me. He did ask me not to talk about him."

"Dr. Shenero told you not to talk about the project, but you still told Alan, didn't you?" Carmen snapped angrily. "It sounds like you're disloyal to everybody, aren't you, Marilyn? Can anybody trust you with anything? Apparently not."

Carmen became deeply concerned and frightened. This little twit had compromised their work and may have sabotaged their chances of bringing an end to the epidemic. How many more lives would be lost? Jeff despised sedition. When he found out, Marilyn would be gone from the department in two minutes.

"What did you tell him about the lab? What did you tell him about who would be where when? What did you tell him about anything we were doing? What?"

Carmen didn't give Marilyn a chance to answer. She pulled her cell phone from her purse and dialed into the Internet. Using her stylus, she searched for a picture of the owner of the OKC newspapers. At last she showed Marilyn an image. "Is this your lover?"

"Why, yes, yes, it is." Marilyn tried to beam, but Carmen's words had hurt her deeply.

"*Madre de Dios, ayúdame, por favor*," whispered Carmen in prayer. "How about this man standing next to him. Who is he?" Carmen was feeling a cruel streak run through her.

"I saw him once at the airport. I think it's his brother. Why?" Now Marilyn sensed Carmen's concern.

"Marilyn, both men are married with children. You got played." Carmen thrust her sword deeply.

"Married...I mean, how do you know? What are you talking about? Carmen? You're wrong," Marilyn screeched, becoming accusatory in defense of her lover.

Carmen suddenly turned around amid the clothing racks and hurried outdoors, crying over her shoulder, "I've got to make a call."

Marilyn watched her leave, puzzlement clearly showing on the young woman's face. Other patrons in the store glanced their way, as the real-life drama unfolded.

Marilyn replaced the blouse in her hands and followed Carmen outside. Carmen punched a single number into the phone's keypad with a shaking hand. A moment later Marilyn heard her say, "Jeff, it's me. I'm shopping with Marilyn. I and just found out the man's she's been seeing is Alan Hood. He set her up."

Carmen paused to listen, at the same time pulling the phone away from her ear in an attempt to soften the volume. A few seconds later she said, "All right. We're on our way."

Marilyn was speechless and dazed, as if in a dream, listening to the conversation, hearing Jeff yelling from his end. Carmen grabbed her arm and marched her to her rental car parked on the street around the corner.

"What's wrong, Carmen?" Marilyn asked as tears started to form.

"Everything," Carmen answered intensely, bitterly, her lips tight.

As Carmen drove to Jeff's office at the university, Marilyn kept asking questions. She received no replies. Carmen's lips remained pursed the entire drive, her eyes straight again, hands gripping the steering wheel in a choke hold.

Carmen parked in the assigned slot. The two women walked into the building and into the office. Only seven minutes had elapsed since Carmen's phone conversation with the man who employed both herself and the troubled young woman next to her.

Jeff was leaving the school library when the call came. He became so animated during the conversation the he dropped most of the pages he was hold-ing which became randomized on the ground.

It took him some time to get them sorted in prop-er order before he could get to his office. When he did arrive, Marilyn was seated in the armchair sip-ping from a bottle of water, and Carmen stood to her right with her left arm around her shoulder.

Jeff promised himself he would try to take the soft approach. The girl was hurting. He needed her to get back in the classroom. The lab was dead. Does an honest mistake this bad count as a seditious act or does it stand alone worthy of punishment?

Jeff closed the door softly behind him and pulled up a chair to face his student some feet away.

"Marilyn, I know this is difficult for you, but you're among friends who are going to help you get through this. Do you trust us?"

"Yes," Marilyn almost whimpered.

But we sure as hell don't trust you, Jeff wanted to say.

Jeff, stop the paranoia, he admonished himself. He had to fix the problem in front of him.

Jeff nodded to Marilyn. "Okay. For openers, if you told him about our lab schedule, he knew when to destroy it."

"What lab?" Marilyn asked. "Who?"

"Your lab. Our lab."

Jeff forced himself to keep his emotions on a slow burn. As one scientist to another, Jeff told her about the attempted burning of his house, and the destruc-tion of each piece of equipment. He tied the events to the theft of Carmen's car. He understood Marilyn's bond with the lab equipment and its destruction must feel as though she had lost an attachment, perhaps even her first lover, the one who would never say no, the one who would always be there for her. The devastation in her face was obvious. She lost two lovers within minutes of each other.

"The topic never came up."

Marilyn tried to hold back tears.

"Fine." Jeff said softy.

It wasn't, but Jeff went on. "Here's what we know about your boyfriend. He and his family are billionaires. They're from Saudi Arabia. Both brothers are married and have children. We think the family is behind the epidemic. Alan was using you to get information. In plain talk, he stole your life to find out about what we know so his family can continue to sponsor the epidemic. And you told him everything we did and everything we knew, didn't you?"

Tears flowed from Marilyn's eyes. The truth slammed her hard onto the pavement.

Carmen rubbed Marilyn's shoulder. Jeff might have gone further than he needed to but how else could he say it?

"Let's see if we can make this work for us, dear. Try to relax and we'll help you," said Carmen.

Jeff picked up on Carmen's action. He backed off a notch. "Marilyn, if you can remember, we need to know exactly what you told him and what he asked you and dates and times and all the rest."

At Jeff's nod, Carmen got her note pad.

Marilyn appeared to be in shock and answered questions robotically. She struggled to recover and took her time, recalling the best she could, while taking an occasional nervous sip of water.

Jeff asked occasional questions without passing judgment. Inside, he was reeling. He had visions of strangling her. The bastards knew. They knew about Parker in the library and therefore his contact with the WHO, possibly about the lab, definitely about the video conference with Brewer and Whitaker and their bunch and certainly how close they were to figuring it all out. The thought of being infiltrated gave him murderous visions.

"When he contacts you again, act as though everything is okay and see him if he wants to get together. Can you do that?" Jeff asked Marilyn.

"Why?" she queried, with a hint of anger born out of a feeling of deep shame. "I have values, and now that I know about him, well, I don't know how I feel."

Jeff stood and paced to the far end of the office and returned back to the women.

"Marilyn, look, the government shut us down and the university shut us down. Paul and I were ordered off the project and back to our old lives. You're going to be flustered when you see Alan so tell him the truth when he asks you what's bothering you. Tell him the authorities ordered us to stop the investigation and tell him the hammer came down on you. You were told to get back to your schoolwork or leave the department."

"Which is all true," added Carmen, softly.

"One request, Marilyn," Jeff added. "Don't tell him we know about the two of you."

"We need you to do this, Marilyn," implored Carmen.

"If it's all right, I'd like to go home and get out of these clothes. Right now they don't feel too comfortable," Marilyn stated, gathering her face into a steely presentation. "I'll be back soon."

Marilyn stood up and left the office. "Now what?" asked Carmen.

Jeff wanted to tell Edgemont they'd been infiltrated, but he didn't know if he could trust the man.

For that matter, could he even trust what Marilyn had told him? Is it possible the whole thing was a setup by Alan Hood, or that he'd paid her off at the same time when the others were recruited or she could be doubling as an actress? Jeff was starting to wonder if he could even trust himself to make objective decisions anymore.

Day 24–Late afternoon

What a day, Jeff thought. Seeking solace, he sat at the microscope, which was wired into his computer. He tried to get some good photos ready for a lab the next day. It could be another long night.

There was a light knock on the office door, and it opened. Billy walked in.

Jeff looked up to see the newscaster. He quickly

stood to greet his guest. "Billy, I thought you were in Jerusalem."

"It was a short stay. I got back a few hours ago. I haven't got a lot of time," the GNN reporter told him. "Can we talk here?"

"Let's take a ride," Jeff said. His friend looked stressed.

"Back in a while," he said, looking at Carmen and winking, trying to convey a sense of total command. Jeff took Billy out to his Mustang and began driving the streets. "Man, I couldn't get out of my mind what you told me. My problem is with Lewis, my boss at the network. He's steering me away from anything to do with the epidemic other than straight coverage. I'm to do no investigative reporting. Screw it. I need you to catch me up to date with what you guys have found out since the last time we talked. All we're reporting now is about perfumes. How did it go from ink to perfume?"

Jeff drove south along Classen Street and found a place to park near the Lloyd Noble Arena where Jeff had worked security there years before during school to earn extra money. He told Billy the story about their arrests, the samples they'd collected, and what they knew about the Hoods. Then he told him about his meeting with Edgemont, the linguist. He left out the part about Marilyn's unknowing betrayal, considering it irrelevant.

Billy listened quietly then said, "The people who handle the papers where they're printed should be the first to react."

"They wear latex gloves," interjected Jeff.

"Where?"

"Here in the city and also, I presume, in Tucson. Jim Harper in production told me."

"Jim's still there? Good for him," Billy responded.

"Unfortunately, by the time the other cities are involved, it won't matter. No reader in this country will want to touch a newspaper. The print media will come to a halt."

"Billy, at this moment, all the ink is at Mid-Western Soy, but it's only there because of the strike."

Billy thought out loud. "Even when it's over it will take time to line up the vehicles and take more time to transport the totes. Once at the plants, they can be changed out in no time at all. Then the presses will roll.

"Hell, people bring papers along with them and leave them everywhere—planes, trains, buses, benches. We're already seeing the collateral damage and it's huge."

"You're wrong about the trucks. Paul and I saw enough of them at Mid-Western to do the job. Check the Internet. They've offered a lot of money for the drivers. They're already flooded with requests."

Then Jeff told his friend about Big Sky Apartments.

"They're in final negotiations to settle the strike, Jeff."

"What?"

"You keep saying, 'What?' Don't you follow the

news?"

"No. Everybody keeps asking me the same question, but I can't seem to find the time."

"You should, especially when your own career and life are at stake. The truckers' union and federal negotiators are about to come to a settlement. The union is out of money to pay their members anything. A couple of sticking points are how big a truck should be to haul various goods and do part time drivers count the same as full time drivers."

"That plan will cost every consumer a lot of money," said Jeff.

"What do you think it's costing us now?" Billy asked pointedly. Jeff scratched his forehead, "Once all those ink totes go out, we're dead, literally and figuratively."

"What are you going to do, set fire to the warehouse?"

"My skills as an arsonist are a little rusty," confided the mycologist. "I'm thinking there may be a way to stop this epidemic and the Hood family."

"I won't ask," said Billy.

"I won't tell," responded Jeff.

Jeff was out with Billy when Carmen pulled up the City of Tucson Health Department data base to check on the latest status of the disease. Another spike in rashes was reported. This time it had occurred at the Tohono O'odham Indian Nation located in Sells, Arizona, some ninety miles to the southwest of the city.

The Indian Health Services, or HIS, reported fifteen children and two adults were affected. All the children were in the age range of twelve to fourteen years. Severe rashes had occurred on their hands with occasional afflictions on the arms and face.

She called the director of the IHS in Sells and identified herself as Jeff Shenero's office manager and he had been assigned by the government to investigate the disease.

The director had never heard of him and had little information to give, however, he did confirm the outbreak.

Carmen delicately suggested that the outbreak might be associated with bad newspaper ink or perhaps somebody had brought in some fliers from the city, also with bad ink.

She knew it was ridiculous to suggest that the affected children were all reading and handling the Tucson Times in a single class, or had fliers made of colored ink, but she had to ask anyway.

Both were denied.

Carmen then asked the name of the teacher, which the director supplied.

Clearly stumped, she thanked him and hung up the phone. An instant later, Jimmy Cantrell called again and asked to speak with Jeff.

Jeff returned to the office by five o'clock. He dropped off Billy at his car.

Carmen met him and Paul sat at the computer. She had briefed Paul regarding what she had found out about the rashes at the IHS.

"Carmen told me you were out with Billy, so I thought I'd hang around to see what's up," said Paul.

Before Jeff could say anything, Carmen offered, "Jeff, Jimmy Cantrell called about fifteen minutes ago asking for you. I told him you'd be back shortly. He wants you to call him."

Jeff remained silent.

Then she told Jeff about the new outbreak and her conversation with the director of the IHS.

Jeff looked at the clock and asked Carmen, "Why don't you make the call. It's three o'clock there and you might be able to catch him."

Carmen looked at both men. She said, almost imploringly, "Is there no one who can stop this?"

"We've started," responded Jeff. It was almost as if he were a turtle withdrawing into itself, yet a turtle full of determination and conviction, rather than one who sought protection from its enemies.

"Starting is not finishing," Carmen said, philosophically.

"After this, it better be," Jeff responded, tersely. "I've made up my mind what to do." As if that were the end of the conversation.

"And?" said Carmen.

"Well..." Jeff began.

"Well?" returned Carmen, looking at Jeff with her head canted. "You don't want to get innocent little Carmen involved. Am I right?"

Carmen glared at him while Paul waited patiently.

Jeff gave in to a superior force. "All right. Here it is." He explained his plan.

"Ah, a new midstream wrinkle," answered the mathematician. "But can you get where you want to go from here, or can you cut across the boundaries and go right to the heart? Remember, short cuts can frequently result in long cuts."

Carmen looked at her employer. "Jeff, you can't be ninety-nine point nine percent sure about this. You have to be totally one hundred percent positive. Taking a chance is not an option. This is your life."

Jeff's mind was made up. "Oh, I'm certain all right."

Carmen gave a brief shrug, picked up the phone, and placed an emergency call to Senator Evans. She said the necessary buzz words to get a direct line to the senator.

The senator would definitely want to take this call and, Jeff prayed, would want to take charge.

Fifteen minutes later Jeff hung up the phone. It was done. "All right. Now's let's call Cantrell."

Carmen placed the call. She identified herself and asked for Dr. Cantrell. She told him Jeff had returned, then listened and said yes one time. She looked at Jeff and Paul and said, "He's expecting to see you both right now."

"I guess you get the honors of talking with the teacher," Jeff said to Carmen. "We've got bigger fish to fry."

"Nyet," Paul said the Russian word for no. "You and I could be the fish in the frying pan."

Two hours after leaving the office, Jeff finally made it home to his dogs and his sanctuary. His mind was spinning with tactical ideas and game plans seasoned with impatience. He desperately needed a break and called Carmen to see how she was doing.

"How am I? Missing you and feeling pretty scared. Give me a chance to get organized and I'll be there in a little while," she said.

"Oh," she added. "It turns out that our teacher had his kids make papier mache´ figures from shreds of the Sunday colored ink section of the paper."

"It's been a long time since I've played with papier mache´," responded Jeff. "Don't you use paper strips and glue?"

"Yes, it's simple. We used to make pinatas out of it all the time. One way to make forms is to tear newspaper into strips. Then you soak the strips into a mixture of flour and water and hand-mold them into any shape you want or overlay them onto a base form to build it up. It's all hand-work—tearing, soaking, molding, squeezing, patting, shaping.

"The teacher had two lessons. For the first, he would use a lot of Sunday front page newspapers for color. The following week they would use normal black and white newspaper print and to paint the forms afterward. They haven't gotten to the second part."

"What did you tell him about the rashes?" inquired Jeff, who already knew the answer.

"I think the director got to him first. They both

thought the theory was pretty stupid and believed they got a bad batch of flour to make the glue so they were going to get different flour but continue to use the colored ink for a while."

It was so sad. Jeff had trouble facing it all. He fell into a dream world thinking of Carmen's melodic voice. He wanted to spend the rest of his life with this woman, if she'd have him.

But for now their future happiness and destiny lay in the hands of the Hoods, and he needed to divest them both of this scourge.

Day 25–Morning

Alan was doing is best to speed up the timetable based on information he'd gathered from Marilyn. He directed his editors to concentrate even more on the epidemic and its possible spread. He also directed them to use more colored ink in every single edition, in order to attract readership.

"I want you to use as much color as you can," Alan told his people.

"Don't worry about the ink supply. I'll get more," he lied.

Harry said, "Your dating this girl Marilyn was a great strategic move, but why did you tell her your name?"

Alan replied, "If I'd given her another name and she found out the truth, the game would be over. I never wanted to hurt her, only use her. Besides, I enjoy her simplicity and her intellect."

"Don't let Father hear you say that. He'll think you're becoming too westernized."

"Harry, it wasn't Father's idea to recruit her, it was mine."

"But not to fall in love with her," Harry stated sharply.

Before Alan could respond, the phone rang at his desk.

"Mr. Hood? This is Jonas Hodgkins with the Food and Drug Administration. How are you today, sir?"

Alan looked over at his brother and whispered, "FDA." Harry mouthed a large "Who?"

Alan held up his hand and motioned for his brother to pick up the extension phone at a second desk several feet from his own.

"Yes, Mr. Hodgkins, I'm fine. And how might I help you today. I'm afraid I'm on a very tight schedule."

"Your email this morning, Mr. Hood."

"My email?"

"Your email telling us about your source for this information and the trouble with Marker."

"Marker?"

"Sir? You do recall."

"I'm afraid it's been a long night and a long day. Perhaps you could get me up to speed."

"Mr. Hood, you are one of the owners of two Oklahoma City newspapers, and the Tucson newspaper, the *Times*, are you not?"

"Certainly."

"Your email address is ahoodokcpapers@inet. org, is it not?"

"Yes."

"Then you sent me the email."

"What email?" Hood looked at his brother and gave an exaggerated shrug. "And why would I send you an email and not call or send you a fax as well?"

"You tell me."

"I can't."

"Sir, I am talking about your letter in which you stated that a confidential source told you about lead being discovered in Marker General Foods batches 071205-85720 and 072831-92361.

"As soon as I received your report, I called Larry Gentry, president of distribution at Marker, whom we've known for a long time. He looked it up and confirmed the fact that they did have those exact batch numbers, but he knew nothing about any lead or foreign chemicals in any of their ingredients.

"Mr. Gentry was adamant that Marker has avoided the use of lead in any and all of their foods, canned goods, processed or otherwise, or box packages for the past quarter century. Nor do any of their cosmetics or toothpastes, the two product lines to which you are alluding. They moved away from purchasing base materials from China years ago for the same reason. He assured me they haven't changed their formulation one iota in a quarter-century and that they extensively test all their products for heavy metals and other contaminants, and finally, that they would have nothing to gain by compromising their product lines. There are a lot of way of making a profit without resorting to taking a chance by making cheaper products containing contaminants, no less.

"Now do you recall your email about lead, sir?"

"Again I say the answer is no, Mr. Hodgkins."

"False reporting is strongly discouraged by our agency, Mr. Hood. I'm not asking you to reveal the source of your information, only a confirmation of your email and a more detailed statement regarding the information you received."

Alan's voice rose in volume. "I tell you I don't know what you're talking about."

"Mr. Hood, this is a very serious accusation against a very large American-based international corporation. You better believe my investigators will get to the bottom of this. I don't care if you are the press. I'll be in touch."

They heard a soft click as Hodgkins hung up.

The brothers looked at one another, perplexed. They sat back in their desk chairs, and each lit a cigarette, puzzled about the call. Aberrant phone calls were commonplace, even expected at a newspaper office. Many newsworthy events got called in by excited citizens. However, this call definitely exceeded the aberrant.

The brothers were concerned, especially about the foreign chemicals mentioned. Soon, laughingly, they came to the same conclusion. There was no email at all and the call was a prank from somebody who works for, or might have been fired from Marker and who wanted to get even with the company—somebody who knew the batch numbers.

Ten minutes later, when Harry was about to leave, a second call came in.

"Mr. Hood, this is Larry Gentry, president of distribution at Marker General Foods."

"Good afternoon," replied Alan, motioning to Harry to pick up the phone again, rolling his eyes upward and throwing his right hand out at the same time. "How are you today?"

"Not very well, sir. This call is in response to an email letter you sent to Mr. Jonas Hodgkins with the FDA."

"Yes, I received a call from him. There seems to be a mistake."

Gentry ignored him. "At the outset I feel obliged to tell you that you are on speaker phone and my attorneys are present. This phone call is being recorded. Do I have your permission to continue with the recording?"

"Of course," said Alan, now totally confused. His authority had never been challenged before and his father had never prepared him for this.

Gentry launched a frontal attack. "I have a problem, Mr. Hood. I have here a copy of the email you sent Mr. Hodgkins. Apparently, you have a source who claims that two of our latest batches are contaminated with lead and foreign chemicals—to wit, batches 071205-85720 and 072831-92361. I categorically deny those claims and demand to know who gave you that false information."

Alan Hood began to sweat. "Mr. Gentry, you must know we cannot reveal any sources of our information, and in this particular instance, I deny any knowledge of any email sent from my office to a Mr. Hodgkins or to anyone regarding this issue. Somebody is playing games. I might suggest it is somebody from your own company. I do not have any source."

"Did you send this missive from your computer?" asked Gentry.

"Absolutely not."

"Really. Is the email address on this report a generic address or one from your private office?"

"It's totally private, Mr. Gentry. And nobody came into my office to send this letter to you. It is locked at night and nobody comes in during the day without me or my brother being here."

"Let's get into plain talk, Mr. Hood. While the FDA does not have the desire or the manpower to respond to every one of the countless complaints they receive each year, they are obliged to respond to those that emanate from the press, which means you, and those that implicate major corporations, which means me.

"That also means that Marker General Foods is going to be investigated and will have to withhold those two batches from the general market until the FDA is finished with their investigation."

Now Alan became angry. "Excuse me, Mr. Gentry, but I don't know anything about any lead or any batches or what you two gentlemen are talking about."

"You are telling me that you never heard of My-Lady face cream or BrighterDay toothpaste?"

"Certainly I've heard of them. Who hasn't?"

"Those are the two batches of products slated to be distributed nationwide. Because of your letter to Mr. Hodgkins, we have to withhold both batches for an indefinite period of time while the FDA mounts an investigation. It's a terribly complicated and expensive process, both in time and dollars. This whole thing is going to cost us a fortune, and you are going to make national headlines when our lawyers file a suit against your newspapers. Excuse the pun, Mr. Hood, but if necessary, we will rip you to shreds."

"Mr. Gentry, forward a copy of this email to me, would you, please?" said Hood, his voice growing noticeably weak.

"Send you a copy of your own letter?"

"Yes."

Gentry could be heard speaking with hand over the receiver, requesting someone to forward the email to Alan's office.

"It's on its way, Mr. Hood. We'll be in touch sooner rather than later." Gentry broke the connection.

Harry spoke first. "That's our stuff, Alan, the toothpaste and the face cream. What the hell is going on?"

Alan remained silent a moment, then shook his head, totally bewildered.

A chime sounding from his desk computer signaled the arrival of Gentry's letter. The brothers read it together:

To: Jonas Hodgkins
Director of Investigative Services
United States Food and Drug Administration
Dear Mr. Hodgkins:
We have secured certain allegations, in statement and written form, regarding a serious contamination problem at Marker General Foods. The issue centers around batches 071205-85720 and 072831-92361. We have very reliable information regarding the presence of metallic lead in these new production lots and that Marker is doing its best to prevent the public from learning about this. This evidence was provided to us by a person who works closely with both of those products and who wishes to remain anonymous.

As a result of our deep concern, we would like to inform you of this in the hopes that you will take corrective action, if necessary, before this story goes public.

Sincerely, Alan Hood,

President and CEO of Oklahoma City Newspapers, Inc. ahoodokcpapers@inet.org.

"What the crap?" exclaimed Alan. Within seconds his emotions rampaged like those of a jilted lover as they morphed from anger to hatred, to murderous rage and vengeance, to confusion, then to objective logic. Like a dream, Marilyn's head and then her naked body swam into view, followed by the image of his father in California, and his wife and his own grown children, safely ensconced in Europe.

Alan paced the office in silence, trying to piece it all together. He stared out the window at the city and then slowly turned back to stare at his computer. Suddenly his face blushed. At last he gazed at his brother and said, "Shenero."

"Shenero?" said Harry.

"The ball-less professor who clings to us like a human leech," said Alan, not trying to disguise the venom dripping from his mouth.

"So what? It doesn't change a thing. So we have a couple of people pissed off at us."

Only moments before the phone call, a reluctant Alan Hood felt somewhat like a warrior, destined to see death splash across the face of a nation and willing to live with the consequences. Now he felt attacked and defensive, indeed, defenseless. "They're worse than a couple of people, Harry. They're starting to make me crazy."

Harry swung his head very strongly back and forth several times. "Wrong. Listen. First of all, the FDA is going to be looking for lead and other heavy metals. Nobody will ever think of looking for mycotoxins in toothpaste and face cream.

"Marker will file suit against us, which will take a lot of time, except by then the other newspapers will be printing with our ink, and we'll be anywhere else but here. It comes with the territory. In a week the whole thing will be over. The seeds will be planted, and we'll be back with our families. Those pigs will take weeks, even months to do anything."

Alan held up a hand and turned to the computer on his desk. He spoke to himself. "How do we check our email records? Obviously we look at the email *sent* file." He quickly took a seat and punched several keys to pull up the email file records. No record existed of an email being sent from his computer.

"What are you doing?" asked Harry.

Alan grimaced. "I thought maybe if somebody had broken into our offices and sent the email from our computer, there would have to be a record of the time and date this act occurred. But there's nothing there."

Harry spoke forcefully, "Alan, I know what you're thinking. Forget Jeff Shenero. The job's done. The perk is, we've got the FDA and Marker pissed at us. As they say, 'How cool is that'?"

Alan stared at his brother. "Really? How do we know this computer jerk, as I called him, didn't get into our computer like Brewer's man did to this Parker in the library? How do you know the email the FDA received wasn't sent with our email address from some hamburger joint and the guy also found out the product codes while he was at it?

"Here's another one, Harry. What's next in their plan of attack?"

To these questions, Harry had no smart answers.

After Harry left the office, Alan hurriedly picked up the phone and called Marilyn. She did not pick up, so he left a message for her to call him as soon as she could.

Twenty minutes later she called back.

"I miss you a lot too, honey," Marilyn spoke into her cell. She stuck her finger down her throat in a make-believe gagging motion while Jeff and Carmen stood by, smiling encouragingly.

"I can't now," she said. Then she told him what Jeff had instructed her to say about her workload and Jeff being pulled off the investigation. "I don't know what's going on. I've missed a couple of big meetings because I was with you," Marilyn said.

Then she said, "Parker? What kind of question is that?" Then she described his physical appearance.

"Richard? Oh, he's shorter than me and very fat. He's a total brainless nerd, if you ask me," she said as both Jeff and Carmen made gestures to her on how to wrongly describe her coworker without trying to laugh at the same time.

Marilyn was hoping her rage would not show through. The man used her—no, was using her—and in all likelihood, to discard her on a moment's notice. What she really wanted to do was to throw it back on him and tell him both Parker and Richard were great in bed to see what he'd say, but now was definitely not the time for reprisal. Someday she hoped to laugh in his face and point her finger at him and tell him that it was she who had used him all along and had passed along everything she knew about him to Jeff. It would be a lie, of course, a lie with which she could definitely live.

"All right, honey, I'll call you as soon as I can," she concluded and hit the off button.

"Bastard," Marilyn said into the dead phone, hoping like hell he was still listening.

Later in Jeff's private office, Frank pulled out a thick envelope from his jacket pocket. Ignoring Richard, he looked at Jeff, Paul, and Carmen as he slowly and dramatically unfolded a number of pages. He flexed his fingers and hands as though he were a magician showing nothing up his sleeve, "I got served with this document this morning, as the representative of you two gentlemen.

"Let's see," he began, "this is from the office of Iverson and Iverson, Attorneys at Law. They are seeking felony charges against us for willful violation of a restraining order, criminal trespass, impersonating federal officers, intent and conspiracy to defame, theft, and . . . should I go on?"

Without giving the others a chance to answer, Frank continued, "And as for me, I may be charged with co-conspiracy, aiding and abetting, and a number of other crimes. I notice defamation of character is ruled out because they haven't suffered any financial loss.

"We're not even talking about Marker or the FDA deal. We're talking about the warehouse job and the restraining order we received. This sure is turning out to be a fun vacation," Frank concluded.

"How long before we have to appear?" asked Paul.

"There won't be an open spot on the docket for weeks, if not months," answered Frank. "These are criminal and not civil charges. The criminal courts are jammed, what with the crime spree we're seeing as a result of the strike. These include break-ins, frauds, armed robberies, shootings, stabbings, and muggings."

Jeff's mind flew elsewhere. "Marker is a great company with great quality control, as far as I know. They'll be in big trouble for a while, but they should climb out of it, once the truth is told."

"Why didn't we come out and tell the FDA that mycotoxins were in the products instead of beating around the bush?" asked Richard, taken aback by what Frank had said.

Jeff said, "Because we've had experience in that regard. They won't accept the truth, at least not that one. Do you think the guy at Marker got bought off and simply went through the motions—not an unlikely occurrence in this game? This way we have a chance. Hell, man, we're the only ones screaming about mycotoxins. Why? Their claim against us would be because I'm a mold man and you're with me and we're trying to promote my business.

"If our names ever became linked with the letter, we'd be arrested again. This way, somebody else makes the discovery and we're out of the loop."

Frank offered, "You'd better hope your names don't get tossed around because what you did was a crime against a corporate conglomerate with infinite resources and connections. The FBI will probably get called into this, if they haven't been already, which, of course, adds to the list of charges." Here he looked at Richard.

"Why is it federal? I mean, after all, the newspaper is Oklahoma-based," asked Richard, extremely concerned.

Frank regarded Richard as a kid who needed to learn about the world. "For a couple of reasons, Rich. Marker is a multistate and an international operation. Our anonymous complaint was lodged with the FDA. That makes it a federal crime and extremely serious."

Richard's face paled.

Jeff felt compassion for the amateur computer hacker now turned pro. "Do you wish you could take it back, Rich?"

"I asked myself the same question many times, doctor. The answer is the word no. It's time for me to use by skills for good and not for fun.

"At the risk of sounding stupid, why didn't any of us yell and scream about the newspaper problem from the start?" asked Parker.

Jeff responded first. "We did for a while, but they shut us down and refused to listen. So it's not a bad question, Rich. Think positively. If we did scream from the start, we never would have found out about the contamination they put into Marker's products."

Paul said quietly, "The clock is ticking."

"What next, Jeff?" asked Frank.

"Now we have to try to stop the presses," came the determined answer. Rich, I hate to say it, but you're in it 'till the end. Run the name Stanley Albert for me. I saw the man at a presentation I gave in Tucson recently, and the damage to our lab smells like him. See if you can find out where he's been for the past twenty years."

Jeff provided Richard with a description of Albert.

"Any age and middle name?" asked Richard in a tone suggestive of a football pile-on, with him at the bottom.

"Same age as I am," said Jeff. "Forty-three, with a birthday on February sixth, three days earlier than mine. His middle name is Boyce."

Forty-five minutes later Richard returned with the information and read from a paper in his hand. "Stanley Boyce Albert left the University of Oklahoma some twenty-one years ago. He was hired full time by Colson Pharmaceuticals out of Los Angeles. He remained employed by them until about four years ago, applied for a passport, gave them thirty days' notice, and disappeared. End of story. Does that help?"

"Definitely." Then the mycologist handed out a document to each person. "Here's a draft of a letter I prepared to the head of the purchasing department at the *Omaha Mirror*. Subject to modification and your approval, this letter will be faxed forthwith to the appropriate persons at their respective newspapers. The fax number will be bogus, but the phone for return calls will be handled by Frank."

Jeff handed each man a copy and began to read:

Dear Mr. Carter:

As you know, over the years, Mid-Western Soy has strived to provide you with the lowest in prices and the highest-quality ink, even amid rising costs for ink in general and transportation in particular.

In an effort to keep down costs to our clients, we purchased a batch of magenta ink from an overseas market. Enclosed please find a copy of a shipping label from MaHoud Enterprises, Riyadh, Saudi Arabia, for verification—translation included.

In our quality control division, we found the magenta ink did not meet our standards of excellence. Our quality control division discovered that these inks will lead to significant bleed-through in all color used, both in the newspaper itself and from the inserts. The color of the ink could transfer to the fingers and hands of the readers. It could cause serious damage to the presses and cause great economic harm.

Should we ship this ink to you in error, please return it, and your bill will be adjusted accordingly. Do not use it under any circumstances. Although we realize that this is an eleventh-hour request, please feel free to shop for another source for magenta and bill us for your extra charges.

We apologize for this inconvenience, and we will make every attempt to rectify this matter with you at the earliest opportunity.

If you have any questions or need further verification regarding this overnight letter and accompanying email and fax, you may contact me at my new position by calling the following number: 730-555-8777.

Sincerely, Robert McBride

Head of Procurement Hood Enterprises

Xc: Jason Veeder Managing Editor *Omaha Mirror*

"I like it," said Paul. "It's going out straight away, isn't it?"

"Yes, as soon as we get coordinated," replied Jeff.

"Frank, you're manning the phone, right?" Jeff confirmed.

"Right. I'll be ready if anyone wants to talk lawsuits and legalities. I figure I'll only need it for two or three days at the most."

Jeff looked at his friend who had joined ranks with them once Jeff had spoken with him in private and explained in more detail about their findings. These included Edgemont's role and even about Marilyn.

"Do we want to reroute Alan Hood's phone calls in case one of them calls him?" Paul asked.

Jeff thought for a second. "I don't know if they will call. To me the letter speaks for itself. If the FDA or Marker wants to give him more grief, hey, go for it. So, I say leave his phones alone."

"Where are you going to get the Mid-Western Soy letterhead for the faxes?" Paul asked.

"Their web site cooperated and had it posted," Richard said, smiling like a crocodile.

"I transferred it to stationery." He reached into his briefcase and pulled out a sheet of paper with the proper letterhead. Beneath it was the printed the Hoods' fax number.

Jeff passed around the copy of his letter along with the paper with the letterhead to his colleagues and collected them as soon as they were read and inspected.

"Aren't we going to need to overnight a hard copy too?" asked Richard.

"The answer is yes," said Jeff. "This needs to be very official."

Frank asked, "What do we do about the perfume and why our same two cities?"

"Could be it's a distribution problem," said Richard.

"Like it got caught up in the strike mess," inserted Frank.

"Which means it came along with the ink," said Jeff. "To me, if it came in before the ink it would have shipped out to wherever and we'd see it in other cities. If it came in after the ink it wasn't going anywhere."

"Did you see any crates in the warehouse when you were there?" asked Frank.

"Now that you mention it, yes."

"When you ran the analysis did you ever figure out how much toxin was in the perfume?" asked Paul.

"Yes," Jeff responded. "It has the same concentration as the ink."

Carmen added, "Except this time women are touching it and putting it directly behind their ears and on their wrists, two very sensitive areas of the body."

"If we had the data, we'd probably find a sharp uptick in the disease among women," concluded Paul.

Jeff reached in his pocket and pulled out a thumb drive, handing it to Rich.

Rich plugged it into his laptop. Jeff's warehouse pictures came up. Rich found a couple of pictures that did have a number of very large crates stacked against one wall. He turned the computer so the others could see it.

"If the warehouse goes down, so does the mother lode. Let other people figure out where it came from and the chain of command," finished Jeff.

"How do we get it pulled from the shelves?" asked Paul.

Jeff rubbed his head. "We don't. It'll have to hit the news first.

Richard said, "Dr. Shenero, if the government knows about it as you're suggesting, why don't they come in and take over?"

Jeff chuckled. "Because they're government, and by definition they're slow and inefficient and cumbersome. For another thing, they don't have enough evidence. Furthermore, the people who do know about this are corrupt.

"Wait," said Richard. "I got so wrapped up in the other stuff I almost forgot."

Richard reached into his briefcase and pulled out a CD in a plastic case and handed it to Jeff. "When I was in Hood's office, I also bugged his phone. So, early this morning, while I'm doing all this other work, Alan gets on the phone and calls somebody, and they start talking in Arabic, I think."

"And?" asked Frank.

"And I don't know what they were talking about. The guy on the other end had a deep voice, and I only understood the word mycotoxin and something like the word Malibu. I don't know."

"Doesn't mean a thing," said Frank, playing Devil's Advocate. "How many words sound like toxin or Malibu are there in Arabic? Got me there."

"Except it was the other guy who started talking about it," responded Richard.

"That does confirm your email suspicions you mentioned earlier," said Paul, "and this time they did mention the M word."

"It certainly justifies our actions," Paul concluded. "Can I have the CD, Rich?" Jeff asked.

"Sure, it's a copy."

"We may need this as evidence later, but it could lead back to us and to you," Jeff told Richard. It's best to let somebody else deal with it—somebody who has power and can keep their mouths shut. At the same time, we need to find out what this says, and there's only one way to do that," stated Paul.

Jeff looked over at his friend, handed him the

CD, and gave him a slight twitch sideways of the head.

As Paul stood, about to leave, Jeff went over to him and spoke to him for a moment. Paul nodded and left the room, pulling out his cell phone as he did so.

Jeff arched his back, cracked his knuckles, and took his seat again. "Okay, let's get back. Where were we?"

Frank said, "Remember, the emails and faxes claim foreign chemicals are present in certain product batches. It'll take time for these claims to be checked out, but the products will be pulled immediately."

Jeff rubbed his chin. "We need to move fast. The trucks should begin to roll again by tomorrow.

"Rich, when it's time, can you erase any evidence of your computer's involvement in this project?"

"Never fear," responded the computer expert.

Jeff looked distracted, staring out into space. "Rich, can we do this electronically?" he suddenly blurted.

Richard frowned. "It would be a stretch. I'd need more information. You're thinking the newspapers?"

"Yes. If no news copy gets to the presses, nothing gets printed. I mean, nobody types a sheet of paper anymore and walks it over to somebody else. Most of it is done by computer now."

Jeff pulled out his phone and made a call. "Billy, I know this is your private number, but I need to talk with you right away. I'll keep it short. Get ready for a major newsbreak. You're numero uno. First, I need to know how the electronic copy from the reporters' desks gets to the print room. Give me as much detail as you possibly can. Trust me on this."

Jeff waited for several seconds and heard a door open and close. He put his phone on speaker. They all listened until he had told what he new, answered an occasional question by Jeff, and hung up.

The group discussed Billy's input in some detail until the office phone rang.

Carmen picked up and handed the phone to Jeff.

"Shenero here," he said.

"Jeff, this is Matthew Edgemont. I'm wondering if you have a free moment to come over to my office."

"I can make it. What's up?" asked Jeff, choosing his words carefully. He knew Richard could hear him and Carmen was the one who had picked up the phone, so she knew.

"I'm listening to the recording Paul gave me, and I want to discuss it with you," Edgemont responded.

"All right. I'll be over," Jeff said.

"You don't need me?" Richard asked, hoping it wasn't this linguist guy he'd heard about. He didn't want to feel as though he were a bug under analysis.

Jeff said nothing as he walked out the door. He arrived at Edgemont's office within minutes and nodded to the two men.

Edgemont was listening to the recording intently and taking occasional short notes. After several minutes, he closed it out and returned it to its protective case.

Edgemont looked at his guests. "Second time through. Think I've got it down. Now, gentlemen, despite what you may read or may hear or believe you may know about our government's lack of efficiency, once in a while we do know what is going on."

Jeff noted the words "we" but let it slide. *Had Edgemont been listening in on their discussion about government inefficiency?* his paranoid mind suspicioned.

"Might I inquire as to where you obtained this?" Edgemont asked, pronouncing each word succinctly.

"You can ask, but let's take it at face value, shall we?" Jeff responded.

Edgemont held up the CD. "The time stamp I found on this indicates it was made shortly after midnight. Is that correct?"

"Correct," said Jeff, now starting to get edgy.

"May I borrow this?" Edgemont asked.

Jeff was rapidly running short on patience. "Yes is the answer, but what are they saying?" Time to get pushy.

Edgemont looked from one man to another. "It is between this Alan Hood and his father. They are speaking about Malibu and a word you introduced to me, gentlemen: mycotoxin. Even though both are borrowed foreign words, they're pronounced the same, but can be lost in the jumble of Arabic words.

"To the layperson who doesn't know those words, the entire conversation will be meaningless.

You have to have a good ear even to catch a single word, so kudos to whoever recorded this.

"The rest of the recording is veiled, but they're discussing the strike and the non-movement of ink. Alan is telling him that their problems will be over soon enough and not to worry. Everything is under control. The father's words are harsh, but beneath it all he seems to be in a jovial mood and wants to see his sons in Malibu in a couple of days."

Edgemont leaned back in his chair. "Sirs, all of this comports with what you have told me to this point. On the surface there appears to be a boatload of circumstantial evidence.

"Let me know if I can be of further help in any way." Edgemont stood as a signal to abruptly end the conversation. The men shook hands and departed.

Outside, walking along the pathway between buildings, Paul said to Jeff, "Edgemont certainly used a lot of vague words. Not here, not there."

"I don't trust anybody anymore anyhow," said Jeff.

"After Brewer and Whitaker and his bunch, I'm a lot more careful about who I trust, which includes the CDC, FDA, EPA, Homeland, and even Edgemont. The good news is that we got information tying in with what we do know."

Paul asked, "But why wouldn't Edgemont be a good guy? Because he says he is?"

In Jeff's mind, if Alan Hood could seduce Marilyn into providing him with information, then Edgemont could be seducing them for the same thing.

Day 25–Afternoon

After receiving Jeff's phone call, Senator Evans thought about it only a few moments and made his own calls, including Rawlins at CIA, who would call Interpol and put them on standby.

Evans sensed Jeff wasn't telling him all he knew, not because of a lack of trust on Jeff's part, but about trying to protect his friends and coworkers. Evans knew from hard experience that real trust was a commodity tough to find in the world of politics.

Sometime after Jeff returned to his office from his meeting with Edgemont, he received a return call from the senator. Once verified, Evans put Jeff on hold while he contacted the general at Tinker Air Force Base out of Oklahoma City, who, in turn, called a security detail down at one of Norman's airports.

After only a couple of minutes with Jeff on hold, Evans got back to him and told him to get ready to fly to Washington and if there was anybody else who could help he should bring them along. A security team would pick them up at Jeff's private office in ninety minutes. This team would enable them to clear gate security and then enter Tinker where a C-130 cargo plane was scheduled to land shortly for refueling. This plane would take them to Washington.

Before ending the call, Jeff remembered to tell

the senator about Edgemont's translation of the recording.

Evans opted against asking them to take a commercial jetliner and wanted the men to be under the watchful eye of the military at this critical point in time. Now that Evans could see a time frame, he began to make arrangements.

Frank declined the trip, noting that he was not a principal player, nor could he add any real information.

Likewise, Parker only downloaded the WHO report and could offer no revelations.

Marilyn, however, had spent personal time with the accused terrorist, and Jeff let Carmen gently talk her into going before Jeff would be forced to strong-arm her, if it came to it. But from what Carmen had told him, Marilyn wanted every chance to go after Alan Hood.

Jeff also brought along Paul and a very unhappy Richard Smith.

Two hours later the group of four boarded the massive cargo plane. They were loaded in the pressurized cargo hold among crates and pallets and four tied-down jeeps. Taking their seats in the net webbing running across each wall, they were strapped in as they tried to prepare for a ride that would turn out to be long, bumpy, and nauseating. They waited an additional hour before the plane's engines were started.

"Why didn't the senator do a video conference?" asked Marilyn, as the props began to start.

Jeff said, "Because video can be hacked and people could be following us and might attempt to, uh, cause us great harm if we tried to get there on our own."

After takeoff and landing protocol, the relatively slow speed of their plane brought them to touchdown at Dulles International Airport early evening, nearly four hours later.

Once they deplaned, the four were guided into a Chevy Suburban and driven to a hotel where two men remained on duty to keep a watchful eye over them. Only Paul expressed an appetite. He found the restaurant while the others settled in to their respective rooms for the night with Marilyn in her own room.

Day 26–Morning

Awakened early by phone calls the four government guests were ushered down to the breakfast bar.

By 8:30 a.m. the Suburban drove them to an unidentified office complex in the heart of the nation's capital.

All of the visitors carried overnight bags, and the men also carried briefcases. With them were notes, recordings, lab data, the DVD from the video conference, Richard's CD of the Malibu call, laptops, photos from the warehouse, a copy of the shipping label, and all materials they could quickly gather that were relevant to the case. Show and tell time.

Or was it? Jeff wasn't sure. Only the day before he had withheld information from Edgemont.

The team from Norman immediately observed several men and a woman in a large conference room.

"Holy crapoly. This is definitely above my pay grade," Richard mumbled.

Those seated all stood as the group entered, and one man approached them. He introduced himself as Rawlins with the CIA. The others seated represented the Federal Bureau of Investigation, Department of Homeland Security, and the United States Public Health Service. A lone woman stood out against the backdrop of men. She represented the Defense Intelligence Agency that grew out of 9/11.

Jeff briefly evaluated her. She wore a game face. Good. No grunts here. Evans sure knew how to throw a party.

Jeff thought about making one of his famous glib remarks about the various agencies finally working together, but instantly decided to keep his mouth shut for a lot of reasons.

In front of each of the seats around the conference table stood a nameplate. Now everybody knew who they were talking to.

Once Rawlins concluded introductions, the two groups were seated on each side of the conference table. Rawlins informed everyone that proceedings were being recorded. Pitchers of ice water stood in convenient locations.

Jeff deftly pulled out an envelope from his briefcase and began to read a letter it contained.

"This is from our attorney, Frank Bennet. It reads as follows: 'Let me go on record as saying that I'm an attorney representing these persons in your presence along with myself in these matters. We are seeking a signed statement granting immunity from prosecution for any and all issues pertaining to these procedures in exchange for all disclosures on our part'."

Rawlins said, "Sir, I can appreciate your attorney's request. Unfortunately, it is up to the attorney general to grant immunity, not us. What is within our purview is to obtain detailed information from you so we can take prompt action to stop these threats to our country. As for the rest, we will do our best to ensure misfortune does not befall you. Now can we proceed, please?"

Jeff felt as though they were defendants in a trial, and he had sudden misgivings about having called the senator in the first place. For a brief moment, he felt as though they were all defensive linemen trying to stop an onrushing attack.

But nobody proceeded, each deep in his own thoughts.

Rawlins continued in a lighter tone. "Dr. Shenero, Dr. Anderson, we understand you have top-secret security clearance, and indeed, Homeland Security and the Department of Defense hired you both to solve this problem, and your own senator directed you to do so. Therefore, I see no issue here. And as for Mr. Smith and Ms. Woods, these two were enlisted by you to be of assistance in any way possible, were they not? Again, I see no problem whatsoever."

Jeff thought what Rawlins said wasn't exactly true, but it was close enough.

"Does that help?" Rawlins concluded in a more relaxed manner.

Jeff pulled out his wallet and found the security card provided by Brewer in their first meeting and Paul followed suit. The laminated cards were passed to Rawlins as proof of the truth behind his words, and they were then passed around the table. To Jeff's surprise the cards were then returned to them. He and Paul had not yet sent them back to Brewer as a show of obstinacy, if not outright defiance.

Jeff took a breath and began the tale. He and his men explained everything, occasionally being interrupted to clarify a timeline or to give more detail. They spoke of their initial meeting with Whitaker and Brewer—Jeff thought he saw one or two people flinch at the mention of those names—then about the warehouse episode and their arrest.

Paul spoke about statistics and epidemiology. They spoke about Edgemont and the shipping label and his translation of Richard's CD, their suspicions during the conference call, their wiretapping, false letters sent by email to the FDA to stop the distribution of the Marker products, and everything they could think of.

Richard told of his crimes explaining that he had no choice but to try to gather evidence, because nobody in the official world they knew of would take action.

Finally, Marilyn told her tale of being tricked and seduced by Alan Hood. Stalwart in her presentation, she knew she would easily be caught in a lie. She appeared to be more like an angry jilted lover than a hurt child.

After Marilyn told of her brief relationship with Alan Hood and their visits together, Denise asked, gently, "Marilyn, when did you last see Alan?"

"Three nights ago," Marilyn responded.

"Could you tell us what transpired during your last meeting with him?" Denise asked.

Marilyn cast her eyes downward for a long moment then said, "After we made love in a hotel in Norman, he continued to ask me about my work and research and wanted to know about everybody's activities."

"How did you respond to his questions?" asked Denise.

"I got a little annoyed with him. He was always telling me how important I was to him and about his love for me and my parents and my education, but the conversation always came back to what we were finding out about the epidemic.

"So I told him I'm always talking about me and if he loved me so much, then he needed to tell me about him and his family and his own background."

"Go on?" prompted Denise, gently.

"He asked me to keep a secret and I said I would and he said he actually grew up with his foster parents in Oklahoma City and it was his father's brother and his wife who had raised him. Well, him and his own brother. He told me his real mother died and his father lived in Malibu a lot and also spent a lot of time overseas. He didn't say where.

"I told him it was time for me to meet his foster parents and his father, too. He said that might not work out because they're very prejudiced, but he didn't say why."

"Do you know if the people who raised him are still in Oklahoma City," Denise asked.

"As far as I know they are. I overheard him talking with them the other day. He'd said he'd stop by to see them real soon because he needed to leave the country for a while."

"Do you have any idea what they were talking about?" inquired Denise.

"Not really. I did hear the word Malibu."

"Why did you break your promise to him not to tell about his background?" Denise asked, gently.

Marilyn said, a little snidely, "Because this time I did it on purpose."

The other questioners looked at her without comprehending.

Marilyn would not be stopped. "See, right when this all started Dr. Shenero told me not to talk about the project, but I told Alan because he seemed to be so perfect and I was so stupid.

"When I asked Alan how he got his money, he said his parents were rich and I asked him if they were millionaires and he said something like, 'Oh, yeah'.

"That made things come together for me, I mean, him trying to impress me with everything he did. I started to get the idea he was a phony. Then Carmen, that's Dr. Shenero's secretary, told me the truth about him and I fell apart."

"Would you be willing to testify to this in a court of law?" Denise asked.

"Gladly," Marilyn replied, simply.

Jeff stared at this woman who had been screwed, blued, and tattooed and felt a new respect for her resolve.

While Paul and Richard knew little or nothing about Marilyn's tale, they earlier inquired as to the reason for her presence and were briefed by Jeff on the plane as to her part in the situation.

Jeff concluded their presentation by explaining their actions were performed reluctantly, but their personal lives were less important than the nation's welfare and the capture of the Hoods.

Nothing like hanging yourself with your own noose. Jeff tried to paint a picture of them having no choice, no recourse, but to do what they did and the way they did it, because even those who hired them could not be trusted.

As Jeff emphasized his points, notes of anger showed up in the faces of the listeners, try as they might to show no emotion. Jeff's words suggested to them that even they couldn't be trusted.

Jeff tried to look at their presentation through the eyes of Rawlins and the others. Were they larks singing to their own tune? Were they stumblebums who perhaps stumbled onto pay dirt? The number of broken laws he and Paul and his team might be charged with were near uncountable. Even a ridiculous charge might be leveled against Marilyn, if the law chose to do so.

And what cute names would Reynolds come up with when she wrote about them in the press? He could think of a few. Some of them could be quite funny, others demeaning.

A light lunch of sandwiches delivered to the served to sustain the group until dinnertime, while the questioning continued into the afternoon with occasional short breaks.

Nearing the completion of the session, Davis from bioterrorism asked, "Doctor Shenero, our people tell us there is no way to get enough toxin into the ink to cause the damage we are seeing. Could you help us understand how that is possible?"

Every head turned toward Jeff. He found himself back at the beginning. In his memory, he heard Paul speaking to him. "Jeff, theoretically, every problem has a solution. What we have is a conundrum, a mystery, a puzzle. Don't rely on what you know. It could be wrong. You're the one who lectures on false beliefs. Don't presuppose that there is no solution to it; accept the fact there is one. Once you admit that poison is in the ink ... well, sometimes you have to force the solution to a mathematical model to get predicted results, a variation of working backward from the solution to develop a model."

Jeff's eyes lost focus for a moment. Suddenly it

all made sense. A large piece of missing puzzle had hidden itself in plain sight. They hadn't added the crystals directly to the magenta ink. That wouldn't provide a high enough concentration to do what they wanted and would be much less than what his people had found. So they added them to something else and added *that* to the ink.

Jeff smiled as the spark of a realization burst into flame. "Did anyone ever hear of DMSO, or dimethyl sulfoxide?"

Without giving anyone a chance to speak, he continued, "A couple of decades ago the chemical was highly touted in the scientific world not only as a great solvent, but as *the* universal solvent. DMSO is a very simple molecule in liquid form that can absorb almost any crystalline compound to a very high concentration. Years ago I used it in research. You could buy it at a swap meet or your local health food store, crush and dissolve a couple of aspirin tablets into a teaspoonful and paint it onto a sore joint with a cotton swab. Today it's widely used as a horse liniment."

"What happened to it?" asked Davis. "If it's so great, why isn't it in common usage?"

"Usual stuff. Researchers injected animals with ten thousand times the recommended concentration and found various harmful effects. In a way it was like oil of cloves. You could buy it almost anywhere for cheap in tiny bottle with the green oil. If you touched the oil to a bad tooth, the pain would go away instantly. It worked, so it was removed from the marketplace, and the painkilling franchise went to the drug companies. Maybe they were afraid people would abuse it.

"The only way I can see for a very large amount of mycotoxin to get into the ink is to dissolve it in a large amount of DMSO and add that to the ink. Done deal. Then it easily enters the skin."

"How would you test for the presence of this DMSO?" asked Rawlins.

"NMR," answered Jeff, now feeling more confident. He saw confused looks. "Nuclear Magnetic Resonance should do it. Ask your people about it."

After the questioning was completed, the visitors were excused and returned to their hotel where they were to remain on call while the government interrogators discussed the meeting. Then each made a very quick call and drove directly to their place of employment to avoid possible interception of their phone messages.

To their great delight, and especially to Paul's, the hotel dining room featured an Italian dinner buffet along with their regular menu. Paul took a bite of meat ravioli, which rested alongside his chicken Alfredo. A glass of wine rounded out the meal. "I'd love to be a fly on any of those guys' shoulders right now," he offered.

Jeff's plate was also full, as were those of Richard and Marilyn. "Did we leave anything out?" he asked.

In fact, he did leave out something on purpose. It

had nothing to do with Marilyn, but it did have to do with a big favor he owed a close friend on a promise—a woman named Ryan with the WHO.

"Excuse me, but all I can see is us hanging on a hook in the same meat locker." Richard tried to joke, but didn't succeed in making any of the others laugh.

Marilyn recovered enough to thrust in a comment. "Oh, don't be such a drama queen, Richard. I mean, there you go again. You're always thinking of your life and family and future. Doesn't that ever get boring?"

The others laughed at her sarcasm. The group was finally winding down and looked forward to eating themselves into oblivion. They wanted to try to get a good night of sleep and not think of what might happen to them tomorrow or any time beyond the moment.

None of them needed to be concerned. Unknown to the group, who laughed and leisurely ate their dinner, satellites were repositioned, numerous government assets in Europe and the Middle East had been notified, and sophisticated electronic capabilities were directed toward specific targets.

In addition, a call was made to Los Angeles SWAT, and a linguist named Edgemont was separated from his dinner at home by a ringing phone on his secure line.

Day 27–Morning

Three Saudis relaxed in the shade of a spacious gazebo that shielded them from the warm morning Malibu sun. Cloudless skies signaled to the Hood family that all was well and that Allah, Praise be His Name, was one with them. The three raised their glasses in a toast.

"Here's to the project," Mohammad said.

He took a long sip from the large glass of iced tea. One of his regrets was that his two sons had picked up the habit of drinking alcohol after having reached maturity. Both sons were permitting their prayers to lapse in frequency, another indication of Western influence, although Harry had come around nicely after his post–high school high-intensity training sessions overseas. A lot of rough edges needed to be smoothed if he was to fulfill his destiny.

Alan and Harry were loath to tell their father about the problems and the possible failure of the project.

Not given to strong emotion, Mohammad allowed himself a smile. Within a few short days, his master plan, the only real plan of his life, would be fulfilled. Countless Americans would be suffering. The strike was over, the ink was on its way, the cosmetics and perfume were poisoned, and their plane tickets back to their homeland were in his possession.

He'd fought with his sons about their decadence, but he was man enough to admit that it was he who created the basis for it to achieve his own goals. Why did Alan have to fall for that redhead? Wouldn't it be enough to get the information he needed and leave her? They wanted to drink socially to be accepted, yet he himself created their careers and placed that demand upon them. Now they could all return to the true faith. The job was finished. Now was the time to gloat.

Alan Hood turned on his cell phone. "I'd better check in with my personal secretary. We have a business to run." He winked at Harry.

Two servants brought new glasses of iced tea, removed the used glasses, and provided clean napkins.

Alan punched in the number to his office in Oklahoma City.

"Where are you? I've been trying to call you," his secretary said. The woman clearly sounded frantic, her voice plaintive.

His call was made with a light-of-heart attitude. Numerous times his father reassured him that jitters were normal near the climax of any project.

"Mr. Hood, we've had calls from the Food and Drug Administration, Marker General Foods, attorneys from hell, the Centers for Disease Control, the Consumer Product Safety Commission; all of our newspaper-ink accounts have cancelled, and two men from the FBI are here along with two people from GNN, with cameras no less!

"Some men are going through your desk and Harry's desk and packing up your computers and files. What's going on?"

As Alan listened, a sickly feeling overcame him.

He blanched and adrenaline pumped into his veins. Suddenly he had to pee.

"Oh, nothing I can't handle. Obviously they've made a mistake. I'll clear it up and call you back." Alan closed the cell phone.

Harry and their father looked at Alan with intense curiosity. Alan repeated his secretary's words.

"What is going on?" asked Harry.

"Shenero. That's what's going on," Alan proclaimed. "That pig at the university."

"Shenero?" said Mohammad MaHoud in the deep, sonorous voice he used in authoritative situations.

Then Alan told him about this teacher who had inserted himself into their lives and wouldn't go away and about the email to Hodgins and to Marker, alerting them to the products that were poisoned and their warehouse infiltration by Shenero and Anderson and the ruination of the project and the loss of contracts. For all he knew, Marilyn might have been a piece of bate he had completely swallowed.

Mohammad MaHoud's mind reeled. Was the project to fail at the last minute after all these years, after an insane amount of money and time spent? The payouts, the bribes, the equipment, the buildings, the years and decades—they passed before his eyes in single-file formation. The man's coal-black eyes bore into Alan and penetrated to the depths of Alan's soul.

To Alan, his life was ending badly. He looked at his brother, who could not meet his or his father's eyes because his head was bowed.

Satellite imagery displayed five un-weaponized men inside the pool area and one with a weapon. Imagery also displayed six persons indoors.

A pair of snipers was located on a hillock that rose above the estate. The men had slowly crawled into place hours before dawn. They wore clothing to protect against scrub oak and chaparral that comprised much of the ground cover. If they had crawled during the warmer daylight hours, the threat of running into rattlesnakes or a mountain lion would be very real and could compromise the mission.

The eyes of the spotter and the shooter were on the weaponized man who patrolled the interior of the grounds.

The FBI Counterterrorism Division combined forces with Los Angeles SWAT, who was familiar with the terrain.

They opted against the use of helicopter assault and roped descent. To alert the enemy in this fashion would result in a forewarning of attack along with destruction of precious documents vital to the case.

Law enforcement was briefed that an act of terrorism could occur in numerous other specified cities now that the strike was settled. Absolute simultaneous coordination was required not only of this domain, but of the two cities that contained the headquarters of the newspaper, including offices of *Your Good Dining*. Law enforcement in numerous other cities were instructed to halt any trucks carrying ink supplies to the newspaper and magazine. Within seconds the newspaper offices in Oklahoma City and Tucson would be shut down, and Mid-Western Soy would be invaded. Arrests would be made.

At the order to do so, the sniper took out the weaponized man. Within seconds, vans drove to the home and assault teams rammed the entrances to the front and basement doors.

The assault teams entering the home had their assignments, some to go to the pool area, some upstairs, and some to the main floor. They were to take prisoners if possible and protect the property.

In the sequence of events, another group of agents arrived to enter the household and to search and seize.

As the MaHouds lounged, their first indication that there might be a problem was when their personal security guard's head exploded and he was blown into the pool.

"We're under attack! Get the files," Harry yelled. He arose instantly and ran toward the mansion. The round from the sniper's rifle caught him in the head before he could run four steps.

Armed and vested men swarmed into the compound.

Alan and his father, both in stunned disbelief, followed orders to get on the ground in the water and blood-strewn pool decking.

This they did, and the elder MaHoud yelled that the pigs would pay for this defilement.

Father and son were searched several times over, manacled, half-dragged to the front of the home, and escorted to special vans earmarked for them.

Servants and household staff were collected and loaded into separate vehicles. No other persons of interest could be located.

Soon numerous visitors would find safes resplendent with cash, documents, and records that would incriminate dozens, including United States senators, house members, along with defense department and health department personnel.

Mohammad MaHoud gave one last backward glance at his mansion as authorities manhandled him into the van, manacles cutting into his flesh and his resplendent robe soaked with swimming pool water and the blood and brains of his youngest son.

The elder MaHoud and his remaining son were loaded into separate vehicles to be questioned individually. Nobody expected the old man to talk. The son might be a different story.

Day 27–Afternoon

"This is Billy Kirk with GNN with a special report. I am standing outside a compound in Malibu, California, where this morning FBI agents have arrested Mohammad MaHoud and one of his sons on terrorism charges and use of weapons of mass destruction. Another son was shot and killed while trying to escape.

"Ranked by *Fortune* magazine as the sixth-richest man in the world, MaHoud was handcuffed and led off for interrogation. He and his sons were the masterminds in a plot to create the ongoing epidemic in two of our cities and planned similar biological attacks in several other cities.

"This morning local and federal agents raided the lavish property of the suspected terrorists. They also raided the offices of the newspapers owned by the Hood brothers, their warehouses, and their private homes."

Here footage panned the front of the OKC newspaper building.

"In an exclusive story, and one that will have repercussions for years to come, a tip led federal investigators to MaHoud and his two sons, Alan Hood, born Ali MaHoud, and Harry Hood, born Hari MaHoud." Their pictures were on the screen.

"The Hood brothers own three newspapers, the *Oklahoma Storm* and the *Oklahoma City Mirror* out of Oklahoma City and the *Tucson Times* in Tucson, Arizona. They also supply ink to several other city newspapers and magazines. Reportedly, the family poisoned the ink supply used in their newspapers, which resulted in the illness of thousands of citizens and caused several hundred deaths.

"International authorities are reviewing evidence that emerged. The evidence relates to a similar epidemic that occurred in the country of Tunisia a few years ago. Fingers are being pointed at the president of the country and the Hood family.

"Sources tell us that federal authorities acted in time to save the lives of possibly tens of thousands, with many times that number who might have become poisoned.

"As incredible as it seems, there is speculation that had their plot succeeded, the newspaper industry would have come to a halt in the United States and possibly in other nations around the world because of concern for the ink supply.

"In this gruesome tale of terrorism, the MaHoud family also allegedly poisoned perfume sold in the two cities. They also poisoned toothpaste and facial cream slated to be distributed nationally.

"In the warehouse, authorities seized the ink supplies and over one hundred thousand bottles of perfume destined to be sent to New York City, Chicago, Dallas, Los Angeles, and other large metropolitan areas. A recall was issued for the same products that, reportedly, were poisoned with the toxin.

"Mohammad MaHoud's billions of dollars of assets are being frozen in every country where they can be found, but experts believe that this will barely cover the lawsuits expected to be filed by victims of their plot. There are reports that authorities are gathering volumes of information in countries overseas and collecting a large number of names linked to the MaHoud dynasty.

"When questioned, Alberto Ruiz, the Attorney General of the United States, stated that it is too early in the investigation to seek the death penalty for the MaHouds; however, this outcome is not ruled out.

"Part of this story includes the arrest of Glenn Lewis, one of the primary producers for GNN, this news network, who allegedly received paid a half million dollars to turn the story away from the truth.

"Finally, federal police in Mexico arrested Stanley Boyce Albert at his home in Puerto Vallarta, Mexico, and is being held without bond for questioning for his possible role in the insidious plot. He was identified as a person of interest after an international watch list posted his picture.

"They also took into custody a Russian man found living with Albert. Early reports are that the Russian may be on the list of top-ten terrorists. Working in concert with the FBI, Mexican Federales seized the home of the pair and froze their assets.

"Both men are suspected of manufacturing the poison used in the ink supply.

"Numerous arrests of high-level officials in the United States government are also expected. Many are believed to be unwilling accomplices in the plot, while others associated with the Department of Defense and the Centers for Disease Control are being detained and their bank accounts scrutinized.

"Local authorities along with Interpol are actively investigating other foreign leads that appear to bring them back to Saudi Arabia. We will follow this important story around the clock.

This is Billy Kirk reporting for GNN."

Day 35

Ten days later Richard confronted his mentor at the university commons where Frank, Paul, and Carmen were seated.

Richard returned from the cafeteria carrying an item in each hand. He looked at his mentor's relaxed demeanor and decided to disturb it.

"You owe me a hard drive, Dr. Shenero," Richard stated as he took a bite of his breakfast lead-sinker donut, which he referred to as his daily dose of LSD.

Today Richard's Tee-shirt read, "Oldie and Moldy, but I'm a fun-gi."

"I take it you transferred your personal files before destroying the old hard drive," said Paul.

"Cheerio, spot on," Richard grinned widely at Paul's question. "And RAM too. Ain't nobody going to link us to nothin' from my end. I'm sticking with plain old snail mail for a while."

"That's a little paranoid, isn't it, Rich?" asked Paul.

"You got that right, boss," Richard said in an imitation of Carmen.

"I think you could get a great job going into computer technology," said Paul.

"No thanks. See, hacking is an addiction with me. Microbiology is my passion. I'll stick with that, for the time being, and try not to mesh the two anymore."

Richard continued, "Incidentally, according to the broadcast I saw with Billy Kirk, well, he didn't report it, but, apparently the three newspapers at the root of the disease incurred internal problems of their own. From what I hear, the entire newspaper works through computers and nobody's copy could get from the story desk to the editor or from the editor to the layout section, let alone get to the presses. In the end they had nothing to print."

"Imagine that," said Jeff, looking as serious as he could without losing it.

"How would that work?" asked Carmen. She knew that Jeff had spoken to Billy about it. She didn't know what Billy told him.

Richard took a breath. "Commercial printers manage their hardware using software packages. If one knows how to do it, all a person has to do is to gain access to the software's control panel and shut off the printers, thereby cancelling all print jobs going to the printers, kind of like a home computer. You do this by finding your way into their database management system. If you hit a firewall, you go in the back door. From what I hear, of course."

Jeff turned to his old friend and roommate. "When are you going home, Frank?"

"I'll take off in a couple of days to see my family, then return. I'll stick around for another month or so to assist you boys and girls"—here he looked at Carmen—"with your personal legal troubles.

"I do suspect that our cases will be dropped, seeing as how there are no witnesses willing or able to step forward to testify against us. This includes the big stuff too. It seems Iverson dropped all charges. I thought that was nice of him.

"Then I'm gone 'till you need me again or until I get the desire to come back home to Oklahoma. Besides, the salmon are running, and I want to catch part of the season."

"What about you, Paul?" Jeff asked.

"It's higher math in Cambridge for me starting next month," said Paul. "I'm going on sabbatical. I need true intellectual stimulation. The company I keep has dulled my senses."

"It hasn't dulled your fists, I hear tell." Jeff had trouble believing that the puzzle master had so much hostility caged within him.

Paul clenched his fists and looked down at them. "My fists are like sharp knives. I do need to strop them every few decades to retain their sharpness."

Jeff laughed at his friend's answer. Then he said, "Got to get back to the old grind. Homeland Security and NIH contacted me a couple of days ago. They want me to head the team doing the mycotoxin analysis on the inks they confiscated. And I mean, right now. Apparently, money is no object. Along with testing a few cosmetics. I told them I could do it, although there would be certain conditions. These would include an independent laboratory dedicated to this cause, along with other causes, of course. So it looks like I'll have enough money to be able to recruit and support my incoming graduate students and build and equip my own lab."

Jeff was thrilled at the thought of contacting Deren Bradford, Javier Cruz, and one or two others. And why not? Together with Marilyn Woods, he would have a terrific group of five-star recruits. It would be fun telling them all about the new laboratory that would be their playground, courtesy of the United States government.

"You poor suffering professor. I'm sorry your name is out there," said Paul, about ready to laugh himself into tears.

"Excuse me, sir. I missed the part where you are not getting national attention," retorted Jeff.

"I admit it," Paul responded. "Actually, I gave all the credit to my department chairman and to the university president who supported us all the way."

"As did I. Welcome to the political world," responded Jeff. "How about you, Rich?" Jeff asked. "You haven't said much about your plans."

"I didn't know for sure until yesterday. I got accepted to the University of New Delhi in India to teach and have a good chance to head a research team, thanks to your recommendation. I'll get a solid salary. My wife and I will have a car and driver, maid, cook, nice home, and full medical. Jenn's pretty excited about it. Anyway, she won't let me stay in school anymore beyond my PhD. So forget postdoctoral research.

"In a nutshell, I'm ready to get more than four hours of sleep a night. So once I've completed my oral exams, I'm out of here."

"Somebody must have put in a good word for you," replied Frank.

"Sure wasn't me," said Paul sarcastically.

"Damn well sure it wasn't the MaHouds," smirked Jeff. At that, they all laughed.

"Did you get any love letters from your buddy Manny Bolton over at Big Sky?" Paul asked.

"No, he's too busy pissing away his money on attorneys to get him out of a dozen lawsuits. They can't get him on terrorism because, in reality, he is an innocent victim because he received those fliers he'd placed on order. I am happy to say that his tenants are having a field day reporting their wet and moldy conditions to ears that are finally listening to them. Too bad things had to come to this to make it happen."

Frank said to Jeff, "I've been wondering about something. What made you suspect Stanley Albert?"

"Three things: the purity of the toxin we kept pulling from every sample we tested and the way somebody destroyed the lab. Both are vintage Stanley Albert. His purity was second to none, and I learned a lot from his techniques. The third reason is that I saw him at one of my lectures. I'm sure he wanted me to see him as a tease.

"As for the lab part, whoever did it knew what it would take to destroy equipment quickly and efficiently. That left out the random criminal.

"In addition, after that lab incident, I suspected it might be him and laughingly asked investigators to keep a wary eye out for a toothpick. I mean, I totally said it as a joke.

"Albert never left a trail of toothpicks that I can remember, but he always stuck one in his mouth right between cheek and gums. You could see the end poking out. I didn't really expect them to find one, yet sure enough, they did. He must have lost it in his enthusiasm. After the DNA test proved positive, well ... now the destruction of our lab is the least of Albert's worries.

"Also, I heard the Russian they picked up along with Albert has a long history. They're casting a wide net on this investigation. Billy told me the Federales found a plastic bag with traces of aflatoxin in it at their home along with passports stamped with Saudi visas.

"Carmen also found out we have a security guard who furnished two key cards to a third party days before the break-in. Unfortunately we can't directly link that to Albert. In time I feel confident we will. That guard is facing a litany of charges, ranging from simple misdemeanor to aiding and abetting terrorists. His newest wife is a little upset about it."

"I'm glad to see our hard work wasn't wasted," said Richard, visibly relieved.

"By the way, how's Marilyn?" Richard asked, concernedly, turning toward Carmen.

"I'm hoping she'll be all right. She's scarred, but the stronger for it. You know, time and all. I'll help her through it. I'm going to introduce her to a new watering hole away from Campus Corner. Marilyn's sick of the Big Coffee Bar."

Unfortunately, when one crisis is averted, a vacuum is created, and in a low-pressure system, another storm can be sucked into the void.

Day 65

Carmen picked up the receiver. "It's Senator Evans, boss."

Jeff took the instrument from Carmen's outstretched hand. "I'm here, Senator."

"Jeff, how are you? And how is the new building working out?"

Jeff knew about the availability of the old Jenkins Medical Building located only a few miles from campus, halfway to Lake Thunderbird. The government bought the building in Jeff's name. This included twenty-thousand-square-feet of workspace and parking, several labs and a basement.

"It's absolutely terrific. We can't thank you enough, Senator. Construction and lab setups are ongoing 24/7. Research is already underway." Two months prior he made the move to resign from his full-time teaching position and wanted to devote himself to doing pure research along with operating his consulting firm.

Jeff's vision for the Shenero Institute for Medical Research was to become one of the nation's top laboratories for analysis of foods and products for the presence of toxins. This would make necessary the hiring of many new staff members and bringing in the best graduate student minds.

"Sir, if it's all right with you, my secretary is the only one listening to this conversation."

"Carmen? Yes, of course," Evans replied.

"I want to thank you, Senator, for all that you've done to speed things up." Jeff felt great humility and gratitude to this man and others who helped him reach his goal of starting his own research laboratory as a reward for his role in taking down the Hoods. Jeff gained the students he sought and hired a number of employees. Parker Johnson now taught Jeff's classes and would be name assistant professor of microbiology and medical mycology.

He also asked Carmen to be the second in command of his new research facility and she willingly joined Jeff to assist him any way she could.

The senator continued, "You know, Jimmy Cantrell, your university president, and I went to school together. Jimmy couldn't say enough good things about you."

"I know that's not entirely true, Senator," suspicioned the scientist. Why did he sense a setup might be in progress?

"All right, not entirely," laughed Evans. "Anyway, along with the good wishes, I want to let you know that with elections next week, there's a good chance I'll be reelected. To be perfectly honest, the arrest of one of my competitors for complicity in this plot didn't hurt my chances either. The grand jury is also convening to indict several House members. Our constituents are enraged, and if it smells like a rat, they will crucify it. Can't say I blame them.

"In case you haven't heard the news, Brewer and Whitaker were found guilty of treason, and Marjorie Reynolds has resigned as press correspondent for the NIH. She'll be on Section 8 after our lawyers get through with her. That is, if she ever gets out of prison for conspiracy."

After a moment of heavy silence, the senator said, "Jeff, the harder we look, the deeper this thing gets. This is the worst corruption scandal this nation has ever encountered. It goes back years and covers election fraud, huge payoffs amounting to hundreds of millions dollars, along with the formation of this prepaid executive committee that you are so familiar with. The only thing they did right was to get you and Dr. Anderson involved, as a result of my suggestion."

"Senator, what's going to happen to the Hoods? A slap on the wrist?"

"Still outspoken, are you? No, Jeff. Not this time. I'm seeking the death penalty for the two of them. My guess is they'll get it. We're going on the offensive, Jeff. Worldwide. And part of my platform will be the call for new laws regarding those convicted of terrorism. Those convicted of treason will never see the light of day. It's what our people want. Hell, man, our people are ready to riot nationwide if we don't quit dicking around, excuse my language. The enforcement of tough laws against those bent on destruction of this country has always been my reputation. That's common knowledge, and I'm going to bet that attitude will take me to the White House someday."

"You'd make a fine president, sir," answered Jeff

sincerely.

"And," added the senator, "I was asked to tell you that you guessed right about this DMSO chemical. Our boys found it in the magenta ink."

"Good news aside, I need to talk to you about an important matter. I know your plate is full, but I'm not sure I can trust too many others at this point, not when the wheels are coming off the United States Congress."

"I'm listening." Jeff looked at Carmen and opened his eyes wide as if to say, "Oh boy, here we go."

Carmen put her hand reassuringly on his shoulder.

Senator Evans spoke in no particular hurry. "We froze MaHoud's assets, at least the considerable amount we could find. We have no doubt he has more money buried so deep we'll never find it. People like him always do. Something the public doesn't know is that the documents we seized in his hidden safes suggest that he had plans for one or two more major attacks. So far, we haven't been able to learn anything more."

"What kind of plans?" Jeff gave a strong look of concern to Carmen, who returned the look.

"From what our investigators could figure out, the numbers don't match. I mean, with what Ochenko and Albert told us they had manufactured compared with the amount you and your people calculated was in the ink, perfume, toothpaste, and face cream. In other words, there's poison left over. Our sense is that something else is going on where those two are concerned, and we can't figure out what it is and they swear they don't know.

"While there is the problem with the missing aflatoxin, we've got our own guys who are pretty sharp and who tell us that there is another angle of attack based on the responses of Ochenko and Albert. These guys are holding out for bargaining purposes, we're guessing.

"Alan Hood is a different story. He came to us a couple of days ago and said that he thinks either Tucson or Phoenix may be involved."

A sense of foreboding overtook Jeff. "Sir, where does Phoenix come into the picture? That wasn't one of their ink clients."

Before the senator could answer, Jeff felt almost breathless. His skin began to crawl. "What about the old man himself?"

"MaHoud? He's not telling us anything. All he does is call us a lot of bad names. I will say, though, that he does look a little different now that he's dressed in a prison jumpsuit and in solitary. I hear it took three men to change him out," the senator chuckled.

Jeff smiled then got serious. "What can I do to help, sir? I mean, you've got the resources of the federal government at your fingertips, ready to go to war if necessary."

The senator retorted, "True, but we don't have you. That's what we need, and I'm willing to get you who and what you need to help us figure this thing out before it's too late.

"Alan Hood made a request. He said he had more information to give if he could visit with this Marilyn girl of yours so we're going to need to contact her. Just to let you know."

"Yes, sir, whatever you need we'll be here."

Although Evans was convincing, Jeff's hands were full running the new lab, his business, and trying to actually build a solid relationship with Carmen.

"Senator, can I get back to you on this, say, serve in an advisory capacity."

"Jeff, let's not wait too long, all right? I'll be in contact tomorrow.

"That will be fine, Senator. I'll be here."

"Thank you, doctor. We'll speak then."

Jeff didn't miss the sudden formality in the senator's voice. At that, Senator Evans hung up the phone, and Jeffrey Shenero did the same.

Instantly a monster realization struck him. Jeff believed he knew and understood what the next plan of attack would be. Indeed, there was an insane component to it that transcended, overrode the poisoning itself—a component so horrific that the terrorists themselves might not have considered it in their grand design.

He needed time to work out the details. This had to be part of the next phase of the attack, a new wrinkle no one had thought about.

Jeff began to sweat and chill at the same time thinking about the diabolical sickness of the enemy.

He needed to talk to the senator and for that, he'd have to wait until tomorrow.

Damn right I'm in.

Day 70

Is Marilyn back yet?" asked Jeff as he walked into his new lab.

"As a matter-of-fact, she arrived a couple of hours ago and texted me that she'd be in as soon as she unpacked," Carmen replied.

The office phone rang. Carmen picked up at the same moment Marilyn arrived. She made a short comment, took a note and hung up.

"Okay, talk to us," said Jeff. What else could he say?

Marilyn casually took a seat. To Jeff a completely different person sat in front of them. Why, he couldn't say.

"Well, as you know, a few days ago after Alan told authorities he had more information to give, if he could see me first, they flew me out east to meet with him in a room at his prison."

"How did you feel about that request?" inquired Jeff.

"Shush, let her talk," Carmen reprimanded her employer.

Marilyn continued, "He said that he needed to see me now because he and his father were going to be sent down to Guantanamo Bay.

"I figured the room was bugged, but I really didn't care. I also didn't care that he was manacled chained to the table, and wore an orange jump suit with two guards stationed in the room. I only wanted to hear what he had to say. I would play any game, well, almost any game he wanted to play to get that information, even if it meant holding hands with him.

"He told me he was sorry for what happened and that he would always love me and he missed me, ya da ya da."

Now Carmen couldn't resist. "So what did you tell him?"

"I told him the same thing, although I tried really hard to keep from vomiting."

"Did he tell you this great piece of information?" asked Jeff.

"Yes," Marilyn responded resolutely, "and the authorities told me not to say a word to anyone about what he told me and I'm going to keep that promise."

Jeff asked, "After he told you this great secret what did you tell him?"

"I asked him if he was finished and he said yes so I stood up, let him see me wipe my hands on my jeans to get his stink off of me, spit in his face, and told him he was a bastard who would burn in hell forevermore and the civilized world will delight in watching him burn. His father, too.

"Before you ask, I'll admit that ten percent of what I said was for me. The rest of it was for the poor defenseless innocent people and the babies who had been his victims. My hurt feelings were nothing compared to their suffering. Then I asked the guards to let me out and take me home.

"Now, if you'll excuse me, I have some research to get back to."

At that Marilyn Woods stood and left the office.

PART FOUR

Jeff expected to get a call from the senator any time in the near future. He leaned back in his desk chair in Lab No. 1 of his new institute and closed his eyes. Damn he was tired.

He couldn't stop thinking about what Carmen had told him about how he needed to let go of his divorce before it ate him up. It made him give serious thought about what other people thought about him and the thoughts weren't pleasant. The concerns spread to Carmen herself. He wondered what lay in the future for them. Would he blow up this relationship, as well?

The phone rang and Carmen picked up. She looked over at her boss, head slumped.

"The president wants to talk with you."

"The president of what?" Jeff mumbled. "Cantrell doesn't own me anymore."

"The President of the United States of America. Should I tell him you're too busy to talk and to call back later?"

Jeff bolted upright. The funk had disappeared. He stored it for later usage, something he was accustomed to doing. In his own view of himself, his mental storage locker had reached peak level. He needed to delete a lot of files. How he could do that presented another problem. He reentered reality. "Sorry. Of course, put him through."

Senator Evans was supposed to call again to see if Jeff wanted to take on the project. Now the president wanted to talk with him, the last person he expected to hear from. Somehow Evans must have convinced the man to personally call him.

Jeff heard a couple of clicks on the phone line while a distant female voice confirmed his presence followed by another click and an instant of silence.

"Dr. Shenero, how good of you to take my call. I hate to interrupt you during a busy workday," quipped the president, with amusement in his tone.

Jeff had to laugh at the man's ongoing sense of humor. "Sir, it's an honor to accept your interruptions."

Jeff's dark mood, his frustration—all vanished in an instant as though a drain plug had been pulled and the foulness flowed away from him like so much detritus.

"Doctor, Senator Evans told me he spoke with you a yesterday about our problem."

Without waiting for a response, the president went on, "Remember Ochenko, the Russian, and Albert, your old friend?"

"No friend of mine," Jeff replied.

The president offered, "Politics and world-class bad guys have occupied my time more than I like, and now the issue has recycled. From what I'm told, our people couldn't account for the entire amount of mold toxin the men produced.

"Thanks to your girl there, Marilyn, I believe, we now know that whatever is going on, it will occur either in Tucson or Phoenix. One of those cities is in imminent danger and the attack would involve a large number of people. He thinks it might happen on his father's birthday, which is coming up on August thirty-first.

"How soon can you get organized and leave for the Southwest?"

Jeff thought furiously. August thirty-first was two days away. He had no opportunity to say no or to ask him for his opinion. Basically Jeff had received an order from the man at the top.

"Give me twelve hours," he said into the phone.

"Good. I'll have a Department of Defense agent meet up with you. Which city are you going to?" the president asked.

Jeff said, "Let's start with Tucson. I have a feel for the place and I was there recently."

"All right. The man you meet will be from my personal team, so we can pull heavy strings if we have to. Call the following number in an hour. We'll have your itinerary for you." The president provided the number and the extension.

"If there are no further questions, I'll wish you Godspeed."

The phone line went dead.

Jeff wanted to tell the president what he believed would happen and how it would happen and with what weapon. What if he were wrong? Besides, he didn't need to take up the man's time with scientific technicalities. With Paul now in England he'd have to go it alone.

Jeff walked over to Carmen's desk. He pulled up a chair next to her and gave her a summary of his conversation.

Then he added, "Why either of those cities?"

Carmen contributed, "Maybe Tucson because they owned the paper there and may have some connections. Maybe Phoenix because it's a very large city."

Carmen put her hand on Jeff's arm. "I don't want anything to happen to you. I'm scared for you. And you know what? I'm always scared for you. I need to take good care of myself so I can stay healthy and take better care of you. You're my doctor."

Jeff needed to man up and tell her that it was their time to be together as partners. He mentally kicked himself, willing to take on terrorists, but unwilling to deal with a simple statement of affections for a woman who wanted to love him. "We'll talk when I get back," he replied, tenderly. *Good, a nice safe middle ground statement.*

Once back at his home, Carmen helped Jeff pack. It would be very hot and the eight percent humidity of the desert summer could and would rapidly suck the moisture from a person.

After packing Jeff called the number he had been given and saw he had time for a couple of hours of sleep. At that point Carmen kissed him deeply and excused herself.

On Thursday morning, at 6:10, the Delta jet that left from Oklahoma City touched down at Tucson International.

Upon entering the concourse, a neatly groomed man approached Jeff. He wore a tailored blue suit over a fit body. He was of middle age with a youthful face and short light brown hair, a man who radiated poise and confidence and who must have shown credentials to get through security. He stood at five-foot-ten, an inch shorter than the scientist.

Jeff's face was no secret, certainly not to the professional who greeted him and stuck out his hand. "Dr. Shenero, I'm Brett Overton. I believe the president mentioned to you that I would be here."

"Nothing personal, sir, but I need to see some proof of that statement," Jeff replied, never in a mood to play games with imposters or impersonators.

"As you please, sir." His visitor produced FBI credentials, Secret Service credentials, a presidential envoy card, a badge on his belt, and a sidearm, which he revealed with discretion.

"My pleasure to make your acquaintance, Mr. Overton. You can call me Jeff."

"And you can call me Brett."

"It's a long flight from Washington," stated Jeff as the men descended to the lower level to the baggage carousel.

"I took a faster plane than you did and actually got here an hour ago. I did manage to get a little sleep on the flight," responded the agent.

Jeff made a quick call to Carmen to let her know of his safe arrival and with carry-on in tow, Jeff went with Brett to baggage claim and picked up a suitcase.

"Got mine earlier," said Brett in response to Jeff's unasked question.

Jeff followed the agent to the car parked in the lot and said, "Why don't you let me drive. I know my way around a little."

Jeff paid the parking fee as they exited the lot. Then he asked, "How's your mycology, Brett?"

Brett said, "A police science major in college takes basic biology and not much more than core courses after the first two years. However, I am up on my terrorist plots, which includes following your adventures."

Jeff laughed at his new friend's statement. The man was what he expected: trim, sharp, and witty. He gave off good vibes. The man could use a little outdoor time to get some color, though.

What a difference between this man and Brewer, destined to spend eternity in prison without any of the money he thought well hidden.

Jeff said, "I've made reservations at the Sheraton Four Points. It's fairly centrally located for our needs."

"Which are?" Brett inquired.

"Not much driving and great Mexican food," Jeff told him. "Next question. How's your knowledge of aerosols?"

"Hairspray or otherwise?"

"Otherwise."

"Not much," replied Brett.

Jeff explained, "When mold grows on something, it sends runners called mycelium into the food source for nutrition like any plant does. Some molds produce antibiotics and some fungal toxins, we call them mycotoxins.

"If it's grown a certain way, say in vats, you can produce a lot of mycelium. The liquid and the mycelium will both have the poison.

"Now, if you freeze dry the pounds of mycelium you might collect over time, you can reduce it to a powder. You now have an aerosol. There would be only one reason to do that in my view.

"Personally, I'd grind the stuff down to a certain size to keep the particles from clumping. If done right, a trillion particles of pure poison will remain a trillion particles."

"I'm impressed," said Brett. A look of deep concern and fear came over the agent's face. "That's some nasty business."

"It gets worse, my friend," prompted Jeff.

"How so?" asked Brett, now staring intently at this scientist he'd read and heard so much about.

Jeff saw the fear in Brett's eyes and his inability to comprehend that things could be worse than what Jeff had presented.

Each time Jeff's mind led him to his conclusions, he became more certain they were right on, and it gave him the cold sweats. "When you look at a pipe it looks flat, right?" Jeff asked.

"Right."

"And when you look at it end on you see it's actually a tube, right?"

"Right."

"Well, mold mycelium looks like that. If you see it under the microscope, it's a thread. If you look at it end on, it's actually tubular and it has segments. Each segment has DNA inside of it. This means that if you mince up the mold and plant it on agar, each of the segments will grow."

"I'm sort of with you. You mean it will grow on something like fruit or bread?" said Brett, not grasping Jeff's point.

"Not just on something, in something," answered Jeff.

"Such as growing into the fruit or bread?"

"No, I mean like growing on human skin and inside lungs," answered Jeff.

"So if I drank it, I'm in trouble," Brett continued.

"Or if enough of it is sprayed into the air to land on your skin or enter your lungs or both," Jeff stated, coldly. Pausing in his narrative, Jeff asked, "Did you bring a laptop?"

"Sure," said Brett.

"So did I. We're going to park ourselves in our room for a while, and we're going to do a little work. Then we'll go to the city waterworks to find out what we can."

"Like any employees they've let go recently, that sort of thing?" responded Brett.

"Right. FYI, no major food manufacturing plants

are in Tucson, and the newspaper here got shut down and may never restart. Cosmetics are out because there is no plant here that distributes only locally. Same with food. I'm thinking that ink is out now, which leaves water and air for anything really big. What do you think?"

"Any sports stadiums?" asked Brett.

"Two that I know of. One is McKale Center, where the basketball team plays, and the other is the football stadium. Both of them are within a half mile of our hotel.

"Anything going on from your end?" Jeff asked.

"Yes, plenty. When I got my directive, I made a couple of calls and found out a lot about the air force base and the defense contractor here separate from the base. The defense facility makes guidance systems for missiles and satellites and half a hundred military items for both incoming and outgoing. You knock down either of those, and this nation will take a big hit.

"You don't simply go online to pull up technicals on either of them, so I asked our own people to pull out the specs. As far as both were concerned, we have a number of people in place so we don't have to do that legwork.

"Now that I know more about what to look for, I'll make more contacts when we get to our room," Brett added.

Jeff maintained serious doubts about people already in place. Brewer and Whitaker were well placed, and so were the senators and congressmen who were paid off in the newspaper scam.

At that moment Jeff pulled into the hotel lot and each man took his luggage to check-in and then to their room where they unpacked and changed into comfortable clothing. They ate a quick breakfast at the hotel restaurant and returned to the room.

Jeff opened up his computer and did some research on Tucson Water while Brett made his calls.

Having finished their work, Jeff said, "Let's see." He punched some numbers into his laptop. "The arena holds about thirteen thousand, and the stadium about fifty thousand."

"The problem with those is that this isn't football or basketball season," said Brett.

"Besides, what can you do in a football stadium with the stuff?" Jeff mumbled.

"A low-flying private plane could drop the powder during a game."

"That isn't our case here," said Jeff. "I suppose you could powder the place when it's unoccupied and wait for the people to come in. That sounds too chancy for these guys. They like a nice clean mass-poisoning job."

Then Jeff said, "Tell you what, in a couple of hours I'll call the city and get us an appointment with the director of water. He should be able to help with some of these issues."

At 11:00 a.m. the two men drove downtown to Tucson Water and met the director. A jovial and portly man, Rich Nordstrom's white baldness was natural compared with Jeff's slightly browned, shaved head. Nordstrom had held the directorship for twenty years and looked forward to helping the men as much as he could. They soon found that he also knew how to run a tight ship.

"Since your call, gentlemen, I asked our people to check the records. In the past year we've lost thirty-seven people—by attrition mostly—and we haven't replaced them, thanks to the economy, which leaves us with around four hundred. I asked one of my staff to print out data on those persons you might want to look at."

Nordstrom continued, "We consider that number a skeleton crew for all the jobs we need to perform to serve the better portion of a million people."

"Such as?" asked Brett. They might have to do background checks on thirty-seven former employees, not to mention the possibility of checking on all of the existing ones.

"Such as ensuring that the water has no coliform bacteria and that it is properly chlorinated, making up tens of thousands of bottles of drinking water for various promotions and sporting events." Nordstrom went on for several minutes listing a score of duties that were necessary to operate a large water supply system for a city.

"Should I go on? How about billings and water meter readings?" Nordstrom was obviously proud of his work.

"What can you tell us about the people who left the last year?" asked Brett.

Nordstrom looked at some papers on his desk.

"Well, some retired, others found better jobs, a couple were fired, a few moved out of state, took maternity leave, that sort of thing. And some we don't have information on their whereabouts."

"How do you have all that information about former employees?" asked Jeff, fascinated with the man's efficiency.

"Because we make an effort to keep up with them. Sometimes we need to gear up in a certain area and have the money to do so. While it's always convenient to transfer somebody over, that takes training and training takes money. Why do that when we can rehire somebody who is local and knows the field? That's worked well over the years."

"Let's talk about your present employees. I mean, do any of them desperately need money?" Brett asked sheepishly.

Nordstrom checked his fingernails. "We all need money, Mr. Overton. And desperation is a relative term."

Brett grinned. "I'll give you that. Here's what I'm getting at. Do any of them need money enough to sell their soul for a very large amount?"

"If they do, it doesn't show on their faces or their actions, as far as I know. They must hide it well," Nordstrom said.

"Those kind usually do," retorted Jeff, now out of his comfort zone. Something about Nordstrom's overbearing presence and sense of security irritated him. He tried to ascribe the feeling to his own problems of insecurity regarding real terrorists who had infiltrated his life. For a moment he felt as though he might be trying to blame Nordstrom for his own weaknesses.

"Tell us about those reservoirs and also about the water bottles," said Jeff.

Nordstrom said, "You mentioned over the phone you were expecting somebody might try to poison the water, and frankly, I don't figure how or where that could happen. See, a good portion of our water supply comes from the CAP, or the Central Arizona Project. We get water from the Colorado River that runs here down a concrete viaduct. Along the way, it picks up a lot of minerals. Those minerals corrode our home pipes. We found that out the hard way. So now we blend CAP water with water from our aquifers. There are millions, if not tens of millions of gallons to deal with and frankly, where somebody might poison the water is beyond me.

"I suppose it might be at the point where we chlorinate the water supply or bottle it. As far as the reservoirs, the water flows in, and it flows out. Theoretically, I guess it's doable. And it is because of that potential problem that we keep tight reins on all those horses."

Neither man liked to hear the words "tight reins" when used in conjunction with terrorism. Their experiences dictated that the bad guys always managed to find a chink, and Nordstrom might be playing the innocent role.

Jeff couldn't get captivated by Nordstrom's enthusiasm, or the prospect of checking out the possible areas where contamination of the city's water system might be initiated. Finally, to display a semblance of interest, he asked, "How many reservoirs do you have?"

"We have six, and there are only a half dozen keys to the fenced yards that house them." Nordstrom stood and pointed to the wall behind him at a laminated map of the greater Tucson metropolitan area. He encircled the areas with the reservoirs using an erasable marker.

"Could you get us a guide who would take us to one or two of them?" Brett requested.

"How about tomorrow morning for that?" agreed Nordstrom. Brett nodded his agreement.

"Also can you give us a list of the employees you let go in the past two years?" asked Jeff.

"Right here." The director handed numerous pages of documents to Overton, who reached out to receive them. "I'm ahead of you," he said.

"Okay, now let's talk about the bottles of water you give out, if you don't mind," said Jeff.

Nordstrom detailed the process of bottling the water from its source distribution to the countless bottles that were supplied to various city-sponsored events.

At last, the two guests stood and prepared to leave.

Jeff suddenly said, "Oh, Mr. Nordstrom, would you know who to contact to get into McKale Center if we want to inspect it?"

"McKale? Sure. But why? The place is under

complete renovation beginning last month and it'll be another month 'till it's finished," replied Nordstrom.

"Thanks," said Jeff. He didn't know whether to have a sinking feeling or to feel relieved.

The two men left the office secure in that they were purview to a lot of new information. Whether or not it had any use was another story.

Once outdoors, Brett asked, "Word has it you were here recently. You didn't know about the arena being renovated?"

Jeff felt chagrined and quickly recovered. "Excuse me, sir. My mission statement at that time was to track down a national terrorist plot, not to keep track of sports venues in the city."

"Apology accepted," returned Brett, smiling.

Jeff laughed. Tragedy and impending doom aside, he began to enjoy himself. At home he would be dragging. He checked his watch. "It's pushing twelve thirty. Let's go out for Mexican and reorganize. How does that sound?"

"Lead on," said Brett enthusiastically. "I'm also thinking that six million gallons per reservoir is equivalent to six hundred backyard swimming pools each. That's a lot of water and too iffy to me. Terrorists don't like 'iffys.'"

"Rumor is, they like to blow things up," said Jeff.

"I heard your sense of humor can be rather droll," said Brett.

Jeff started the car and turned on the air conditioning. Even though they were in a covered parking lot, the temperature on the car dash read 90 degrees.

Jeff pulled up the calculator on his cell phone. "Hang on a sec, Brett. I want to run some conversions. Let's see, fifty pounds is how many micrograms in six million gallons?"

A minute later he looked up and said, "Given that it's evenly mixed, all you need to drink is a half a glass or half a bottle of water to be dead five times over. Aflatoxin is one of the most toxic naturally occurring chemicals known to man."

"Can you test for that little?" asked the agent.

Jeff paused, then said, "Something doesn't feel right and I can't tell you why and yes, I can test for that little.

"Let's look around tomorrow morning anyway. Tonight we can check on the employees."

"Let me make our lives easier," said Brett. "I've got a secure wireless fax with my laptop. Let me fax these documents to my people and have them take care of it. By the time we get back from lunch we'll check and see what they've got."

After Brett faxed the information Nordstrom had given them, Jeff drove the rental car and took them to a restaurant on south Sixth Avenue, laced with Mexican restaurants. He picked one and parked in the lot.

The men were seated and moments later were brought chips and salsa, which Jeff tore into. Brett followed suit and quickly gulped water.

"Consider yourself initiated," laughed Jeff. "Water won't help. Try salt to neutralize the oils in the peppers. I call salsa the Chernobyl hot stuff if it glows in the dark. Then there's the lighter Fukushima salsa and the mild type I call the Three Mile Island. Let's order you some light salsa, unless you want me to ask the waiter to bring you some plain ketchup."

"Moderate will be fine, thank you," responded the agent, a bit defensively, as the top of his head began to sweat.

Jeff called over the waiter and ordered moderate salsa in Spanish.

"Can you tell me more about your last visit here?" Brett prompted, trying to deflect attention from the sweat dripping down his neck.

Jeff took several minutes filling Brett in on most of the details of the MaHoud plots. Then Jeff began to chuckle.

"What's so funny?" asked Brett.

"I don't think I ever told this story to anybody. The short version is that a few years ago in the city I ran into a woman who owned and operated a fishing fleet in Nome, Alaska, where women outdrink the men. She said she came down to visit her sister and got three DUIs in two weeks. At the time I met her she was headed for the courthouse to see the judge.

"I told her 'Get ready to check into the courthouse; just don't plan on checking out. Either that or to take off and go back to Alaska and don't make plans to come back to Oklahoma in this lifetime'."

"What did she do?" asked an intrigued and curious federal agent.

"She offered to buy me a drink if I ever got to Nome. Then she turned around and went back the way she came. One of these days I want to go up to Alaska and see what happened to her. What do you think she should have done?"

"Can't say. It's not my area," said Brett.

After lunch, Brett received information on former water company employees. Jeff looked over his shoulder as the agent scrolled through the data.

"What's that, shorthand? I can't understand most of it."

"Right," responded Brett. "We get in a lot of information in a small space. None of the people we checked on so far has displayed an unusual amount of money or has any overseas connections or long stays in the Middle East."

"If somebody got paid a lot of cash, they might have hidden it from the government for a rainy day," contributed Jeff, not quite willing to let it go.

"You mean hide it from the Internal Revenue Service?" asked Brett in all apparent seriousness.

Jeff narrowed his eyes, dropped his head to a forty-five-degree angle, and raised his eyes to stare at the agent from beneath dark eyebrows as if to say, "You're kidding." Then he broke out in laughter which caused Brett to begin laughing in turn as if it were a surprise that people actually hid money from the IRS.

After a moment, Brett sobered up and said, "Let's get back to our Tucson problem. We'll call Nordstrom and tell him we'd like to check out one or two of the water storage units and also the water bottling plant and see what turns up."

Jeff slipped off his shoes and lay down on the bed, hands behind his head.

"Today's the thirtieth," Brett offered.

Then Jeff looked at his watch and said, "It's two thirty now." He checked his computer. "That makes it twelve thirty in the morning on the thirty-first in Saudi Arabia. They're ten hours ahead."

"Which means it could be happening here right now," responded the agent with a note of urgency in his voice.

Jeff remained silent.

Brett looked long and hard at the man on the bed with the deep scar on his forehead. "It's your call."

Jeff told him his thoughts and Brett made a call. He gave some authentication codes, waited a moment, listened, and then spoke for several minutes.

He made a second call to book a room in downtown Phoenix, satisfied that his instructions to local FBI personnel were clearly understood.

When he phoned the hotel in Phoenix, he received a less than courteous reply by a gum-chewing secretary with apparent nasal congestion. That is, until he identified himself as an FBI agent and a member of the Department of Homeland Security personally assigned by the president, and he would appreciate some assistance. "'To ensure compliance, would you mind providing me with your name?' She stopped chewing gum, apparently having bitten her tongue, and graciously presented her name." Within seconds she had made Brett's reservation for later that same evening.

At least that was how Brett reported it to Jeff.

Jeff could envision the poor woman on the other end of the line. He didn't care how cool Mr. FBI Man appeared on the surface, it must have felt nice to have that much power.

Within the hour, the two men were aboard a Southwest Airlines flight to Phoenix. Both were busy working their laptops, scouring locales where an attack might take place. When they finally landed, they had a fair idea of where to start.

Once in their downtown hotel, Brett removed his jacket, tie, and shoes, and lit up his laptop. He went to his favorites. "We've got a full dozen places where concerts are held, but most of them are outdoors. The new stadium has a roof that opens and closes. Here in the Southwest it's almost always open, I would imagine."

Jeff said, "Which leaves us with the Copper State Arena about two blocks from here. We passed it coming in from the airport. It's got a huge seating capacity of around 19,000."

Jeff's mind calculated. "If you want to mess with an enclosed sports arena, you don't have to worry about wind currents blowing away and diluting your powder. Instead, you've got a place where air is re-circulated.

"Now, you get your phony repair crew to check the air conditioners when the game or whatever is getting started, and you load the fresh-air intakes with powder. While the event is in progress, you have a full three hours to saturate the crowd with your mycotoxin. I would call that a captive audience.

"I'll leave the rest to your imagination because, in all honesty, a part of me doesn't want to know. I will say this ain't no anthrax scare. You can get vaccinated for that. You can get vaccinated for rabies, the bubonic plague, smallpox and diphtheria. You can't get vaccinated for this, either before or afterward. Although you work for our government, you should understand what I am saying. For your edification, did you know we now believe the plague was spread by the human body louse, and not by the rat flea?"

Brett Overton's review of Jeff's profile included the fact that when he mockingly belittled a person, that person should appreciate him. He should consider that as a compliment. Through his own experience, he also understood that his charge would be an impossible man to interrogate, should it come to that, and that the man was totally trustworthy and a patriot in the truest sense.

Jeff stretched and yawned. "My friend, it's been a long day. Let's set it up for the morning, do some more research, have a good dinner and get some sleep. In the morning we'll get over to the arena to see if that one holds any possibility."

At eight thirty the next morning, the two investigators parked in a slot marked "Staff Only" at the venue, climbed up a ramp, and knocked on a set of double doors. In a moment one door opened and two persons wearing hard hats greeted them. Each wore gray work clothes and brown work boots.

Jeff wore his usual brown loafers, khaki slacks and a polo shirt. He wore a sports watch was on his left wrist and carried a small briefcase. Brett chose a short-sleeve shirt and lightweight tan suit for an August desert day that would prove to be very warm.

"I'm Brett Overton, and this is Doctor Shenero. I'm the one who called," said Brett to the larger of the two. The other was a woman.

"I'm Bob Hinton, facilities manager here at Copper State, and this is Janey Swan, my first in command." The group shook hands all around.

Hinton looked fairly fit, although his craggy face suggested years spent on the hard side of life.

Soldier in the field? thought Jeff. Curiously, the man's hands were not as calloused as Jeff might have suspected. He noticed that the man also spoke with the slightest of accents that did not suggest a Southern drawl or an East Coast R depletion. If anything, his Rs were slightly rolled. This suggested a foreign language influence at some point in the man's life, for whatever value that held.

Hinton's partner was a fit woman about fiftyish, whose brunette hair spilled out of her hat. She possessed an all-business set to her jaw yet carried a friendly sparkle in her dark eyes.

Hinton said, "I understand you think we might have a problem of some kind. Do you mind if I see some ID? Sorry. Rules are rules."

Without a word, Brett pulled out several credentials, showed them the badge at his belt, and let his sidearm be seen without being obvious. "I'll vouch for him," he nodded toward Jeff.

Hinton looked over the credentials as if he could recognize a fake presidential seal from a real one "Okay with me."

"Who does the scheduling?" asked Brett.

"Let's go into my office," offered Hinton. "We can be more comfortable talking there. After that I'll give you the tour."

The four walked about a quarter of the way around the upper concourse to an inconspicuous door that Hinton unlocked. He turned on the light.

The office consisted of file cabinets, two desks, and several adjustable desk chairs. A whiteboard hung on one wall, and a detailed colored map of the exterior and interior of the facility hung on another.

Hinton motioned for everyone to be seated while Swan went to one of the file cabinets and pulled a manila folder from a slotted file holder on top of one of the cabinets that held a number of other folders.

She brought the folder to Brett and said, "This is a record of the concerts and various events we've held here for the past couple of months. The upcoming schedules are there too. The upcomings are also listed on the whiteboard."

"How far in advance do you schedule these events?" Brett asked, looking from one to another.

"Sometimes weeks, sometimes months," replied Hinton. "They're either cast in stone because of a contract arrangement, or we pencil them in depending on a lot of factors.

"Last month we had a couple of exhibition basketball games between Russia and the United States, even though it's not the season; also a rock concert, two political lectures, and a tech seminar with some great video."

"The real question is, what's coming up?" Jeff asked.

Hinton pointed to the whiteboard and read the red lettering. "Let's see. Today is Friday, so we've got Branch Hoag tonight, a rock concert tomorrow, and nothing till next weekend when we have a car show."

"Branch Hoag!" exclaimed Jeff, a little more intensely than he intended.

"Yeah, he sure packed 'em in about four months ago during that terrorist thing. Took home better than a half million after paying arena rental fees.

"You remember that terrorist thing, the one run by the Hood brothers? If I remember right, some art dealer guy caught on to them."

Jeff glanced at Brett who smiled.

"What's so funny?" asked Hinton, glancing at Swan and back at Jeff. "You didn't know about Hoag coming here? Don't you read the papers?"

"No," said Jeff.

"And I'm stuck back East with limited exposure," said Brett.

Stuck, as in a member of the president's personal team stationed in the White House.

"Wait, hey, I know you," Hinton declared, looking at Jeff. "You're the guy, aren't you? I thought I knew your name."

Hinton stuck out his hand and Jeff took it. To Jeff, the hand seemed a little clammy.

Swan ignored the banter and returned to business. "Well, we had a full house at his last show, although we didn't have enough security then. Tonight we'll be packed again, this time with a dozen uniformed police, and our entire staff will be working," as though she had been the one who might have dropped the ball on deciding how much security was necessary and didn't intend to let it happen again.

"I thought Hoag was tied to racist rants," said Jeff.

"He is. He's added Muslim stuff to his repertoire," replied Hinton. "Don't worry, we have it covered. And, say, if you gentlemen are in town, why don't you be our guests?"

Hinton turned to Swan. "Janey, see what we've got for VIPs left over down front, would you?"

Swan went back to the file, pulled out a drawer, and flipped through wads of tickets.

Brett said, "We'll take you up on your offer. Can you find us seats, say midway up, if it's all right."

"Got it," she said a moment later as she pulled out a pair of tickets. She walked over to the wall map, where she pointed to the seats they would have. "How about halfway around and midway up?

"That'll be section twelve, seats seventeen and eighteen on the end. That'll give you aisle seats, and you'll be close to the concourse, bathrooms, and concessions."

"Perfect," said Brett. "Now, I take it your physical plant is in the basement," said Brett.

"Yes and no," Hinton quickly responded. "In the basement we have electrical, water, sewage, some fire, cold storage for food, a couple of battery-powered golf carts for hauling, storage for extra chairs, general storage, a couple of forklifts, and a medical office.

"Up here, we have a half dozen food concession stands, another medical office, our office, a meeting room, and more fire control equipment.

"On the roof we have the air conditioners and connections to the air ducts. They go on every afternoon and go off an hour after the concert or the game, depending on our setting for the day.

"Janey, let's take these gentlemen where they need to go," Hinton said to his partner.

"Roof," said Brett.

Hinton walked to the door. "Okay, follow me. There're three ways to get up there, two access ladders and an elevator, unless you want to come in by helicopter, and it hasn't happened yet. The elevator holds only two at a time, and it gets stuck once in a while."

He walked them to where the elevator stood and then led the group past one ladder to a second one.

"This one will be fine," said Brett.

Hinton began the climb followed by Swan, then Brett, followed by Jeff.

When they opened the trap door to push it back, a

wave of hot reflect heat struck them. "When was the last time you serviced these?" asked Brett, squinting somewhat, as they headed toward the nearest of ten air conditioning units. He reached in his pocket and pulled out dark sunglasses. An occasional gust of hot wind caught the four.

Hinton said, "Serviced them? How? The coils are cleaned as needed and the filters are changed every three months according to specs. We get ample fresh air through these louvres, and the air passes into a mixer of recycled air. Then it's all run through a series of steps, which includes pre-filtration, molecular filtration, and HEPA filtration. We're talking surgical room air filtration before the air enters the arena. This facility is state-of-the-art."

Swan added, "Basically, we slow down the cycle when the place is unoccupied, then speed things up before the crowds come in."

They reached the first unit, and Jeff squatted down to look at the intake. "When did you physically open any of these and look inside?"

Swan scratched her head behind her hardhat. "Oh, a couple of months ago when we cleaned the coils.

"We need to look inside them," said Jeff.

"All of them?" asked Hinton.

"Yes, every single one," responded Jeff.

"Okay. This is going to take some time," said Hinton with a twinge of frustration in his voice.

Hinton and Swan consulted their all-purpose tool kits hung on their waists and began to open the units.

Jeff and Brett visited each one of them together. Neither man saw any powder.

"It would help if you told us what you're looking for," said Hinton somewhat impatiently.

Brett stared hard at Hinton. "We're looking for something foreign, anything unusual. Is there any way to introduce, say, perfume into the air conditioning system?"

"Perfume?" Hinton repeated.

"Just an example," said Jeff.

"No," said Hinton definitively. "That is, not unless you do it from the fresh-air intake here."

Swan remained silent.

"We're going to need to secure this roof for the next couple of days and nights," stated Brett in such a manner that it put him in authority over everyone. "And I'm going to need a copy of the files on each of your employees, including yourself, sir."

Hinton shrugged. "Come on down, and I'll give you the files to copy. As for security, we can padlock the hatches and pull the key on the elevator. If you want, we can get campus police to watch the ladders and the elevator. I don't have any more ideas."

Brett said, "We'll cover both days and hit it heavy tonight. We'll have plainclothes people in the audience along with your local police. Let's have a couple of police stand by the two ladders and the elevator to be sure nobody gets to the roof without our knowledge."

"Okay, I'll set it up," said Hinton. "If we're finished with the air conditioners, we'll put them back together again."

Thirty minutes later, with file copies in hand, Brett and Jeff walked the arena by themselves, trying to get a feel for the place.

Finally, by mutual consent, they left the building, and Brett pulled out of the parking slot, having removed a parking ticket from his windshield, to Jeff's great delight.

"I need to fax these off to Washington away from prying eyes, so let's get back to the hotel," suggested Brett.

"Good. I need to think," answered Jeff. The hour approached eleven o'clock.

After Brett completed his work in the room and Jeff made a few calls of his own, the men seated themselves in the hotel dining room and ordered a pot of coffee.

Brett said, "I'm starting to get fixated on this arena thing. Fixation and gut feelings are two separate entities; right now I'm trying to tell the two apart. I can't. They keep merging."

At that, Brett pulled out his phone and made a call. After a short conversation, he hung up.

"The consensus is that water's out. Video camera around the storage units shows no activity except for a maintenance person who only carries a clipboard. Besides, it's not solid enough for me. Water flows in, and it flows out. And they're bottled up for their next couple of activities. To me water is a long shot.

"That leaves out Tucson," said Jeff, "unless your guys come up with something at the base or at the defense contractor."

"Guess we're stuck with Hinton and company," concluded Brett. As if to reinforce his beliefs, they could learn little about the former employees of Tucson Water and nothing from that avenue appeared to offer any leads.

The men spent the remainder of the morning, each in his own world. Brett spent most of his time on the phone, while Jeff made must-do lists for if and when the mycotoxin would be found.

Hoag's program was slated to begin at eight that evening. By two o'clock Jeff changed into blue jeans, polo shirt, and sneakers. He brought a small briefcase. Brett wore a clean white shirt and a casual, smart, lightweight tan suit.

"Better leave your weapon here, Brett. I don't think they allow guns in the arena," Jeff chided.

"Don't tell on me, all right?" The agent and retained firearm.

Brett insisted on driving to the sports arena despite its close proximity. He wanted to have a vehicle ready at hand in case he needed to drive somewhere in a hurry. Once more, he parked in a staff-only slot directly in front of the arena. This time he posted a government tag in the windshield that he pulled from a pocket.

"Forgot to use it last time," he confessed.

The men found their seats in the deathly quiet of the empty arena.

Jeff looked hard around him, scanning. "Something is bothering me, something I saw earlier and I can't figure out what it is."

An instant later, he exclaimed, "I know. Look up there, Brett. What do you see?"

Brett answered, "You mean those large slits?"

"Yes. They're air registers and they're part of the air return system that houses the ductwork. That should be in the mezzanine. Why didn't Hinton tell us where the filters are located? Asking that simple question escaped me when we were looking for the powder on the roof."

"That's the problem with simple things," philosophized Brett.

Jeff said, "Well, let's take a look. Swan should be around here somewhere."

The men got up from their seats and took the broad stairway down to the lower concourse. Swan was on the office phone when they got to Hinton's office. She saw them and hastily hung up the receiver.

"Ticket sales," she said defensively. "What's up?"

The men could see her curly brunette hair was graying at the roots. Jeff wouldn't hold that against her. He was impressed with her personal strength in a job where she worked in a world of men. No rings adorned her fingers.

Brett asked her about the mezzanine.

"No big deal," said Swan. "Let's go."

Fifty feet from the office she opened a steel door with a key on her belt keychain. They ascended a short stairway until they were standing in an area that encircled the arena. Every fifty to seventy-five yards, galvanized steel ductwork could be seen descending from an air conditioner in the roof. These transitioned to horizontal flexduct as they branched into separate ducts and air registers.

Brett inspected an area where a branch began. A fitting connected the vertical to the horizontal shaft. "Open that," he said. He wasn't polite.

"That's where the filters are located," she said. She reached into a case on her belt and pulled out her multipurpose tool. She opened it to a position and used the tool to remove the connecting portion of the ductwork.

"Slowly and very carefully, please," said Jeff.

She removed the two-foot portion of connecting duct. Brett pulled a small powerful penlight from his pants pocket. He peered into the curved ductwork where it ran horizontally from the vertical down shaft to the main horizontal feed.

"My God!" he said and crossed himself.

Jeff looked into the shaft. The filters were gone, and what he saw was not God, but the devil: a two-inch-high and four-inch-wide strip of tan-hued powder.

"It looks like somebody poured the powder from wide-mouth bottles. How seriously demented is this?" Jeff tried to visualize the action.

Swan forced her way next to Jeff and looked at the mound of dust. "What is it?" she asked.

"Where's Bob?" asked Brett.

Hinton? I don't know," she replied.

"Let's open another one," ordered Brett.

One by one the ducts were opened, inspected, and closed. The filters were gone from each of them, and in their place was powder.

"Janey, I need you to listen to me," said Brett.

Swan's instincts told her they were looking at big trouble. "Yes, sir."

"The program is off tonight. We have a terrorist scare. We don't know if it's real or not so we need to take precautions. You are not to say anything about what we have seen to anybody, not now and not tomorrow and not to Hinton if he returns. However, I am asking you for assistance to do exactly what I tell you to do. Can you do that?"

"Yes, sir. I have the campus police and city police on speed dial at my office." Her lower lip began to tremble with fear.

"Hold on until I make a few calls of my own. We'll meet back here in a little while."

"One more thing, Janey," added Jeff, trying for a little personal touch. "When are the air handlers supposed to turn on?"

Swan checked her watch. "It'll be several hours yet."

"Okay. You must make sure they stay turned off. Can you do that too?"

"Will do," she said.

The woman meekly walked to the stairway like a whipped dog.

"I'll be right back," said Brett. He walked outdoors into the heat of the desert air.

"And I'll go with Swan to watch her turn off the equipment. We'll meet you back at the office," returned Jeff.

Several minutes later Brett returned to find Jeff sitting at a desk making notations with Swan at another desk, looking despondent. Ignoring her, Brett asked, "What now, Jeff?"

"Let's go back to the mezzanine so I can run some tests," said the mycologist.

The men returned to the ducts, where Jeff explained, "My guess is they poured this garbage in here with large-mouth bottles, something like fruit punch or sports drink bottles you buy anywhere. The bottles were probably filled from a master container which we may find if we look hard enough. That is what I would do if I was stupid and ignorant. Quite frankly, I don't think whoever did this had enough guidance as to proper procedures and may have inhaled some of it, or gotten it on their skin."

Jeff looked around. He placed his briefcase on an electrical box. From it he unzipped a leather pouch and pulled out a small test tube rack with miniature test tubes. Into each test tube he added a little of the powder he collected with a miniature spatula, holding his breath as he did so.

Jeff took out a vial labeled sulfuric acid and added a few drops to the first test tube. To the second he added a few drops from a vial labeled methyl alcohol. He carefully tapped the tubes at the bottom to ensure the ingredients mixed thoroughly. He pulled out a small clamp and held the first test tube and passed a tiny butane torch back and forth across the bottom. Within seconds the mixture turned bright red.

He repeated the process with the second test tube and dipped a test strip into it, which also turned red.

"How does that work?" asked Brett, fascinated by the process.

"They're basic chemical tests for aflatoxin. They are very specific thanks to technology.

"And yes, it is definitely aflatoxin—B1, the worst of the worst. We have double proof." Jeff capped the test tubes and put the case back together again.

"How's hazmat going to remove the stuff? I can't picture any way for them to do that," said Brett, clearly concerned.

Jeff thought furiously. "Unfortunately, you can't inactivate it with bleach or at five-hundred-degree temperatures. I might have another idea.

"They're not going to remove it. They're going to open the ducts and cover the ends with several layers of heavy gauge polyethylene sheeting, the same kind that's used to set up containment barriers during mold and asbestos removal. Then they're going to secure it with duct tape. After that they're going to cut the duct back about four feet and cap the other end the same way. Then all the duct pieces get hauled out to storage for later analysis and weighing. We'll worry about repairs later.

"Why don't you put me in touch with someone over at hazmat, and I'll tell them what to bring," said Jeff.

Brett did so, and Jeff gave the directives.

"Let's see if there are any more places where they've seeded the toxin," Brett added.

"There's another problem," Jeff continued.

He quit looking at the powder and backed off. If he was going to die, he wanted it to be from basic health problems, which to him would mean a heart attack as a result of running too far or eating too many hamburgers. He made a call back to his lab and spoke with his graduate students and gave them some dimensions of the pile. While he waited he took out his phone and worked the calculator on it.

A return call came within ten minutes. Jeff listened and hung up. "We've got a wide variation in our calculations for a lot of reasons. Our rough guess is that we're missing another five to ten pounds. That's huge. Not counting what we're missing, what I'm seeing right here is a hundred to a thousand-fold overkill."

Brett pulled out a small digital camera from his left front pocket and began photographing a closed and an open duct system and the powder inside. "I'm going to stay here a few minutes and, like, make some calls. Why don't you get together with Swan and I'll meet you in her office."

Jeff got caught by surprise. Brett had let slip the word "like" in a manner similar to that of a teenager. A teenage daughter at home would be a likely suspect to influence a parent's vocabulary. Either that or a soccer mom who picked it up and helped pass it along.

"What stuff is it?" Swan asked, seated upright in a well-worn rollaway chair when Jeff walked in.

"It's a powder-like substance that somebody purposefully put into the duct system. It may be harmful." He certainly didn't want to talk about mycotoxins or anthrax when the initial press release might use the term "bomb scare," at Brett's directive.

"What can I do?" she asked.

"Janey, I'm sure Brett is going to ask you a lot of questions, either that, or one of his people will be here shortly to ask them."

"I didn't do anything," the woman pleaded, tears welling.

Jeff felt compliant and totally on her side, yet he understood the magnitude of the situation. He wanted to aid her in any way he could, yet the circumstance dictated otherwise. His experience with the MaHoods was integrated onto his emotional hard drive to the extent that he believed anybody might be culpable of wrongdoing or murder, not excluding himself.

Jeff forced himself to respond calmly. "Nobody is saying you did anything. If you can help us find out who did, you'll be a hero in my eyes. How about that?"

Jeff was making it up as he went along. He was definitely out of his comfort zone. He had to experience interrogating people. That element belonged to others; research and investigative procedures were his domain.

Sirens sounded as fire trucks and police cordoned

off the neighborhood around the sports arena and re-routed traffic.

"Hazmat is on the way," said Brett. "Janey, I need you to relax. What time did you get here today?" asked Brett.

"About eight this morning."

"Were you here all day?"

"No. Right after you guys left, Bob asked me to pick up some valves for a water flow problem we started having a few days ago. The leak happened out of the blue. It took me a good three hours or so to find the right parts. I guess I got back here before noon.

"Wait a minute." She pulled out a drawer and retrieved receipt for the parts she had purchased and handed them to Brett.

He looked at the receipt and handed handed it back to her.

"And Bob stayed here with how many men?"

"He was here alone, as far as I know."

"How long have you known Hinton?" Brett continued.

Swan started to relax a bit. This questioning wasn't about her. "He started here about six months ago."

"Who hired him, if you know?"

"Somebody in the city council got him in, I think," she said. "He's a pretty quiet guy when he's not talking shop."

Jeff said, "Janey, there's a lot of this dust that is missing. Where do you think somebody would put it here if they wanted to hurt people?"

"I don't know. I can't think," she said.

"Is Hinton here all day every day?" Brett asked.

"We all come and go. It's the nature of the job," she replied.

Brett worked at trying to get the most information from the woman. "We suspect him but we're not accusing him. Now, you're saying that you've had recent activities here in the arena and everything was fine. Then he sends you for new valves and you're gone for some time. Then we find the stuff in the ducts. "Is that correct?"

Swan simply answered "Yep."

"The air handlers are run every day you have a performance, is that correct?" Brett asked.

"Yep."

"And obviously you both have the keys to come and go if you need to. Is that right?" asked Jeff, kicking himself for letting it come out as an accusation.

Swan became defensive. "I told you, sir, we all come and go. "I probably do more than he does."

"What do you do when you're not here?" asked the agent.

"I do have a life, you know," she replied.

"Which means what," persisted Brett relentlessly.

"Which means reading and working out."

"What about Hinton. What does he do when he's not here?"

"He has another job," Swan said.

"Which is?"

"He works maintenance at the airport," she replied.

"What does he do over there?" Brett asked.

"I have no idea," she said. "Maybe he sweeps floors. I don't know."

"Guess we'll find out, won't we." Within sixty seconds, Brett told the two, "He's in charge of filtration systems for the airplanes and for the terminal itself," he reported.

Hinton wouldn't be back. "Checking them over for what?" Jeff asked.

"Preparing for insertion into the air-handling systems of jet liners and for the entire airport. He likes to inspect them to make sure they're up to his specifications," he said.

Four men from the fire department hazardous materials division arrived, dressed for duty. Accompanied by Swan, Jeff and Brett led the group to the areas that required their attention. Jeff briefed them on what they needed to do to remove the threat.

Brett's phone rang as he and Jeff were returning to the office. "They picked up Hinton at the airport when he checked in with his supervisor. He was carrying a satchel."

"Tell them to confiscate any boxes that look like they have filters, large or small, and not to open the boxes or the satchel under any circumstances," Jeff said. "My gut tells me that a lot of the missing aflatoxin is in the satchel he brought with him. I'm also thinking that there's more of it here."

The men were conversing inside one of the main

entry doors to the arena. Flashing lights from fire engines and police cars filled the streets and the early evening sky, while news helicopters circled like vultures riding the edges of rising hot-air bubbles.

Jeff stuck up his finger as a point to be made. "Hinton showed the air conditioning system. What we also needed to look at is the forced-air heating system. I mean, if you're rigged to run A/C and the weather switches from hot to cold with a thirty to forty-degree temperature drop, you'll have to make sure your heater is brought into play. If that doesn't happen for a few months, it *will* happen when winter rolls around."

Jeff wasn't finished. "Man, in addition to the human tragedy, if it did happen, there would be absolutely no way to clean it up. Even if you blew up the building or blew it down, you'd release a cloud of poison. I wouldn't know what to do if we had to face that scenario."

Calmly, Brett called Swan, who was on the mezzanine with the work crew, and asked her to come down to the office. "Why didn't you tell us about the heating system when we asked about your air handlers, Janey?" asked Brett the moment she entered the room.

"I'm not in the habit of correcting my bosses anymore," she responded, crossing her arms defensively. "Every time I used to say or add something, I got fired or demoted, so I learned how to stay out of trouble. Job security is better that way."

"Where is your heating system?" Jeff asked.

"In the basement." She jerked her head in the direction of a stairwell. "It connects with the other ducts from underneath."

Without saying another word, she got up and led the men downstairs to the first of two large unit which served as one of the two heaters for the complex.

"It's set to go on when the outdoor temperature drops below sixty degrees, and that won't be for a few months from now."

"Disconnect the entire heating system," directed Jeff.

Brett gave another order and watched her turn off the timer to the unit, and he followed her to ensure that she did the same to the second unit.

"Now let's open it up," said Jeff.

Hinton never mentioned the heating system.

Once again, Swan unscrewed the front panel of the heater. She pulled it off and pulled out the flashlight. They all peered inside.

No powder was visible and no filter present.

"Damn, Jeff, nothing here," exclaimed Brett with great frustration.

"Where's your return air?" asked Jeff.

Swan stooped down at the rear duct of the unit and unscrewed it to reveal a flat area that permitted air to return from the arena into the unit, to be reheated and sent out again through a vertical duct that led into the main ducting system. In that flat area, large mounds of powder stood like a line of foothills.

Jeff took off at a sprint to alert the hazardous materials team of their find. When he returned he found that Brett had opened a door to a storage locker and found all the missing air filters.

The three of them discussed and devised a method of disconnecting the ducts that led from the heaters to the primary ducting system and encapsulating the return air system. Then they would overlay the return air with polyethylene, cut a slit into it, and insert a closely controlled vacuum hose to remove the majority of the toxin. Detailing the area would have to wait for another day. So would buying another vacuum.

"Jeff, is there anything else you need from her," Brett asked?

Jeff shrugged. "Not from my end."

Brett turned to Swan, spun her around and pushed her up against the wall, face first, saying, "All right, then, Swan, or whatever your name is, you're under arrest. Hands behind your back. Now!"

She did as requested without uttering a sound. Deftly, Brett removed a zip tie from his pocket and tied her wrists together. "Let's go to the office," he ordered, as Jeff stood watching, dumbfounded.

Brett said to Jeff, "We ran Hinton's prints. His real name is Gregory Polterak, a Russian. He may be the intermediate man whom the MaHouds contacted to obtain Ochenko, who hired Stanley Albert to help him make the mycotoxin in the first place. We've been after him a long time before then. The man reads, writes, and speaks Arabic fluently. Along with his Russian and English skills, he is very dangerous, as we've seen. Obviously, the man gets around and fits in well. He's the worst kind of sociopath.

"Swan's his sister. Her specialty is blowing up school buses with children on board. A real smooth piece of work. Now let's go catch us a bad guy."

Hazmat completed the work in four hours. Jeff couldn't wait to return to the relative calm of his lab and the welcoming arms of Carmen. Brett would remain behind to brief other state and federal agents who would soon be arriving. Two federal officers came to take Swan to a secure location.

Jeff thanked his friend and his agency and said, "I'll walk back to the hotel. I need the fresh air. Oh, and, one last thing, Brett. Could you do me a favor?"

"If I can," Brett answered.

"If you see old man MaHoud, tell him that his life is over, and it was completely wasted. One of his sons is dead, and the other one turned him in and helped us guide him to death row. Tell him his empire is finished, and so is he. After you tell him that, tell him that if there are any investors in his enterprise, they will be looking for a way get compensated for their loss. Then tell him.to have a nice day."

"Should I mention your name?" asked Brett, smiling.

"If you could be so kind," Jeff grinned, broadly.

The weather was clear and warm in Phoenix when Jeff's plane departed from Phoenix to Oklahoma City after arriving in Tucson only the morning before. He would have to return soon to oversee the destruction of the toxin and to ensure that all the toxin was gone. For now he could get back to the old lovable workload.

"Any comments on your adventure?" Carmen asked with her arms wrapped around her man's neck as she met him at baggage claim.

To Carmen's surprise Jeff kissed her deeply and then said, Now, hon, I'm ready for some Chinese."

Jeff walked through four of the six laboratories that were now in use in the building.

He spoke with each student and professional high-end scientists, giving encouragement and guidance to each person he met. And learning from them.

Jeff knew their strengths and weaknesses, perhaps better than they did. *Researchers attach to their inner strength when encouraged by those whom they have high regard for*, Jeff knew.

Lab 5 was reserved for foreign medical scientists who strove to better humanity with the final lab reserved for the unexpected.

The phone rang.

"Jeff, it's a Mr. Brett Overton on your secure line." Jeff took his mind from research to focus on the caller.

"Brett, what a pleasant surprise."

"Jeff," Brett began with sincerity, "it is my duty to inform you that on the street you are considered bad luck."

Jeff's stomach sank. He paled. Had they discovered more powder, more mycotoxin, something he missed? How did he screw up? What would be the public's retribution against him? Against his company? Against Carmen?

"Brett, where did I screw up?" Jeff almost stuttered.

Brett gave a hearty laugh. "Not you, Jeff. The word among the terrorists is that you are big trouble. They have superstitions too. Not only did you get the MaHouds and their cronies, we're recovering tens of billions of their dollars. How does it feel to be unappreciated?"

Jeff laughed, permitting oxygen to enter his lungs. "Brett, I couldn't have been a loser without your help."

"The president told me you'd probably try to transfer the blame to someone else," retorted the agent.

There was a pause then Brett continued. "Here's what we've got so far. The short version is that Hinton's an Al Qaeda player of the worst sort. World class bad guy. We followed his footsteps back to Saudi Arabia, Syria, Russia, and Yemen. He operates – correction —*operated* his own network of terrorists that intermeshed closely with old man MaHoud. As far as MaHoud's sons, their role was as described; to pass on the poisons that were created by Albert and Ochenko.

"And while we're talking about Hinton, we might as well talk about Janey Swan, sister to Hinton; first name Afizah. Her specialty is explosives; blowing up buses filled with school children. They were both hired at the same time. Included in their hiring were city council members, state representatives and on up, people who were imbedded for years in some cases.

"I hate to admit it, but Swan had me totally fooled. We caught up with her at the airport later that evening heading for Paris."

Brett paused in his narrative.

Jeff remained speechless.

"I know you're thinking of something. Want to share it with me?" the agent asked.

"I'm thinking that Whitaker and Brewer were foul people and that I never actually met the Hoods. Now I come face to face with two the lowest scum on the planet earth with Hinton ... I don't want to know his real name, and his sister, and I spoke with them and shook hands and saw them in action and right now I feel very dirty. How do I deal with it, Brett? How do I scrub off the filth?"

"For me it's a little different because I have to deal with it head on so I have to train myself to be objective or I'd never remain sane. For you, you might try training your mind to flip to another sub-ject when the thought of those two comes up. It takes a little practice but it's doable. The simplest thing is to think of it as the world getting purged of a whole lot of filth."

"Sorry for the interruption. Go on with your tale," said Jeff, who wanted to hear more details.

"Okay. MaHoud spent hundreds of millions of dollars, possibly a billion dollars or more on these projects in terms of payoffs all the way up into the core of our government, including the purchase of Kirk's newspapers. He was backed by nations with unlimited resources at his disposal. For a long time, he used to be the man, as they say.

"MaHoud's plan went back decades and he planted his sons with his own brother and sister-in-law who were totally in on the entire enterprise. They were the ones who contacted a man in Madrid named Alvarez to pay off Senator Rossman. This Alvarez and a lot of his bunch are in tow now.

"At that time, the senator headed the Subcommittee on Crime and Terrorism. He was in the perfect position to do what MaHoud needed done, by his way of thinking, although I might have chosen someone else.

"We come up with some fifty million in payment to the Senator.

"The subcommittee has a dozen duties. One of them is oversight of anti-terrorism enforcement and policy, and another ws oversight of Homeland functions, as they relate to anti-terrorism enforcement and policy.

"He'd been around a long time and knew who could be dirty. At the right time he, along with a couple of his people on the subcommittee, would announce their discovery of a terrorism plot and they would get their contacts with the USPHS to agree."

"So what?" Jeff asked. "That wouldn't change anything that happened or change the crimes or the punishments."

"Actually it would," Brett answered. "Terrorism unto itself is a bad thing. An epidemic is also a bad thing. Now you'd have a multiplier effect where one plus one equals ten. The public would absolutely freak.

"Rossman would come out on top after the worst had happened, because he'd take the 'I told you so' position. But it never happened because the worst never happened. The ink never got to the other cities and the bad face cream and toothpaste shipments had been halted.

"With that man at the top virtually every aspect of our country would rapidly spiral downward.

Jeff stopped his friend. "Wait a minute, Brett. I mean, what if Rossman had said 'absolutely not' and told about the meeting to whomever?"

"Then every single member of his entire family would meet with separate accidents. Each of their names and current locations were told to him. He had no choice but to cooperate, with a lot of money as a reward and the presidency as the ultimate prize."

"He could be that evil?" Jeff asked, disgustedly.

Brett replied, "He could and he was. It's the presidency, Jeff. People will do anything to get there.

"Where Whitaker fits in is because Rossman had pharmaceutical connections. Because of these leanings, he already knew Whitaker and also knew he was in desperate need of money of his own to pay for a daughter's surgery. Rossman provided the money through MaHoud along with additional financial incentives. So Whitaker took an early retirement from his CEO position as soon as he could and headed the committee.

"Once installed, Whitaker believed he needed a grunt, a yes man, who knew how to follow orders so he contacted Brewer over in Homeland. He'd asked around and heard the man was no Brainiac, but a good person to have by your side and will back you to the end. So he gave Brewer a whole lot of money along with several orders, and we were off and running."

"It sounds like money flowed from a large spigot," Jeff observed.

"Yes, which was connected to a huge reservoir—MaHoud himself and foreign government investments.

"Rossman put together a typical investigative team headed by Whitaker and Brewer, who served as compliance officers and administrators, and brought in Homeland so it was all up and up. Then he brought in Simon and Schmidt who were microbiologists. Both men were respected in their field wouldn't hurt a fly on the wall. They would, however, take home a few hundred thousand dollars extra for maybe a month or so of work, so what's the harm in that?

"Of course you know that an epidemiologist is critical during an outbreak, food borne or otherwise, so that meant Anderson, and you were there because Evans wanted you.

"Whitaker got Marjorie Reynolds to spin the webs while he oversaw and misdirected the CDC investigative teams that were under himself and Brewer.

"Those are the basics. You should watch GNN tonight. I think this guy Billy Kirk is going to present the details."

"I might just do that," offered Jeff, still in shock at Brett's tale.

"Have you ever watched him?" asked the agent.

"Who, Kirk? I think so. Maybe once or twice," said Jeff.

"Personally, I'd like to meet him," said Brett.

"Brett, you know how these things work. He's probably the dullest guy on the planet outside the newsroom."

Brett continued. "For what it's worth, Hinton started having the shakes and is seeing visions every few hours. He beats and tears at himself, as if trying to remove all-too-real creatures that cover his body. I'm told the attacks seem to be more frequent as time goes on. Also, he has developed rashes on his face and arms that he scratches incessantly.

"And here's the really strange part," added Brett. "He has a heavy growth of white-brown threads coming out of all of his body openings. Our people say it's mold mycelium. Is that possible?"

"I'm happy to say it is," said Jeff with more than a fleck of sadism.

Then he grew deadly serious. He seemed to be doing that a lot lately. "Brett, that mycelium is highly contagious in its present form. He needs to be in total isolation and anybody who examined him in his present state needs to go on antifungal medication as soon as possible."

Brett contacted the necessary people to give them Jeff's directives.

Thousands of people had escaped the horror of inhaling the countless fragments, each of which could reproduce into mold colonies within the body while the entire body and mind received poison at the same time.

"Expect his medical problems to get worse," Jeff threw in for good measure.

Jeff took a flier. "I'm thinking you have a daughter. Tell her I said hello."

"How did you know I had a daughter?" Brett was truly surprised.

"Brett, have a wonderful day. Feel free to call anytime."

Clearly puzzled, Brett became almost flippant, "I almost forgot a small detail. The president asked me to thank you for your work in this case. He said to tell you to expect a present. He wants me to send you some tickets to come to Washington for a visit. How many would you like?"

Floored at the complement and the request Jeff thought, *Let's see. Paul is in England, Richard is in India, and Frank is knee deep in an environmental case up in Alaska. That leaves himself, Carmen,*

Parker, Marilyn, and of course, Billy.

"Would five work?" Jeff asked.

"You got it. Oh, one last comment. The president is talking about awarding you the Medal of Freedom."

"Not without Paul Anderson" inserted Jeff. *And a lot of others.*

"See you." Brett hung up.

Jeff turned to Carmen. It was her turn to receive a favor from him. "Excuse me, ma'am, are you ready to meet to take a flight and pay a visit to someone?"

"To where? Back to Tucson? I thought..." Carmen said absently.

"One guess," replied Jeff. "He lives in Washington, DC. And like it or not, you're going to get one hell of a pay raise," Jeff said, as he put his arms around her.

"Oh, hon, before I forget, you got a call from a scientist up in Lincoln, Nebraska, by the name of Jason Randolph."

"I heard the name. Has his own lab like us. Rich guy. Came into family money. A little too smart for me, though. Did he say what he wanted?"

"I asked him that and he said something about wanting to learn about fermenters, and wanting to buy some.

Jeff stopped and stared at her, remembering about Albert and Ochenko. "And?"

"He said he wanted to learn about growing a large quantity of virus.

"Viruses in a fermenter? I didn't think you could

do that, but what do I know? In any case, that's kid's stuff. What can be worse that what we've been through.

Carmen laughed. She had her man.

Synopsis of other books by Mark R. Sneller

The Mars Virus
(Sequel *to Dying to Read*)

Cancer researcher Jason Randolph and his geologist friend, Don Jennings, decide to search for life in a meteorite the geologist found in Antarctica years before. What's the worst that can happen? Everybody tried it, from NASA to the Russians, *and nobody found a thing.*

Suddenly, in Lincoln, Nebraska, a nightmarish discovery by the scientists threatens not only mankind and all life on Earth, but the stability of the planet itself, while Randolph and Jennings try to make hay before the sun stops shining.

Toxic Exposure

Dr. Jeffrey Shenero, rough-hewn professor, adventurer, and mold expert, finds himself embroiled in a lawsuit by a man-eating shark because he didn't find mold in her home. She is circling. He is blindsided by the attack.

At the same time he becomes embroiled in a national scandal surrounding a school controversy in which a demonic teacher is hard at work poisoning the educational system of the country. Do the two women know each other?

Jeff is partnered with Frank Bennett, his best friend and an environmental attorney with his own dark past, and Billy Kirk, a handsome television broadcaster, who wants to play by the book, but has an eye on his own future. He wants to move up the ladder of success and will bend the rules, if it becomes necessary.

Greener Cleaner Indoor Air 2nd Edition

Re-edited and enlarged, the 2nd Edition boasts over 120 articles written by award-winning scientist Dr. Mark R. Sneller. Greener Cleaner Indoor Air is an invaluable reference guide promoting longer life. Covering virtually every aspect of the range of particles (and toxic gases) we breathe every day, you will learn how to reduce, if not eliminate, them from your home air and save money at the same time.

Considering the book to be of such value, the country of South Korea purchased the rights to download the e-version to its citizens.

www.ingramcontent.com/pod-product-compliance
Lightning Source LLC
Chambersburg PA
CBHW070929100726
47908CB00001B/157